Deadly Gray

A Mystery / Thriller

by

Ed Day

Ed Day

Deadly Gray by Ed Day is a work of fiction. All names of characters, places, and events are products of the author's imagination. Any resemblance to real persons, living or dead, is purely coincidental.

ISBN: 978-0-9974555-7-1

Deadly Gray

By Ed Day

A Deadly Discovery

Tucker and Maya's discovery has the potential to change the world for the betterment of humankind. So why do they need protection from state sponsored assassins?

Ed Day

Deadly Conspiracy

An investigation by the Tucker Cherokee extended family into seemingly two unrelated events uncovered an international conspiracy of epic significance.

Quote: "The older I get, the less life in prison is a deterrent." -Unknown

Dedication: This book is dedicated to Dawn Marie Cashion, a sweetheart who passed away too young in life.

To Terminally Ill Seniors: Live vicariously through this book and know that there are criminals who now need to continuously look over their shoulders in fear of you.

NOTE: To aid the reader to keep track of *Deadly Gray* characters, the author provided a list at the end of the book.

Deadly Gray

Prologue

April 10, 2024
Santa Clara County, California

Despite the continuous presence of hostile and aggressive California drivers, 23-year-old graduate student, Kurt Rainwater, rode his top-of-the-line Pinarello road bike daily from Menlo Park to Stanford University on Sand Hill Road. The dry wind in his face, the sun slapping his polycarbonate sunglasses, and the sensation of quadriceps strain made him feel almost transcendental. Kurt wore a bright yellow cycling jersey and a bib shorts kit over his tall lanky frame to ensure that he was visible so that vehicle drivers could not miss seeing him.

He was accustomed to people flipping him a bird or yelling obscenities at him as they passed him in their disdainful gas guzzlers, heavy electric cars, diesel trucks, and nearly empty municipal buses. He never quite understood the irrational hatred people had toward bike enthusiasts. But because he loved biking, he endured the abuse. He thought, *They just don't understand the sense of one he feels with the universe when he rides—it is their loss.*

Until now.

Rainwater hit the pavement hard. The pain in his right shoulder was excruciating and he was dizzy from pounding the concrete with his helmet, but nothing prepared him for the pain he experienced when the front tire of an unabated 7600-pound vehicle ran over his left calf while his foot remained clipped to the pedal. Kurt screamed in agony and knew immediately that his fibula was crushed .

Without braking or slowing down, the back wheel of the large SUV ran over the same leg. This time bike wheel spokes jabbed into his stomach and part of the chain embedded in his hip. Pieces of the broken carbon fiber bike frame smacked his mouth and cracked his top central incisors. Kurt's pain receptors were in over-drive magnifying his surreal experience.

The Cadillac Escalade that assaulted him finally braked and pulled to a stop.

Kurt Rainwater, blinded by the hatred he felt toward the careless driver and crying from fear that the driver crippled him for life reflected, *At least this asshole is coming back to help me.*

He couldn't have been more wrong.

The driver put the SUV in reverse and backed-up and over Rainwater's leg a third and fourth time. The anguish and shock Kurt felt from the assault caused him to pass out. The motorist then put the vehicle back in drive and ran over the student again; this time the white-haired hit-and-run driver made sure he maneuvered the vehicle over the bicycle rider's chest with both the front and back wheels. Witnesses at the scene testified that the senior vehicle operator drove off with a satisfied smile.

Twelve vehicles drove past Rainwater's lifeless body before anyone stopped to check on him.

PART ONE

Chapter 1

April 12, 2024
Northern Virginia

Star Cherokee passed through Quantico's guard gate, under the I-95 overpass, past the Quantico National Cemetery, through the hairpin back roads of Prince William County, and past intelligent agencies' safe houses known to but very few. She could have taken another route to the FBI Northern Virginia Resident Office outside Manassas, but she enjoyed negotiating the sleepy hollow-like road where the sunlight occasionally flickered through the dense forest onto the tinted window of her electric Rivian sport utility vehicle.

Agent Cherokee's lifelong protector, Ram, a 100-pound military trained German Shepherd, sat in the back of the SUV, and growled a millisecond after her personal cell phone rang. She did not recall Ram ever growling after her phone rang and it gave Star a chill down her spine, so she let the call go to voice mail. She thought, *Ram has saved my butt on multiple occasions with his uncanny sixth sense.*

She brought her SUV to a stop where the two-lane winding road teed onto a less challenging four-lane highway. She turned left, headed north, and waited until she hit a stop light before she checked to see if she recognized the number of the caller. She didn't but decided to check to see if a message was left. The stop light turned green and just as she began to accelerate through the light, the voicemail began to play on her

Bluetooth. The voicemail proclamation mesmerized Star.

She pulled over to the side of the road and listened to the message from an apparently elderly man three separate times. "Ram," she said, "You called that one right. It is a disturbing statement, isn't it?"

She put her vehicle back in drive and continued her commute until she pulled into the FBI Field Office parking lot. After Star attached a leash to his collar, Ram lead her up the steps to the entrance and into the building lobby. Ram was infamous inside Washington Field Offices and was the only FBI K9 with an access badge attached to his collar.

Agent Cherokee was somewhat in a trance as she thought about what she should say to her boss about the unusual voicemail. She was a head-turner and always wore clean, pressed, sharp-looking clothing with her badge prominently displayed on her belt. After Star placed her handgun on the x-ray belt, FBI security dutifully checked the contents in the tray. The FBI security guards let Star and her K9 pass through without a hitch; no guard wanted to pass a wand around Star to check for other weapons with Ram by her side. Afterall, if even a fraction of the legendary stories about Ram were true, the guards did not want to risk the appearance of threatening Star.

Cyber Division Special Agent Rusty Winemiller's first floor office door was open, so Star knocked on his door frame to get his attention. "May I come in?"

Winemiller did not look up, instead, he looked at his watch. He said, "You're kidding, right? You are five minutes early. I didn't expect the end of the world would come so soon."

Star said, "Wasn't it you who taught me to alter my pattern to be less predictable so that bad guys couldn't take advantage of my repetitive movements?"

"Maybe so, but when before did you ever listened to me?"

Star said, "I listened to you the time you explained that it is best to get right to the point. I know you called me here to give me a new assignment, but first I want to share with you a call I just received on my personal cell phone while on the way here. Listen to this."

"Hello, Star. I am going to kill a man who has managed to avoid justice for his crimes. I tell you this so that you will investigate not only me but also the motive for my transgression and why I chose this victim. I trust you will get to the bottom of it."

Ram growled again at the sound of the person's voice who left the message. At the end of the recording Star pushed stop and said, "That's the entire message. Intriguing, don't you think, sir? Why do you suspect the caller, who sounds like an old man, sent this message to me?"

Winemiller, a paraplegic who always wore a suit and patent leather shoes wheeled his electric wheelchair around his desk without responding.

Star said, "What do you mean, 'That's a stupid question?'"

Special Agent Rusty Winemiller stopped his wheelchair's progress, pulled off his glasses, rubbed his hazel eyes, lifted his handsome gaze toward his protégé, and made eye contact with Star's penetrating blue eyes, but said nothing.

Star shifted uncomfortably on her feet, ran her hands through her curly auburn hair and said, "Sorry, I promised you I wouldn't do that, didn't I?"

He said, "It was, in fact, a condition of your employment agreement. We agreed that I would accept you back into the Bureau if you never used your special mind reading skills on me. I'll terminate all our in-person conversations and communicate with you only remotely if it happens again."

"Yes, sir."

Winemiller said, "Listen, someone would have to have a double-digit IQ not to pick you first to investigate an unsolved mystery—you with all your unofficial sleuth family resources and all."

Rusty wheeled back behind his desk, punched a few strokes on his keyboard and asked, "You don't have to continue standing, pull up a chair. Now, what's the phone number of the guy that called you and said he would kill someone; you know, the number that popped up on your incoming cell phone screen?"

Star looked at her cell phone and gave it to him. He punched in the ten digits into his computer and waited for roughly a minute during which time he petted Ram to reinforce that they were friends. Better to be Ram's friend than not.

Finally, Special Agent Winemiller said, "Your caller's name is Colby John Manion of Blytheville, Arkansas, age 79. He is a retired Air Force Colonel who maintains a blog critical of the government's investigation into the 2017 Las Vegas massacre. I see where he lost a granddaughter who attended the outdoor country music festival on that awful fatal day."

Winemiller continued to read the background information on Manion and said, "Star, I bet he's going to kill someone associated with the Las Vegas massacre; he appears to be obsessed with it. He may kill someone he suspects is responsible for the shooting, or maybe an individual who he suspects covered up the crime.

"Ah," continued Winemiller as he read information on his computer, "he has stage four pancreatic cancer—he does not have much longer to live."

Star asked, "Sir, did you say he has a blog page? Does that mean it could be a cybercrime and fall under your authority?"

Rusty said, "Yes, it may. In fact, it may dovetail with your new assignment. The reason I called you into my office today is because I want you to investigate the alarming increase in murder committed by senior citizens and decide if cybercrimes are committed to encourage seniors do what they are doing. We think there might be a subversive organization out there that encourages vulnerable terminally ill seniors to commit vigilante type crimes through email, social media, or ordinary telephone contact. People at the end of their lives have less to lose and may be susceptible to manipulation. I have dubbed this development as the "*Deadly Gray*" phenomenon. It's not a stretch for this Manion fellow to fall under the overall *Deadly Gray* case umbrella. Your caller is a terminally ill senior who claims he will execute a vigilante murder."

Star asked, "What do you mean by alarming increase in murder by seniors?"

"Suffice it to say, the murder rate by men and women over the age of 65 has quadrupled over the past five years. Most of the murders are committed by people who seek revenge for some perceived injustice in their lives. It sounds to me like Manion fits the mold."

Star said, "So, you suspect he wants to exact vengeance on his way out and have us investigate the victim."

"True, but the FBI, the Las Vegas Metropolitan Police Department, and the Bureau of Alcohol, Tobacco, Firearms, and Explosive have investigated the Las Vegas massacre extensively. It's hard to justify spending too much more money and energy on that well-worn path. However, maybe we can stop the murder before it happens. We don't get many opportunities in our business to do that.

"Star, seventeen murders were committed this week alone by seniors. A 23-year-old Stanford post-graduate student just riding his bicycle to the university campus was intentionally run over by a senior driving a Cadillac Escalade; a 75-year-old woman mutilated a rapist who was on parole; a 72-year-old man killed a ransomware thief; a Vietnam-era sniper killed a retired *New York Times* editor; an attempt on the life of a former Virginia governor was tried by an 84-year-old radical right winger; etc., etc. etc. I want you to investigate whether there is a cyber thread to these crimes. Who knows, you might discover a thread that leads you to Las Vegas?"

Star said coyly, "Let me guess, the FBI is getting pressure from Congress. The government leadership is afraid that they will be targeted by this group called *Deadly Gray* if, in fact, it is organized."

Rusty Winemiller said, "Bingo," though he suspected Star had not deduced that assessment on her own, but that she had again, read his thoughts.

Star said, "Do I have Carte Blanche? May I use pre-approved consultants?"

Rusty said, "As long as she doesn't shoot anybody."

Star responded, "Now look who's reading other people's thoughts."

◆ ◆ ◆ ◆ ◆

April 13, 2024
Blytheville, Arkansas

Colonel Colby Manion took four 325mg Percocet pills ten minutes before his Uber driver arrived. Even before the death sentence diagnosis, Colby had difficulty moving his body—too many old college wrestling injuries and unnecessary wartime antics. At 79, his gait was downgraded to the senior shuffle. Ten steps out of his senior living condominium, it hit him. He was quite sure he would not make it back to the bathroom in time.

The Uber driver nodded in acceptance—it would be a while before the rider would re-emerge. She understood it was one of the many indignities the terminally ill, who injected chemicals into their bodies just to extend their lives a few more precious weeks, had to suffer. She wore tight jeans, a long sleeve blouse, a silk scarf, and a Star of David necklace.

Twenty minutes later, the old man who now wore a golf hat, golf shirt, black pants, white shoes, carrying a gym bag shuffled down the ramp to a late model white Chrysler 300. The rear door was open for him and before he bent down to slide in, he said, "Well, aren't you a sight for sore eyes. I think this the first time in my long life that a pretty lady opened the door for me. This is an omen."

She smiled and asked, "Omen about what?"

"End of times, young lady. End of times."

The driver asked, "To the hospital, right? That is what the dispatcher said. How much time do we have for you to make your medical appointment?"

Manion said, "Change of plans, young lady. Can you drop me off at the airport, instead?"

Colby had lived a blessed life for most of his years. He had a healthy active childhood, grew up in Dayton, Ohio, played catcher on the high school baseball team, was district wrestling champion in the 175-pound weight class, never got in trouble, never smoked cigarettes, or drank alcohol, and had loving parents. He graduated from Ohio State University with a degree in mechanical engineering and was in the Air Force ROTC program. He joined the Air Force but fortunately never saw the horrors of the Vietnam War as the Air Force assigned him to aircraft maintenance in Guam.

He fell in love and married an old high school classmate when he returned from the war effort and subsequently was assigned to Air Force Bases in San Antonio, Texas; Tucson, Arizona; and Minot, South Dakota. He wasn't pure and made some stupid mistakes along the way, but in general had lived an honorable and fulfilled life. He retired as a colonel at age 48 and accepted a position with a defense contractor for which he was stationed at Nellis Air Force Base outside of Las Vegas until he retired at age 65. He was a good husband, good father, and loving grandfather.

His blessed life changed on October 1, 2017. He became fanatical to find out what the real story was about the Las Vegas massacre and ventured into the shadowy world of hate and conspiracy. His present was unlike his past.

♦　♦　♦　♦　♦

April 13, 2024
Blytheville, Arkansas

The Uber driver, Sonja McLeod Vincente, Star's closest and most trusted friend, doubled back to Manion's condominium after she dropped him off at the airport, donned latex gloves, let herself in, and took thirty or so digital photos before she called Star as instructed.

Star answered, "Hit me."

"He will not come back here. He prominently displayed his Last Will on the dining room table. I photographed all pages."

Star asked, "What else?"

"He left the password to his computer in big black magic marker letters on a notepad."

Star asked, "What did you find on his computer?"

Sonja answered, "Damnit, Star, you know that is not my skill base. I'm not a geek. Where do you want the computer delivered?"

Star laughed and said, "Harpers Ferry."

Sonja said, "Warn Jimmy Ma that I'm coming to his home. Otherwise, he may have a coronary when I show up."

Jimmy Ma, a short dark-haired man with a round baby face, baggy pants with lots of pockets and who eccentrically wore bowties, worked for Star's father, Tucker Cherokee. Jimmy is an unparalleled computer hacker assigned as a contractor to the Department of Treasury to assess all department firewalls and to break through firewalls of known criminals for the Secret Service. He envisions himself as a ladies' man and spends an inordinate amount of his resources to dress up to attract the fairer half. That is when he is not gambling.

Star said, "Roger that, and Sonja, where did Manion say he was going?"

Sonja answered, "Only that he would play his last round of golf."

Silence.

Sonja added, "Yes, of course I placed a GPS transmitter under the back of his shirt collar. We'll know where he is when he lands.

"You know, Star, you are my best friend and I love you like a sister, so I must ask: is what you're doing sanctioned? We're breaking and entering, stealing personal property, and invading this old man's privacy. You're going to get yourself in a lot of trouble."

Star answered, "The old man announced that he is going to kill someone. It was not a hard sell to get a warrant. The judge just didn't know we would use a consultant that was a former Mossad sniper to do the search and seizure."

Chapter 2

April 15, 2024
Boothbay, Maine

It's all about acceleration. At six feet - seven inches tall and 310 pounds of low body-fat and honed muscle, Jorge (Tank) Alvarez whipped out his weapon of choice, a 28 cubic inch club head at the end of an extra-long titanium shaft, with added lead tape and three 15-gram weights. Tank said to the others in the foursome, "Force is equal to mass times acceleration."

When the club head met the ball as it sat on a tee on the men's whites of the 13th hole, Tank drove the ball over 375 yards—in the wrong direction. He hooked it to the left into and through an adjacent fairway.

Tank's golf cart partner, Adam Heinz, Deputy Director of the Bureau of Alcohol, Tobacco, Firearms, and Explosives, said, "After I put my Titleist in the middle of the fairway, I'll come help you find your wayward ball."

Tank responded, "Anyone can put it in the middle of the fairway if you drive the ball only 150 yards. I bet you can't make it past the women's tee. You know what that means don't you?"

Though Heinz stood nose to nose with Tank, he weighed a good 85 pounds less. Tank playfully taunted him and said, "I've yet to see you drive a ball more than 200 yards. I guess you were just a desk jockey with the ATF. You're all gas and no speed."

Adam Heinz smiled, winked at the other two in the foursome, pulled his driver from his bag and teed up. He spent the next two minutes adjusting his belt, practicing his swing, stepping around his ball, stretching, picking up grass around the tee area and throwing it in the air to confirm wind direction until Tank said, "I'm sorry I put so much pressure on you to hit the ball like a man."

Ultimately, Heinz sliced his drive 150 yards to the right; still a good 250 yards from the green. Adam pulled his 7-iron from his golf bag on the back of his cart and said, "Tank, you can take the cart and go find your ball assuming it landed somewhere on the golf course. I'll catch up with you."

Tank smiled and drove off while Heinz searched for his ball only to find it behind a big oak tree. The ATF executive resigned himself to the fact that he had to suffer an extra stroke and chip back onto the fairway.

Star's parents, Tucker and Maya Cherokee, rode the other golf cart in the foursome. Tucker was Tank's best friend since high school where they grew up in western North Carolina. Tank was considered part of the overall Cherokee "virtual family." In their teenage years Tucker saved Tank's sister from drowning in a lake back before Tank learned to swim. Tank would march across hell for Tucker ever since.

Tucker said to Maya, "Deputy Director Heinz sure is slow. Every damn stroke takes him forever. He needs to practice on the driving range, not on the golf course. The older I get, the more I am unimpressed with people like Heinz"

Maya said, "Calm down sweetheart, enjoy the outdoors in this unseasonably warm Maine weather."

Maya Li Cherokee received her Doctorate in particle physics from the University of Chicago. She met Tucker at a Department of Energy lab in Illinois where he provided consulting services for the company he now runs, Entropy Entrepreneurs. Together Maya and Tucker discovered a revolutionary method to produce electricity, incurred the wrath of threatened nation-states, and ended-up extremely wealthy but forced into witness protection in New Zealand for years to protect the two of them from technology thieves and state-sponsored assassins.

Tucker waited for what seemed to him to be an interminable amount of time for Heinz to chip out from behind the tree. The ball never came out onto the fairway.

Tucker said, "This is ridiculous. Do we have to let the foursome behind us play through or what?"

Maya said, "Let's go see what Heinz is up to. Maybe he can't find his ball; golf has turned into the adult version of an Easter egg hunt."

They found Adam Heinz's golf ball. They also found Heinz face down in pine needles, the back of his head split open, and blood on a pitching wedge that laid beside him.

Maya immediately grabbed her cell phone and called 9-1-1; Tucker checked Adam Heinz for a pulse.

There was none.

He looked around for a perpetrator and saw a golf cart move away on a parallel fairway of the 16th hole in the direction of the clubhouse.

Tucker said to Maya, "Stay here. Pull your gun out of your pocketbook and be at the ready in case the killer is nearby and not the guy I'm chasing." He gave hunt and yelled for the fleeing golf cart to stop.

It did not.

Tucker pushed the pedal of the golf cart to the floor, pulled out his cell phone, and called Tank. "Head to the clubhouse, Heinz is dead. I believe I've got the murderer in sight."

Tucker eventually caught up with the gray-haired driver of the escaping golf cart before they reached the clubhouse and shouted, "You, stop, right there, mister."

Colonel Colby John Manion had a satisfied yet fatalistic smile on his face as he held up his hands in submission and said, "Ah, Mr. Tucker Cherokee, it is an honor to meet you. Where is your beautiful wife?"

Tucker said, "I am at a disadvantage; I do not know who you are nor why you murdered a man in my golf foursome. Please, enlighten me."

"I'm Colby Manion. I recently left a message on the phone of your daughter, Star. Did she mention this to you?"

"No."

"Well, I don't trust the upper echelon of the FBI, but I do trust your daughter based on my background check, your and Maya's history as patriotic Americans, and your crack team of genius investigators. I'm sure Star will eventually reach out to you."

The Lincoln County police showed up at the Boothbay Harbor County Club. The county sheriff asked repeatedly of golfers as he walked briskly through the lobby, "Who here called 9-1-1 to report an alleged murder?"

Tucker heard the sheriff's plea and responded, "My wife did. She is with the deceased to make sure the crime scene is untouched."

Tank arrived at the clubhouse just in time to hear Tucker say, "Tank, would you escort the good police officers to the crime scene? You don't mind, do you?"

Tank concluded from his request that Tucker needed time with the perpetrator before the police discovered that the old man with Tucker was a person of interest and arrested him.

Tucker watched Tank and the police ride golf carts down to the 13th fairway. Manion said, "Boy, that Tank fellow is even bigger in person than he looks in interviews on TV."

Tucker asked, "Why did you call my daughter, why are you here, and why did you kill Deputy Director Adam Heinz?'

Manion said, "My granddaughter was a victim of the shooting referred to as the Las Vegas massacre. Why do you suppose Paddock with all the weapons he had in his possession in Mandalay Bay Resort and Casino stopped shooting? Why not empty every magazine within reach? What do you think is the real reason he had all those weapons up there? He didn't need or use the vast majority of them. You know there were multiple shooters, right? Have you ever heard of 'Fast and Furious?' Have you ever heard of an FBI or ATF sting gone bad? A government black hole has sucked the truth from all of us."

Tucker asked, "Just what is it you think Heinz did, what role do you think he played that you want us to investigate? Do you suspect that Heinz covered up the truth about the Las Vegas shooting that killed your granddaughter?"

Colby said in a very accusatory tone, "The bigger question is why were you golfing with Heinz? You were already investigating him, weren't you? Why?"

Tucker ignored the accusation and asked the old man, "How did you know we intended to golf with Adam Heinz, today?"

Colonel Manion answered, "In today's world, it is impossible to keep almost anything a secret. Yes, I knew you would play golf today with that piece of shit."

Tank arrived in his golf cart back at the clubhouse with Maya in the cart with him.

Manion beamed as they approached and said, "Dr. Cherokee, I want you to know it was worth my crime to see you in person. You are even more lovely than you appear in magazines."

Maya is a stunningly beautiful woman with an unusual mix of ethnicity inherited from a Taiwanese father and Norwegian mother. Maya is five feet, nine inches tall with an athletic body, long silky black hair, and exotic almond shaped eyes with bright blue irises. She easily could be a model.

Manion turned back to Tucker and said, "I am confident now that you, Dr. Cherokee, and Tank Alvarez will help guide Star to discover the truth about Adam Heinz, the ATF, and even the FBI's role in covering up the truth about the Las Vegas massacre. I've teed it up for you; don't shank it."

Col. Manion started to shake uncontrollably, and said, "I'm not alone" just before he foamed at the mouth and collapsed onto the floor.

Maya said, "Cyanide."

Tucker said, "Guess he finished his mission and wanted out of his pain."

♦ ♦ ♦ ♦ ♦

April 15, 2024
Quantico, Virginia

"Sonja," asked Star, "I understood from you that Manion was in Nashville according to the GPS tracker you attached to his shirt collar. What gives?"

Sonja responded, "He must have changed in Nashville and left the shirt with the transmitter on it there. You know, he was prone to change outfits often. Frequent diarrhea is a symptom of pancreatic cancer."

Sonja was part of the overall virtual Cherokee family. Sonja's natural father, Powers, was Tank Alvarez's security services mentor and ultimate business partner. Together, Tank and Powers started White Knight Personal Security, LLC which grew to become the nation's premier security contractor. Powers learned that he had a daughter, Sonja, late in life. Sonja's grandmother raised her in Israel, pushed her to join the Mossad where her inherited skills ultimately turned her into an internationally feared sniper. Sonja learned about her father, Powers, after her grandmother passed away. Sonja was a petite, brown-eyed blond who was deceivingly tough.

Sonja said, "I dropped the computer off with Jimmy Ma in Harpers Ferry. What did he find?"

Star said, "As you know, Jimmy Ma is an eccentric genius who works for my dad but is emotionally unstable. He is scared shitless of you. It took him hours to regain his composure after you left. But eventually he learned that Colonel Manion was a very clever man. He had a following of over 50,000 seniors over the age of

75. He had a blog page called '*Senior Vigilantes.*' Let me read to you his final blog:

> "The older we get, the less the threat of life imprisonment means to us. We have won life's lottery if we managed to live to our age. I assumed getting old would take longer. For those of us that have lived too long, that is, to the point where we have no control of our bodily functions, to the point where pain is our constant companion, or to the point where the quality of life is questionable, we have a chance to change our final image from one who couldn't control his or her bowels to someone who is committed to achieve justice for loved ones.

> "Has a loved one of yours been mistreated, abused, defrauded, or harmed? Has a family member been raped, murdered, disabled, or mentally tortured? At the end of your life, you can achieve justice. I will demonstrate by example. We are an army and more powerful than anyone suspects. Expose the truth."

Star said, "Based on these findings and his dying statements at Boothbay Country Club, my boss wants the investigation to be low key which means he wants very few people at the FBI to be aware of the case. It's a trust issue. Therefore, he has authorized me to involve only contractors he trusts: my dad's company, Entropy Entrepreneurs, LLC and Tank's company, White Knight Personal Security."

Star asked, "You do still have a consulting agreement with Tank, right?"

Sonja said, "Yep. We girls know how to have fun, don't we?"

♦ ♦ ♦ ♦ ♦

April 16, 2024
Wiscasset, Maine

"Dad," asked Star on FaceTime, "Why, exactly, did you play golf with ATF Deputy Director Adam Heinz?"

Tucker asked, "Is this my daughter asking me this question or is this the FBI asking the question?"

"Dad, come on. You know I love you and that I would willingly give up my FBI career before I would question you on a case. I am, however, very curious. Do you think Colonel Manion knew in advance that you and Tank would golf with Heinz when he contacted me?"

Tucker answered, "I don't believe in coincidences."

Silence.

"Dad? You and Tank were investigating him, weren't you?"

"Sweetheart, sometimes there are things I can't share with you. I have signed non-disclosure agreements that prohibit me to share information with anyone, including you. I'm about to have a Microsoft Team meeting and I'll invite you to join. Maybe some of the answers will emerge from the meeting."

Five-minutes later, several of the greater Tucker's and Maya's extended virtual family were on the conference call. Tucker started the conversation, "Jimmy, what new information can you tell us about Colonel Manion? We know you've already looked through his laptop."

Jimmy Ma, a 37-year-old employee of Tucker's company answered, "Yes, I am the genius of the 'extended' family."

"Wait a minute," said Tony Vinci, Entropy's chief scientist, "you have a little competition, here. I'll bet you $20 that I have the highest IQ on the team?"

Tucker said, "I'll take that bet."

Tony said, "Uh, oh" while Jimmy stayed silent.

Tucker continued, "I happen to know Maya's IQ."

Jimmy's boyish round face frowned. He cleared his throat and said, "To answer your question, boss, Col. Colby John Manion had numerous communications on the dark web with someone who uses the hashtag '#Steel.' They discussed numerous conspiracy theories about the Las Vegas massacre which ranged from an FBI sting gone bad to an attempt by the CIA to frame a Saudi Prince who stayed at the Mandalay Bay Resort and Casino at the time of the massacre. They agreed they couldn't trust federal law enforcement or intelligence agencies to reveal the truth, whatever it is, so #Steel convinced Manion to find another entity to investigate the event."

Star said, "It doesn't make sense that Manion would reach out to the FBI, me, based on his distrust of the FBI."

Maya said, "He didn't just reach out to the FBI, he reached out to Star Cherokee, the key to accessing the overall Tucker Cherokee family."

Jolene Alvarez, Tank's better half, a former marine and Chief Operating Officer of White Knights Personal Security, LLC said, "Star, we are so pleased that you are back at the FBI, but it has to be less exciting than working in the White House."

Star said, "Thanks, Jolene, but I'm glad to be out of there, too much pressure as the Assistant Press Secretary. I have some stories you wouldn't believe."

Tucker interrupted the sidebar and said, "Manion trusted us to get to the bottom of 'it', whatever 'it' is. He didn't trust law enforcement or the judicial system."

Tank said, "It's about time someone released a credible statement about the Las Vegas massacre. Like everyone else, I want to know the truth. Sonja, did anything show up in Manion's Will that supplies a lead?

Sonja answered, "He left the bulk of his estate to his daughter in Ohio, a key to a safety deposit box to his attorney, and a $20,000 reward to anyone who unveils the truth about the murder of his granddaughter."

Tank said, "That's good enough justification for me to get involved in the investigation of the Las Vegas massacre."

In the background, you could hear Star's protector, Ram, bark in agreement.

Jolene added, "Tank, you don't need a justification if it fits your idea of fun. You love a challenge."

Tony Vinci, a genius in his own right, said, "Boss?"

Tucker answered, "Yeah, Tony."

"My research indicates that ATF DD Adam Heinz played almost no role into the investigation of the Las Vegas massacre. So, why murder him? Jimmy, does your information imply anything different?"

Jimmy answered, "No, his name does not show up on any joint FBI/ATF report."

Maya interrupted and said, "Isn't that the point?"

Silence on the phone.

Maya continued, "In his position, he should have had a more active role. Why didn't he? Maybe that's what Col. Manion wanted Star to investigate. There is probably an unacceptable reason for it."

Tony said, "Glad I didn't take your IQ bet, Tucker."

Tony Vinci is four feet, ten inches tall; mostly upper body. He had dark dull eyes, short-cropped salt and pepper hair, and abnormally large head and hands for a man with dwarf-like legs. He was handsome in a Sicilian sort of way and wore an Outback hat but was most respected for his intelligence; Tony had 76 patents either pending or outright awarded by the time he was 32 years old.

Jimmy added, "Me, too. But I bet I have the second highest IQ on the team."

◆ ◆ ◆ ◆ ◆

April 16, 2024
Wiscasset, Maine

Maya approached Tucker who sat on the back porch overlooking the Sheepscot River and offered him a cup of coffee. Tucker said, "Thank you, sweetheart." He often sat on the porch to meditate and contemplate solutions to indeterminant problems. Maya admired Tucker who was half Cherokee Indian and half of Irish decent, a lean 185 pounds on a six-foot, one inch frame, and blessed all his life with good health. His green eyes on his decisively Native American face gave him a unique, if not handsome, appearance.

Maya said, "We just received a copy of the list of people who were invited by the family to attend Adam Heinz's funeral. It's an eclectic group of people for sure but what stands out is that nobody from the FBI associated with the investigation into the Las Vegas massacre is on the list of attendees."

Tucker said, "That is curious. Either no one liked Heinz or there is something else going on. Is Tony Vinci set up to deploy the drone as I asked? We still want to get a video of all who do show up at the funeral including the uninvited."

Maya asked, "When has Tony ever let you down?"

Tucker lowered his head, looked at Maya over his reading glasses but didn't say a word.

Maya said, "Never mind."

Chapter 3

April 17, 2024
Quantico, Virginia

Star sat in an empty meeting room with the door closed so that she could spread out papers on a conference table and give Ram space. She scrolled through the list given to her by Winemiller of 17 recent victims attacked by alleged senior perpetrators. She looked for a common thread that tied the crimes together and a starting point for her investigation.

As she reviewed the material, she contemplated, *There seems to be no universal theme linking the victims to each other. Some of the victims were well known to the public, most were not. Some were convicted felons, most were not. Although all the victims had past dark shadows in their lives of one form or another, the only concrete thing each of the victims had in common is that a senior committed the attack against them. Most of the perps were over 70 years of age; well past their 'use by' date.*

Ram laid at Star's feet.

Star said, "Ram, I don't know where to start. I see that Adam Heinz and Col. Manion are not even on this list. I guess, all the crimes on this list were committed before Colby Manion made his infamous call to me."

Ram lifted his head off his paws to look at Star as if he wished he could speak but he made no other move.

Star continued, "Let's see, all the perps are older than the Sun and there is no evidence any of them knew each other. Maybe if I send their names to Jimmy Ma, he can find an interrelationship between the senior vigilantes.

"Ram, pay attention?"

Ram did not move a muscle or even blink.

"I see that one of the victims was a defense attorney. I sort of get that. I'll cross-reference the people the lawyer defended with the *Deadly Gray* person that killed the lawyer. The attorney must have successfully defended a powerful but guilty criminal and denied justice from being served, at least as far as the killer was concerned.

"Hmm. I see one of the victims was an MS-13 gang leader. Wow, you got to respect the old geezer that took that challenge on. Death by cop killers.

"One of the crimes committed by a *Deadly Gray* vigilante was the attempted murder of a California State Senator. I will not touch that one with a ten-foot pole unless the Director forces me to investigate it.

"Ram, you're no help.

"Here's one you'll like." Ram stood up on all fours and nuzzled against Star. "A Vietnam era marine sniper placed a round through the head of a long-retired editor of the *New York Times*. Winemiller mentioned this *Deadly Gray* crime to me earlier. The marine sniper even wrote a letter to the *Times* where he took credit for the assassination. Yet, to date, he has not been apprehended by law enforcement. Hmmm, I hope he's done with his revenge. Otherwise, he may continue to commit more murders.

"One of the *Deadly Gray* victims was a 31-year-old rapist on parole mutilated by a 75-year-old vigilante woman from Paris, Kentucky. Let's see, she was clever enough to hunt the parolee down in Cincinnati, Ohio but she didn't kill him. Instead, she shot the man in the groin. I should talk with her to see if she was influenced by someone via the internet which would make her crime an FBI cybercrime. You ready to go for a ride?"

Ram was at the door before she finished her sentence.

April 17, 2024
Quantico to Charlottesville, Virginia

Ram lay in the cargo area of the Rivian SUV on a specially made bed as Star started her leisurely trip from Quantico to Cincinnati via I-64 and I-75. She had only reached Richmond before she received a call from Winemiller. "Have you heard?"

"Probably not. I've been listening to an entertaining audiobook. It allows me an opportunity to escape from reality. What have I missed?"

Winemiller said, "A terminally ill commoner was murdered a member of the House of Lords in the United Kingdom. We might want to coordinate with our friends across the pond to see if they are experiencing the same phenomena as we are with the *Deadly Gray* vigilantes. This problem may spread internationally which reinforces our suspicion that *Deadly Gray* is a universal cyber problem."

Star asked, "Exactly what do you want me to do with this information? Do you want me to contact MI-6 or Scotland Yard or something?"

Winemiller said, "Good idea, Star."

Star considered the impact of the international aspect to her case when she stopped in Charlottesville to let Ram out to do his business. She checked her phone messages, emails, and texts and noticed that one of the texts was from Sonja: *Call me*.

Star called back at once and asked, "What?"

Sonja said, "I heard you are going to Cincinnati."

"It wasn't a secret. Why?"

"Because my husband will be in Cincinnati to play against the Reds at the same time you're there. You should go to the game. He'd love to see you."

Star said, "I have Ram with me, do you think they'll let him in the stadium?"

Sonja said, "Who in their right mind would try to stop him? Anyway, if you have problems getting Ram into the game, let me know because Troy can make it happen. I'll call him now. Love ya." Sonja hung up.

April 18, 2024
Cincinnati, Ohio

The Hamilton County Corrections facility originally refused to allow Ram to stay by Star's side when she attempted to meet with their oldest female inmate. The county police ultimately acquiesced but only if a guard accompanied Star and Ram.

A weak old woman with fat cheeks, decayed teeth and a scarf shuffled into the interrogation room wearing a bright blue jumpsuit and a big smile on her face. She said, "Hello, young lady, are you really with the FBI?

You are so young." She looked apprehensively at Ram, paused, but said, "May I pet your dog."

Star said to Ram, "Good, good."

Ram took on a docile posture and allowed the woman to scratch his head.

"Yes, ma'am, I am with the FBI. I have a couple of questions for you, Mrs. Cloud. But before I ask them, tell me your story as to why you maimed the man whose injuries resulted in your incarceration."

"You can call me Alice, Agent…..," She hesitated.

"Cherokee. Star Cherokee."

"Oh, what an interesting name. Are you Cherokee Indian?"

Star answered, "Actually, about one quarter. My grandfather on my father's side changed his name from Mankiller to Cherokee. I guess you can understand why? I'm also part Irish, Taiwanese, and Norwegian. The virtual American melting pot."

Mrs. Cloud said, "You are way too pretty to be an FBI person. You look a little like my daughter when she was your age. You know, the daughter that was viciously raped and left for dead by that less-than-human criminal that I hurt. My daughter recovered physically from the rape but was never the same mentally. And she couldn't have children afterwards and so I have no grandchildren.

"I was very happy when the police caught the butt-wipe and sent him away to prison. I felt like justice had originally been served and hoped he'd be raped himself in prison. You know, if I had gotten away with my crime against him, I was going after the judge who set him free. I guess the judge will get away with his crime.

Why would the judge do that; I never understood his reason?"

Star said, "I have no idea. How did you find the rapist after the asshole was released? He could have gone anywhere."

Thirty-seconds of silence passed before Alice Cloud said, "You can find just about anybody on the internet these days. It's amazing, don't you think?" Star read the old woman's mind, *I'm not going to tell her about my great nephew.*

Star responded, "True. Did anyone encourage you to commit the crime?"

The old woman said, "Oh, no, it was all my idea. Even my daughter didn't know I was going to find the piece of shit and kill him. It was only at the last minute that I decided to shoot his thing off, rather than kill him."

Star asked, "Where did you learn to shoot a gun?"

"Agent Cherokee—I do love your name—I live in eastern Kentucky."

Star learned nothing new from trying to read her thoughts and asked, "Did you know a man named Colby Manion?"

"No, I don't know anyone by that name."

"Have you ever heard of #Steel?"

"What does hashtag mean?"

Star asked, "Have you heard of the *Deadly Gray*?"

"No."

"Are you ill?"

Mrs. Cloud smiled and said, "I imagined getting old would take longer. I'm only 75 you know. I guess my bald head gives away that I'm ill. Before I was place by the courts here in this Cincinnati prison, I got chemotherapy treatments on the outside."

Star asked, "Has you daughter and/or great-nephew visited you since you entered the detention facility."

Alice Cloud's demeanor changed from a friendly old woman to an angry, hostile person. She said, "We're through here, return me to my cell, please."

Star reflected, *Sometimes I just don't know when to keep my mouth shut. I should never have mentioned her great nephew since she never mentioned him in our conversation.*

After Mrs. Cloud was escorted back to her cell, the thirty-something policeman who oversaw the interview asked, "Agent Cherokee, would you be interested to join me for dinner before you return to Quantico?"

Star took a deep breath, looked the policeman in the eye and said, "First, you have to get Ram's approval."

Ram bared his teeth.

The cop said, "Never mind."

April 18, 2024
Cincinnati, Ohio

"Rusty, I think the investigation of the old Kentucky woman, Alice Cloud, is a dead end. Though by definition, she is a *Deadly Gray* criminal, I don't believe she is part of a broader movement. I may need to talk to her great nephew to close this case out, but Alice protects him like a grizzly protecting her cub. It's a low probability anyway that the great nephew will provide a meaningful lead."

Agent Winemiller said, "It is just as well because I want you to go to California and follow up on the Stanford student who was a victim of the Cadillac Escalade hit-and-run crime. Witnesses at the scene said the driver intentionally killed the bicyclist. There were no tags on the Escalade and witnesses also said the driver was a white-haired Caucasian who wore dark sunglasses. That's all we've got."

Star said, "It sounds like an anger management issue; California road rage and all. "

Winemiller said, "An older man targeted and intentionally killed someone; that sounds like a *Deadly Gray* murder to me. Head out there as soon as you can."

Star said, "First, Ram and I are going to a baseball game."

April 19, 2024
Wiscasset, Maine

An armed guard at the entrance to the Cherokee estate, shouldering an M4 carbine by a strap, forced the Fed Ex delivery driver to stop. The guard held out his hand to accept an envelope. The driver's voice cracked as he said, "I'm supposed to hand deliver this to a Dr. Maya Cherokee and get her signature."

The guard rolled his eyes but made the call over the intercom, "Dr. Cherokee, there is a package here for your signature from, let's see, A. Vinci. Do you want me to follow protocol and x-ray the package?"

Maya spoke into the intercom and said, "No, don't x-ray it. I'll be right out."

Maya's long black silky hair swung back and forth synchronized with each step. She wore a tight-fitting dark blue silk kimono over her tall athletic body. Her beauty stunned the driver. He pondered, *She could easily be a movie star or a model*. She signed for the package, smiled at the driver, and said to the guard, "Thanks, Jason." Maya turned around and returned to the estate. The driver stood still and watched her walk back to the house."

The guard cleared his throat and said, "Don't you have something better to do?"

As the man slid into the driver's seat of his van, he said, "No."

Maya found Tucker pensively working on his computer in his home office and handed him a thumb drive. She said, "Compliments from your most trusted employee."

Tucker said, "Let's look at the contents together. Let's see if anyone who attended Col. Manion's funeral also attended Adam Heinz' funeral.

"Why didn't Tony just send this to me electronically?"

Maya said, "I suspect it contains too many megs."

Tucker said, "Let's view each funeral on the big screen. There is no reason why someone who attends Manion's funeral would also attend Heinz's funeral."

Maya, said, "Except a reporter or a detective."

They viewed the Heinz funeral first which took place in St. Albans, Vermont. It was well-attended by what looked to be family members and a few obvious ATF colleagues. No one looked out-of-place. Then the video panned out when Tony Vinci lifted the drone an additional 50 feet in elevation, rotated it, and focused on more distant non-attending people. The drone captured the faces of cemetery employees, taxi drivers, the hearse driver, and flower delivery type people. The video zoomed in on one person, obviously alone, near the entourage of service people. He was dressed casually in jeans, wore a Red Sox ball cap while scanning the funeral attendees through a monocular.

Tucker said. "Can't see his face. How much more time on the video?"

Maya said, "Looks like we're only about halfway through it."

The video from the drone operated by Tony Vinci days earlier continued to survey the field of attendees. Toward the end of Tony's MP4, the drone caught the mystery man with the monocular as he entered one of the taxis. Tucker said, "His face is too blurry, but he is roughly six feet tall, 190 to 200 pounds, white, with brown hair based on his sideburns."

Maya said, "Tony got the cab plates. Maybe the driver could work with an artist."

Tucker said, "Let's see if this spook-like character also attended the Manion funeral."

Chapter 4

April 22, 2024
Las Vegas, Nevada

"Exactly what is it you expect to find here with your investigation? You should just read the comprehensive reports filed by the joint team that investigated the tragedy." An irritated Sheriff Lakota continued his rant at Tank and Jolene and said, "After almost twelve months of analyzing evidence and information, the FBI concluded its investigation without finding a clear motive for Stephen Paddock's bizarre actions from the 32nd floor of the Mandalay Bay Resort and Casino. He had no identifiable grievances and apparently had a desire to die by suicide.

"The FBI's Behavioral Analysis Unit determined that Paddock acted alone, and that his attack was neither directed, inspired, nor enabled by ideologically motivated persons or groups. They concluded that there was no single or clear motivating factor behind the attack. The jerk acted alone."

Jolene said, "Sounds amazingly similar to Lee Harvey Oswald's assassination of President John Kennedy. He allegedly acted alone, too."

Tank added, "As did Jack Ruby who acted alone to kill Lee Harvey Oswald. How convenient. Sheriff, we are not conspiracy theorists. New light has been shed on the case based on the murder of ATF Deputy Director, Adam Heinz. Did you work with him, discuss the case with him, or interact with him in any way?"

Sheriff Lakota narrowed his dark eyes, stood up and said with undamped anger, "We are through here. I have a job to do and cannot spend my life in a 'Groundhog Day' reinvestigation of a closed case. Investigate all you want but do not tie up my Las Vegas Metropolitan Police staff. Good day."

Tank and Jolene remained seated.

Lakota said, "Must I have you forcibly removed from my office?"

Tank said, "You could do that. Or you could share with us the evidence the evil doers forced you and Adam Heinz to suppress."

Jolene added, "Did you fear for your life or was your family threatened? The massacre was more insidious than just a man gone mad, wasn't it?"

The sheriff ran his hand through is silver hair, stood his ground and said, "Please excuse yourselves from my office. You two sound more and more like the very conspiracy theorists you protest that you are not."

Tank stood up, looked down at Lakota, smiled, and without saying another word, left the sheriff's office. Jolene, however, did not leave immediately. At six feet, one inch tall, the attractive, blue-eyed blond marine who wore a purple sweatsuit and cowgirl boots said, "It was not a good idea for you to throw Tank out of your office. Based on your reaction to our visit, he now suspects you are covering something up. Bad move on your part; he is a tenacious investigator. Whatever are your fears, he will make damn sure they ultimately are exposed." Jolene then left Sheriff Lakota's office.

As she and Tank walked down the strip, Jolene said, "The fear in the man's eyes is palpable. It reinforces what Jimmy Ma said after he read the documents on old man Manion's laptop. Col. Manion believed the investigators were threatened by someone.

Lakota sure acts like someone who has been threatened by people to be feared. The question is who could successfully threaten an ordinarily tough police officer?"

Tank ruminated pensively and walked a few steps before he said, "Maybe it was Adam Heinz who threatened Sheriff Lakota. Maybe it was the FBI. Maybe it was the real massacre killer. Whatever, he probably has a shitty attitude because he has his head up his ass.

"As you are aware, I did a little research about the Las Vegas massacre before we arrived. Lakota never got the massacre timeline right when he briefed the press, he never admitted to the fact that there had to be multiple shooters based on calculated trajectories of bullets, he never explained how there could be so many head shots from a shooter randomly firing out a window, he never explained why they didn't attempt to match ballistics with the weapons in Paddock's room, or why three helicopters hovering around the Mandalay Bay that night turned off their transponders fifteen minutes before the shooting began.

"What could possibly be the motive for randomly killing people you don't know? Why would Paddock need multiple assault weapons with bump stock devices when he only needed one or two assault rifles since all he had to do was insert new fully loaded magazines? And why would he stop shooting when there were thousands of rounds left in magazines in his Mandalay Bay Resort and Casino room? Why would Colby Manion kill Adam Heinz instead of someone else to lead us on this wild goose chase? What did Manion know?"

Jolene said, "All good questions, Tank. But what bothers me most is why the case is closed by authorities."

Tank's cell phones rang. He saw his call was from Tucker who asked, "Have you heard the news?"

Tank answered, "Maybe not, I'm here in Las Vegas to try to gather information about the massacre."

Tucker said, "There has been a suicide bomb detonated in Berkeley, California at the headquarters of a gun control advocacy group. It's all over the cable news networks."

Tank said, "OK. There must be more to the story. Otherwise, you would not call me."

Tucker said, "The suicide bomber was 87 years old. Jimmy Ma told me that the old man announced his intent in advance to Colonel Manion in an e-mail."

Star Cherokee was tied into the same call with her father and said, "Hi, Tank. I am headed to California. I have got some investigating to do on the suicide bombing in Berkeley and a hit-and-run case of a Stanford student. Have you learned anything there in Las Vegas that could be relevant to my cases?"

"Only that *Deadly Gray* Manion succeeded in his attempt to get us involved in investigating the Las Vegas massacre. I am definitely sucked into finding out why he killed the ATF guy, Adam Heinz. The hook is firmly planted in the roof of my mouth."

Jolene received a call from Maya who asked, "Can you add a couple of White Knight guards to protect our estate? Tucker is a man possessed by both Star's *Deadly Gray* vigilante case and Tank's goal to find out the truth about the Las Vegas massacre. He will kick over a hornet's nest which usually results in the need for more security here at the compound."

Jolene said, "Of course, but your premonition scares me."

Chapter 5

1966
Laos

#Steel, Steelman, had been through hell and back serving the country he loved. Looking back at his naiveté 58 years later, he had to smile. He was full of 'shit and vinegar' back then; and he believed he was immortal. He lost forty pounds during Navy Seal training that landed him at a trim 220 pounds. He believed his country and his government were pure, honorable, and did everything with the best interest of its citizens in mind. For the most part he still believed some of that was true. Like all good Special Forces operatives, he followed orders explicitly; he did not question what he was instructed to do even when he was instructed to assassinate a potential leader of a foreign nation. At the time, back in 1966, he had no idea why a charismatic Laotian was a threat to America, but he trusted his leaders, his captain, and his team.

It was a trust he regretted now for almost six decades. Steelman, as his teammates referred to him, was the most junior on the Laos mission as they crawled through the jungle and approached an unassuming typical Laotian home. He observed no guards, no apparent resistance, no obvious risk to the Seal Team at the target's location. One team member alone could have completed the mission; let alone five Navy Seals.

The target was, maybe, 32 years old with a healthy-looking wife and three kids ranging from three to seven years of age.

Captain Werner, the Seal Team leader said, "Our orders are to take the entire family out, not just the father. Apparently, it's supposed to look like a gang-killing—nothing that could link back to America. Laotians will turn against the opposition party which is backed by the communists. We must plant the evidence to support the premise."

Steelman stopped and asked, "Captain, do we have to kill the kids? I did not sign up and work to become a Navy Seal to kill children."

Captain Werner asked his team, "Are any of you refusing a direct order?"

Steelman shook his head, said nothing, but thought, *The captain has more acid in his veins than blood.*

The mission leader said, "On the count of five, move and complete your mission assignment."

♦ ♦ ♦ ♦ ♦

April 23, 2024
Great Falls, Virginia

Nature's fireworks sounded like artillery shells fired from cannons. Storm water drowned traditional drains; water droplets bounced a quartet-inch off the asphalt, branches surrendered to the wind, and oak tree leaves upturned to GOD. Light flickered seconds before the next artillery volley, dogs whined, and rain pounded everything in its way.

#Steel wondered, "*Long before people of science understood that when there is a layer of warm air near the ground hovering underneath a layer of colder air, thunderstorms occur. What did indigenous people think 1,000 years ago when a thunderstorm overwhelmed them? What do deer think when thunderstorms occur?"*

Old man #Steel smiled and thought, *What a great environment in which to kill the bastard. I have to be one crazy MF to enjoy being out in this weather.* He wore fireman's rain gear acquired years ago from an Indianapolis fire department. He wore trout fishing boots, slickers, and carried a weatherproof bag to protect his 9mm Walther PPQ and its attached homemade silencer from the severe weather.

His computer search about his target's family revealed that they had no children and enjoyed only cats, so he did not have to contend with a barking dog. He searched the property for surveillance cameras but only spotted a trail camera from which he removed its scandisk. #Steel approached the basement sliding glass door of the exclusive 4,500 square feet house and prepared to pick the lock. It was unnecessary—the door was unlocked.

He cautiously eased himself into the basement but left the sliding glass door open—just in case he needed a fast exit. #Steel listened for sounds of movement in the house but could only hear the cacophony of noises produced by the thunderstorm. At his age, he was lucky to hear anything.

He searched for and found the power cabinet, then flipped the main circuit breaker off. He was confident that his target would assume that the power loss was due to the storm. He pulled down his Night Vision Goggles and wandered in the direction of the basement stairs that lead up to the first floor. #Steel was big man who had added too many pounds to his frame over the years which amplified the sound of his own wet boots sloshing around on the basement cement.

Suddenly, his target opened the door to the basement and yelled back to his wife, "I'm going down into the basement to get our Coleman lamp, more flashlights, and candles."

#Steel's target absent mindlessly flipped the useless light switch to the stairway, laughed at himself, donned a flashlight, and headed down the stairs into the basement.

#Steel waited near the bottom of the basement steps and contemplated, *How lucky am I?*

He pulled his 6-inch K-Bar knife and waited until his target reached the bottom step. He did not want to just kill this guy, he wanted him to know why.

From the shadows he dragged the knife across his target's back to maximize the man's pain while he covered his mouth with his gloved left hand to muffle his scream.

#Steel said, "Do you recognize my voice; do you remember me? Well, I remember you and I know who you became. I know what you did and what you do. This is for all the innocent people including children whose lives you helped ruin or killed."

Former Seal Captain Werner moved quickly for a man at his age. His Navy Seal training kicked in; he turned and dropped quickly, tackled Steelman with a double-leg takedown and then rammed his shoulder into Steelman's stomach. But Steelman did not drop his knife, instead, he jabbed his victim again in his back before he slit Werner's throat. Werner reflexively tried to stop the bleeding with his hands as Steelman said,

"You never should have ordered me to kill those children 58 years ago."

His victim, Paul Werner, was a highly respected man in his community who had concealed his true character. He facilitated the death of innocent children in Laos and moved on to human trafficking and child pornography. He reaped rewards from Mexican drug lords who supplied the kidnapped children for nefarious reasons.

The captain did remember who Steelman was just before his heart stopped beating.

#Steel, Steelman, was a *Deadly Gray* justice warrior and a leader of the senior vigilante movement. He not only talked the talk but walked the walk.

◆ ◆ ◆ ◆ ◆

April 23, 2024
WMAL, Woodbridge, Virginia

Breaking News:

Fairfax County's Sheriff just announced that former Congressman Paul Werner was found dead in his basement by his wife, Angela. Mr. Werner was a veteran, a public servant, and successful lobbyist for three of the nation's largest tech companies. Law enforcement is withholding information about the cause of death. Foul play has not been ruled out by investigators. More to follow.

Star was studying new data collected by the FBI contained in the *Deadly Gray* file until her personal cell phone rang. It was Jimmy Ma.

"Either Colonel Manion communicates from the hereafter or someone else has administrative rights and access to his blog page."

Star asked, "Jimmy, have you been drinking again?"

"Yes, of course."

"So, what are you talking about?"

Jimmy said, "A message from Colonel Manion showed up on his blog page today. Quote: *Like Adam Heinz, Paul Werner paid for his evilness. Justice is sweet.*

"You know, Star, I heard that Colby Manion said quote, 'he was not alone.' Whoever the killer was that had a grudge against this old Werner fellow for something he did who knows when, the perp may be as old as Manion."

Star asked, "Did you uncover anything on Manion's blog page or in his laptop that is relevant to the Werner case?"

Jimmy said, "I compared writing styles using a program that our mutual friend Tony Vinci wrote and compared the style to Manion's historical blogs. The blog was not written by Manion."

Star said sarcastically, "Well that's a relief."

"The writing style matched one of his frequent contacts: #Steel."

"Anything else?"

Jimmy answered, "Yes. I will send you a link to another message to Manion from someone currently unknown except as 'Angel'."

Star clicked on to the Angel link and read aloud:

"You are never too old to be a vigilante. I intend to kill an evil person in the sunset of my life. I have observed over my 84 years a number of eligible candidates. My current list of targets includes MS-13 gang members, pedophiles out on parole, abortionists, criminal defense attorneys, human traffickers of children, and even a couple of politicians.

"I have never hunted an animal; never shot a deer. I do not like to fish and when I did fish, I threw it back so it would live another day. I am squeamish about killing a mouse or a snake. I have always been a non-violent type of guy.

"Until now.

"Though in good health for my age, I recognize that I am mortal. I still play racquetball once a month and ride a bike. I have no terminal illnesses and am of sound mind yet I'm realistic enough to know my days are numbered as I approach the end of my life.

"It is not how long you have to live but how you spend the rest of your life.

"I have decided to be a vigilante. If I can avoid it, I refuse to die in a nursing home with the inability to wipe my own ass. I want to go out with a purpose, exact justice, and eliminate evil.

"GOD forgive me."

And it is good to know I am not alone in my waning days.

Star said to Jimmy Ma, "Angel definitely falls under my investigation into the *Deadly Gray* case."

"Star," said Jimmy, "There are hundreds of similar correspondences between Manion, #Steel, and other blog participants."

"Hundreds?"

Jimmy answered, "At least."

"Jimmy, could you corroborate the blogs associated with Manion and the Las Vegas massacre?"

"As FBI Agent Mulder said many times in the program 'X-files,' the 'truth is out there'."

Star asked, "What is the truth, Jimmy?"

"I do not know. I am searching for it."

◆ ◆ ◆ ◆ ◆

April 23, 2024
Minneapolis, Minnesota

82-year-old Mrs. Hoffman who lived in Minnesota's 5th district in Minneapolis received a text message on her old flip phone. She was a short, thin grandmotherly woman with a slight limp and who was the wife of a former Minneapolis police department captain, the mother of a son who made police sergeant, and a daughter who made police detective. She had not shared with her loved ones that she had terminal ovarian cancer—she had only three weeks to live. The text was simple: call me at 702-555-7705.

She did.

The person on the other end of the phone said, "Mrs. Hoffman you have an opportunity to make a difference in your life that reinforces the honor of your late husband, as well as your son and daughter. Your representative in Congress supports defunding the police, proposes Sharia law in your community and the elimination of our southern border. She will have a fund-raising lunch at the Hilton Hotel Minneapolis on Tuesday. Your $500 plate has been paid by your benefactors. You still have your husbands service revolver. Use it."

Chapter 6

April 23, 2024
Oakland, California

Before he retired, 87-year-old Jacob Cohen taught history at a Ralph J. Bunche High School in Oakland. He taught his students that a year before Adolf Hitler took power in 1933, the German Interior Minister directed that gun registration records be made secure to keep them from falling "into the hands of radical elements." The Minister's efforts proved futile, and the records fell into the hands of the Nazi government, The Nationalist Social German Workers' Party, which used the information to disarm its political enemies and the Jews.

Cohen taught his students that the disarmament of the German Jews was initially limited by the government to local areas. The major target was Berlin, where large-scale raids in search of weaponry took place. Cohen's own father was a victim of the raids.

Starting in 1936, the Gestapo prohibited German police officers from giving firearms licenses to Jews. In November 1938, the Nazi's prohibited the possession of firearms and bladed weapons by Jews. Also in 1938, the Nazis deprived Jews of the rights of citizenship and were ratcheting up measures to strip them of their assets—including the means to defend themselves. The horrific consequences have names etched in history's consciousness. Cohen shared the following often-cited passage, from the doctrine, Part Three: 6 February – 7 September 1942:

"The most foolish mistake we could possibly make would be to allow the subject races to possess arms. History shows that all conquerors who have allowed their subject races to carry arms have prepared their own downfall by so doing. Indeed, I would go as far as to say that the supply of arms to the underdogs is a sine qua non for the overthrow of any sovereignty. So, let us not have any native militia or native police."

Cohen taught his students that the 1938 German Weapons Act lowered the age upon which German citizens could own firearms, but stripped Jews of any rights to own firearms. Cohen said, "Jews were never allowed to fight back. Learn from history and control your own destiny."

Jacob Cohen posted on an anti-gun control website the following:

"I was 12 years old when the Allies freed me at Auschwitz. The fascists in Berkeley attempt to follow the model established by Nazi Germany. I will fight back in my father's memory. History cannot be allowed to repeat itself."

Star called her boss, Rusty Winemiller, and said, "The Oakland bombing of a gun control organization is definitely a *Deadly Gray* case after reading the perpetrator's post, but I don't find evidence that he was coerced or cajoled into committing the suicide bombing by #Steel or any other cybercriminal. I will continue to research the Cohen crime but that is where I am today on the case. Do you have any information to the contrary?"

Winemiller said, "Actually, yes, I do. I think one of his students is active on a dark web site entitled *DanielWebsterWorldView.* I am trying to learn what his IP address is. When I do, I would like for you to interview the student."

Star said, "Roger that."

April 23, 2024
Harpers Ferry, West Virginia

Jimmy Ma's encrypted satellite phone rang. Very few people knew his number, so he took a deep breath before he picked it up. "This is Jimmy. How can I help you?"

"Jimmy," said Tucker, "I promised some of your time to help Star, Tank, and the FBI; roughly 15 hours a week. Are you OK with that? Will our Treasury Department customer blink?"

Jimmy said, "I can do in 15 hours what most people take 40 hours to do."

Tucker said, "I love your self-deprecating humor. That is good because I want you to do what you do best—follow the money. Search the financial records of Adam Heinz, Sheriff Lakota of the Las Vegas Metropolitan Police, and Paul Werner of Great Falls, Virginia. Also, contact Tony. He is in the process of identifying a man on a video taken from a drone of a guy that attended the funeral of both Heinz and Manion.

Once Tony identifies him, I want you to follow the money on him. They will be more later."

Jimmy asked, "Do I get a bonus?"

Tucker said, "Tell you what Jimmy, I'll let you keep your job and, maybe, give you a free trip to Las Vegas. I understand they have 'Go' tables there. Tank can protect you when you cheat."

"I do not cheat boss. I'm just good."

Tucker said, "Sure, that's why you're persona non gratis at most 'Go' tables in New York City and Washington, DC. The only reason you are still alive is because it is illegal to shoot you or because someone saved you from the mob."

Chapter 7

April 24, 2024
Wiscasset, Maine

"You're not here."

"No, I'm here."

"Where is here?"

"Las Vegas, Nevada."

"That's a long way from here, isn't it?"

"That depends on where you are."

"I'm here."

"Stanley, where is 'here'?"

"I am at the front door to your house, Jolene. Can I come in?"

"I am not there. I am thousands of miles away. Why are you at the front door of my home? You have not spoken to me in weeks."

"That is why I'm here. I have not spoken to you in weeks. I want to talk."

"OK. OK. Stay at my front door until someone comes to let you in."

"Then we can talk?"

"No, not until I come home."

"Who will cook for me? I am hungry."

"Just stay at the front door until someone comes by to let you in. Can you do that, Stanley?"

"I'll stay right here."

Jolene hung up the phone and sighed with exasperation.

Tank said, "Don't tell me that was your brother on the phone and he's at the front door to our house? How did he find his way from Huntsville, Alabama to Wiscasset, Maine?"

Jolene shrugged her shoulders as she made a call. "Maya, I need your help. My special needs brother, Stanley, currently stands on the front porch of our home. Would you send one of our White Knights who guard your estate over to our place to let him in. And, if you would, see if Chef Rhino can rustle up something for him to eat. I will fly home as soon as possible to take care of him."

Maya said, "Of course. I did not know you had a brother. You never speak of him. Special needs?"

Jolene said, "Let us just say he's unique. Thanks, Maya."

Tank said, "Unique? That's an understatement."

"I will head home while you do your pit bull stuff here. I know you cannot let go. I must help our business manager run the White Knight operation anyway. Our business is booming. You need to take some time off from this case and interview people to hire. We cannot seem to keep up with the demand ever since the "defund the police" movement took hold."

April 24, 2024
Quantico, Virginia

"What have you found?"

Star answered, "Jacob Cohen, the gun control organization bomber left a suicide note on his desk in his home in Nice on Clear Lake. He definitely had a grudge against the activist organization who attack the people's 2nd amendment rights. He left a Will. And oddly, he left his laptop to the FBI. That's got to be a first."

Special Agent Rusty Winemiller said, "Actually, Star, it has happened before. Bring the laptop back with you and we will have our computer forensic staff look at it. What else have you discovered?"

"He posted a manifesto on his son's Facebook page. In the narrative, he mention's #Steel's leadership."

Winemiller asked, "Did you interview the Cohen's student as I instructed?"

"No. He has disappeared."

Star added, "Are your forensic experts any closer to discover who #Steel is?"

Winemiller said, "Unfortunately, no."

Star said, "You might want to engage Jimmy Ma and Tony Vinci."

"Yeah, I have thought about that, but our computer forensic team assures me they'll find #Steel in the next few days. I will give them that much rope.

"What's the status of the Stanford hit-and run case?"

Star said, "The local police found the Cadillac Escalade with no plates in San Jose; it was wiped clean; no fingerprints, no fibers, no nothing. It was stolen same day the unsub who ran over the kid on the bike. I spoke with a couple of the witnesses and then with people who interfaced with the biker but learned nothing useful. The local police got a warrant to look through his home and allowed me to join in the search for someone who hated him enough to run him over. We have a couple of incredibly good leads. To our surprise, the Stanford student, Kurt Rainwater, lived by himself in a $4 million home on a golf course in Sharon Heights. We checked his parents out and they are not financially well off except for the $10,000 check he sent them every month."

Winemiller said, "He must be doing something illegal to achieve that kind of wealth as a grad student."

Star said, "We agree."

"Can we get a warrant to check his computer?"

"Already done."

"Well, keep me posted."

April 24, 2024
Washington, DC

The Secret Service designated Asa Frank as a person-of-interest. The old man stood outside or walked around the Capitol, the Congressional Office buildings, and the Senate buildings, every day for the past three weeks. He appeared to be a thin, short homeless man with long unkempt hair and a beard. He wore a fishing hat as he pushed a shopping cart containing only a large canvas bag. Asa, however, was too articulate to be a homeless person or a mentally ill case when confronted by the Secret Service who asked him to move on and go elsewhere.

His response always was, "The Mall, the Smithsonian, and the Capitol belong to the people. I have every right to be here. It is still a free country, right?"

He watched intently as Congress members, senators, lobbyists, and tourists paraded around the center of power day after day. He finally spotted his target get into a limo and shuttle down Pennsylvania Avenue in the direction of the White House. Traffic kept the VIP limo from traveling at a speed too much faster than Asa could follow on foot pushing a cart. Blocks later he saw the limo turn right on 15th street. The Speaker of the House stopped at Old Ebbitt Grill for lunch.

Asa sensed; *This is my chance.*

He left his grocery cart on 'G' Street, grabbed his canvas bag, and started to wait at the corner of 'G' and 15th until the Speaker finished her lunch meeting and come back out to get in her limo to return to the Capitol.

Asa thought, *Damn, the Secret Service is everywhere around this restaurant. I better stay on the move.* He decided to turn around and walk a block to 14th Street, back to 'F' Street, and then turkey-peak on 15th to see the status of things. On the way, he checked the contents of his bag.

Before Asa made it back to 15th street, three Secret Service officers surrounded him. One officer asked, "What's in the bag?"

Asa answered, "Do you have a warrant to investigate my possessions?"

The officer said, "We have probable cause based on the fact that you stalked the Speaker of the House."

Asa reached into his bag.

All three officers pulled their weapons. The lead officer said, "Whoa now, be careful, hand over the bag, now." One officer grabbed Asa, wrapped his arms around his shoulders, prevented Asa from lifting his arms and from using whatever was in the bag. The other officer grabbed the bag.

"Well, what do we have here?" asked the lead officer. "Looks like a stick of dynamite to me. Where did you get this and what did you intend to do with it?"

A disappointed and dejected Asa Frank defiantly stuck his chin up and said, "My malfeasance is justified had I been successful. I intended to eradicate one source of tyranny and abuse of power in our overreaching government. We must stop government excesses before we lose all our freedoms. I want my grandchildren to live and prosper in the same country I grew up in."

One of the officer's asked, "What mental institution did you escape from? Did you really think we would let you that close to the Speaker?"

The first officer asked again, "Where did you get dynamite? It's illegal to buy or sell."

"So are guns in Washington, DC but the use of guns here by criminals is still a problem, isn't it because the fascists that run this place have taken away our freedom to protect ourselves."

"OK, I have heard enough. You are under arrest under the domestic terrorism statue 18USC2331. You will be in a federal penitentiary for the rest of your life."

Asa said, "So what. There is no dignity to die without a purpose or cause."

One of the Secret Service agents said, "I really wonder why we look for intelligent life on other planets when it is so hard to find intelligent life here."

Chapter 8

April 25, 2024
Washington, DC

FBI Director, Brad Naylor, sat in the Oval Office in front of the President of the United States, Timothy Lamb. Naylor never enjoyed coming to the White House because it usually meant he would have his anus enlarged. He was of medium height but muscular and carried his square jaw line and perpetual two-days of facial hair growth with pride. His intelligent eyes, dirty blond hair, and natural smile endeared him to many, but not POTUS.

"Director," POTUS said, "I understand we have a problem. Apparently, seniors are taking the law into their own hands. I am told, not by you, that there is a trend by seniors to commit murder or other crimes. One tried to assassinate the Speaker of the House. Is that correct?"

Director Naylor responded with a deep gravelly voice, "Yes, Mr. President, there is an alarming increase in murders by seniors over the last few months."

President Lamb waited for Naylor to continue.

"The FBI is investigating the trend under the umbrella case called *Deadly Gray*."

Still, POTUS waited.

"This may be an anomaly, or it may be organized."

President Lamb said, "What do you recommend I do about this? Why is it happening now and what action should I take?"

Director Naylor asked, "If you could reach out to big tech, encourage them to allow us to investigate certain elements of their cookies, it could be helpful."

"I will have to use a little reverse phycology on them to get them to cooperate. After all, they've even banned me from their sites. Brad, keep me informed. I do not need to hear this shit first from others."

"Yes, sir."

POTUS stood six feet, five inches tall and carried a fit 230 pounds. He projected his intimidating former military policeman confidence with an intense, midwestern, all business management style. He said, "I also understand the man who tried to kill the Speaker intended to use dynamite. Where did he get it and what do we need to do to prevent explosives from entering the city? I was under the impression we had methods to prevent that."

Naylor said, "We have learned that the domestic terrorist was a professor at the University of Missouri. He taught Explosives Engineering and had a blasting certificate. It was legal for him to buy dynamite. He shielded the stick in a schedule eighty pipe so that chemical sniffers and K9s didn't pick up the scent of explosives. Fortunately, Secret Service officers were vigilant and stopped the event before it happened."

Director Naylor left the Oval Office and immediately called Special Agent Winemiller, "Rusty, I just left the Oval Office. Someone has informed POTUS about the *Deadly Gray* problem. He will want answers immediately. The question is 'Why is this happening, now.' I will need a daily briefing from this point forward."

Rusty Winemiller subsequently called Star and passed the information on to her. He said, "You know shit flows downhill, right?"

Star said, "Give me the tools I need. Let me increase the size of the contract for Jimmy Ma and Tony Vinci. I need the professor's social security number and physical address as soon as possible."

Winemiller said, "OK."

Star called her father and said, "Dad, I need to increase the use of Jimmy Ma and Tony Vinci to assist me on the *Deadly Gray* vigilante cases. I got approval from Winemiller. Can you spare them from their day job with Entropy?"

Tucker said, "Actually, no. Both are tied up on some very important national security type contracts. You can have Jimmy Ma, maybe 25% of his time and Tony closer to half time."

"Oh, thank you Dad. I do not think you'll regret it."

"Star," said Tucker, "Will you come home anytime soon?

"We will see, Dad. We will see."

April 25, 2024
Wiscasset, Maine

"Well, it is about time. I came all the way here to see my big sister and she was not here."

Jolene said, "Stanley, you should have let me know you were coming, I would have made sure I was home when you arrived. How did you get here all the way from Alabama?"

Stanley stood in front of Jolene wearing dungarees pulled up over his navel, a long-sleeved plaid shirt with a hole above the pocket, beat up working boots, and a ball cap turned backwards. He said, "I wrote your address down on a piece of paper."

Jolene looked at her little brother and asked, "Who did you give the piece of paper to?"

"Truck drivers. You know, Peterbilt, MAC, Volvo, the big guys."

"So, you hitchhiked all the way here. Does the home you were staying in know where you are?"

Stanley hung his head and said, "I never want to go back there." He looked anxiously at his older sister and happily asked, "Can I stay here?"

Jolene grudgingly said, "We'll see."

Stanley said, "I can help you. I know things."

"Oh," said Jolene with humor in her voice, "what kind of things?"

Stanley said, "I am really good at solving mysteries. I always know the ending to every movie I watch on TV before it ends."

Jolene laughed and said, "Well, that would come in handy in our business."

A warning light appeared on a panel in the hallway. It announced that someone had passed through their intrusion detection system. Before Jolene checked to see who it was, Stanley said, "Oh, that was just a deer."

Sure enough, when Jolene checked the video camera, it was a group of three does. Jolene pondered on how Stanley could know but let it pass.

◆ ◆ ◆ ◆ ◆

April 25, 2024
Town and Country, Missouri

Sonja walked into the playroom and yelled at her 4-year-old son, "Powers, stop tormenting Runner. One of these days he will bite you."

Of course, the 85-pound off-spring of Ram would never do that. Sonja noticed his tail was wagging as Powers tried to lay on top of Runner while the German Shepherd tried to sleep. Powers' twin sister, Li, was oblivious to the event as she played with an empty cardboard box and jabbered in some unknown language to a stuffed elephant.

The famous sound of ZZ Top's "La Grange" interrupted Sonja's scolding of her son. It was the tune she picked for when Tank called. She ran to pick up her cell phone on the third ring.

Without introduction, Tank asked, "You busy?"

She answered with thick sarcasm in her voice, "No less busy than any mother raising twin four-year-olds. I got all the time in the world. Why?"

"Can you come to Las Vegas for me?"

"Tank, the baseball season has begun. You know I've fundamentally lost Troy until October."

"Your MVP shortstop husband is stinking rich. You probably have three full-time nannies and a cook. Powers and Li can do without their mother for a couple of days."

"Two nannies and a maid."

"Whatever."

Sonja asked, "What is it you need me for in Las Vegas that one of your numerous Special Forces employees can't do."

"Forensics."

"Tank, what are you talking about. I know nothing about forensics."

Tank said, "But you know a thing or two about shooting rifles. I would like you to dive into the Las Vegas massacre event and investigate the forensics associated with the shooting by Paddock out the 35th floor of the Mandalay Bay Resort and Casino. Who knows more about shooting than you? Ask for Sheriff Lakota when you get there. It will rattle his cage."

April 25, 2024
Las Vegas, Nevada

Las Vegas Metropolitan Police Department detective Mike Tursky, Jr. sat at his desk in his cubicle on Martin Luther King Blvd., when he overheard Sheriff Lakota complain to one of his subordinates about the never-ending conspiracy theorists that consume his time surrounding the 2017 Route 91 country music festival mass shooting. "Can you believe that even Tank Alvarez of White Knight Personal Security was in my office this week investigating the crime. I have lost respect for him over that. What was it Einstein said, 'The difference between intelligence and stupidity is that there is a limit to intelligence' or something like that?"

Detective Tursky lifted his large frame—heavy in the shoulders with a beer gut—off his chair and out of the office to his home in Henderson. He went into the kitchen grabbed a beer and a bag of chips before he sat down in front of his home computer. He looked up the White Knight Personal Security web site and called the listed number.

"Hello, this is White Knight Personal Security, how can we help you?"

"This is Mike Tursky of Henderson, Nevada. I am trying to reach Tank Alvarez who I understand may be in Las Vegas. I would like to speak with him about information I have on the Las Vegas massacre. I will give you my cell phone if you can ask him to call me at his earliest convenience."

The office manager called Tank and said, "A man called about information on what you all are investigating out there. He might be just looking for a job under false pretenses, but I thought I better give you his number just in case."

Tank said, "Thanks, I'll give him a call."

"Hello, this is Mike Tursky."

"Mike, this is Tank Alvarez, I understand you want to speak with me."

"Yes sir. I am a detective with the Las Vegas Metropolitan Police Department. This call is not an official police call. In the past I investigated a fraud perpetrated in Pioche, Nevada involving claims of gold and silver in a mining waste pond. People claimed to have ownership of the pond when they did not. Millions of dollars were paid to the perpetrators when they sold the claim they did not own. One of the perpetrators was Stephen Paddock. He was never accused of being an accomplice to the crime and he never served time for his role in the fraud.

"I brought this to the attention of Sheriff Lakota, but it never made it into any of the investigative reports. I do not know if this is of any value, but I reckoned I would share this with you."

Tank said, "All information is useful. Do you still have the evidence, or did Lakota expunge the data as part of the overall cover up?

"I can show it to you, but I will not give you a copy. You will have to come to my home in Henderson to view it."

April 25, 2024
Harpers Ferry, West Virginia

Tucker asked, "What's the status on the follow-the-money projects I asked you to investigate?"

Jimmy said, "You don't believe in coincidences, do you?"

"No."

"Tony identified the man in the drone video at the funerals as Spencer Blessing, a CIA analyst who happens to be the son-in-law of the Speaker of the House whose life was threatened by a *Deadly Gray* vigilante just yesterday. The plot thickens."

Tucker says, "This is convoluted. I cannot immediately see the relationship between the Speaker and the murder of Adam Heinz by a *Deadly Gray* vigilante.

"What have you found out about Adam Heinz?"

Ma said, "Nothing so far unless you think it odd that he and his wife made a trip to Crete in the Mediterranean. Could be a vacation or it could be a non-ATF sanctioned meeting with someone."

"Hmmm, check the manifests of people flying in and out of Crete on the dates Heinz was there. His trip smells bad to me."

Jimmy said, "I'm way ahead of you this time, boss; that's why you pay me the big bucks. A big shot with the Iranian Revolutionary Guard Corps flew in and out of Crete during the time Heinz was there. I have no idea if they met or know each other or if is just a coincidence."

Tucker said, "I don't believe in coincidences."

Chapter 9

April 26, 2024
Near Smithsburg, Maryland

Using an app that distorts the sound of the voice from a person #Steel did not know, he or she asked, "What availability are you getting from the satellite dish that was delivered to you?"

#Steel said, "Between 90 and 95 percent. Sometimes thunderstorms block the signal."

The voice said, "Good. I note with satisfaction that the membership of our army of seniors is increasing exponentially. I see you shared my manuscript on the study of evil, psychopaths, and sociopaths with selected *Deadly Gray* army candidates. "

#Steel asked, "It is effective. Are you the one that leaked the story to Newsmax? Since it aired, hundreds of new seniors have logged onto our site. Too bad Asa Frank failed. Do you think he will sing?"

"Yes, but I do not think it will matter. What will they find, a web site they already know exists? As long as we keep the IP addresses fluid, it is unlikely they'll find us. My dear puppet master, at your age, why do you care?"

She reflected, *It has been a long time since I dressed up. My Harry always loved me in these pearls. I am so glad I will see him soon.*

White-haired Martha Hoffman removed her apron as she looked at her husband's loaded police revolver on her vanity and reasoned, *I will never get past security with that. But I bet they will not stop an 82-year-old lady and take her cane away from her.*

Mrs. Hoffman grabbed her 1-million-volt Zap cane, added the cloth sleeve to cover the shaft, put on her rose-colored glasses, donned her cashmere sweater, and headed for the waiting taxi.

There were hundreds of people at the entrance to the Hotel Hilton Minneapolis when she hobbled weakly out her taxi. A gentleman who wore a head scarf helped her up the steps as she waited to tell security personnel her name and that she had a seat at one of the tables. The hotel servants escorted her to a folding chair near the walkway in the back of the ball room.

Twenty minutes later, the congresswoman walked down the walkway, shook hands with contributors and headed to the podium. When she got near the table at which Mrs. Hoffman sat, Martha lifted her cane, poked the cane in the congresswoman's chest, and pushed the button. Mrs. Hoffman said in a surprisingly loud voice to make sure the congresswoman could hear, "You really shouldn't support defunding the police. My Harry who died in the line of duty would have disapproved."

The congresswoman screamed in pain before she hit the floor, face first. The ballroom erupted in panic, people ran for the door and Mrs. Hoffman was grabbed forcibly by a Secret Service officer.

♦ ♦ ♦ ♦ ♦

April 27, 2024
Minneapolis, Minnesota

The front page of the **Minneapolis Star Tribune**:

Headline: **Congresswoman Huda Mohammed Attacked at Fundraiser**

A senior white woman whose deceased husband was a Minneapolis policeman assaulted Congresswoman Huda Mohammed at a fundraiser in the Hotel Hilton Minneapolis. Currently, the Minneapolis police are considering the attack a hate crime. Huda Mohammed is in the intensive care unit of a non-disclosed hospital under tight security. She was physically shocked with one million volts from a concealed weapon.

♦ ♦ ♦ ♦ ♦

April 27, 2024
Manassas, Virginia

Rusty Winemiller said over the phone, "Star, there has been another high visibility *Deadly Gray* event. We need to get in front of this one since it involves another congressperson. I will be called on the carpet any minute now. What can you tell me?"

Star answered, "Mrs. Hoffman has no computer, no iPad, no electronic devices. We are trying to get a judge to get access to her telephone records. We'll go from there and I'll keep you posted."

"While I have you on the line, any progress on the Stanford hit-and-run case?"

Star answered, "Actually, yes. Our student victim, Kurt Rainwater, was an identity thief. He was successful at stealing the identity on no less than 129 victims that we have uncovered so far. He stripped 401(k)s, bank accounts, IRAs, and even cryptocurrency accounts. He was good; he stole millions."

Winemiller said, "That means there are at least 129 potential unsubs, one of whom is the killer."

Star said, "Rainwater, was not in the FBI Cybercrimes headlights. He escaped our net. So how did the Escalade driver know who he was? Unless, of course, he had outside help."

Winemiller said, "We need to narrow the list down from 129. Let us start with flights into San Francisco, Oakland, and San Jose around the date of the hit-and-run who are also on the list of 129. Also, can we narrow the list demographically by age?"

Star said, "I have got a lot on my plate. Can your crack cyber team help narrow the list?"

"Crack?"

Chapter 10

April 28, 2024
Harpers Ferry, West Virginia

Tucker asked, "Jimmy, what more have you learned about the CIA guy who attended the funerals of Manion and Heinz?"

"Blessing."

"What?

"The guy's name is Spencer Blessing."

Tucker asked, "What new do you know about him?"

"Not much. I have asked Tony for help. This guy is invisible."

Tucker asked, "What have you learned about Sheriff Lakota?"

Jimmy said, "Ah, that is another story. I would not trust this guy as far as I could throw him. Did you know that you can leverage a sheriff's salary into part ownership of a beach front hotel in Cabo San Lucas?

"And guess who else has partial ownership of the 5-star hotel?"

Tucker said, "OK, I give up."

"Melinda Johnson."

Tucker said angrily, "Jimmy, quit playing games with me. Who the hell is Melinda Johnson?"

Jimmy could not contain a smile when he said, "Gee, that name is identical to the maiden-name of Adam Heinz's wife. Am I good or what? Do I get my trip to Las Vegas, yet?"

Tucker said, "No."

Tank was on the phone with Jolene when Sonja entered the small conference room Tank secured in the Mandalay Bay Resort and Casino as their forward operating base. Tank said, "Let me put you on speaker since Sonja is scheduled to give me a progress report on what she has found."

Jolene said, "Hi, Sonja. Try to keep my husband out of trouble while you are there."

Sonja said, "I think that should be an episode of "Mission Impossible."

In the background, Tank and Sonja could hear Jolene's younger brother, Stanley, say "Can we watch it again? Do you have it here?"

Jolene said, "Excuse me, I'll try to keep him under control."

Tank said, "So, Sonja, you've been here a couple of days, what do you think the police, FBI, ATF, and Marshall's have overlooked?"

Stanley yelled in the background, "Maybe the killers were really after only one person. Everyone else was just for fun."

Jolene said, "Stanley, go watch TV or something until I am done. Then I will cook you something.

"Sorry, we've got to do something about him before he drives me nuts."

Sonja said, "You know, his idea is not so ridiculous, especially after I tell you what I discovered. Most of the victims were hit by rounds from semi-automatic and automatic rifles. The direction of the line of fire were consistent with firing from here in the Mandalay Bay Resort and Casino."

In unison, Tank and Jolene said, "Most?"

Sonja said, "Most. Two people standing in close proximity of each other were shot in the head with .300 Winchester Magnums probably from a Christensen bolt action tactical rifle. Think about it. Two head shots from a sniper rifle from a different angle."

Tank asked, "How did you learn this? I have not seen that information in any of the reports filed by investigators."

Jolene added, "Which itself tells us something about the investigators."

Sonja said, "I went to the Clark County Office of the Coroner/Medical Examiner and persuaded them to let me interview the four medical examiners engaged by the LVMPD after the mass shooting."

Tank said, "Persuaded?"

"Sometimes I can be charming. It is an act of course but I can turn it on. Anyway, I reviewed the autopsy reports, interviewed the medical examiners, and discovered this anomaly. When I asked the Chief M.E. why this did not show up in the investigative reports, he just shrugged and said, 'They had their killer. Case closed. Nothing dies harder than a lie that people want to believe.' It is possible that there is another reason the investigators would cover-up this piece of information. That would be because the government or someone in the government knows or knew the truth—whatever that is?"

Tank and Sonja could hear Stanley say in the background, "Has no one ever heard of the CIA?"

♦ ♦ ♦ ♦ ♦

April 30, 2024
Shaker Heights, Ohio

It was only 0630 when twelve senior men and one ageless woman dominated the seating area of the town's only breakfast diner. The breakfast club included mostly retired military veterans, businessmen, a psychiatric nurse, bankers, entrepreneurs, and former government civil servants. To a member of the breakfast club, not one was happy with the new America. Ed, a 94-year-old Korean War army veteran asked loudly of his wheelchair bound compatriot, "Where's George this morning; he never misses weekly breakfast meetings?"

Over the diner's 1960's background music, one of the club members answered, "You have not heard, Ed? Wow, it is the talk around town, here."

Ed answered, "You know I am almost deaf. I was an artillery officer, remember?"

"Well, George is in jail for murder. He always said he would get even."

Ed responded, "Well good for him. He was terminally ill anyway. Did he get that guy who carjacked his wife's car with her in it and still walked the streets?"

"Yep."

Ed stood, tapped his coffee mug with a spoon and said, "Here is a toast to George for achieving his goal of justice for his wife before he died. May all of us be as successful."

"Hear, hear."

Another breakfast club member said, "Hey, Ed, I hear more and more of this senior vigilante stuff is happening. What are you going to do on your way out?"

Ed said, "I'll figure that out when I get old."

Chapter 11

May 1, 2024
Harpers Ferry, West Virginia

Jimmy Ma completed the task of cross-referencing a list of people who filed a complaint with the FBI that their identities were stolen by someone in the past two years with flight manifests to San Francisco, Oakland, and San Jose. Then he called Tony Vinci. "Tony, I have a list of six names. I'm slammed and need a little help. Could you identify the age and address of the six names I will give you? This is for Star's hit-and-run *Deadly Gray* case."

Tony said, "What is your IQ anyway?"

Jimmy said, "Tony, I know you and that you already researched it, you're just testing me to see if I tell you the truth."

"So, you bet me because you already knew I would lose the $20 bet?"

Jimmy said, "Guilty as charged."

Tony said, "Tell me the truth, do you cheat at the game of 'Go'?"

Jimmy said, "No but only because there is no way to cheat."

Tony said, "Your secret is good with me. Give me the names."

Jimmy did. Two hours later, Tony returned the call and said, "Only two of the six people are over sixty-five. One is sixty-eight and flew into Oakland from New Orleans. The other is seventy-seven and flew into San Francisco from San Diego. My bet is it is the guy from New Orleans; he is a retired drilling roughneck and pipefitter. The guy from San Diego is a retired elementary school principal. I'd go with the roughneck."

Jimmy asked, "Any way that you could help me get a line on how he knew Rainwater was his identify thief?"

"Jimmy, I am not the dark web genius, you are. Besides, I am helping Tucker and Star get background on this guy Werner who had his throat cut in Virginia. Talk to you later."

Jimmy called Star and said, "It is not certain, but it's a high probability that the unsub in your hit-and-run case is a roughneck from New Orleans. Here is the address of the guy." Jimmy gave her the address.

Star said, "Great, I will get the local FBI office to pick him up as a person-of-interest. Have you hacked his computer yet?"

"Do you have a warrant?"

"When has that ever stopped you before."

Jimmy said, "Why break the law if I don't have to?"

Star said, "OK, I'll see if I can get a warrant."

May 1, 2024
Mount Vernon, Virginia

Star was at home in a beautifully renovated 60-year-old house which overlooked the Potomac River. She needed some down time, a chance to relax, and share a meal with a male friend no one in her close circle of friends knew about. Star had learned a little about cooking from Chef Rhino, her parent's chef for over a decade. She made veal parmesan, garlic bread, and a spinach salad. She opened a bottle of wine and served herself as she sat in a comfortable lounge chair on the back porch. The breeze was warm for this time of year, and she looked forward to non-shop talk with a man she met shopping at a local grocery store and knew virtually nothing about. He appeared to be gentle, soft-spoken, intellectual, and damned handsome.

The doorbell rang and Star anxiously went to the front door to let her guest in with Ram by her side. She wore a pair of tight jeans, a white blouse that exposed a little cleavage of her ample breasts, and a necklace that highlighted her blue eyes. She opened the door with a bright smile which quickly faded. It was Rusty Winemiller, with a young agent behind his wheelchair and another agent standing by Winemiller's van.

He said, "Sorry to disappoint you. I will not stay long, but we have an urgent case to address; new crimes have gone down. I want you to lead the investigations into the bomb that exploded in New York University yesterday and a sniper attack that occurred this morning involving *The Washington Post*."

Star furled her eyebrows and asked, "You want me to lead an investigation of crimes that surely belong to the Criminal Justice Division?"

Special Agent Winemiller answered, "I want you to lead the cyber-side investigation for these crimes. You will work under the direction of Agent-in-charge Chris O'Connor."

Star asked, "Why do you suspect those two crimes are cyber related?"

"That's your job, Star, investigate it."

"Sir, you know I am investigating multiple *Deadly Gray* vigilante cases to establish a thread that connects Col. Manion to the Kentucky woman to the Stanford student hit-and-run perpetrator to Joel Cohen to Asa Frank to Mrs. Hoffman to #Steel, to whomever killed Werner, and others. Do you really want to take me off those cases?

Winemiller said, "No, I'm just changing your priorities."

Star nodded and said, "OK, whatever you say."

Winemiller said sternly, "You did it again, didn't you?"

Ram rose to all four in response to Winemiller's tone of voice.

Star asked innocently, "Did what?"

"Read my thought."

Ram growled.

Star said, "Good, good." Ram stood down.

"Sir, I am sure you have good reasons to convince the Criminal Justice Division to add a young agent from Cybercrimes to tag along. I do not need to read your thoughts to understand that."

He stared at her for a few minutes but let it go.

Winemiller left only minutes before her friend, Brooks, arrived. He said, "Looks like Feds just left the neighborhood."

She gave him a hug, quickly changed the subject, and said, "I am so glad you are here; you have no idea how much I need to get my head out of my work. I hope you like Italian food. I just rustled up something for us."

He said, "Isn't that a coincidence? I happen to own and operate an Italian restaurant in Ole' Town Alexandria."

Star thought, *Oh no, no pressure here.*

Star's mood changed to melancholy.

Brooks said, "A quiet man is a thinking man. A quiet woman is usually mad. You, OK?"

She said, "As W.C. Fields once said, 'I cook with wine, sometimes I even add it to the food'." In actuality she was reminiscing about a much too short personal trip she made across the country with a male friend four years earlier.

Four years earlier
Niagara Falls, New York

Star Cherokee was the youngest person in history to be employed as an agent by the FBI. She was a teenager when Rusty Winemiller observed, firsthand, Star's mind reading skills which made her a quantum leap better than anyone else at the FBI during interrogations or interviews. Rusty could lead the interview while Star would know if the interviewees were lying or not. Often, she could tell Winemiller whether the person on the other side of the table was guilty of the crime or not. She was damned good at her job.

The skill, however, was a double-edged sword. She read the thoughts of her parents, the mind of any potential romantic relationship, and the brainwaves of people who were just ships passing in the dark. Tucker and Maya built a home in which Star's bedroom was at the other end of the house and shielded to prevent her from reading her parents minds in adjacent rooms.

Star felt cursed that she could use a part of her brain that few if any others have access. She knew she was abnormal, a freak of nature. At age 23, she decided she needed to "find herself" and explore her boundaries, act like a normal person.

For the first time in her life, she met a man that she believed could accept and live with her curse. They headed west from Wiscasset, Maine in a brand-new conversion van donated to the trip by Tucker and Maya.

The sound of thirty-eight million gallons of water falling every minute was deafening. Star said, "Sweetheart, I find this experience indescribable."

Her friend said, "I have read about Niagara Falls in magazines and had seen it on TV but to see it in person is entirely different. I am so glad to share this moment with you."

Star asked, "Where to now? What state or national park do we have on our list to visit next?"

"Cuyahoga Valley National Park in Ohio is next. Let us spend the night at a hotel here and start out in the morning."

Before Star, her friend, and Ram reached their van, her friend started to run while hollering, "Ram, go get them."

Two thieves wearing ski masks ran away from the conversion van with plastic yard bags thrown over their shoulders. A side window on the van was smashed in.

The two criminals could not outrun Ram, but Star feared one of the thieves would knife or shoot the German Shepherd. Ram grabbed the slower of the two runners by the right calf. The hooded person screamed and tried to hit Ram with a fist. Star and her friend were at Ram's side in seconds. Star said, "Go" while pointing in the direction of the faster thief. Ram took off while Star's friend kicked the first thief into unconsciousness. Star pulled out her cell phone and called 9-1-1.

Star said, "Follow Ram and capture the other guy. I'll secure this guy until you return." He followed Ram. Star pulled her Ruger and held it at the ready to hold the first thief at bay.

The faster thief came to a 6-foot-high chain-link fence and scrambled over it before Ram could reach him. "Stay," the friend yelled as he too climbed over the fence after the first thief. Whatever was in the black yard bag was too heavy for the first thief, so he threw the bag to the side and increased his speed. Still, Star's friend continued to gain on the thief. 45 seconds later, he tackled the person from behind, rammed an elbow into his groin, and headbutted the guy into the dark. He pulled the ski mask off the thief to see it was a teenager. He checked the kid's pulse. He said aloud, "At least your still alive."

Four years earlier
Niagara Falls, New York

Star had never before sat on the wrong side of the table in an interview room. She waited in a classic seven feet by nine feet space with a one-way mirror for an interminable amount of time for someone to join them. She was unsure what the Niagara Falls Police

Department had done with Ram and worried about not only his safety but the safety of whomever was holding him.

The ugly dirty yellow room smelled of sweat, the reference table appeared to be older than Star, and the overhead florescent light flickered every three seconds or so.

A door to the claustrophobic room opened. In walked two officers. One was an unsmiling Police Sergeant in his late forties, the other was an even more solemn-looking young woman in serious need of Head & Shoulders shampoo. A little underarm deodorant would not have hurt either.

The Sergeant adjusted his glasses and addressed Star, "Looks like the boy will live. You two beat the snot out of him. Was it really necessary?"

Star said, "Sergeant, I am glad the boy is all right. He had a ski mask on, we did not know who broke into our van to steal our stuff. It could have been a much more dangerous person."

The Sergeant said, "First of all, I did not say he would be all right. I said he will live. He will suffer through some long-term injuries. You two seem to know how to handle yourselves; maybe a little too well."

Star spoke up, "Sir, we are the victims here. Do you want our statement? If not, are we free to go?"

The Sergeant said, "I will ask the questions here, young lady, not you. By the injuries sustained by the two boys, it does not look like you're the victims. It looks to me more like they are the victims of brutality inflicted by the three of you. Is that German Shepherd your dog?"

Star read the Sergeant's thoughts: *He is a dangerous animal that needs to be put down.*

Star asked, "Are you charging us with a crime? If so, you need to mirandize us, and we need to call our attorney. If not, we are ready to leave."

"Ms. Cherokee, if that is your real name, you are not in charge here, I am. Now shut up and speak only when spoken to.

"Now, which of you instructed the killer dog to maul the first victim? That is a criminal offense."

Star said, "We want a lawyer. Now."

Someone tapped the one-way mirror from the outside. The young female officer followed the Sergeant out of the room. While alone in the interrogation room with her friend, Star pulled out her cell phone and called Tucker and Maya.

Three minutes after the Sergeant and the female officer exited the interview room, the police captain walked into the room. "Ms. Cherokee, I am deeply sorry that you two were treated like criminals. Serge just does not trust outsiders. Anyway, you and your friend are free to go but we would appreciate it if you'd stay in the State of New York until your case is closed."

"Captain," he heard over the office speaker, "you're needed out front."

Five White Knight Personal Security agents (referred to as White Knights) and an attorney who represented the Cherokee family stood at the entrance of the police station. All five White Knights were former military Special Forces and intimidating in appearance. The attorney said, "Sir, we are here in the hope that you would allow us to pick up our team's K9."

The captain remembered a quote by Euripides: "Fortune truly helps those who are of good judgment."

Four years earlier
Bad Land, South Dakota

Star, her friend, and Ram continued their exploration of America's national parks. Star's friend drew closer to and fonder of Star over time and Star, in turn, experienced a sensation never before felt—being normal. But that ended when they visited the Bad Lands in South Dakota.

"Star," said Maya Cherokee on the phone, "something especially important has come up. Would you fly home for a short visit? You can fly back and continue your adventure."

"Mom, is Dad alright?"

Maya answered, "Yes, he is fine. It is nothing like that. But it is important that you visit with us as soon as possible."

Star asked, "Can you give me a hint as to what this is about?"

"No, honey, not over the phone."

Star's friend drove their conversion van to Rapid City Regional Airport where Star caught a flight to Chicago and eventually on to Portland, Maine where she rented a car and drove up to her parent's estate in Wiscasset.

Ram's offspring, Algorithm, greeted Star first by slobbering on her face, then Maya and Tucker hugged

Star. A visitor to the Cherokee estate waited for an introduction. Tucker said, "Star this is Nate Sinclair." They shook hands and Star said, "Mr. Sinclair, it is a pleasure to meet you, but if you do not mind, I need a few minutes to clean up. Mom, could you join me so we can catch up on a few things before we meet with this gentleman?"

"Sure, sweetheart."

Before the two ladies could enter Star's bedroom, Chef Rhino offered Star a glass of her favorite wine. He said, "I suspect you will need this today."

"OK, Mom, who is this guy and why is it so important that I had to abandon my trip, which has been wonderful except that experience in Niagara Falls, to meet him."

Maya said, "Star, he is the Chief of Staff in the White House for President Taylor. He wants to make you the offer of a lifetime."

Star downed her glass of Pinot Grigio.

Four years earlier
Wiscasset, Maine

"Thank you, Ms. Cherokee, for taking time away from your vacation to meet with me. I have read your dossier on the time you were assigned to the FBI and met with Special Agent Randy Winemiller, who is a big supporter of you. He suggested I meet with your parents, both of whom are well respected by President Taylor. The general consensus by all the people I've interviewed is that you could become the most important advisor any president in history could possibly have. America needs you and I am here to offer you a position in the White House."

Star nodded at Chief of Staff Sinclair and glared at both Maya and Tucker. She felt betrayed.

"The White House would benefit if you were present at meetings attended by heads of state, national security advisors, and cabinet members." She read his thought, *And leaders of the opposite political party.*

Star also read her father's thought, *It is the most patriotic thing she could ever do. I do wish I had her skills so she would not have to do this for our country.*

Star read her mother's thoughts, *Though this is an opportunity of a lifetime for her, I don't want her exposed to the cesspool of Washington.*

Star asked, "Mr. Sinclair, who told you about my special skills?"

"The United States Attorney General questioned FBI Director Brad Naylor as to why cybercrime arrests are down while cybercrimes themselves are up. He learned from your boss, Randy Winemiller, that a particularly good interviewer had resigned. Naylor pressed Winemiller as to why the agent who resigned was so invaluable. Ms. Cherokee, please do not be too disappointed and angry that Winemiller disclosed the details of your skills, he was under serious pressure at the time."

Star read Sinclair's thoughts, *Winemiller's position at the FBI was at risk.*

Star asked, "How do we contain the knowledge of my capabilities; I don't want it to become common knowledge if I work at the White House?"

"Ms. Cherokee," Sinclair stated, "No one will agree to meet with President Taylor in your presence if it becomes common knowledge. You will be the Assistant Press Secretary and invited to meetings POTUS requests you attend."

Star said, "As a condition of my employment, I require Ram, my K9 protector, to be always at my side. Will that be a problem? Will Secret Service agree to that?"

Sinclair said, "If the President so instructs, yes."

Chapter 12

May 2, 2024
Baltimore, Maryland

The chief operator of Baltimore's refuse derived fuel facility worked long hours. It was a challenging job to keep the plant operating profitably; people threw all sorts of things they should not into their garbage so that making fuel for power plants out of trash was problematic. Today, for example, a customer threw a half-full propane tank into the trash. The tank entered the plant shredder, exploded, and damaged the shredder, the feeder, and the structure supporting the waste feed equipment. He thought, *You just can't fix stupid* and shut the plant down, ordered waste redirected to the parallel feed system and then ordered the plant maintenance personnel to ready line one.

The chief had to deal with news reporters, his superiors, and waste haulers before he called it a day. Before he got in his car, he received a call from his wife. "Can you pick up a pizza on your way home? I am stuck in the office until the captain returns from his current investigation. Sorry, babe."

The chief called in an order to Dominos on his way home and then called his daughter. "Sweetheart, I will be home in ten. I will bring you your favorite meal."

She responded, "Whatever, Dad."

He sat in the parking lot of Domino's Pizza, called them to inform them he was there and waited for them to deliver his order. A young man with tattoos displayed on his neck and wearing pants down below his crack came out to the parking lot to deliver the pizza. He wore a leather jacket, a ball cap on backwards, and a Covid mask. The chief rolled down the window of his Chevy Volt as the delivery person asked, "This is an extra-large supreme pizza. Is that what you ordered?"

He answered, "Actually, no. I ordered a ...."

The chief's brain matter was splatted onto the inside of the windshield. The boy tucked his revolver into his waistband, dropped the empty pizza box and ran.

♦ ♦ ♦ ♦ ♦

May 2, 2024
Baltimore, Maryland

Alexandro Rodriguez, Clica leader of the Baltimore Mara Salvatrucha or MS-13 said to the young pizza delivery boy, "You passed your first test by killing a random person. Now I know you have what it takes to join us. See Zee, he will tattoo your fingers. See me tomorrow and I will give you your next assignment."

"Alexandro," said one of his soldiers, "Cheesesteak wants you to call him." Cheesesteak was Alexandro's counterpart in Philadelphia.

In Spanish, Rodriquez said, "I understand you wanted me to call you. What is up?"

Cheesesteak asked, "Our supplier of young cows is out of business, his throat slashed. Who will take Werner's place and who took him out? Has someone discovered our network? We need to find out who killed him and what the killer knows."

Rodriquez said, "True, but I am more concerned about how to replace Werner. The Council of Nine will not be happy with us if we don't find a replacement soon. Did he have a second in command?"

Cheesesteak said, "I bet his wife knows something."

Rodriquez said, "I will take care of the wife, you learn who killed Werner. And Cheesesteak, no more calls. In person or nothing."

"Got it."

Rodriquez yelled for the soldier who remained in the compound while he spoke to Cheesesteak, "See if you can find the boy that I sent to get tattooed. I have a new job for him."

♦ ♦ ♦ ♦ ♦

May 2, 2024
Great Falls, Virginia

The MS-13 wannabe boy admired the tattoos on his fingers as he surveyed the front entrance to his new target's home. He thought, *I have never been in a house like this. Bet I can find some good stuff in there after I complete my job.* Only the 17-year-old illegal immigrant from El-Salvador wasn't alone. A news reporter with her cameraman sat in a van twenty-five yards away waiting for Mrs. Werner, the wife of the recently murdered former congressman, to show herself. The boy knew he could not do what he was instructed to do with the news media performing surveillance; he'd have to go around the block and come in through the back yard. Twenty minutes later he jimmied the basement sliding glass door open, silently moved to the basement steps, and crept up the steps to the first-floor door.

He heard voices and froze until he realized it was the TV in another room. The boy turned the knob and pushed ever-so-slightly until it was open enough for him to slip through. He thought, *Wow, the kitchen is bigger than most homes.*

The boy was grateful for the soft-soled sneakers he wore, and he moved in the direction of the sound from the TV. He turkey-peeked into the large family room and saw an old woman asleep on a huge couch with her mouth unattractively open. The boy silently slid over to the window, parted the curtains, and looked to see if the news people were still out front. They were.

He pulled out the Smith & Wesson M&P9 he used on the guy in the pizza parking lot and approached his victim. "Hey, lady, get up." He kicked the sofa cushion to make sure she would awaken.

Angela Werner was an unattractive matronly 75-year-old blue-haired woman in relatively good health. She wore bright red sweatpants and a matching sweatshirt, both of which matched her long fingernails perfectly manicured. Her eyelids flittered open to reveal glittering grey eyes that screamed an awareness of her situation.

"What do you want? Jewelry? Cash?"

The boy said, "My boss wants to see you. Get up."

She asked, "Who is your boss?

He said, "You'll find out soon enough, now get your car keys; we're driving to Baltimore."

She said, "Ah, so your boss is Alexandro Rodriguez. I am surprised he sent a boy to do a man's job."

The boy started to hit Angela but hesitated, unsure how his boss would handle the knowledge that he hit her.

She said, "You tell your boss, that if he wants to see me, to come in person. I will tell him what he wants to know."

The MS-13 killer said, "That is not what I was instructed to do. Now come with me."

Angela Werner said, "Sure, whatever you say." Then she bolted for the front door, swung it open, and stepped outside before the boy tackled the old woman on the brick steps in view of the news van.

The news reporter said as she stepped outside the van, "Quick, get the camera rolling." The camera person was prepared for rapid response and aimed the camera at the event in front of the Werner home.

The boy hit Angela with a jaw crushing uppercut that broke her dentures and knocked her unconscious. Then he focused on the news people.

The camera was on, and the event taped live in the studio. The killer did not know what to do so he pulled his gun and approached the newscasters—he shot them both, the reporter in the head, the cameraman in the chest. He took the camera out of the arms of the cameraman and threw the camera inside the front door of the Werner's house. Then he dragged the old woman through the front door. He searched for others who may have witnessed his crimes but saw no one.

The MS-13 killer found the entrance to the garage from the house, put the camera in Werner's Audi, tied old lady Werner's ankles with plastic ties, and placed her in the back seat—face down.

He drove the Audi back to Baltimore unaware that half the people in the DC and Baltimore greater metropolitan area knew what he looked like and witnessed his murders of two prominent news people. He drove up to the headquarters for the Baltimore MS-13 operations only to find no guards protecting the building and no evidence of security. He checked on Angela Werner and found her to be lucid but silent. He cut her ankle ties and said, "Get out, I'm taking you to the boss."

The assault broke Angela Werner's jaw, damaged her hip, and fractured her wrist from bracing herself from a fall. She limped out of the Audi in pain as he pushed her from behind with his weapon drawn.

The young MS-13 killer recruit was confused, no one was in the operations center; no Alexandro Rodriguez, no soldiers, no one. He turned to Angela Werner, the money launderer for Werner Enterprises and saw that she tried a smile as much as she could achieve with a broken jaw and in pain from the hip injury.

He asked of her, "What?"

She used her long sharpened and manicured fingernails to slit the carotid artery on the neck of the young killer. As he bled out, he shot the old lady in the left eye.

The young killer attempted to return to the Audi but was too weak from his loss of blood to make it. The Baltimore police surrounded the car and watched the boy killer die. No one called for medical backup.

Chapter 13

May 3, 2024
New York City

It felt like de ja vu, like 9/11 all over again to Special Agent in Charge Chris O'Connor. Firemen dug through rubble in the hope of finding someone still alive while New York's finest protected the crime scene from pedestrians and the media. O'Connor was hypnotized by the scene, wondering how to even begin to identify who the bomber was using forensic data collected and analyzed by the FBI team flown in from Quantico.

He stood on West 4th Street contemplating his next move when he sensed the presence of someone standing next to him. He looked down at a roughly 27-year-old woman with auburn hair and captivating blue eyes staring back at him while she held tightly to a leash attached to an intimidating looking German Shepherd.

Special Agent O'Connor said, "Young lady, I'm unsure how you got past the police crime scene barrier, but you need to leave the premises before I have you arrested."

Star displayed her FBI badge as she said, "You do not have a clue what to do next do you SAC O'Connor? And no, I am not a "fucking" reporter as you suspect. What I do know is that the bombing was not well-planned, more likely an impulse suicide bombing."

SAC O'Connor, a large overweight agent past his prime responded, "You must be the help I have to babysit from Cyber."

Star said, "I am here to make you look like you know what you're doing, which will be a challenge for me, I know, but those are my instructions. What do you know so far, my leader? What great discoveries have you made?"

Ram bared his teeth.

O'Connor said, "Ok, OK. My fault we got off to a bad start. Let's start over. I am glad to have you on my team. All and any help are appreciated. I just expected a more senior and experienced agent to help me. What I know so far is that the center of the explosion occurred in the journalism school faculty lounge."

Star said, "That is consistent with what we've uncovered so far."

"What? You just got here. How could you have uncovered anything, Agent, uh?"

"Cherokee, Star Cherokee."

O'Connor lit up, "Oh, I have heard about you. You used to be part of the press team for the last administration. Now I recognize you. And you are related to Tucker and Maya Cherokee, correct?"

Star just nodded her head.

"You are close to Tank Alvarez and the White Knight Personal Security group, right? I hope to join them after I retire from the FBI. Wow, I am sorry I was such a jerk and we got off on the wrong foot. So, what have you uncovered?"

Star said, "We think we know who committed this heinous crime."

SAC O'Connor, who rarely was lost for words, just stared back at Star, and waited for an explanation.

Star continued, "You said the explosion occurred in the faculty lounge. How many bodies have we discovered? How many were Arthur L. Carter Journalism Institute professors?"

O'Connor said, "So far, we have discovered the remains of six victims but nine people are missing. Hopefully, we'll learn the other three were not in the faculty room. Forensics has not identified names yet and won't until DNA test results are finalized. We do not know if any were from the School of Journalism."

Star said, "It is a low-yield explosion. Maybe not intended to kill many or bring the building down. I bet it was a targeted killing, focused on taking out specific professors."

O'Connor asked, "And what is the basis of that conclusion."

Star said, "Because Gregory Jack posted a threat two-days ago on the dark web. We have traced him to an IP address in Sparta, New Jersey. Cyber further traced the IP address to a library so it is a dead end. But Mr. Jack, if that is his real name, did supply one piece of information in his threat that we may find useful: he was a Vietnam veteran who hates or hated the mainstream media."

"Hated?"

"I think you'll discover that one of the victims is the bomber."

SAC O'Connor said, "Are you saying this was a suicide bombing? We do not see many of those in this country."

"Mr. Jack posted a manifesto of sorts on a web site on the dark side entitled *DanielWebsterWorldView*. You should read it."

◆ ◆ ◆ ◆ ◆

May 3, 2024
In-Flight between LaGuardia and Reagan
National Airports

The Learjet 75 leveled off on the short flight at 28,000 feet. SAC O'Connor thought, *I fail to see a connection between the New York University bombing and the Washington Post assassination. I wonder if my partner here has not shared with me what she knows. I have to walk on eggshells with her. How do I approach her?*

Star looked over at the SAC and suppressed a smirk. She did not want him to learn about her special skills. She waited.

"What do you know about this case you have not shared with me, Agent Star? Anything you want to say to me? And why do you travel with the dog?"

Star responded, "I wondered when you would ask about my knowledge of the case. The shooter accessed the same black web site as the New York University bomber hours before their attacks. It turns out the *Washington Post* sniper also posted a statement on *DanielWebsterWorldView*. We think they coordinated their attacks. We also suspect that both were over seventy and both claimed to want justice for a corrupt media. As you know, there is a thin line between legal justice and vigilante justice.

"As far as the 'dog' goes, Ram is my protector. It was a condition of my employment that he stay by my side at all times. He comes in handy when I interview suspected persons-of-interest."

O'Connor asked, "Any reason to expect more attacks on journalists?"

"Yes."

Star's cell phone rang. It was Sonja McLeod Vincente.

Sonja asked, "Can you talk?"

Star answered, "Yes, I can hear you."

Sonja understood that Star could not talk but could listen. Sonja said, "The Washington shooter used a 30-caliber rifle, probably a Remington 700 XCR with a suppressor. It is good from 250 to 400 yards. Not my first choice but it obviously got the job done. The rumor in the sniper community is that the shooter is a Vietnam vet who promised to pull this assassination off. He hated the editor of the *Post*. Back at you when I know more."

Star looked over at SAC O'Connor and said, "A reliable contact of mine just told me that the sniper was also a Vietnam vet."

O'Connor asked, "Who is your contact?"

Star said, "Do you reveal all your sources?"

"Listen, Agent Cherokee, I am the Special Agent in Charge. You are not running this investigation; you need to share all pertinent information with me. Do you understand?"

Ram growled.

Star said, "Yes, I do." But she did not reveal her source.

Star's satellite phone rang, it was her boss, Rusty Winemiller. "Yes, sir."

"Are you with O'Connor?"

"Yes, sir."

"Put it on speaker."

Star did as instructed.

"Fifteen minutes ago, a Molotov cocktail was thrown through the picture window of the editor's home of the *Portland Observer*. He survived and his family was not at home, but his home was destroyed. Though we have not completed our search, I suspect this action was coordinated with the other two attacks on journalists. Director Naylor is on my ass for answers. I want a report by 1600 EDT tomorrow."

Winemiller disconnected.

O'Connor's satellite phone rang, it was his boss.

"Chris, what do you know so far? We have had another event that seems connected to the New York and DC crimes against the media."

O'Connor answered, "Yes, I have heard. We know that these crimes are coordinated and that whatever nefarious organization sponsors these crimes has a vendetta against the mainstream media."

O'Connor's boss said, "You have all the resources you need to find the underlying cause of these acts of terrorism. Both the Washington and Portland field offices await your direction. I want a report by 1600 EDT tomorrow."

O'Connor looked over at Star and said, "Everybody gets shit on them in a shit storm."

Ed Day

77-year-old Corey Robertson was writing a blog piece to share with his ideologically like-minded friends about how 50-years later the mainstream media learned nothing from their wrongheaded misinformation and intentional disinformation of the Vietnam War Tet offensive when he received a life-changing epiphany in the form of an email.

The email was from someone who used the hashtag, #Steel, and who proclaimed he was assembling an army to defend the Constitution, right wrongs the Justice Department ignores, defend the Bill of Rights, and realign the country's moral compass back to where it belongs. "Corey, are you willing to play an important role in the movement; can I count on you to use your impressive skills to help save our country from falling into the same chasm as Venezuela or North Korea? If so, I have an assignment for you."

Corey responded, "I did not just fall off a turnip truck, the government monitors emails. I am unwilling to take part in this treasonous anarchy event. Sorry."

He continued to blog on *DanielWebsterWorldView*, "The media could not be more wrong during the Vietnam war, yet, to my knowledge, no one has ever paid a price for their incompetent and treasonous editorial crimes. Since that time, I have listened to talk radio hosts constantly and repeatedly whine and complain with justification about the lies and disinformation presented in newspapers and by TV commentators. However, no one has ever proposed a solution, a way to reverse the trend. With today's social and other electronic media, the mainstream media has even gotten bolder in its misuse and abuse of the first amendment. Someone must do something about it. The media is like a jock rash you cannot get rid of."

The next day a courier delivered a package to the doorstep of blogger Corey Robertson. The package was anonymously shipped from Ping of Phoenix, Arizona which appeared to be set of golf clubs. Upon opening the package, Corey discovered a Remington 700 XCR with a suppressor. And an envelope which contained a note, a passport with his photo, plane tickets, a credit card, and a photograph. The note stated: "Corey, I know your real name. I know you were an Army sniper during the Vietnam War. I know that your wife passed and that you are at the end you your life. I share your hatred for journalists. The suppressor will limit accuracy to around three hundred yards. I hereby give you the tools to 'do something about it.' The photo is of the editor of The Washington Post. The plane ticket is from Reagan National to Ottawa, Ontario. The credit card is good for $50,000. Go somewhere even I do not know about. Hit 'em straight. You have no future without a past."

Chapter 14

May 4, 2024
Wiscasset, Maine

Tucker sent Star, Tony Vinci, Jimmy Ma, Tank, and Jolene an invite to a Microsoft Team meeting scheduled for 7:00 PM EDT. Jolene brought her brother Stanley over to the Cherokee estate to attend the meeting with Tucker and Maya in person rather than to listen to the call from her home.

Stanley said as he arrived, "Is Rhino here? What specials are on the menu?" Jolene, embarrassed by Stanley's lack of etiquette just shook her head.

Maya said to Jolene, "Do not worry, Chef Rhino wants nothing more than to have a new food connoisseur to entertain. Now, come on and let us assemble in Tucker's office for the call."

As Maya and Jolene entered the office, they could hear Tucker say, "I see Tank, Star, and Tony are on the line—the good, the bad, and the ugly."

Tank said, "You shouldn't talk to Star like that."

Jolene yelled from the back of the room, "Hi, honey."

Tony said, "Isn't that an oxymoron—Tank and honey?"

Tucker interrupted the banter and said, "Will someone please call Jimmy, wake him out of his stupor and give him a shot of adrenaline."

Star said, "Already called him. He is predictably late. I bet he was playing 'Go' online."

Jimmy said, "I'm on the call, sorry I am late."

Tony said, "We agree that you are sorry."

Tucker said, "Turn your video on, I want to see what you're doing while you are on this call to discuss the Deadly Gray vigilantes."

"Boss, I'm hurt."

Tucker said, "Let us get this meeting started. First, I want all on the call to know we are not conferencing with the FBI, we are on a conference call with Maya and my daughter; understood?"

All nodded on the video call except Jimmy. Tucker said, "Earth to Jimmy Ma."

Jimmy said, "Yes, understood."

Tucker said, "I need your full attention, Jimmy, because this call is about you."

Jimmy said, "Uh, oh."

"Maya and I have been thinking. Mostly Maya. Sweetheart, would you fill in the team with your postulate."

Maya said, "My theory affects both the investigation into Adam Heinz and the analysis of the overall *Deadly Gray* set of cases. For an exponential increase in senior crimes over a brief period of time that transcend closed data points, there must be a forced anomaly."

Tank interrupted and said, "Maya, I am sorry, but could you speak down to my level. I have no idea what you just said."

In the background you could hear Stanley, who stood in the doorway without anyone noticing, say, "She means someone is organizing the *Deadly Gray* killers."

Jolene took Stanley by the hand and led him out of the office, returned and closed the office door.

Maya continued, "It may be this #Steel guy, or it may be someone else, but whomever it is, he or she has cross-referenced people with life-threatening illnesses with their history and found that there are serious grievances of which to take advantage. Somehow, the conductor of the *Deadly Gray* orchestra knew both that Colby Manion had a grievance about his granddaughters' murder at the Las Vegas massacre and that Col. Manion was a stage four cancer victim. He played Manion like a violin.

"Same may be true with the Kentucky woman, the man who tried to assassinate the Speaker of the House, and the woman who zapped the congresswoman in Minneapolis. If we explore this, maybe more of the people on Star's list, which is growing, will fit the formula."

Jimmy Ma said, "How is all that about me?"

Tucker said, "Because you are going to recreate the algorithm the person who is manipulating the ill seniors is using. He or she may be smarter than you, but I doubt the person is smarter than you and Tony combined."

Tony said, "No one is that smart."

Maya said, "IQs are not additive gentlemen, but the difficult part will be to build a data base using information that is protected by HIPAA or the Health Insurance Portability and Accountability Act regulation."

Tucker added, "If #Steel or whomever can do it, I am sure Jimmy and Tony can get it done. If the algorithm the two of you build is as good as I suspect, we will be able to predict future *Deadly Gray* victims and perpetrators."

Tucker asked, "While I have you on the phone, Tank, how is your investigation proceeding?"

Tank answered, "I have proof that Sheriff Lakota suppressed information about the case against Paddock. I have suspicions that the CIA played a role in the coverup, but I have no proof yet. It is work-in-progress."

Tucker asked, "Anything new on Heinz?"

"No, still trying to figure out why a CIA guy was performing reconnaissance at Heinz's funeral."

Tony interrupted, "Just for fun, I investigated the ATF guys at Heinz's funeral. Both worked for Heinz, and both were signatures to the joint FBI/ATF/LVMPD reports. You might want to interview them, Tank."

Tank said, "Will do. Has anyone learned more about this #Steel person?"

No one spoke.

"Tank," asked Jolene, "Are you coming home anytime soon?"

"Yes, but it will be a round trip ticket."

Star asked, "When do you, Jimmy, and Tony, expect to complete the algorithm?"

Jimmy said, "We work best under pressure and with a little bourbon. You buying?"

May 4, 2024
Wiscasset, Maine

As Tucker and Maya were relaxing on the back porch of their estate watching a couple kayaking down the Sheepscot River, drinking wine and nibbling on a plate of Chef Rhino's stuffed mushrooms, Tucker's phone rang. Maya said, "It's late, don't answer it."

He looked at the phone number displayed on the smart phone; it was the United States Attorney General. Tucker showed the display and said, "You tell him I'm too busy to answer his call."

Maya shrugged, answered the phone, and said, "Hello, Mr. Gannon, this is Maya Cherokee. It is an honor to speak with you."

A.G. Gannon said, "Please, Maya, you can call me Arthur. Is Tucker available or have I called too late?"

"No sir, you did not call too late. I will get him."

Tucker smiled and mouthed while reaching out for the phone, "Coward."

"Sir, I have been expecting your call. My phone is secure so ask away."

Arthur Gannon, the top law enforcement person in the nation said, "When I asked you to investigate potential corruption within the Federal Government, I did not expect one of our top executives to end up dead while golfing with you. It has been three weeks since his murder. You have not contacted me to download information. You have failed to submit a report on your findings on the task I awarded you. This is highly unprofessional of you, Tucker."

Tucker said, "The task, as you put it, you asked me to perform for the Justice Department was quote, 'highly confidential and not to be shared with any third party.' It was between you and me. I did not even share knowledge of the assignment with Maya. I was not about to call you at your office and tell your assistant that I was trying to reach you. I surely was not going to author a report that could and necessarily would become public record. I expected contact from you weeks ago. I honored our agreement."

A.G. Gannon said, "Is Maya listening to our conversation?"

Tucker said, "No, but she is nearby. Would you like me to find a more private area to continue our discussion?"

"No, besides, I would like to hear her side of the murder. I understand she was there and guarded Adam until the police arrived."

Tucker said, "That is correct. Can I put the call on speaker? No one else is within ear shot."

"OK. So, what have you learned? Do we have a fundamental problem within the ATF?"

Tucker said, "DHS pays their leadership way too much money."

The A.G. said, "What are you talking about?"

"Well, Adam Heinz and his wife are part owners in a 5-star hotel in Cabo San Lucas. I was unaware that government employees could afford such a luxury. That and the knowledge that Sheriff Lakota of the Las Vegas Metropolitan Police Department also owns a share in the hotel reinforces my belief that Heinz was corrupt. The question, of course, is does it end there?

"Sir, if anyone hears things that are suspicious, it has to be you. You gave me this task for a reason. What can you share with me, rumor or otherwise, about the real goings on surrounding the Las Vegas massacre?"

Gannon rebuffed Tucker and said, "I will ask the questions here. You know I cannot share with you everything I hear."

Tucker said, "OK, you have set the ground rules, but know that a CIA agent or employee took photos of everyone at Heinz's and Manion's funeral. I conclude that there was a relationship between Heinz and the CIA. Is it possible that Heinz was also CIA?"

A.G. Gannon did not answer the question, but instead asked, "How thoroughly have you investigated the background of Col. Colby Manion? It is a little too convenient that he had only a personal vendetta against Heinz and that he wasn't working for someone else."

Maya said, "Sir, you have the entire Justice Department behind you to investigate Manion. Do you really think Tucker can be as affective all by himself?"

Arthur Gannon ignored Maya and asked, "Tucker, is there more?"

"I have suspicions of more but no proof. Do you want me to continue?"

"Yes, but first, I want to hear Maya's story about Heinz's murder."

Maya shared her story with the A.G., and he was satisfied that Manion committed the crime but remained skeptical that he worked alone.

Gannon said, "One last question, is there any evidence of corruption with the Director of the ATF."

Tucker said, "None as of this moment."

"Let's meet in person next time."

Tucker said, "Are you sure you want to be seen with me in public?"

"No, I'll come to you." He hung up.

After waiting a moment Maya said, "He's scared to death about something."

Tucker said, "We just poked a stick in the eye of a bear. I need a wine refill."

Chapter 15

May 4, 2024
Katonah, New York

"Mr. Judas, your guest has arrived."

"Send her in."

Judas' butler escorted into his study a tall slender conservatively dressed lady in her mid-forties who was formal in her mannerisms.

Penny Clark said, "Mr. Judas, it is an honor to meet you. I am so grateful that you selected me to write your autobiography."

He said, "Please, call me Victor. Was your experience getting through my security too harrowing?"

She said, "I was a tad embarrassed by the thoroughness and invasiveness of your guards."

Judas said, "You would be surprised at the number of daily threats on my life. Would you like anything to drink before we get started? I am having a little Scotch myself."

She said, "No, but thank you. Would you mind if I spread my notes on your beautiful coffee table?"

Judas nodded 'yes' as she brought out a bottle of germ-free hand lotion and cleaned her hands energetically. She pulled out a can of bacteria fighting spray and applied the contents on the coffee table. Penny said, "I'm sorry but I'm a bit of a germaphobe."

Victor Judas crunched his bushy eyebrows and eyed Ms. Clark as if she were mentally ill but said, "Let's get started."

Penny said, "You have lived a long and eventful life. You are well known worldwide as a philanthropist for ideological causes. What do you consider to be your greatest accomplishment?"

Judas said, "I believe I have had significant success in changing America and to a lesser extent the world. It has taken decades for me to convert millions of people to believe in a one-world society with no national borders. I sponsored, financed, and got two United States presidents elected. But I have to say, my greatest accomplishment has been my influence in changing the American education system. I was able to alter what is taught to young students who later became journalists. Well educated journalists believe in my open society concept."

Penny said, "What is your core belief and how did you arrive there?"

Judas took a sip of his Scotch before saying, "The journey was short, actually. You see, I am an atheist. Once you believe that there is no GOD that is controlling our world, then you can stand back and view what is wrong in the world and arrive at a way to fix it. In my youth, I was ashamed of being Jewish, after all, I grew up in Germany when being a Jew was stigmatic and disadvantageous. To survive I had to leave my religion. I did not believe in it anyway. All religions are foolish. How many people have died in the defense of their religion? Is that what people think GOD wants? What kind of GOD wants people to kill as a form of worship? Hence my core belief is that there is no GOD. Somebody must fill the void. It might as well be me.

"At an early age, I wanted to create a new world order in my vision. Instead of hundreds of tribes or countries protecting their little fiefdom, there should be no borders, no armies, no significant wealth disparity between peoples of the world. The United States, Bangladesh, and Chad would all have the same level of prosperity. The world would share resources instead of hoarding them."

Penny picked up her can of disinfectant and sprayed the coffee table in front of her again before she asked, "How does underwriting Black Lives Matter, the teaching of Critical Race Theory, and violent protests to defund the police play into your world view?"

"Ms. Clark, no revolutionary change in culture is achieved without violence."

Penny said, "Is it true that in your youth you confiscated property of Jews for the Nazi's?"

"It's true and I feel no remorse for my action; I had to survive."

Penny asked, "Is it also true that you shorted MGM stock two weeks before the Las Vegas massacre? Did you know that the attack on innocent people was going to happen?"

Victor said, "I am accused to be involved in almost every right-wing conspiracy theory. I had nothing to do with the missing Malaysian aircraft either. Can we get back to the autobiography, please?"

"Mr. Judas, I am sorry, Victor, let's go back to what you consider to be your greatest accomplishments. On a personal level, your sons are following in your footsteps. How does that rank in terms of other great accomplishments such as your ability to manipulate currencies?"

She picked up the can of disinfectant and sprayed the area again and said, "OK, sorry for the diversion."

Judas asked, "Do I smell or something, what are you doing with the disinfectant. I have had enough of you, please find your way out. I will get another writer."

Penny stood up, picked up the spray can and sprayed it directly into Victor Judas' face. He was too shocked to respond; no one treated him like this. He yelled, "Security, get this woman out of here."

A guard entered the study, grabbed Ms. Clark by her elbow and escorted her out. She had an odd smile on her face.

Within a few hours of inhaling the alleged disinfectant, Victor began to have difficulty breathing. A fever set in, he began to cough uncontrollably, felt nausea, and experienced a tightness in chest.

Judas' personal doctor was called by Judas' security to treat him but by the time he arrived Judas began to experience heavy sweating and his skin started to turn blue.

The personal doctor said, "Victor we need to get you to an emergency room to have an x-ray. You may have fluid building up in your lungs or pulmonary edema. Also, your blood pressure is way too low."

On the way to an emergency room the doctor had to document Judas' time of death.

Penny Clark knew she would die and that her symptoms were consistent with the Ricin she sprayed in the room with Victor Judas. She made no attempt to call a doctor or go to an emergency room—she knew the consequence of her actions. Besides, she had Amyotrophic Lateral Sclerosis or ALS. Her final act was to post a comment on #Steel's web site, *DanielWebsterWorldView*:

"One monster down, maybe my greatest accomplishment. May GOD forgive me. Victor Judas attempted to destabilize and commit acts of sedition against the United States and its citizens. He created and funded dozens of organizations whose sole purpose was to apply Alinsky's model terrorist tactics. He facilitated a movement to reconfigure the government of the United States and developed unhealthy and undue influence over party politics to drive the nation from capitalism to socialism or communism. Yet, he made his fortune as a capitalist. What a hypocrite.

"He was a domestic terrorist. There are more. Maybe his sons. Get them.

"We all die alone."

♦ ♦ ♦ ♦ ♦

May 5, 2024
New York City, New York

New York Times Headline: ***Billionaire Philanthropist for Leftist Causes found Dead – Ricin Suspected***

Victor Judas died in his Bedford Hills mansion of symptoms consistent with exposure to Ricin, a biological warfare agent. The Bedford Police Department, the New York State Police, the New York Bureau of Investigation, and the U.S. Department of Homeland Security are collectively investigating the crime. Currently the Judas estate is under quarantine until further notice.

Ricin is a poison found naturally in castor beans. It can be in the form of a powder, a mist, or a pellet, or it can be dissolved in water.

Terrorism has not been ruled out.

♦ ♦ ♦ ♦ ♦

May 5, 2024
Quantico, Virginia

"Sir," said Star, "I am calling to give you my status report as you requested at 1600 EDT. Before you ask, I will address the recent murder of Victor Judas. Though not technically a *Deadly Gray* event, I understand the killer left a message on *DanielWebsterWorldView* according to Jimmy Ma."

Rusty Winemiller said, "Yes, I know. I read it myself."

Star said, "OK, but did you know the killer was a 44-year-old woman with ALS? This may mean the influence of #Steel has transcended seniors into the general population of terminally ill patients. This is scary."

Winemiller asked, "How does Jimmy know that?"

"He and Tony Vinci are trying to build an algorithm that cross-references terminally ill patients with recent victims and discovered a correlation with Judas."

"Good to know. This will be covered with Director Naylor on our next meeting. It is good to be out in front of this one."

Star said, "By the way, the woman, Penny Clark, who also died of Ricin poisoning challenged fellow bloggers to take out Judas' sons. Someone needs to alert the sons of the threat against them."

Winemiller said, "I will take care of that. What is the status of your investigation into the New York University bombing, the assassination of *The Washington Post* editor and the bombing of the home of the Portland journalist?"

Star answered, "All three crimes were committed by people who post on #Steel's web site. They are all connected. Has your crack cyber team discovered who this person is?"

"No, I guess it's time to engage Jimmy and Tony on this task."

Winemiller heard Ram growl in agreement in the background.

Chapter 16

May 5, 2024
Jefferson City, Missouri

Dr. Angel Brown missed his blog friend, Colonel Colby Manion. Over the past months he had grown close to Manion as they were near the same age, had similar military experiences, both had lost loved ones, and shared a similar world view. Col. Manion had once blogged a narrative entitled, "*I Miss My Country.*" The blog resonated with Angel, and he began to follow Manion's bold position that seniors should do something meaningful on their way out.

Dr. Brown was an Army K9 warfighter veterinarian stationed at Fort Leonard Wood, Missouri. Twenty-five years ago, he retired from the military as a Lt. Colonel and set up a private sector practice in Jefferson City. Fifteen years ago, Angel also retired as a veterinarian after training his grandson to run the business.

Angel and Colby Manion met once to golf and share experiences at a location halfway between Blytheville, Arkansas and Jefferson City, Missouri. They hit if off famously. After Manion followed his own advice and took out ATF Assistant Director Adam Heinz, 84-year-old Angel Brown looked for a purpose.

That was before he received a call from his grandson. "Gramps, I need your advice."

"OK but you get what you pay for and my advice to you is free."

"There is no one whose opinion I trust more than yours."

Angel said, "Tadpole, you need to get out more; meet more people. What can I do for you?"

"One of my, ah, our customers knows about an animal abuser. She has called the police and an animal rights groups with no obvious result—no saving of these animals. She asked me what I recommend she do next. I told her to stay away from the abuser because more likely than not, he or she is also a people abuser. What would you do, Gramps?"

Angel responded, "I know of an organization that removes animals from their abusers. Do you have an address where the animal abuser lives? I will take care of it."

"Yes." He gave his grandfather the address.

Angel thought, *I am the organization that handles animal abusers.*

♦ ♦ ♦ ♦ ♦

May 6, 2024
Jefferson City, Missouri

Through binoculars Angel conducted reconnaissance at the address given to him by his veterinarian grandson. The 50-year-old 800 square foot house badly in need of paint had a small chain-link fenced-in backyard. An undernourished German Shepherd and a limping Pit Bull were tied by its owner to a post on opposing six-foot-long chains. No water bowls were visible. Dog shit sat in clumps on the grassless clay. The owner obviously did not understand the joy of having pets, the benefit of reciprocating love.

At his ripe old age, Angel was unsure exactly how to proceed. Should he call authorities? Should he try by himself to set the dogs free? Should he just take them a water bowl and leave some treats? After twenty or so minutes of contemplation, a decision was made for him. An obese middle-aged man exited from a door on the back of the house with a beer can in one hand and what looked to be a fireplace poker in the other hand. Both dogs cowered down as he yelled something Dr. Brown could not hear.

The dog owner reached down and removed the leash from the Pit Bull and apparently ordered him to attack and fight the German Shepherd.

Angel had had enough and thought, *It is the owner that needs to be tested for rabies*. He got in his four-wheel drive SUV, revved it up, pointed the vehicle in the direction of the chain-link fence, and let the clutch out. He drove through the fence being careful not to hit the dogs but missed his target, the abusive owner, who had jumped out of the way. The pit bull escaped, running as fast as his limp allowed him, but the German Shepherd was still on a chain. The fat man screamed at old man Brown and said, "You idiot, don't you know how to drive? You are going to fucking pay for the damage you've done. DMV needs to deny you old farts a license."

Angel rolled down his window and said, "Let the German Shepherd off the chain."

The man said, "What? That is my dog; you can't tell me what to do with my dog. Wait a minute. Did you drive through my fence on purpose? You son-of-a-bitch.

I will teach you a lesson." Anger seemed to be the dog abuser's only emotion.

The hate-filled obese man came around to the driver's side of the SUV, lifted his fireplace poker, and started the swing down when he was greeted in the face with a 9mm round from Angel's Sig Sauer P365X.

Angel thought, *My buddy, Colby Manion would be proud of me.* He got out of the car, stepped around the dead fat man, and spoke with gentleness to the abused German Shepherd, "Would you like some water and something to eat?" The dog whimpered. Dr. Brown entered the dead man's home, looked in the nasty kitchen for a bowl to put water in and found luncheon meat in the disgusting refrigerator.

The German Shepherd lapped up the water first and then turned to devour the meat. His tail wagged, so Brown felt free to remove the latch on his collar and asked the dog to get in the back of the SUV. Angel pulled out his cell phone and called the local animal shelter for direction. Then he called 9-1-1. "This is Dr. Angel Brown. I killed a man in self-defense. Please have the police meet me at the city animal shelter."

Dr. Angel Brown smiled as he thought, *All of us will be remembered more for the mistakes we made in life than all the good we did. This last act is how I will be remembered, and I am good with that.*"

He backed his scratched-up SUV up onto the road and headed for the animal shelter. On his way he saw the pit bull standing confused on the side of the road. He stopped to save the dog, but he ran away.

The police were waiting for old-man Brown when he arrived at the shelter. The shelter volunteers rescued the German Shepherd as the police cuffed Dr. Brown who agreed to show them where the man lay that he killed.

Ultimately, he was taken to the police station where he was interviewed, read his rights, and allowed to make his call. Angel called his son who proceeded to call the family attorney. The attorney negotiated Angel's freedom until the trial date.

Prior to the trial Star interviewed Angel Brown who confirmed his relationship with Colby Manion and his knowledge of #Steel's website. Angel said, "I am not suffering from intellectual dishonesty. Killing that hateful animal abuser was like shooting a rabid fox but no good deed goes unpunished. I would do it again in a heartbeat. My alleged crime was not due to this #Steel person or my friend Colby Manion. I had to defend myself and the two dogs who I understand now have good homes."

◆ ◆ ◆ ◆ ◆

May 6, 2024
Las Vegas, Nevada

Tank asked, "Sonja, who were the two people killed with the sniper rifle? You know, the two killed from a different angle than from the Mandalay Bay?"

"Bradley Schwann and Dan Delaney were both private sector businessmen. One was a California real estate tycoon, the other a distributor of Taiwanese computer chips from Chicago. There is no obvious overlap in their professions or personal relationship. Yet both were targets."

Tank said, "Let's get Tony on the line."

Tony Vinci answered the phone on the fourth ring. "Hi, Tank, what's up?"

"I'm in Las Vegas with Sonja and we're trying to uncover the relationship between two victims of the Las Vegas massacre."

Tony said, "You mean Schwann and Delaney?"

Sonja asked, "My God, Tony, how can you know that?"

"Tucker and Maya are ahead of you. They asked me to investigate the dead and wounded and find any anomalies. Two guys standing together who were in their fifties without family members at a country music concert stood out like a sore thumb."

Tank asked, "What can you tell us about them?"

Tony said, "Well, first of all, Schwann and Delaney are not their real names."

♦ ♦ ♦ ♦ ♦

May 6, 2024
Mount Vernon, Virginia

Though Star was home, she could not turn her head off. Winemiller overloaded her with too many concurrent *Deadly Gray* cases. She had to categorize the cases—those cases that are confirmed to be tied to #Steel; those cases that have no relationship with #Steel or the web site *DanielWebsterWorldView;* and those cases that could go either way.

She thought, *Who is #Steel and how is he orchestrating the* Deadly Gray *army*?

She said to Ram, "Let us see, the Heinz/Manion case and the Werner murder are absolutely related to #Steel. The media related crimes in New York, DC, and Portland are related to #Steel as was the sniper who killed the *New York Times* editor. The same guy who killed him killed the Washington Post editor.

"The guy who ran over Kurt Rainwater was probably, though unconfirmed, a murder by a *Deadly Gray* vigilante.

"The Berkley bomber, Jacob Cohen, was connected to #Steel as was Mrs. Hoffman who shocked the Congresswoman in Minnesota with her Zap cane.

"Ram, pay attention. There is no evidence yet that the Kentucky woman, Alice Cloud, who mutilated the rapist is tied to #Steel though I still need to speak with her nephew. Nor is Asa Frank's attempt to dynamite the location of the Speaker of the House tied to the *Deadly Gray* cases.

"I am confident the assassination of Judas and the murder of the MS-13 boy were not related to # Steel. Yet can it be a coincidence that Mrs. Werner's husband's murder is related to #Steel? I have not had a chance to investigate the House of Lords, the defense attorney, and the California State senator murders by seniors yet so they are still open.

"The one that is curious is the murder of the animal abuser by a veterinarian who was friends with Colby Manion. All and all, of the seventeen cases I must close, nine are definitely tied to #Steel and three more may be. You are a good listener, Ram."

Star's cell phone pinged—she received a text: "You cannot stop us. You have only scratched the surface. There will be more senior vigilante events tomorrow."

Star tried to determine the phone number of the text but was unsuccessful. She was not looking forward to tomorrow.

PART TWO

Chapter 17

May 8, 2024
Atlanta, Georgia

Old man Maurice Milner who resembled Willie Mays sat in the passenger seat of his grandson's ten-year-old Ford F-150 listening to rap music as they were driving the country roads from Macon to Atlanta to attend an auto show. Maurice ran his fingers through his thinning gray hair as he observed several cemeteries on the trip and thought, *So many headstones of people who died decades ago. I wonder if anyone alive remembers who they really were. My grandfather was born in 1893; I remember him fondly. When I pass, there will be no one left on earth to remember him. A hundred years from now, there will be no one who will remember me. That is unless I do something meaningful that will make me famous.*

Maurice said to his grandson, "Do you know that I write poetry and lyrics to music?"

The grandson said, "You are kidding. No, I did not know that."

Maurice added, "I think my lyrics would make good rap music. Do you think it is possible to put my lyrics and poetry in front of one of these rap artists? Do you know how to do that?"

"No, Pappy, but I would like to read them. What are they about?"

Maurice said, "Many of the lyrics are about what it was like to be a poor black man in Georgia before the civil rights movement. Have you ever heard the Allman Brothers song 'Whipping Post'?"

"No."

Maurice started to sing, "I feel like I'm tied to the whipping post, tied to the whipping post; I feel like I'm dying" or something like that. Anyway, I wrote lyrics very similar to that. They would make good rap songs.

"Did you know I used to play the slide guitar?"

"No."

Pappy said, "you do not know much about me, do you? Aren't you a little curious?"

The grandson said, "I know you were a good mechanic."

"True, but did you know I once bowled a perfect 300?"

"Get out of here, Pappy, you're pulling my leg."

"True, I am about bowling but not the rest of the stuff. On a serious note, I wrote my Last Will this week. I don't have much, but I left my poems and music lyrics to you, but you have to promise me you'll try to get them published. I do not know how to do that but you're smarter than me about stuff like that. Promise me, OK?"

"Sure Pappy, I promise. We are almost at the auto show. Do you want me to drop you off while I try to find a parking spot? I'll meet you at the Ford exhibit."

"Good idea."

Maurice's grandson had difficulty finding a spot in the coliseum lot—it took him twenty minutes to find his way to the Ford display. He could not find his grandfather. Thirty minutes later, he grew concerned. An hour later he began to panic.

◆ ◆ ◆ ◆ ◆

May 8, 2024
Atlanta, Georgia

Maurice did not enter the auto show on Market Street, instead, he caught a bus that dropped him off near the Atlanta Police Department on Peachtree Street, SW. He waited on the steps of the police station for only 45 minutes before he saw the man, he came to Atlanta to see, Officer Smyrna, who apparently was now Lieutenant Smyrna; the man who tied him to a post and beat him mercifully for a crime he did not commit—a dirty cop. It took Maurice 18 months to fully recover from that beating decades ago.

Old man Milner positioned himself where Smyrna had to walk around him to avoid running into him. Maurice said, "Lieutenant, may I speak with you for a minute?"

Smyrna said, "I'm sorry, no, I'm late for an appointment."

Maurice said, "Do you remember me?"

Smyrna kept walking as he said, "No, should I?"

Maurice said, "We met when you were a Macon cop."

"Well, that was a long time ago, now leave me alone."

Maurice said, "But I have something that belongs to you."

Lieutenant Smyrna stopped just long enough for Maurice to plant a knife deep into the dirty police officer's chest. Maurice said, "I lied, but I'm not sorry."

Smyrna died at the scene and Maurice was arrested by police on the spot. He smiled knowing his grandson would publish the lyrics of the song, *Dirty Cop*, which forecasted the crime.

◆ ◆ ◆ ◆ ◆

May 8, 2024
Hoboken, New Jersey

"Who is dumber, Congresswoman Lake, or the people that keep re-electing her. She is an idiot. On one of her congressional hearings, she asked if too much military hardware on one of our small Pacific islands would cause it to tip over. You got to be kidding—this is one of our representatives? She stated that there would be less crime if there were fewer prisons. Dah! She supported defunding the police and then complained that crime increased in her precinct. Where do we find these people? She could not paddle a canoe by herself. And the media, of course, give her a pass. So, what is new?

"Darn, it's time for a commercial break."

Talk radio host Lynn Barkham looked over her reading glasses on her nose and reviewed her notes during the break to prepared for the next segment. She was a tall thin blond attorney turned radio commentator who became enemy number one on far-left media outlets. She required more security than the President. But it was time to share the bad news with her audience.

"Ladies and gentlemen of the listening audience— note that I did not include people who prefer transgender pronouns—I am ordered to cease and desist as a talk show host. The State of New Jersey passed a law sponsored by State Representative Anthony Dow, III to silence conservative talk radio hosts. The State believes we promote anarchy, instigate violence, support opposition to the Critical Race Theory, openly challenge the past COVID-19 vaccine mandates, and question the science behind climate change. I do not think I've incited violence, but the rest is clearly true. This is a clear violation of the First Amendment to the Constitution, but I will have to remain on the sidelines until the US Supreme Court takes up the argument. No talk radio host will be allowed to discuss controversial issues as defined by the State of New Jersey.

"This is my last segment until the issue is cleared up. However, I have been offered a spot on a Pennsylvania radio station. I hope you join me next month. Until then, keep the faith."

◆ ◆ ◆ ◆ ◆

May 8, 2024
Trenton, New Jersey

Three hours after talk radio host Lynn Barkham made her announcement, a crowd formed in front to the State House Annex with posters and signs expressing their displeasure on the attack on the First Amendment. Signs included: "*Impeach Dow*," "*Free Speech*," "*Totalitarian NJ*," and "*Is this what we pay taxes for*?".

The steps of the legislative building were filled with media from TV, radio, newspaper, streaming entities, and self-appointed YouTube types with smart phone cameras.

New Jersey State Police were present and controlled the small crowd of approximately 250 protestors when a smug, arrogant Anthony Dow III came out to make a speech. He grabbed the microphone that was set up on the steps and listened to 90 seconds of boos before he tried to address the hostile crowd.

"Dear New Jersey citizens, we cannot allow people who want to violently overthrow our duly elected state government to mislead you, drown you with disinformation, and promote hate for our legislators. The legislation I sponsored protects you from abusive speech. I….." Dow heard the unmistakable sound of metal scraping across the concrete steps as someone screamed, "Hand grenade!"

Panic ensued, the crowd tried to escape, but the grenade did its job. State representative and one old man died while four others at the scene were injured from the blast from the exploding grenade: one trooper, a couple from Parsippany, and a student at Rutgers. It was later determined that the fatally wounded old man left a message on his kitchen table that stated, "I lost a son who valiantly fought as a marine. He fought for the United States. He fought for the preservation of the Constitution. I love my country. Apparently representative Dow does not. The fall of America is our fault if we do nothing about it. "

◆ ◆ ◆ ◆ ◆

May 8, 2024
Wiscasset, Maine

"It feels good to be home."

"It's great to have you home, Tank."

"Can I stay here?"

Jolene, said, "Stanley, Tank just got home. We need to discuss this in private."

Stanley said, "I will not eat too much, I promise. Besides, you need me to help you solve mysteries."

Tank said, "Stanley, if you're so good at solving mysteries, what happened to the missing Malaysian Airlines back in 2014?"

"Oh, that one's easy, North Korea's SSD threatened the pilot's family's lives if he didn't take the plane down over the Indian Ocean."

Tank asked, "Why would North Korea do that?"

Stanley said, "It was all about who from Japan was on the flight. Do you want to watch TV?"

Tank said, "You go start without me. I'll catch up."

Stanley left and went into the family room.

Jolene said, "I am so sorry Stanley invaded our home. Have you given it any thought as to what I should do about him? I am his only family, so he falls under my responsibility."

Tank asked, "Where is the closest home for the mentally challenged to Wiscasset?"

Jolene said, "In South Portland."

Tank said, "Hmmm, too far from here. Do you think he could hold a job?"

"Unlikely."

Tank said, "Let's look into getting him a small apartment in Wiscasset."

Jolene said jokingly, "Maybe he could move in with Jimmy Ma."

♦ ♦ ♦ ♦ ♦

May 8, 2024
Boston, Massachusetts

Tank said, "Tony, are you calling from the Entropy office and why are you calling me so late? I just got home."

"Sorry, Tank, I forgot you were not still in Las Vegas. Do you want me to call back tomorrow?"

Tank said, "It depends, whatcha got?"

"I think I know why the two guys were assassinated by a sniper from another hotel at the same time the massacre was on-going from the Mandalay Bay Resort and Casino."

"I'm listening. Let me put you on speaker so Jolene can hear your assessment."

Tony said, "Both the men assassinated were retired Chicago Police Department officers who started their own private detective company. Apparently, a Saudi Prince hired them to investigate a threat on his life if he went to Las Vegas."

Jolene said, "Yet, the Prince went anyway?"

Tony said, "Yes and as you know, he stayed at the Mandalay Bay Resort and Casino."

Unknown to all, Stanley crept to within earshot of the conversation and said, "That makes about as much sense as a steering wheel on a donkey."

An exasperated Jolene said, "What are you talking about, Stanley?"

"Didn't I hear Tony say that a Saudi Prince was in Las Vegas when the massacre at the country music festival occurred?"

Jolene said, "Well, yes. What is your point?"

Stanley said, "I know you do not believe in coincidences. And what is the Prince doing in sin city? Looking at scantily clad young girls at the concert out his window with binoculars?"

Tony said, "No doubt, he was gambling."

Stanley said, "The real gamble was that no one would make the connection between the massacre and the assassination on the same grounds. When are we going to eat? You know carrot cake is my favorite veggie food."

Jolene asked Tony, "Did anyone take credit for the massacre?"

"No. Returning to the topic of the two Saudi hired PIs, someone must have learned that they were working for the Saudi Prince."

Tank asked, "Who do you believe was threatening his life?"

Tony said, "I don't have enough evidence yet, but I think it was the Iran Revolutionary Guard Corps, the IRGC."

Tank said, "I am confused. Iran wants to kill the Saudi Prince, the Saudi Prince hires a couple of American PIs, the Iranians kill the PIs, all this while the massacre is on-going. This is like mental jujitsu. I am having trouble putting this all together."

Tony said, "Unless the weapons in Paddock's hotel room were intended for the Iranians and the PIs figured this out."

"How does Adam Heinz, the ATF, the FBI, and CIA figure into all of this?"

Tony answered, "Work-in-progress."

Tank said, "Thanks, Tony, you have given us a lot to think about. I feel like I am on a vodka high even though I haven't had a drop to drink. "

Chapter 18

May 9, 2024
Near Smithsburg, Maryland

"I sent Agent Star Cherokee a text message."

The mechanical sounding mystery voice, he or she asked, "I do not think that was very smart, #Steel. What were you thinking and why would you do that?" Again, the person on the other end of the phone used an app that distorted the sound of the voice. #Steel was frustrated with not knowing with whom he was speaking.

#Steel said, "There is no way to track the text I sent. The FBI is trying desperately to find me. They are convinced I am the lead conductor for this *Deadly Gray* orchestra. They know the senior vigilante army is growing faster than they can manage, especially when they have assigned the case to a single FBI agent. I want her to give up trying to solve the *Deadly Gray* vigilante acts of honor and focus on why. It serves no purpose unless the world knows why it is happening."

The voice said, "Shut down the *DanielWebsterWorldView* website, open a new one, rename yourself with a new hashtag, destroy your computer, and establish a new IP address. Somehow, make your followers and the FBI think you are dead."

#Steel asked, "If I do that, how will we make the *Deadly Gray* army grow?"

The amplified voice laughed and said, "We no longer need to; it will be self-sustaining. The mainstream media will make it grow unintentionally as they beat their own drum. And the Government will reinforce the media megaphone. I am going to make that happen. Watch and learn.”

May 9, 2024
Quantico, Virginia

Star called Winemiller and asked, “Do you want me to come by and give my report in person.”

Rusty Winemiller said, “No, let’s do it over this encrypted line.”

Star said, “You don’t trust me anymore, do you?”

“I do not think you have control over your special skill, and I have thoughts I’d like to keep to myself. Go ahead and give me your report.”

Star was hurt but accepted the rebuke. She said, “I asked Jimmy Ma and Tony Vinci if they could figure out who sent me the text that warned us that more *Deadly Gray* crimes were going to overwhelm us. They said the firewall was too good even for them to break through. Jimmy and Tony tracked the thread and got as far as Djibouti before they lost it. Any thoughts as to why #Steel would risk sending me a text?”

Winemiller said, “Yes, I have thought a lot about it. #Steel wants us to know that he is untouchable and that he is smarter than us. For him to be this good, I believe he must be employed by the National Security Agency or a private firm in Silicon Valley. He or she is domestic, not foreign.”

Star said, "A rogue NSA agent? I had not thought of that. Should we share this theory with the Director of the NSA?"

"No, at this point I trust no one in our government with this knowledge. However, I do trust your dad, Jimmy, and Tony. See what they suggest we do to infiltrate the NSA."

"Infiltrate the NSA? You must be kidding. Even Jimmy and Tony are unlikely to be successful without being discovered, arrested, and tried for treason."

Winemiller said, "I will document that they were hired to perform an audit to evaluate the NSA's security.

"Now, update me on the status of each of your cases."

Star said, "We will start with the most visible cases. Asa Frank, the guy who tried to assassinate the Speaker of the House with dynamite confessed to knowing about #Steel and the *Deadly Gray* movement. He was a follower of #Steel's blogs but has no idea who the person is and how to contact him. It is another dead end.

"Mrs. Hoffman who tried to kill the Minneapolis congresswoman with a Zap cane confessed that she was called by #Steel and encouraged to commit the crime. We investigated every call received by Mrs. Hoffman and discovered only one phone call of interest from a gas station in Harrisburg, Pennsylvania. No one there remembers the caller. It is also a dead end.

"The suicide bomber who attacked the New York University School of Journalism faculty lounge was a *Deadly Gray* vigilante. We performed forensics on his personal computer, his laptop, his I-pad, and his smart phone. He was definitely influenced by #Steel though there was no hard evidence discovered that #Steel suggested a suicide bomb attack.

"The sniper attacks on *The New York Times* and *The Washington Post* editors were committed by the same person; Corey Robertson, a Vietnam vet who has serious issues with the media. He has not been found and is still out there and likely to continue his vendetta. Again, he followed the blogs of #Steel. In fact, we think #Steel had a sniper rifle delivered to Robertson's home in Culpepper, Virginia. Though there is not a formal chain of custody for the package, we are still interviewing people in the supply chain. This is currently our best lead so far at finding #Steel."

Winemiller said, "Keep me posted on this one. We need a break since Brad is being asked to brief the President at the White House 0900 tomorrow. Director Naylor wants us there by his side in case he needs us."

"Yes, sir. Aren't you concerned to be in my presence?"

"Don't be a smart ass and you can't bring Ram with you to the White House."

Star thought, *Better than being a dumb ass*.

"Next on the list of cases is the murder of the New Jersey State Representative Anthony Dow III by an old man with a hand grenade. The old man had a history of mental health issues. There was a tornado running through his brain. There is no evidence he even knew how to start a computer or manage a smart phone, so we think that murder was unrelated to the *Deadly Gray* cases."

Winemiller said, "The President is likely to ask about the murder of Judas. How should Naylor handle it?"

Star said, "I suggest that he tells the President that the woman who killed Judas with ricin was a *Deadly Gray* vigilante even though she was comparatively young."

Winemiller said, "OK. I do not need to hear the status on the rest of the cases. POTUS will ask the question, 'what should he do to help mitigate the rise in terminally ill seniors committing vigilante crimes'. Any ideas?"

Star said, "That is a question best answered by the Director, but I would think we need our best hackers in the country to help us find #Steel. And maybe, make some sort of statement about improving our justice system so they don't have to take the law into their own hands."

Rusty said, "I think I will pass on the justice system advice. See you tomorrow."

♦ ♦ ♦ ♦ ♦

May 9, 2024
Hollywood, California

"I bet my life on you, you fucking whore. I trusted you. We shared the beauty of music, the artistry of sunshine through the trees, the majesty of hummingbirds, the innocence of fawns, and the magic of metamorphosis. Did you fake it all?"

"Tom, you are so fucking naïve. I bet you believe in Santa Claus and the Easter Bunny."

"Cut."

Director Wayne Moore took his glasses off, rubbed his eyes, and yelled to the actors, "Can't either of you say 'fucking' with passion. You're supposed to be angry. The audience is not going to believe that you mean it unless you conjure up heartfelt anger. Now let us try this again. Pretend you are angry with me for making you do it over."

Both actors thought, *I am angry with you, Moore, you fucking whore.*

After the third cut, Moore said, "OK, let us call it a day. It is past dinner time. I have a scheduled meeting at the Musso & Frank Grill. See you tomorrow at 10:00 a.m. and people, practice your fucking lines."

The obese producer and director gradually and carefully removed himself from the director's chair with the help from his bodyguard and driver. Moore was planted in the backseat of his limousine and driven to the restaurant. The maître de was expecting the famous producer and escorted him along with his bodyguard to a reserved table where a young twenty something aspiring actress awaited his arrival.

"Mr. Moore, I am so glad you made it. I was afraid you got detained by your work. I am on my third Margarita waiting for you."

Wayne Moore lecherously eyed the voluptuous want-to-be actress and said, "Do not worry, I am sorry I'm late. Remind me, what is your name?"

I am Taylor Sanders from Toledo, Ohio. I want to audition for a role in your next movie. Here is an mp4 which contains my qualifications."

Moore said, "Thank you Taylor, I am sure you have ample qualifications. Let us order, eat, and go to my place where I can watch your acting in real time."

"Sure."

Moore said, "You know I am on two diets, right. I cannot seem to get enough food on one diet."

Though Taylor did not get the joke, she said, "Whatever you say, Mr. Moore."

Taylor ordered a spinach salad while Wayne ordered a rare 16-oz steak, a loaded baked potato, a side of fried onion rings, and a large martini. He ordered a hamburger and French fries for his bodyguard.

The waiter told Moore that his martini would be right out as he went to the kitchen to process the food order. An older gray-haired man with a towel over his left arm brought Moore his Martini. Moore did not acknowledge the bar tender's existence and continued to fawn over his next young conquest. After a couple of long sips of the martini, Wayne's meal was presented to him and his protégé.

The famous Hollywood director's chin started to quiver, his hands shook uncontrollably, and his speech became unintelligible. Beads of perspiration formed on his forehead and froth started to escape from his mouth. The bodyguard yelled for medical help, called 9-1-1 and laid the big man on the floor. By the time the ambulance arrived, Moore was comatose. He died before the medics could put him on an ambulance gurney.

Police arrived a few minutes later and asked everyone to stay put while they investigated the circumstance of Moore's death. The bartender was nowhere to be found.

A Hollywood police detective went to the home of the bartender as shown on his restaurant application only to discover that the address listed was fake and that the location was that of a local high school.

♦ ♦ ♦ ♦ ♦

May 10, 2024
Klamath Falls, Oregon

The bartender's wife placed flowers on the grave of their granddaughter. They had raised her from the age of seven until their granddaughter left to be a star in Hollywood. She was full of life; she exhibited a turbocharged metabolism and a unity of purpose.

They had driven her all the way to Hollywood to show their support, set her up in an apartment, supplied her a means of transportation, and gave whatever help she asked for. She was full of love and was a joy to be around. They were shocked to get a call from the Santa Ana Police Department stating that their granddaughter had committed suicide. They never saw it coming and doubted its authenticity.

The police sent the bartender and his wife a copy of the suicide note: "I have never been so humiliated and ashamed in my life. I think I would have been a good actor in my own right. But Wayne Moore said he would not even consider me unless I went down on him and gave him a Lewinski. When I said I would not do that, he held a gun to my head. I cannot live with what I did to that ugly fat man."

The rest is history. The bartender did what he felt compelled to do.

The bartender said to his wife, "You know we are going to have to roll soon, right? The Hollywood, California police no doubt already know that I put rat poison in Moore's martini. One form of law enforcement or another will be here soon. The RV is gassed up, the refrigerator is stocked, the propane tank and freshwater tank is filled, and ready for our trip east. We will be on the road the rest of our short lives but at least we won't be here when the police show up.

"#Steel was right. I feel vindicated. Let us get on the road, honey before the snow melts on the daffodils. I have always wanted to see Yellowstone. It is on our way anyway."

The bartender's wife said, "We are going to another country, right? Do we need a passport to get to our destination, West Virginia?"

Chapter 19

May 10, 2024
New York City, New York

Wall Street Journal Headline: **Justice Department Announces Drastic Increase in Crime by Seniors**

Over the past few months, crimes by seniors over the age of 65 years has dramatically increased. Crimes such as the attempted assassination of the Speaker of the House by a university professor from Missouri, the attempt on the life of a congresswoman from Minneapolis, the assassination of a New Jersey State representative, and the recent murders of liberal philanthropist Victor Judas and Hollywood producer and director Wayne Moore are just a few of the recent crimes committed by seniors.

The Wall Street Journal asked a Justice Department spokesperson why they thought the sudden increase in seniors committing serious crimes has developed. They said the following: 'We have reason to believe the crimes are instigated by a third party via the dark web. It should be noted that in every case you described the senior vigilante was terminally ill. Someone is preying on our grandparents. It is disgusting.'

New York Times Headline: **Seniors Targeting Journalists**

Vietnam vets have long memories. A Vietnam era army sniper assassinated a retired New York Times journalist for the journalist's coverage of the Tet offensive during the war. The same army sniper assassinated a Washington Post editor and is still on the run. Law enforcement knows who he is but is unable to find the aggrieved veteran.

A Vietnam vet also entered the faculty lounge of the New York University School of Journalism wearing a suicide bomb vest that resulted in the killing of school professors. A Molotov cocktail was thrown by an irate senior into the editor's home of the Portland Observer.

We asked our Washington correspondence to inquire about why these events were happening now and he concluded after interviewing several government officials that a private social-media non-governmental organization is conspiring to build an army of seniors who quote, "want justice and want their country back." Unquote.

New York Post Headline: **Seniors are Fighting Progressives for their Country**

We interviewed a 75-year-old woman from Kentucky who resides in a Cincinnati jail for mutilating a man on parole who had raped her daughter. She said, 'He ruined my daughter's life, yet a demented misguided judge let him out on parole. Where is the justice in that? I am at the end of my life, I'm terminally ill, what do I have to lose in my quest for justice? I could have killed him, but I did not. My moral compass is not broken. The judge that set him free, well, he is one sick bastard. Getting old is not for sissies. I made the best of the rest of my life by seeking justice unavailable thorough the alleged legal process'.

The Post also interviewed 82-year-old Mrs. Hoffman who electrified Congresswoman Huda

Mohammed with a 1-million-volt Zap cane. She said, "Huda shames my family with her anti-police and Sharia law rhetoric. She is statistically blind, has left the universe of truth, and is unaware of the true benefit of law enforcement. What she thinks is fair, I do not. I want to be remembered by my loved ones as a person who fought for law enforcement. It makes my life meaningful to know I defended my police-oriented family. My Harry was a police captain and took his responsibilities seriously. By my action, I support him."

May 10, 2024
Near Smithsburg, Maryland

The mechanical voice said, "#Steel, our recruitment into the *Deadly Gray* army just got a fantastic boost. You wait and see; senior vigilantism has transformed into a grass roots movement. All you must do to maintain momentum is to keep posting pro *Deadly Gray* narratives."

#Steel said, "By the way, as you instructed, my new handle is #Star and my new website on TOR is *DeadlyGrayJustice.*

The voice said, "I love it when a plan comes together."

May 10, 2024
Washington, DC

Special Agent Rusty Winemiller was 45 minutes early at the White House to allow for his van and his motorized wheelchair to be inspected by Secret Service and his credentials verified. Director Naylor and Agent Cherokee also arrived early and waited for POTUS to start the meeting. In attendance was the National Security Advisor and POTUS' Chief of Staff. President Lamb started the meeting with, "Director Naylor, how do we contain this crisis with seniors. You know seniors have supported me more than any other demographic group in the last election. What is going on?"

Naylor said, "Sir, it has nothing to do with you or your administration. Someone, some group, or some organization has convinced seniors that there is honor in being a justice vigilante in the sunset of their lives when they have nothing to lose; when they have an opportunity to correct an injustice in their lives and do something meaningful before they pass. Most of the new senior crimes are committed by people with stage four cancer or other debilitating diseases."

POTUS asked, "Do we know the source of the group encouraging vigilantism?"

Naylor said, "We only know his or her hashtag name; #Steel."

The National Security Advisor asked, "Is this a domestic issue or is there a reason to believe a foreign entity is involved?"

Naylor said, "It is an international problem in that other countries are experiencing similar senior vigilante crimes, but we do not see it as a national security problem. The United Kingdom, Australia, Brazil, and Japan are experiencing the same senior vigilante problem as we are. You may have heard that a senior commoner murdered a member of the House of Lords."

President Lamb asked, "Was the attempted assassination of the Speaker of the House influenced by this quote 'group or organization'?"

Naylor said, "Yes, sir."

POTUS asked, "Was the murder of Judas and what's his name Moore related to the *Deadly Gray* vigilantes?"

"Yes, we think so."

"Director, what are we going to do about it? What is your plan?"

Star read the thoughts of Naylor, *Nothing I say will satisfy the President.*

She read the thoughts of Winemiller, *There is nothing President Lamb can do to stop it.*

She read the thought of the Chief of Staff, *This is an election year game changer.*

And finally, she read the thoughts of the President, *I have walked this road before. There is no satisfactory answer.*

Naylor looked over at Winemiller for help as he said, "Sir, our goal is to find this #Steel and limit his future influence over ill American seniors. It would be beneficial to the crisis if we could encourage the media to issue editorials stating that there is no honor in committing vigilante crimes."

POTUS looked at Winemiller and asked, "You are responsible for bringing cybercriminals to justice, correct?"

Winemiller responded, "Yes, Mr. President."

Lamb continued, "This is obviously a cybercrime problem whereby an organization is manipulating seniors to commit crimes. Our older generation must be catching up on the use of the internet and social media. Special Agent Winemiller, why can't we find this #Steel guy? Who is he? What is his motive? What is his beef?"

Winemiller said, "Good questions, sir. The fact is, we do not know yet. He or she is good. What we do know is that the cybercriminal intends to build an army of people approaching the end of their mortality who are willing to commit crimes to address what they believe to be grievances or injustices in their lives."

The National Security Advisor asked, "Could he or she be Chinese, Russian, North Korean, or Iranian?"

Winemiller said, "Unlikely sir. More than likely, domestic, maybe even NSA."

POTUS said, "Agent Star, do you have anything to add to this conversation?"

Star said, "Mr. President, in my opinion it has nothing to do with your administration. It has everything to do with a buildup over years of frustration with the perception by some who believe our justice system has failed Americans. Most of the crimes by seniors were committed by the aggrieved."

POTUS asked, "What do you advise me to do about this problem?"

Star looked at Director Naylor and then at Rusty Winemiller for guidance before she answered the question but received none. She thought about the famous Winston Churchill saying, 'Life is full of opportunities to keep your mouth shut,' but instead said, "Secure the best hackers in the nation to find #Steel."

President Lamb said, "Thank you, Agent Star, finally someone advised me what to do about this. Consider it done."

◆ ◆ ◆ ◆ ◆

May 10, 2024
Wiscasset, Maine

Tucker and Maya requested a Microsoft Teams meeting with Jimmy Ma and Tony Vinci. This time Jimmy called in on time. Maya said, "Miracles never cease."

Jimmy said, "Maya, that's not fair."

Maya said, "Nothing is more relative than fairness."

Tucker said, "The reason we asked for this conference call is that we want to know the status of the algorithm you and Tony are building. What are your roadblocks and is there anything we can do to help knock them down?"

Tony Vinci said, "Jimmy and I have made a lot of progress in a short period of time. The problem is that the algorithm we created has identified thousands of potential vigilantes and multiple thousands of potential victims. We are trying to find a way to narrow the lists down to something manageable."

Jimmy added, "We've successfully cross-referenced seniors over 65-years-of-age with people with life-threatening illnesses. There are hundreds of thousands of people in that group. Then we cross-referenced that group of seniors with those who have filed complaints with law enforcement entities. That narrowed the list down to only thousands of people. To get it to a smaller group, we need to find a way to determine how many of them observe the #Steel blogs. We have not figured out how to do that yet."

Maya asked, "How did you get past the HIPAA issue?"

Tony said, "To protect you and Tucker, I would rather not say. You know, plausible deniability and all."

Tucker said, "I know of only one person I can trust at the NSA. Do you want me to contact him and see what he can do to help with the #Steel website and get a list of IP addresses that visited the site?"

Jimmy said, "Give us a couple more days. Tony is a genius and I think we can work through our issues."

Tony said, "Wow! Jimmy, you have never complimented me before. How many bourbons have you had?"

Maya said, "I have a private sector contact in Silicon Valley who is contracted by various entities in our government to hack the pentagon and the NSA to test their firewall protection and security. Would she be a valuable asset to our team?"

Tony asked, "Why should we trust her?"

Maya said, "Because she is my sister."

Jimmy said, "Are you talking about Suzzanne?"

Maya answered, "The very one."

Jimmy said, "Yes, add her to the team."

Maya said, "But Jimmy, you have no chance in hell of dating her."

Tony said, "By the way, #Steel has shut his web site down and replaced it with a new website, *DeadlyGrayJustice.*

"And sadly," Tony continued, "I think he is catfishing and operating under a new hashtag--#Star."

Tucker said, "So the evil one knows Star is on to him. Do you think she is in danger?"

Tony said, "It is possible. You might want to warn Star if she doesn't already know that #Steel knows who she is. If I were you, I would consider putting a couple of Tank's White Knights down there at her home in Mount Vernon."

Maya said, "Tony, give Suzzanne a call, she probably won't answer a call from Jimmy."

"Yes Ma'am."

Jimmy said, "I guess I'm the color of doom when it comes to Suzzanne."

◆　◆　◆　◆　◆

May 10, 2024
Mount Vernon, Virginia

It was late when Ram woke Star with a bark. Her phone was ringing, but Star had not heard it. She looked at the call number on her phone display and saw it was from her parents. She answered the call and said, "It is unusual for you to call me at this hour. Is everything all right?"

Maya said, "Are you aware that #Steel has reinvented himself as #Star?"

"Oh, No. I am not surprised that he knows who I am but somewhat surprised that he is so arrogant, so confident that he would use my name. When did this happen?"

Maya said, "Unsure, but Tony discovered the change, he also changed his website."

Star said, "#Steel texted me a few days ago. He is feeling empowered, invulnerable."

Tucker asked, "What did he say in his text to you?"

"That I was not going to be able to stop the army of senior vigilantes seeking justice."

Maya added, "We are concerned that your life is in danger from this person, so we've asked Tank to post a couple of White Knights to guard your home around the clock. Do not be surprised when they show up."

Star said, "They must already be here because Ram barked a few minutes ago."

Tucker said, "Warn the White Knights about Ram, we don't want him chewing on Tank's staff."

"OK, Mom and Dad, thanks for taking care of me. Love ya, bye."

After she hung up, she went to the front door and started to open it when Ram became animated, barked ferociously, and bared his teeth. Star stopped, grabbed her 9mm, put a round in the chamber, and yelled, "Who is there? Are you a White Knight?"

There was no answer. Star turned the flood lights on, parted her blinds, and surveyed the premises for persons unknown. Ram ran to the back of the house barking and growling with enough fierceness to frighten even Star. She turned the lights off in the house and crept to the back door of the deck. Star slowly turned the doorknob, eased the door open ever so slightly, and said, "Bad, Bad." Ram bolted through the opening at Mach speed and threw his 100-pounds jaws at a figure standing on the back deck."

"The deafening crack of gunfire erupted."

Star was petrified that Ram was shot. But Star could hear a man scream in pain and Ram thrashing and growling. Star said, "Stop, Stop." And he did. She knew that in less than a second, Ram had probably ripped the throat of whomever was out there.

Star moved stealthily out the back door with her gun at the ready and surveyed the area in case the person was not alone. After she was confident the invader was solo—Ram would have warned her anyway—she looked at the body on the ground who had both of his hands around his neck trying to stop the bleeding. He was an old man, maybe in his late seventies. He was trying to speak but found that he was unable to do so.

He mouthed the words, "You can't stop us."

Star kicked his 22-caliber Beretta away from his hands, checked to make sure Ram was not shot, called 9-1-1 and requested medical assistance.

The old man lost a lot of blood but was still alive when the ambulance took him off to the emergency room. The police were interviewing Star when two White Knights finally showed up.

One of the White Knight guards, a large muscular man, asked Star, "Are you hurt? Apparently, we're late for the opening scene. Good to see Ram was with you."

A local detective asked, "Who are you and why are you here? I am conducting an investigation."

The former Special Forces security guard said, "We are here to protect FBI Agent Cherokee from further attacks. We will wait outside until you're done."

The detective asked, "Who is the old man that we hauled to the emergency room and why did your dog maul him? We may need to remove the dog until this investigation is over."

Star said, "Please observe the gun lying on the deck. You will discover it has been fired recently, that gun residue will be discovered on the old man's hands, and that only his fingerprints are on it. The dog, as you refer to my military trained K9, did what he was trained by the military to do and saved my life. If you try to remove Ram from me, you will incur the wrath of the FBI. Good luck with that."

The detective asked, "Why did the man want to take your life and why do you need protection?"

Star said, "Have you heard of the *Deadly Gray* vigilantes? It has been all over the news. I am the lead agent in charge of investigating the reason for an increase in crimes by seniors like the one who tried to attack me tonight."

The detective said, "Have you ever seen this man before?"

"No."

Star's cell phone rang, "It was her dad's number.

"May I take this?"

He nodded, yes.

"Hi, Dad."

Tucker asked, "Are you alright? I received a call from one of your guards."

"Yes, I am fine, thanks to Ram. The detective here is thinking about removing Ram from the premises."

"Let me speak with him."

Star reached out to give the detective her phone and said, "My dad would like to speak with you."

The detective took the call and listened for a minute and a half. During that period of time, his face expressed anger, then embarrassment, and finally fear. He handed the phone back to Star.

Tucker asked, "The White Knights are there, right?"

Star said, "Yes. What did you say to the detective?"

"That is between him and me, but he won't remove Ram from you. Call me if you need anything." Tucker hung up.

The detective was collecting his things and headed for the door as he said, "I'll be back in touch with you, Agent Cherokee."

Star asked, "What did my dad say to you?"

The detective said, "That's between him and me."

Chapter 20

May 21, 2024
Las Vegas, Nevada

After Tank returned to the Mandalay Bay Resort and Casino, he re-read a 2017 newspaper article from the *Los Angeles Times*:

Spraying the crowd with bullets, Stephen Paddock killed or wounded about five hundred people and then took his own life before police breached his hotel room door. The steps Paddock took were calculated with suicide in mind. He had surveillance cameras to alert him to approaching officers, had one handgun and accelerated the attack based on his perception that law enforcement response to his room was imminent.

Investigators determined Paddock's attack was not motivated by a grievance against any particular Las Vegas casino or hotel, nor was it against the Route 91 Harvest music festival or anyone killed or injured in the rampage.

Throughout his life, Paddock went to great lengths to keep his thoughts private, and that extended to his final thinking about this mass murder. Active shooters rarely have a singular motive or reason for engaging in a mass homicide.

Analysts determined that the shooter experienced a decline in mental and physical health and his finances over the last years of his life.

The findings match those of the final criminal investigative report by the Las Vegas

Metropolitan Police Department, which also could not determine a motive for the attack.

Tank said to Sonja over the phone, "There is always a motive. How does the author of this article reach her conclusions; she is bullshitting her readers. There is no basis for her claim that she completely understands Stephen Paddock's psychology. Sonja, what have you concluded?"

Sonja said, "We must ask ourselves that if Paddock had no obvious motive, then maybe he did not do the shooting. That is deductive logic, something foreign to most journalists. He might be a victim. Who would have a motive? Who would enjoy killing and wounding all those people? Excuse me, all those infidels. All those girls exposing their legs and faces.

"What if the overall plan by a duplicitous cadre of powerful people was that all the weapons in Paddock's hotel room were intended for a group of Jihadists? What if Paddock who needed the money to pay off his gambling debts was just a convenient fall guy? What could Paddock do if the terrorists double-crossed him? What if the Shiites who were after the Sunni Prince failed both in their mission to kill the Prince and the mission to collect weapons to supply a domestic branch of terrorists and decided to make some kind of demented point?

"Why do you suppose Paddock with all the weapons he had in his possession in the Mandalay Bay Resort and Casino stopped shooting? Why not empty every magazine within reach?

"Because he did not do it. A coordinated attack on the victims of the concert by a Shiite terrorist group and the Shiite snipers from a different angle occurred. Anyway, that is my theory."

Tank said, "Well, that is a bold conclusion but how come nobody said they saw evidence of the terrorists and how does Adam Heinz and Sheriff Lakota fit into this theory? And what about the claim by Tursky that gold is involved?"

Sonja said, "My theory is that that Adam Heinz and the CIA were trying to catch the terrorist group buying weapons from Paddock, but the deal went bad and so they tried to cover it up. They had to threaten or pay Sheriff Lakota to take part in the embarrassingly failed operation."

Tank said, "Proof; we need proof."

Sonja said, "All it takes is for one person to sing."

Tank asked, "Lakota?"

Sonja said, "I know just the person who could make him sing."

Tank said, "No, at least not until we have more evidence that your theory holds water. See if you can find out what the two assassinated private investigators from Chicago discovered."

May 21, 2024
New Orleans, Louisiana

The white-haired man sat in his modest kitchen in his rented apartment a block off St. Charles Avenue. Though in his sixties, he retained a powerful body in good physical health. His mental health was another story. He worked 40 years as an oil platform drilling roughneck, saved a good portion of his pay, and did a yeoman's job of investing it in the stock market. He and his Mary were very much looking forward to traveling the world, taking cruises, and living the good life in retirement.

But Mary got dementia. When he needed the money, he saved over a lifetime to treat and care for her, there was no money in his accounts. Some fucking jerk stole his identity, stripped the contents of his life savings, and even redirected his social security checks into the thief's account.

The roughneck had nothing but hate and vengeance in his heart after Mary died. He heard about #Steel at a local bar and discovered, with #Steel's help, the identity and location of the cyber thief. He felt proud and vindicated to have killed Kurt Rainwater by running him over with the stolen Escalade. He just knew he saved the financial lives of many others with his action.

But it did not bring his Mary back or replenish his lost savings. He was alone, broke, and bitter.

Roughneck was thinking about getting a part-time job in the drilling industry when a loud knock pounded on his door. The old roughneck went to the door wearing his ubiquitous yellow polo shirt, opened it, and was greeted by two Feds standing on his front porch.

Roughneck asked, "What can I do for you two?"

"May we come in?"

"What is it that you want?"

"We want to speak with you about your recent flight from Oakland, California."

"Why is that any of your business?"

"Have you ever been to Stanford?"

The roughneck knew that, somehow, he had been caught. He had nothing to lose. He accelerated his meaty fist into one of the FBI agent's jaws with an unexpectedly powerful force generated from heightened anger and adrenaline. The FBI agent's teeth shattered, jaw broke, and hit the concrete slab with a concussive blast to the back of his head. The second FBI agent went for his shoulder holster but was too slow; the roughneck kneed him in the groin, reached in and grabbed his gun-hand wrist and snapped it. He proceeded to give the agent a round-house punch to the side of his head.

The roughneck took the guns from both FBI agents, their car keys, and their wallets. He went back in the house, pulled out whatever cash he had and ran for the FBI's SUV. He drove the vehicle into the poorest section of New Orleans and left the car to be stripped by opportunistic residents.

The roughneck was surprised at his will to live. He headed to the Mississippi River with no idea how he would disappear.

But he did.

♦ ♦ ♦ ♦ ♦

May 22, 2024
Melbourne, Australia

HEADLINE ON OBSERVERSUN.COM.AU: DON'T MESS WITH AVA

Ava Ester was so angry after she learned that two hoodlums carjacked her 18-year-old granddaughter's car and dumped her on the side of the road 30 kilometers away from the crime, that she tenaciously tracked the ex-cons down and shot each of them in their knees; crippling them for life. The old woman spent weeks hunting the criminals down to exact a protective Grizzly mother's type revenge. After achieving her vigilante justice, Mrs. Ester drove to the nearest police station, turned herself in, handed the on-duty sergeant her weapon, and told him as calmly as she could that the 'bastards' that hurt her granddaughter will never walk without a cane again.

Interviewed police officers stated that the two mutilated carjackers were felons, prosecuted thieves, and former prison cell inmates. Rambo Granny as she was later dubbed by Australian law enforcement, swung into action after her granddaughter was carjacked in broad daylight by two knife-wielding creeps in a section of town bordering on skid row.

Ava said, "When I saw the look on my granddaughter's face that night in the hospital, I decided I was going to go out and do something about it myself since a weak-kneed judge went easy on them. I had heard about the *Deadly Gray* vigilantes in America on the news and thought, well hell, I can be one. I was not afraid of the two felons because I carry a gun for my own self-protection. I'm a real supporter of gun control. I control my gun just fine, thank you. I've been practicing all my life."

Using a police artist's sketch of the suspects and her granddaughter's description of the criminals, angry as hell Ava spent ten days prowling the drug-infested neighborhoods where the quote 'scumbags' were known to buy drugs until she spotted the two entering their seedy hotel.

"Though I knew it was them the minute I spotted the evil pair, I double-checked with my daughter. I took a cell-phone picture of them and sent it back to my granddaughter to confirm it was them," the old woman recalled. "She cried and said she was sure it was them, so I found their room, knocked on the door, and shot the big one right square in the knee with my 9mm the minute he opened the door. Then I went in and shot the other one as he backed up pleading with me to spare him. I only wished I had been able to carry my shotgun with me. I left the building and went down to the police station to turn myself in."

Melbourne lawmen arrested Ava Ester amidst howling locals who want Mrs. Ester released. An officer said, "She committed a crime, broke the law, and must face the consequences but it is difficult to throw an 81-year-old woman in prison; especially when millions of people in the city see her as a hero, not a criminal and want her elected to office."

◆ ◆ ◆ ◆ ◆

May 22, 2024
Mountain View, California

"Hi, Suzzanne, this is Tony Vinci. I am chief scientist at Entropy Entrepreneurs, your brothers-in-law's company. Do you remember me?"

"Hi Tony, it's good to hear from you. What's up?"

Tony said, "How secure is this line?"

Suzzanne, a tall slim woman with long curly brunette hair, and a rosacea skin condition, answered, "It's not secure. It's intriguing that we need to speak on a secure line. Give me five and I'll return the call."

Five minutes later Suzzanne called Tony and said, "This line is encrypted and secure."

Tony said, "Maya suggested we give you a call. She said you are now a government contractor who evaluates military and security agency firewalls and internet security."

Suzzanne said, "That is not supposed to be public knowledge, Tony. I'm disappointed Maya shared that information with you."

Tony said, "She had good reason; you are the only person she trusts; Star's life may depend on us."

"Us?"

"We need your expertise; your background is safe with us."

Suzzanne asked, "Besides you, who else is included in 'us'?"

"Tucker, Maya, Star, Jimmy Ma, you and me."

"Oh, no. Jimmy is going to constantly hit on me throughout this effort. Please, if you keep him away from me, I'll join the team."

"OK. We need to find out who has visited a dark web site, is that doable?"

Suzzanne answered, "Well it depends on the sophistication of the people who visit the site and the technical expertise of the site administrator.

"Tony, as you know the dark web is a part of the internet made up of hidden sites that can't be found through conventional web browsers. Instead, you must rely on browsers and search engines designed specifically to unearth these hidden sites.

"Sites on the dark web use encryption software so that their visitors and owners can remain anonymous and hide their locations. It's why the dark web is home to so many illegal activities. If you tap into the dark web, you'll find everything from illegal drug and gun sales to illicit pornography, stolen credit card and social security numbers."

Tony asked, "Have you heard anything about the *Deadly Gray*?"

Suzzanne said, "You had to be hiding under a rock not to have heard of the *Deadly Gray* vigilantes. Is that what this is all about?"

"We're looking for the people that visit the primary web site used for the *Deadly Gray* to communicate with the organizer of the movement."

"What is the web site you want to monitor?"

Tony said, "It's a bit complicated. It was *DanielWebsterWorldView* on TOR but has been shut down by the site administrator and replaced with *DeadlyGrayJustice*."

Suzzanne said, "Why don't you give me an assignment that's challenging or something. If I'm able to help you with this, what are you two going to do with the information?"

Tony said, "We've built an algorithm that predicts the next vigilante killing. This information will help the FBI narrow the list of suspects down to a manageable level."

Suzzanne was a survivor of a kidnapping by a psychopath and sociopath that killed her and Maya's parents, tried to kill Star, battled Ram, and attacked Maya. The sick son of a bitch who committed the crimes died a horrible death, but Suzzanne still feels a need to achieve justice and revenge. If she could, she would be a *Deadly Gray* vigilante.

◆ ◆ ◆ ◆ ◆

May 22, 2024
Orangeburg, South Carolina

"Dad," said Drake Earl's son, "Todd has searched the dark web for information about Rebecca and discovered a website called *DeadlyGrayJustice*. Apparently, someone using the hashtag #Star posted pictures of Rebecca and Joshua and asked the followers of the website if anyone has seen Joshua."

Law enforcement spent months with no success trying to find Joshua and bring him back to South Carolina for questioning about the death of Rebecca Earl. She and this creep, Joshua, toured the west, visited Yellowstone, took part in a Dude ranch, and went on to Glazier National Park. She sent back photos and messages describing the joy of the experience.

Until the correspondence stopped. Until his granddaughter was found murdered in Montana near the Canadian border.

Drake asked, "What is a dark web and how does my grandson know anything about it?"

Drake's son said, "Actually, the U.S. government created the dark web to allow spies to communicate with each other anonymously. Since then, the use of the dark web has grown where encryption software is used so that their visitors and owners can remain anonymous and hide their locations.

"According to Todd, a specific user of the dark web site posted that the killer, Joshua, was seen near Orangeburg. Dad that's only 45 miles from where you live."

Drake said, "Finally, a lead. This is too good an opportunity to pass on. Do you still have some clothing that belonged to Joshua; that may be all we need for my bloodhounds to find the asshole if this tip is correct. Son don't notify the South Carolina State Police or the FBI about this rumor; I want to deal with Joshua myself if I get the chance. My semi-automatic 12-gauge Mossberg shotgun will do the trick."

"Dad, that's not a good idea. Let law enforcement handle this."

Drake said, "Right, they have done such a good job so far. No, I'm at the end of my life anyway. What is that saying, 'the older you get, the less life in prison is a deterrent'? Be on call. I'll want you to bring my loyal and loving bloodhounds to me at some point. And tell Todd I'm proud of him. He's never given up trying to get justice for his sister. I'm headed to Orangeburg. Why in the world do you think Joshua would return to South Carolina?"

Drake's son said. "Maybe he has some unfinished business, like taking care of us. He knows we'll be relentless even after it becomes a cold case. Or maybe he has a stash somewhere and he needs to collect it before he moves on to parts unknown."

Old man Drake wore his best bib overalls and boots as he went from bar to bar for days in the Orangeburg area, showing photos of Joshua with his granddaughter to bartenders, patrons, and waitresses until he got a hit. An *Unwoke Gentleman's Bar & Grill* server recognized the photo of Joshua and said he'd only been there once or twice. "I pay attention to people's conduct; he was constantly looking around like he was afraid of something or somebody."

Drake sat on a barstool for ten straight evenings before Joshua showed himself, grabbed a beer, and wandered over to a pool table. Upon seeing him, Drake picked up his phone and called his son and said, "Got eyes on 'em. How long will it take to have the bloodhounds ready to rock'n'roll?"

"Give me an hour."

Drake said, "I hope he hangs around here that long. If he sees me, he's going to run." Drake went out to his car parked in the lot and secured his shotgun, disengaged the safety, and made sure a round was in the chamber.

The hour felt like a week, but finally Drake saw his son's pickup pull into the parking lot with the dogs in the truck bed. He got out, petted the dogs with love and said to his son, "Take the boys around the back, just in case he tries to escape."

Drake entered the *Unwoke Gentleman's Bar & Grill* with his shotgun pointed up in the air, searched for Joshua, his granddaughter's killer, spotted him and walked in his direction.

The bartender yelled, "Gun. Get down. Gun."

Two patrons with concealed carry permits pulled their weapons and aimed them at Drake.

Drake said, "I mean no harm to anyone except that man." Drake pointed the shotgun in the direction of Joshua. The killer ducked down under a pool table, crawled out one side and tried to escape out the back of the bar. Drake didn't want to injure any bystanders, so he didn't fire. But one of the concealed carry permitters did and shot Drake in the side of his stomach with a 9mm round.

Drake's shotgun blasted three times in the direction of the fleeing Joshua before the old man was shot by both a patron and the bar tender.

Drake didn't go down easily and took a couple steps toward the back of the bar, got one more 12-gauge buck shot off before he collapsed to the floor.

Joshua was hit by the blast, his back ripped apart, but he managed to escape out the back door before he tripped and fell—in front of four barking dogs and one mad father who beat the killer with a car lug wrench until there was no more life left in the man.

Drake's son went to his father's side while the dogs guarded the dead killer and said, "You did it, Dad, you did it."

Drake asked in a weak voice, "Is this what they mean by going out in a blaze of glory?"

Tears were streaming down his son's face, but the son managed to say, "You exacted justice, Dad. Say 'Hi' to Rebecca for me."

Chapter 21

May 23, 2024
Washington, DC

The Speaker of the House called a session to order and said, "The Speaker recognizes the congressperson from Rhode Island."

The congressman stood before the podium and said, "I'd like to bring to the attention of the House the issue associated with the *Deadly Gray* vigilantes, the drastic increase in violence by seniors, and the corresponding increase in threats received by lawmakers from the alleged *Deadly Gray* vigilantes. Personally, I've received more threats on my website, in my email, and even in texts over the past two weeks than I did over the prior two years.

"I've taken a private survey with some of you and have determined that my case is not an anomaly. And it is not a partisan issue. Madam Speaker, I propose that we caucus in committee and see if there is something we can do to mitigate this potential anarchy by seniors who, in the past, as a group were supportive of our policies. Thank you."

The Speaker said, "The floor recognizes the congressperson from New Mexico."

"Thank you, Madam Speaker, I share the concern expressed by the Congressperson from Rhode Island. You of all people must be concerned about the threats on our lives. Fortunately for you, Secret Service prevented a catastrophic event. Which brings me to the point I'd like to make. I propose that Congress triple the budget for the Secret Service. There are so many threats on so many of us that the Secret Service cannot possibly follow all the leads with its current staff. Thank you."

"The Speaker recognizes the congressperson from Tennessee."

"Thank you, Madam Speaker. I agree with both my colleague from Rhode Island and my colleague from New Mexico. I propose that we name a Special Counsel to determine the root cause of the uprising by seniors as the first course of business. Before we decide 'what' we're going to do or 'how' we're going to do it, we need to determine 'why' this is happening. It is not just the House that is under assault, it is not just the U.S. Government that is under assault, but Governments and private citizens throughout the world that are suddenly under assault by seniors. This is incoherent. Is the root cause something we've done or are doing to our seniors? We need to assess the headwinds to understand why someone would try to assassinate you Madam Speaker. I understand from reports that the Professor from Missouri said, 'I was going to eradicate one source of tyranny and abuse of power in our overreaching government.' I understand the man who killed the State Representative from New Jersey said, 'The fall of America is our fault if we do nothing about it.'

"Threats on my website end like this, 'I want my country back.' Others I have spoken to have similar statements embedded in threats on them. This is not going to end well if we don't understand why the *Deadly Gray* movement is happening now. Otherwise, we are pushing a supermarket cart with a busted wheel. Thank you."

Star turned off C-Span and said to Ram, "The pressure is going to be on me now. I think Congress is missing the point. It's all about justice. Policies around the world have placed justice second to protecting criminals. They should just ask me to explain the problem instead of assigning a Special Counsel who will take years to complete a report too late to be useful and which will contain ideological conclusions. There is no way to put lipstick on this pig."

Ram cocked his head as if he understood.

Star's encrypted satellite phone rang. She answered it, "I'm surprised it took you more than one minute to call after watching C-Span?"

Winemiller said, "They're missing the point. They think it is all about them; it's intellectual dishonesty."

Star said, "Exactly."

Rusty said, "You know we're going to be called before this pathetic cross-pollinated Congress, right?"

Star said, "What do you mean 'we' Kemosabe?"

May 23, 2024
Lexington, Kentucky

I see trees of green, red roses too, I see them bloom, for me and for you. And I think to myself, 'What a wonderful world.'

I see skies of blue, and clouds of white, the bright blessed day, the dark sacred night. And I think to myself, 'What a wonderful world.'

78-year-old Sarah listened to her favorite song, one by Louis Armstrong, while she donated blood to her life-long friend of the same age, Melinda, who suffered from advanced stages of acute leukemia.

Melinda once asked Sarah, "Why do you do this for me? You know it's futile. I'm not immortal."

Sarah answered, "Because you would do the same for me. You have helped me throughout my life to ensure that I maintained good values and that my moral compass remains pointed in the right direction."

Melinda laughed and said, "Funny you should say that. Currently my moral compass is pointed in the direction of vigilante justice—I want to be a *Deadly Gray* justice warrior. Maybe I've morally decomposed but I feel like my body's engine check light is on. I want to do something meaningful before there is no tick left on my clock.

"Do you remember Caesar Kuffin?"

"No."

"He was the volleyball coach at the University of Kentucky. He thought volleyball meant to ball his young girl athletes.

"For almost 55 years, I've thought about how I'd like to get even with him. I checked, he's 92 years old. Can you believe it, the godless criminals get to live forever while we victims suffer the injustice? Anyway, Sarah, I want to confront him. I want some sort of closure before I die. Promise me you'll get even with the goat fucker if I die before I am able to achieve justice."

That was two weeks ago. Today, Sarah had to decide whether or not to fulfill Melinda's wishes or to let the criminal get away with his crimes. Sarah, wearing a white lab coat, went to the senior living center outside of Lexington where Caesar Kuffin currently resided.

"Hi Caesar, weren't you my volleyball coach at Kentucky when I attended in 1963?"

Caesar said, "What is your name? It's hard to correlate faces from 50 years ago to now."

"I'm Melinda. You remember, you bedded me a couple of times."

"Ah, yes. I remember you. I'm so sorry. I was misguided and foolish back then."

Sarah, pretending to be Melinda said, "Let's talk about it. Do you want to go outside; I'll push you in your wheelchair? It's a wonderful world out there."

Sarah pushed Caesar around the senior living center campus populated with dogwood trees and rhododendron bushes and asked, "Have you heard of the *Deadly Gray* movement? Have you thought about what you would do given the opportunity to be a vigilante on your way out?"

"Actually, yes. I'd like to have an opportunity to kill one of my team players who tried to castrate me 20 years after she was one of my setters."

Sarah pushed Caesar's wheelchair down to a campus lake and said, "Look at the ducks, aren't they beautiful?"

Caesar said, "Maybe for dinner."

Sarah pulled an ice pick from her pocketbook, placed it Caesar's left ear, and jammed it as hard as she could into his brain.

On her way to the car, she looked up into the sky and said to Melinda, "I think my talk with him fell on deaf ears."

◆ ◆ ◆ ◆ ◆

May 23, 2024
Las Vegas, Nevada

Tank organized a conference call with Tucker, Jolene, and Sonja and started the meeting by saying, "I went to Henderson and met with Officer Tursky. If you remember, he's the guy who presented evidence to the investigative team that Stephen Paddock was involved with a gold mine tailings scam. Tursky showed me the evidence and his investigation report submitted to but ignored by LVMPD Chief Lakota."

Tucker asked, "What do you think the relevance of the discovery of Paddock's involvement in another crime has on our task of investigating why Colonel Manion killed ATF Assistant Director Heinz?"

Tank answered, "The relevance is that Lakota displays a trend to cover up events and that, maybe, are inconvenient to his career."

Tank asked, "Sonja, any luck finding out what the two assassinated private investigators who were former Chicago police officers found out? Whatever it was, it was bad enough to get them assassinated."

Sonja said, "What I've learned is that there were 22 Iranian nationals in Las Vegas on the day of the massacre. Seven of them were Iran Revolutionary Guardsmen. Another three were part of a cell established in Phoenix."

Tank said, "So, your theory is that the two PIs were killed by the Iranian Revolutionary Guards because the PIs uncovered their mission which was....."

Tucker finished Tank's sentence, "to kill the Saudi Prince, to arm the Phoenix cell, and place the blame on Paddock."

Jolene asked, "Sonja, how did you manage to uncover what you learned?"

Jolene's brother, Stanley, could be heard by the call participants in the background saying, "In the past, Sonja was part of Israel's Mossad. Israel keeps close tabs on Iranians, right? How else could she know how many Iranians were in Las Vegas?"

Sonja said, "Jolene, your 'Special Needs' Brother always comes up with the right answers. How does he do that?"

Tucker said, "If what Stanley said is correct, then the CIA knows that there were Iranian Revolutionary Guards in Las Vegas at the time of the massacre. Do you know what that means? It means that if Iran sanctioned the assassination of two Americans—which would be considered an act of war—then the CIA covered it up to avoid war with Iran."

Sonja said, "And if the CIA covered it up, they had to include ATF Heinz and LVMPD Lakota. How do you suppose Manion knew about all this?"

Jolene said, "He knew enough to put us on the investigation of why he killed Heinz?"

Tank said, "OK, it's a good theory but how do we prove it, and what are the consequences of us proving this?"

Sonja said, "If you remember Tank, I suggested that we make Lakota sing?"

Tank said, "You mean torture."

Stanley said, "Oh, boy, we get to go to Cabo San Lucas. Can I watch?"

Sonja said, "Lakota must have to go there occasionally to see how his partial ownership in a hotel there is doing."

Jolene added, "There is a dark pool of money involved. The hotel is a good place to have secret meetings."

Tucker said, "And the consequence is that we've just made Star, the lead FBI investigator into Heinz's death, a target."

May 23, 2024
Perugia, Umbria, Italy

After a few ugly years of pandemic shutdowns, The Global Investigative Journalism Conference in Italy was finally held. The robust conference agenda included sessions, workshops, and breakouts on topics such as Disinformation, Flight Tracking, Cyber Investigations, Culture of Peace, Online Sleuths, Video Forensics, How to Follow the Money, The *Deadly Gray*, Stress and Burnout, and Femicide.

The conference Keynote Speaker was a senior journalism professor from Oxford, United Kingdom. He opened his monologue with "Everyone has the right to be stupid, it's just that some people abuse the privilege."

Deadly Gray

The overflow audience laughed. When the laughter calmed down the professor said, "Blaming the messenger for the message is as old as humanity itself. We journalists are responsible for ensuring that the message is shared with as many people as possible. Well, I have a message for all the hateful, ignorant, and violent *Deadly Gray* seniors, 'Don't shoot the messenger'."

The audience yelled, clapped, whistled, and applauded the Keynote Speaker. The professor went on to say, "I recently went to my doctor for my 350,000-mile checkup."

The audience applauded.

"He said I had a few components in my equipment that are failing and that cannot be bought on Amazon."

Again, the audience laughed.

"I definitely qualify as a senior. Frankly, I have never minded getting older, though my body is taking it badly. My doctor told me that the leading cause for injuries in old men is thinking they are still young. I can't touch my toes or clip my nails; I take pills for everything, but I still can't hear; and I can't stay awake, nor can I sleep. But I have never thought it possible that getting old qualified me to take it out on other journalists. That illusion is found only in dark shadows. Do not fear to be a journalist because a few crazies blame us for their failings. It is social disinformation for journalists to be responsible for wars lost, science discredited, or nations rebuilt. We're the Jersey Walls that keep people from running off the ideological road, we're the force multiplier that hounds mischief, and we're the magnifying glass that focuses on injustice.

"Hang in there. Fear Not. And keep your fingers on the keyboard. Thank you."

The Oxford Professor received a standing ovation from conference attendees. He shook hands with many famous journalists around the world, idolizing students, and investigative journalist wan-a-bees. One man clasped the speaker firmly and wouldn't let go. The man said to the professor using a thick eastern European accent, "Do you know who said, 'Make the lie big, make it simple, keep saying it, and eventually, they will believe it.'?"

The Keynote Speaker said, "Yes. Adolf Hitler."

The man said, "That was a big lie you just told out there to a fawning youth. Your ideological predisposition contaminates an open mind. You are blind to the real truth.

"You will be my *Deadly Gray* victim before the night is over. You won't see me coming."

With that the man who threatened the Oxford professor disappeared into the crowd. The Keynote Speaker could not enjoy the banquet dinner in his honor, he was distant, anxious, and paranoid company. He asked a young conference organizer to escort him to his fifth-floor hotel room and thanked her as he slipped into his suite. He quickly locked the door, turned the deadbolt, and slid the chain in place. It was only 10:45 p.m. He thought, *I am going to be a nervous wreck until the time reaches midnight. What did the man with the thick accent say, 'You will be my Deadly Gray victim before the night is over?'*

The Oxford journalism professor felt a chill and went to close the sliding glass door to the balcony. "Awe!" The professor had never felt so much pain. He was hit in the back where the kidneys were located with a billy club. Then he was hit on the side of his head with a fist holding a roll of coins. When he laid on the threshold between the hotel room and the balcony, the man stomped on his stomach, making the professor vomit on himself.

The man with the eastern European accent said, "Professor, do you remember writing a narrative on benefits of a strong KGB? Do you remember writing about the how great the Soviet Union was by prohibiting free speech? The KGB took my wife from me and sent her to a Siberian labor camp because she was outspoken about the suppression of free speech. She died there. And you have the gall to standup in front of a misinformed audience and talk about the message. The message you promoted were lies. I am your *Deadly Gray* justice warrior."

The Oxford Journalism Professor took an assisted swan dive off the fifth-floor balcony.

◆ ◆ ◆ ◆ ◆

May 24, 2024
Europe

The Wall Street Journal Europe Edition and digital version of the *Wall Street Journal* had the following headline: **Deadly Gray Vigilantes Reach Expands**:

The keynote speaker from Oxford attending a journalism conference in Italy stated, "I have a message for all the hateful, ignorant, and violent Deadly Gray seniors, 'Don't shoot the messenger'." Later that same evening he was found dead from an apparent fall five stories below his hotel balcony. A note was left on his nightstand that stated, "Don't believe his lies." and signed by someone claiming to be a part of the Deadly Gray movement. As of the time of this writing, Interpol had no comments.

Chapter 22

Star called Rusty Winemiller from her office and said, "Sir, since you put me in charge of the case of the *Deadly Gray* back on April 12, literally hundreds of potential new *Deadly Gray* crimes were committed not only here in the states but worldwide. The individual crimes are solvable in that almost all of them are admitted to by the vigilante who committed the crime. They are not trying to hide from the law. But the reason for the exponential increase in *Deadly Gray* crimes is evasive. I'm no closer to understanding the crime growth by seniors than I was six weeks ago. I'm not going to make progress without some help. Frankly, we need an increase in our FBI cyber staff assigned to this case. Jimmy Ma and Tony Vinci are great but only available as part time help. If you want us to investigate the NSA and keep Director Naylor and the White House off your ass, I need help."

"Star, I told you up front, I want non-government employees and contractors investigating cases that involve the Las Vegas massacre, the attack on law makers, and even on cases involving the failure of the justice system to keep rapists, cyber criminals, and billionaire criminals off the street. I've authorized you to retain the people you trust. Let's keep it that way.

"I have to go now, Brad is calling."

Rusty Winemiller hung up on Star and answered the call from his boss, "Hi, Director, what's up?"

"I know you know about the proposed resolutions by the House of Representative. I know you know about the recent *Deadly Gray* murders in Australia and Italy. I know you know POTUS is on my ass. Explain to me why you are leaving Star, one of our least experienced agents, on this case? It's time to up our game. Assign someone else and give Star a major role in supporting the more senior agent. I'd like Chris O'Connor, the Special Agent in Charge of the New York University bombing, and the sniper attack on the *Washington Post* editor to take the lead."

Rusty said, "Director, you are more and more a politician and less and less a manager of agents with each passing day. O'Connor may look good on paper, but Star led him around by his nose and solved the cases before O'Connor knew what hit him. If you want to make it look like you're doing something without really doing anything, put O'Connor in charge."

Brad Naylor said, "It's an order, Rusty."

May 26, 2024
Washington, DC

On the seventh floor of the Hoover Building, FBI Director Bradley Naylor convened a meeting with Special Agent Chris O'Connor, Special Agent Rusty Winemiller, and Agent Star Cherokee. Naylor started the meeting with, "Agent Cherokee, I want you to know that I think you're doing a good job on solving individual *Deadly Gray* crimes. By my count, you solved 10 crimes in six weeks. I don't know any other agent who has done that."

Star said, "Twelve, sir."

Naylor's blond eyebrows raised, his face flushed, and he gritted his teeth when he said, "Don't interrupt me again, Star.

"OK. Twelve. But the problem is no longer solving who committed crimes. It has grown to who is orchestrating anarchy in our country and how do we stop it? So, I have asked Chris O'Connor, who I understand you already know, to be the SAC for the bigger *Deadly Gray* issue. Give him your complete and total support. Do you understand?"

Star was trying to read the thoughts of Rusty Winemiller, but he was trying too hard to think of waves crashing on the beach. She said, "Yes, sir, I understand."

Naylor went on to say, "I have a meeting at the White House tomorrow and plan to take O'Connor with me. Star, you debrief O'Connor so that he knows what you know and so we don't look like fools in front of the President. Understood?"

Both Star and O'Connor said, "Understood."

Naylor said, "This meeting is adjourned."

In the elevator, on the way to the ground floor, SAC O'Connor said, "Listen, Star, I didn't ask for this. I was ordered to do this so please don't get your back up with me. OK?"

Winemiller was in the elevator with Star and O'Connor but said nothing. Star tried to read her boss's mind, but he was intentionally thinking this time about the Washington Commanders.

Star said, "We all have to follow orders, don't we Rusty?"

Winemiller did not respond which gave Star a bit of the creeps. She thought, *What is going on with him?*

O'Connor sensed the drama and said, "Let's get a cup of coffee before we have to talk in a closed soundproof room."

After the elevator door opened on the ground floor, Winemiller said, "I'm headed back to my office. You two do your thing."

Winemiller operated his electric wheelchair in the direction of a waiting van without saying another word to Star.

O'Connor asked, "What gives with him?"

Star said, "I think he didn't appreciate the director overruling him and doing his cybersecurity job. At least that is my best guess. Now let's skip the coffee and get on with it. I want to start by saying that Congress, the White House, the Justice Department, social media, and the mainstream media have it all wrong."

O'Connor said, " What do you mean? What do they have wrong?"

Star's phone rang; it was her dad. If it had been anybody else, she wouldn't have taken it. She said, "Excuse me," to O'Connor and accepted the call.

"Yeah, Dad, what's up?"

Tucker said, "I want you to know that the Chicago defense attorney killed this morning by a senior who just got out of federal prison is someone I know. I can give you background on the guy. Frankly, if I were older and at the end of my road, I might have killed him myself."

"I have no idea what you are talking about. I've spent the last hour in the Director's office being reassigned to support rather than lead the *Deadly Gray* case."

"Oh, you are not in a position to talk, are you?"

"No, I'll call you soon, OK?

"OK."

Star started to speak to O'Connor when his phone rang.

May 26, 2024
Chicago, Illinois

Sean LaKerry was found guilty of money laundering and racketeering in 1993. He was incarcerated at the federal high-security prison at Thomson Correctional Center where he received constant and continuous abuse from sadistic inmates. He was a physically small man and became even smaller and more pathetic as the years passed. LaKerry spent every moment of every abusive day during all of his years in prison plotting revenge for this day; the day he was released from prison.

His target was Fred Glenson, the defense attorney funded by the Outfit or Chicago's La Cosa Nostra organized crime family. Glenson defended the Outfit's nefarious activities when law enforcement finally had enough to bring them to court. LaKerry was a victim of the crime family's high-pressure extortion of businesses for their alleged 'protection'—he paid 15% of his revenues to the Outfit.

LaKerry eventually had enough of the abuse and notified the FBI who, in turn, used him to testify against the Outfit. He was not offered Witness Protection and was coached by an amateur prosecutor. On the stand, LaKerry said, "Typically the La Cosa Nostra get into running restaurants and other legal businesses that they can use to hide money gained from their illicit activities."

Glenson fabricated evidence against LaKerry, and even had a video photoshopped showing that LaKerry was the man extorting money from other businesses. He learned in prison from other inmates that the judge was in the pocket of the mafia and that the weak FBI prosecutor's family was threatened by the La Cosa Nostra.

Here he was, 31 years later in front of Glenson's Lake Shore Drive building. He researched Glenson's continued history and discovered he had a 10,000-square-foot full-floor penthouse unit with 12-foot ceilings and the best skyline view in Chicago. LaKerry thought, *Crime pays. Members of the mob will go to almost any length to conduct their criminal activity.*

LaKerry watched from across the street when Glenson got out of his Tesla with a lady much too young to be his wife, tipped the parking valet and sashayed into his favorite restaurant, the Found Kitchen and Social House. While his target was imbibing, LaKerry threatened the parking valet for the keys to the Tesla, further threatened the kid if he spoke to anyone about it and placed two packages in the back seat of Glenson's electric vehicle. He opened the packages before he shut the doors.

He said to the young valet boy, "Your life depends on you doing just what I say. Under no circumstance do you bring the Tesla to the driver. Give the keys to the driver and tell him you couldn't get his car started. I mean it, your life depends on doing just that."

Ninety minutes later, an angry Glenson left his dinner partner standing at the entrance, stormed off to his parked car, opened the driver's side door, and pushed the button to start the EV. It started with no problem. He said to himself, *I will insist that the restaurant fire that incompetent parking valet.* He squealed tires as he pulled the Tesla out of the lot and proceeded to ram the electric car into another car parked on the street.

People ran to the scene of the accident only to realize that the driver, the famous defense attorney, Fred Glenson's head was leaning on the steering wheel.

But that was not the scary part. Around his neck was an orange snake with darker dorsal blotches and lateral spots. Another grey looking snake sat in the back seat.

It was later determined that the two Saw-Scaled Vipers were the world's deadliest snakes responsible for more human fatalities than all other snakes put together.

Sean LaKerry stood across the street from the restaurant, whooping it up, celebrating and saying loudly, "I did it; I did it."

The Chicago police arrived, interviewed the valet driver who pointed at the celebrating LaKerry; he made no effort to run. He did what he wanted done.

LaKerry said to the police, "I heard about the *Deadly Gray* vigilantes and decided to be one of them.

Do what you want with me but I'm going to plead insanity."

May 27, 2024
Las Vegas, Nevada

It was 2:30 a.m. but Tank couldn't sleep. He was thinking about what else he could learn about the Las Vegas massacre from his room in the Mandalay Bay Resort and Casino. *Maybe, I should go home and work from there. I'm sort of at a dead end here.*

It was then that he heard the distinctive sound of a card being slid through the card reader to his room. His first thought was that a drunk was trying to get into the wrong room. But the card opened the door. The person on the other side of the door tried to push the door open ever so slightly but the dead bolt lock prevented it from opening.

Tank pulled his Sig Sauer out from under his pillow, slid out of bed to his knees and aimed the gun at the door.

The person trying to enter the room began to tamper with the deadbolt; Tank could hear the slight scraping of metal on metal—someone was trying to pick the lock. Tank knew a deadbolt could be picked using a long metal pick and a tension wrench. But it took time and some skill. Though Tank was dressed only in his boxer shorts he moved quietly to the door so that when and if the door opened, he'd have the element of surprise.

The invader took seven minutes before he successfully rendered the deadbolt useless and pushed Tank's hotel room door further open until the security chain was fully extended. Another 30 seconds of silence went by before the guy put enough continuous pressure on the chain for it to pull the screws on the door frame mount to loosen.

That's when Tank pulled the door open from the inside, broke the chain mount free and clobbered the invader with the butt of his gun. With his huge powerful left hand around the wrist of the assailant's knife-wielding hand, Tank viciously pulled the assailant inside the room. But the smaller man was lightning fast and hit Tank on the side of his head with a wrench held in his free hand. Fortunately, the blow did not render Tank unconscious as he brought his Sig Sauer to the face of the unknown assaulter.

Again, the man was an experienced professional and used the wrench to knock Tank's gun free from his hand. The Sig Sauer fell to the floor out of reach of both fighters.

Tank never let go of the predator's wrist and twisted it until he heard it crack, the man screamed in pain, and the knife fell to the floor. The invader tried to kick Tank in the throat, but Tank caught the foot before it landed. Tank lifted the man's foot high into the air and he fell on his back.

Tank stomped on the man's right knee knowing the man would never walk the same again.

The man screamed in pain and cried, "I have diplomatic immunity."

Tank said, "Not in here you don't" and hit the man in the jaw with all the strength his 310 angry pounds could muster. While the man was out cold, Tank cuffed his ankles and wrists together with plastic ties and inserted a gag in his mouth.

Two of the Mandalay Bay Resort and Casino armed security guards stuck their heads in Tank's room with their guns at the ready and asked, "What is going on in here? We have had calls from concerned hotel occupants. We have notified the Las Vegas Metropolitan Police. What is going on?"

Tank came to the door and said, "I'm sorry. A colleague of mine drank too much, lost too much money, and got violent with me when I wouldn't loan him anything. He forgot how big I am. Anyway, I have things under control. I am sorry if we have caused the hotel any trouble. And say hello to Chief Lakota for me. I'm Tank Alvarez. owner of White Knight Personal Security, LLC."

After the placated hotel security staff left, Tank slapped the knife-wielding invader awake, removed his gag, and asked, "Who are you, who sent you, and why did you try to kill me?"

The man said, "I have diplomatic immunity."

Tank laughed and said, "So you think that means I'm going to stop and let you kill me? No, it is the other way around. I am going to kill you unless you tell me what I want to know. Let's start with 'who hired you to kill me?"

"I have diplomatic immunity."

Tank replaced the gag on the invader and said, "OK, have it your way."

Tank called Sonja and said, "You are on speaker phone. Looks like we're not going to have to torture Lakota for information, we have a new candidate. How soon can you get your Mossad interrogator here to Las Vegas? I'm not sure but I think the guy he'll interview wants to kill all Jews and eliminate Israel off the map."

Sonja said, "He's already in Las Vegas. I'll contact him and send him to your room. Do you have a place we can take the interviewee where sound is not a problem and where we can cover the floors with plastic sheets?"

The invader was trying desperately to get Tank's attention, but Tank ignored him. Tank said, "I have a contact here who can find a place in the desert where the interview can be conducted by us. It's in a town called Pioche."

The fear exhibited by the man assigned to kill Tank was palpable. Tank looked at the man and said, "They didn't tell you who I was, did they? Don't you see? They didn't send you here to kill me, they sent you here to be killed by me. You need to reach deep into your soulless existence and decide how much pain you are willing to endure to protect the people who sent you here on a suicide mission. Your destroyed knee will seem like a minor scratch compared to what is about to happen to you.

"I won't be in the desert warehouse when the Mossad agent interrogates you. I don't have the stomach to watch. I just want the information. You have only minutes to decide how this proceeds.

Three black Ford Expedition XLTs pulled up to the gate of the Cherokee Estate. Two large official-looking men in suits, dark sunglasses, and spit-shined patent leather shoes exited the vehicles, approached the guard shack, and displayed their credentials to the White Knight Personal Security guard. The guard had pushed the panic button before the two men even left their vehicles to alert the other White Knights in the compound as well as Tucker and Maya of their presence. Three guards aiming automatic weapons at the visitors were prepared to protect the Cherokees if so ordered. The lead guard had activated the land mines just in case.

A man got out of one of the bullet-proof Expeditions, held up his hands and said, "Tell Tucker the U.S. Attorney General is here to consult with him. Stand down. I see I should have told him in advance that we were coming."

Tucker drove a golf cart up from the estate entrance a quarter of a mile to the guard gate, stopped, got out, and stood there with his arms crossed. He yelled across the gates to his visitors and said, "Arthur, you have no idea how close we just came to an armed conflict. You must have forgotten that in the past this compound has been breached by armed forces from nation states. You might also remember that we spent six years under Witness Protection in New Zealand because countries didn't like our energy discovery. It was stupid of you not to call before you came, or do you live in an alternative reality?"

Tucker looked over at the guard at the gate and said, "Disarm the Gatling Gun, deactivate the land mines, tell the snipers to stand down, and open the gates to allow the Attorney General to pass through. The vehicles stay outside, Arthur can ride with me in the golf cart."

Tucker could hear one of the Secret Service agents ask, "Holy shit, Gatling Gun?"

Tucker said, "Yes, it's a 50-caliber version controlled by Artificial Intelligence; it's not manual."

Another agent said, "One of us must join A.G. Gannon. We must always maintain visual contact with him."

Gannon held up his hand to the agents and said, "It's OK, men. I'll be back out in less than an hour."

Tucker said, "You can maintain visual contact by watching the monitor in the guard gate." Tucker turned to the gate guard and said, "Jarrod, turn camera 6a on and put it on one of the monitors. Thanks."

Tucker and AG Gannon rode the cart to the main entrance to the estate where another armed guard stood. They walked into the foyer where the AG was greeted by Maya and Algorithm, one of Ram's offspring.

Maya said, "What a pleasant surprise. Chef Rhino will bring refreshments to the study. What is your poison, Attorney General?"

He said, "Scotch on the rocks, thank you."

In Tucker's study, Arthur Gannon said, "You seem a little agitated Tucker; surely, I'm not the first person to just drop in on you."

Tucker said, "What I'm agitated about Arthur is that you showed up with a squadron of Secret Service agents or U.S. Marshals when you told me that our meetings had to be secret and where no one could see you with me. Was that just BS? How many people in the Justice Department know that I've been asked to investigate government corruption? What gives here Arthur?"

Arthur said, "I assume the video feed to the guard shack does not include audio."

Tucker said, "They have no audio, your words will stay here in this room."

The AG said, "Recently, I have received literally thousands of death threats. For my own protection, I had to drastically increase my security staff. The team I brought with me do not know why I am here with you. They think I'm here to offer you a top-level position within the Justice Department, which of course I would do if there was even a remote possibility that you would accept it. Anyway, that is my explanation.

"I came here to learn what progress you have made with the assessment of potential corruption in the Justice Department."

Chef Rhino knocked on the door and asked if it was OK for him to deliver their drinks. Tucker nodded his head. Rhino placed drinks and a plate of miniature crab cakes in front of the two men.

Mr. Gannon asked Chef Rhino, "How did you know this is my favorite food?"

Chef Rhino was afraid to answer the question without approval from Tucker and made eye contact. Tucker nodded his head.

Rhino said, "We maintain a comprehensive data base of preferences by important people. You'll also determine that the Scotch in your glass is your favorite, Glenlivet."

"Thank you, Rhino," said Tucker.

Upon Rhino's departure Tucker said, "Yes, you have a corruption problem. The Justice Department may not have a problem greater than any other department, but your department is chartered to fight corruption, not take part in illegal activities.

"You have more than 100,000 attorneys alone in your staff with an almost $30 billion annual budget. That alone is a formula for disaster. There is no conceivable way to stop corruption where there are that many well-educated people. Sociopaths makes up approximately 3 to 5 percent of the general population. That means you have probably between 3,000 to 5,000 sociopaths working for you. Good luck managing that."

Gannon said, "You are scaring me, Tucker. Is my job to end corruption in the Department of Justice impossible?"

"Yes, it is. We need to lower your expectations; lower the bar so to speak. My suggestion is that you have zero tolerance for corruption at the highest levels. The general public has lost confidence in the FBI because of a past corrupt director and other high level FBI officers. In my opinion, you must prove that justice is applied equally regardless of their fame or political ideology. Prove that by indicting criminals within your hierarchy."

Arthur asked, "Have you identified anyone that needs a thorough examination of potential corruption?"

Tucker answered, "Yes. Check the head of your Anti-Trust Division, your second in command at the DEA, the Head of your Immigration and Naturalization

Service, and several in the FBI whose names I will withhold until I've fully vetted them.

"As far as the Department of Homeland Security is concerned, the ATF appears to be the most corrupt. Not only was Heinz corrupt but several of his minions were co-conspirators and benefitted financially from the Heinz/CIA operation. I'm still gathering data; I'll provide you specificity at a later date."

Gannon said, "Keep this under your hat until I decide how to proceed."

Tucker said, "You do the same. You haven't tried the crab cakes."

The Attorney General said, "I'm a little sick to my stomach. Nothing another Glenlivet won't fix."

◆ ◆ ◆ ◆ ◆

May 27, 2024
Washington, DC

FBI Special Agent in Charge, Chris O'Connor asked Star Cherokee, "Can you continue to share information with me? The murder of the Chicago defense attorney distracted us and interrupted our conversation."

Star asked, "Did you learn anything from that event? What was the real reason LaKerry killed Glenson? Was it just because he was an old man under the influence of a *Deadly Gray* puppeteer like the media and Congress would like you to believe?"

SAC O'Connor said, "LaKerry was exacting revenge."

"Revenge for what?"

O'Connor said, "Revenge for being set up for a crime he claims he didn't commit."

Star said, "There is a thin line between revenge and justice. The truth is somewhat evasive, but it appears to me that all of the *Deadly Gray* vigilantes are achieving both. Not one of them have committed crimes for money. Not one of them have committed their crimes for greed or evil. They commit them to achieve justice and with it revenge. Unlike how the media has portrayed their crimes, unlike how Congress and the White House envision their crimes—as anarchy. Most are trying to achieve justice unachieved through the legal process which failed to get down with the victim but instead protected the criminal. That's what I recommend you tell POTUS when you and Director Naylor meet with him."

♦ ♦ ♦ ♦ ♦

May 27, 2024
Las Vegas, Nevada

"Listen to me Mr. Diplomatic Immunity," said Tank, "is it OK for me to call you Dip for short? Let me tell you what the Mossad interrogator will do to you to get you to talk. His methods border on creative thinking.

"First, he'll make sure you are secured in a way that you will not be able to move. Then he will put your feet in a glass lined pail. He'll ask you a question. If you don't answer he'll pour sulfuric acid into the pail. Just a little at first so you get the idea of the pain you'll endure. Then he'll ask you another question. If you don't answer he'll put more sulfuric acid in the pail until your feet and ankle are covered with it. As your flesh and cartilages are eaten away until only bone is left, he'll ask you which eye you want to lose sight from first. If you don't answer questions, he'll put an acid-laden patch over the eye of your choice. That's going to hurt, and you will go blind in that eye. He'll ask you a question. If you don't answer, he'll put a patch on the other eye. He'll treat you like you are the bottom of the food chain.

"It seems to me, Dip, unless you were born with the stupid gene that you might as well avoid all that pain and damage to your body and tell me what I want to know now before he opens his toolbox. It's your choice. You need to abandon your ideological blindness and your ignorant willingness to be a martyr. Otherwise, I'm going to gag and stuff you in a large suitcase that the Mossad agent is bringing to take you to the Pioche warehouse. He's committed to a couple days of his time. What do you say, talk now, or later?"

Dip said with unwarranted self-confidence, "You are bluffing."

Tank said, "If you never talk after two days of agonizing torture, if you are that tough, he'll leave you in a cage, put a dozen rats in the cage with you, and leave you alone there. It doesn't sound like fun to me. You need to give up your neurotic pride and answer my questions. You have to be brain dead to suffer through what is planned for you."

Tanks phone rang, he answered it, and said, "Hi, Daniel, did you bring the large suitcase?"

On the other end of the phone, Jimmy Ma, said, "What?'

Tank said, "Great, I'll prepare him for transfer. It will only take me a few minutes."

A perplexed Jimmy Ma said, "OK, I get it, I'll call back later."

Dip said, "OK. OK. What do you want to know?"

Chapter 23

May 28, 2024
Boston, Massachusetts

Tony Vinci sat in his office at Entropy Entrepreneurs contemplating when his boss, Tucker Cherokee, walked in wearing a $3,500 power suit.

"Sir, I didn't know you were going to be in the office today. Good to see you."

Tucker said with a smile, "I'm actually glad to catch you working. Can I take a photo on this rare moment?"

"Gee, I thought you were coming in here to tell me you're giving me a raise."

Tucker said, "Good one, Tony, but you really shouldn't drink on the job. Before we get into your progress on Entropy contracts, tell me where you and Jimmy are on the *Deadly Gray* algorithm."

Tony said, "First, I want you to know that Jimmy and I with Suzzanne's help think we've narrowed the location of #Steel to one of two IP addresses."

Tucker said, "Fantastic."

"One is located near Smithburg, Maryland. That is remarkably close to Camp David. The other IP address is located in Maysville, West Virginia. The first one is associated with the *DanielWebsterWorldView* website. The second is associated with the *DeadlyGrayJustice* website. My guess is that the Steelman is currently in West Virginia. Do you think Star could assemble an FBI team to raid the Maysville site?"

Tucker said, "Star is no longer in charge of the case. I don't think we want the new SAC to know what we're doing. Do you think you could get one of your nanodrones up there and get a read on things? Maybe get a video or photo of the guy?"

Tony said, "There is a regional airport in the small town of Petersburg only ten or fifteen miles away. Can we use your Learjet to get me close enough to control a drone?"

"It's here at Logan. I'll notify the pilot to get a flight plan together. I'll go with you—it sounds like fun."

♦ ♦ ♦ ♦ ♦

May 28, 2024
Chevy Chase, Maryland

Supreme Court Justice, the honorable Randolph Atkinson, entered his limousine for the ride into Washington DC with Secret Service protection. As they left the gated community, the limo ran over a line of spikes that were not there only minutes earlier. The tires flattened immediately bringing the bullet-proof vehicle to a stop. The security detail pulled their weapons and surrounded the hardened Chevy Suburban limousine suspicious of the tire deflation device they learned about in training. Thirty seconds went by without incident. The Secret Service dispatched another specially built vehicle to transfer the Supreme Court Justice into the city.

Fifteen minutes later, still no new threats were evident, the transfer was complete, and Randolph

Atkinson was swiftly escorted by the Secret Service to the Supreme Court Building without incident.

Two Secret Service agents went to the home of the justice and discovered a letter in a plastic slip pinned to the front door. The agents put on nylon gloves and slipped the paper out of the sheath. The letter started with "Dear Constitutional Traitor," but before they could read on, they both smelled smoke. One agent entered the house while the other ran around to the back of the house. Smoke seeped into the first floor of the main building. The agent inside the home called the limo and said, "Let me talk to the Justice."

Justice Atkinson said, "Yes?"

The agent asked, "Is anyone home at your house?"

"No, Imelda is visiting with our daughter in Pittsburgh."

The agent said, "Good." He hung up and called the fire department. The second agent discovered two separate fires raging: one on the back deck of the house, the other in the pool gazebo. He smelled it before he saw that the valve to a 400-gallon propane tank used to heat the pool was wide open with the line disconnected spewing out propane into the atmosphere. The agent said, "Holy shit" and started to run away from the gazebo as fast as possible. The explosion was horrific.

By the time the Chevy Chase Fire Department arrived at the Atkinson home, firefighters were able to save only a fraction of the home. When the fire was finally under control, one of the agents began to read the rest of the letter originally tacked to the front door.

"Dear Constitutional Traitor, you voted to allow the greedy people that sat on the board of the City of New London, Connecticut to abuse the Fifth

Amendment of the Constitution and steal everything I own in the shadow of Eminent Domain. You wrote a blank check for local and state governments to abuse property owners. You voted to give power to the government to take private property and convert it into public use. The City of New London did not provide fair compensation to me for the property; the City stole it from me in the name of 'economic development.'

"In time, I will take from you everything you own in the name of public interest. I will ruin your life just as you voted to allow a greedy city to ruin mine. You committed legal arson of the Constitution. I committed legal arson of your home. The Secret Service will not be able to protect you from me. Check your bank account.

"I am a *Deadly Gray* justice warrior."

♦ ♦ ♦ ♦ ♦

May 28, 2024
Washington. DC

Special Agent in Charge, Chris O'Connor was a nervous wreck. He'd never been to the White House much less met in the Oval Office with the President. He and Director Naylor passed through security and waited for 20 minutes before the Chief of Staff agreed to let them through. President Lamb had an intimidating presence, not just because he was 6 feet, 5 inches tall, and 230 pounds, but because he had a bearing that constantly said, "Don't fuck with me."

O'Connor was perspiring when the Chief of Staff asked him, "You ready, it's your turn in the barrel?"

The President didn't shake hands with either of the FBI attendees and started out by asking, "In the last six weeks, how many serious crimes were committed by seniors over the age of 64?'

There was no answer.

"SAC O'Connor, I asked you a question."

"I don't know sir; I've just been called in to take over the *Deadly Gray* cases."

"And just how many cases are unsolved?"

"I don't know the answer to that, sir."

POTUS asked, "Director Naylor, I understand a Justice of the Supreme Court was attacked by a *Deadly Gray* criminal; is that correct?"

"Yes sir, a looney toon set fire to his home. We're in the process of determining who he is. The number of people affected by the New London eminent domain judgement is small."

The Chief of Staff raised his hand. POTUS asked, "You have a question?"

"Yes, sir. What is the FBI's plan to end the *Deadly Gray* attacks on government officials?"

Neither Naylor nor O'Connor spoke for about ten seconds before the Director said, "First, we need to discover the root cause of the sudden uprising by seniors. Then we need to address that root cause."

POTUS looked at O'Connor and asked, "Are you up to this challenge?"

"Yes, I am. I'm confident the *Deadly Gray* problem is not a fault of anything associated with your administration. The problem is systemic and accumulated over years, maybe decades. This is not anarchy; it is anger and disappointment over lifespans. We are not going to solve the problem tomorrow. But it is solvable."

Naylor looked at O'Connor like he just committed a felony.

The President said, "Interesting statements but what do you base your position on?"

O'Connor said, "Not one of the *Deadly Gray* crimes I reviewed were crimes committed for greed, evil, or money. There is a message in that observation."

POTUS said, "I want your plan O'Connor by June 1st. See you then."

May 28, 2024
Las Vegas, Nevada

"You're smarter that you look, Dip. So, answer my first question, who sent you to kill me?"

Dip took a deep breath, started to say something, stuttered, and said, "Allah, forgive me."

Tank slapped Dip with his open hand. Dip fell to the floor unconscious. When he woke up, he said, "I want to pray. Please allow me prayer time."

Tank said, "What is your real name, Dip?"

"Mohammad."

Tank said, "Yeah, no surprise there. Listen, Moe, you'll get all the time you need to pray after you've answered my questions. Now, who sent you to kill me?"

Colonel Darius Mosoudi, Colonel in IRGC."

Tank asked, "What is the IRGC?"

"The Islamic Revolutionary Guard Corps."

Tank continued, "OK, why does the Colonel want me dead?"

Mohammed answered, "I do not know. I just take orders."

Tank said. "Hazard a guess."

Mohammad scrunched his eyebrows up and asked, "What do you mean, hazard?"

"Why do you think you were sent to kill me?"

"I told you, I do not know."

"Guess."

Mohammed said, "He must think you are a threat to the Caliphate."

Tank said, "I may not be a threat to the Caliphate, but I will be a threat to you if you don't give me straight answers."

Mohammed asked, "Straight means correct?"

Tank said, "Yes, I want correct answers. Is the colonel in Las Vegas?"

"Oh, no. He would never come here."

Tank asked, "Are you the highest-ranking soldier here in Las Vegas?"

"No."

"Who knows you're here in the room and expecting you back with a statement of mission complete?"

Mohammed hesitated.

Tank said, "You've been stalling, haven't you, until others come to rescue you and eliminate me."

Tank hit Moe as hard as he could in his jaw, cracking teeth, and rendering his ability to speak marginal. Moe, still tied to a chair, would be out for a while. Tank then dressed, grabbed his gun, a knife, a flashbang, and his phone. He left the room, went to the hall to the stairway and left the stairway door cracked slightly so he could observe anyone entering the hallway from the elevator.

It was still very late or very early depending on one's perspective, but the elevator opened and two people exited drunk and giggling.

Or so it seemed.

One was male, one female. Both looked middle eastern. They walked past Tank's room for about three doors and then doubled back still laughing and giggling. But it was not genuine laughter—it was forced.

The stairway was too far from his room door to grab one of them. He thought, *Moe didn't know who he was or what he looked like. Maybe these two didn't know either.*

Tank left the flashbang in the stairway, tucked his gun and knife in his waistband and started to walk casually to a room across the hall from his. The two fake drunks watched him closely as he pulled out a keycard to slide through the reader across the hall.

Tank exploded into the male half to the team sending the back of his head into the wall and then grabbed the woman with a bear hug to keep her from using her hands to find a weapon. He pinched a nerve in her neck that rendered her unconscious and turned back to the man who was trying to get to his feet. An elbow to the man's right ear put him down for the count.

Tank removed their weapons, brought both of them into his room, tied them to chairs with plastic ties and waited for the first of them to awaken so he could restart his line of questioning.

May 28, 2024
Hamilton, Bermuda

The Chief Executive Officer of *The New York Times* sat at the head of the table in a reserved conference room at The St. Regis Bermuda Resort with the publisher and chairman, editor-in-chief, managing editor, and marketing manager.

The CEO said, "I sure enjoyed the camaraderie we experienced at the banquet last evening, but I guess it's time to get down to business.

"The first order of business is to address a proposal submitted by our marketing manager that we add a section to our paper called 'The Other Viewpoint' which I understand is to attract conservative readers and grow the number of subscribers. Comments?"

The publisher and chairman asked, "What basis do we have that our readership would increase with such an addition? It may, in fact, decrease our readership."

The marketing manager answered, "Half the readers of news are of the other persuasion. Attracting a small percentage of them might also attract new advertisers. I don't see how we could go wrong. If our subscribers are angered by this addition, well, they can just not read this section."

The CEO said, "I propose we commission a study to determine its impact before we add said section. Do I hear a second?"

The publisher and chairman said, "I second the motion."

The CEO said, "The next order of business is a proposal by the managing editor to allocate funds to protect the people sitting around this table from the *Deadly Gray* vigilantes. Comments?"

The managing editor said, "As you all know, there has been a drastic increase of violent attacks on editors and journalists around the country over the past several weeks. One of our own colleagues was assassinated by a Vietnam-era sniper. A *Washington Post* editor received the same fate. And as we have published, members of the New York University journalist faculty were killed in a suicide bombing. There are more. We are sticking our heads in the sand if we think we are not targets. I propose we hire a private security firm to help prevent our demise."

The Editor-in-chief said, "How do you suppose bodyguards could protect us from a sniper a half mile away?"

"Maybe they can't but they could protect us from crazies that operate closer to their targets. Remember, most of the seniors involved don't give a flying f-word if they get caught or if they die in the process."

The publisher and chairman said, "We don't have time for a study on this subject, but we do need a cost estimate and a list of potential private security companies to provide bids. Let's get this done. Anyone want to second the motion?"

All attendees said, "Second."

The CEO said, "The next order of business is to address the lawsuit against us by….."

The lights went off. All attendees in the conference room were in the proverbial dark. The double doors to the conference room swung open and three men entered.

The management team of *The New York Times* just knew their time was up. Each dove under the table in reflex to the invasion as if the table was going to save them.

But the three men were only resort employee. One said, "We're sorry for the power failure. We have an emergency generator which will come on in just a few minutes. We apologize for any inconvenience this outage has caused you. Are all of you alright?"

The marketing manager was first to climb out from under the table and said, "Yes, can you help a couple of our more senior executives back into their chairs?"

After he was helped back into his seat and the resort security personnel left, the publisher and chairman said "Get a security team on board as soon as possible. We will go out for bids later."

Chapter 24

May 29, 2024
Petersburg, West Virginia

On the flight from Boston to Petersburg, Tony Vinci asked, "It is unusual for you to do field work; why this time?"

Tucker said, "As you know, before Maya and I were married we discovered an energy technology with the potential to drastically reduce the world demand for fossil fuels like oil and natural gas. The economy of Russia and OPEC nations were seriously threatened by our discovery and China wanted to steal the technology's intellectual property. We became targets of assassination and/or kidnapping and were hunted by multiple nefarious parties to stop the discovery from quote, 'falling into the wrong hands.' I hid out in a log home very close to where I think #Steel is now residing. Is this a small world or what?"

Tony said, "That was not really why I asked the question. Why is it so important to you that we catch this guy that you are willing to do field work? I kind of empathize with #Steel's goal of achieving justice. He is performing a service as far as I'm concerned."

Tucker answered, "A part of me agrees with you. But there are multiple reasons for my pursuit of this guy. First, the world has a bad history associated with vigilante justice. Suspected horse thieves were strung up by self-appointed vigilantes in the old wild west without proof of guilt. We do not know if all the *Deadly Gray* victims actually got even, or the vigilantes were incorrect in picking their targets. We don't need thousands of vigilantes running around the country.

"Second, #Steel is no better than a conman who preys on seniors and convinces them to give money for alleged charitable causes when the money is actually embezzled by the conman.

"Third, I want to help Star. Sure, she can make it on her own, but Maya and I enjoy assisting her.

"The fourth reason is a selfish one; I love to solve a good mystery."

As the Cherokee-owned aircraft approached the Grant County Airport, Tucker couldn't help but admire the beauty of the green mountainous landscape. The jet landed on the short runway without incident but not without notice. It was not often a Bombardier Learjet 75 Liberty arrived in Petersburg, West Virginia.

Tony said, "This does appear to be a good place to hide if you don't want to be found. Are we able to get a car here?"

Tucker said, "I just happen to know someone in the area from my previous life. In fact, he works for Tank. There is a vehicle waiting for us."

Sure enough, a young man handed Tucker the keys to a beat-up Ford F-150. Tony said, "You know in my dwarfish situation, I won't be able to get into the passenger seat easily."

Tucker smiled and said, "That's been taken care of and don't think for a minute that beat-up exterior is any sign of its safety or engine reliability. It's a cover for its various undercover uses. You would not want to sneak around this county in your Jaguar and expect to be inconspicuous."

Tucker opened the passenger side door to the truck, grabbed a three-step stool in the bed of the pickup, and placed it such that with Tucker's help, Tony could climb into the truck cab.

Tucker asked, "How close to #Steel's IP address do you need to get to operate the nanodrone?"

Tony said, "Within five miles."

Tucker drove for 20 minutes before he pulled over onto Possum-Hollow-Lawyers Road. Tucker said, "We'll park the truck here. This is a safe location for you to set up and do your magic."

Tony said, "They don't really name roads like this, do they?"

Tucker said, "Welcome to West Virginia."

Tony activated his portable router hot spot, pulled out his laptop, connected his joystick, activated the insect size nanodrone with video capability and let it loose. Tony said, "It's a good thing it is not windy today. It'll take five minutes for Florence to arrive at her destination."

"Florence?"

"I give all my nanodrones names."

Both watched the laptop screen as Tony navigated Florence to the GPS coordinates of #Steel's IP address. The small and unimpressive cabin was on a dirt road at the top of a long and steep hill.

Tony said, "Good hiding place. No one would expect this place to be the center of so much drama."

Tucker asked, "Don't you think he is clever enough to know he can be found?"

Tony said, "I bet the place is wired to explode by Steele if anyone enters it. That is why an insect size drone is perfect for our surveillance."

Tucker said, "I don't see any vehicles. He's probably not home."

Tony said, "Do you see that tarp over by the wood pile? It is covering something. I bet it's a dirt bike or an ATV and Steel has an escape route we can't follow if we drove up there in the truck."

Tucker said, "Well, I think we may be here for a while before anything happens. What's the battery life of the drone?"

"Three hours. I'll send a second nanodrone up before we have to call this one back."

Tucker pulled his laptop out and said, "I'm going to do some work while we wait."

Ninety minutes later, an old man wearing a ball cap with a WVU logo embossed on it walked out of the cabin, stretched, and wandered over to a shed on the hideout's property.

Tony said, "OK, let's get a close up, take a few photos, and send them to Jimmy. His facial recognition app might give us this guy's real name and background." Tony manipulated the joystick and took several photos of the large man with a long grey beard wearing bib overalls unlock a shed. Tony's drone then followed with some photos inside the shed.

Tucker said, "Looks like an armory in there." The man took out a shotgun, relocked the shed and headed back to the cabin.

The insect size drone, Florence, followed him into the cabin where several computers, monitors, keyboards, routers, and satellite phones were strategically located around a room with a fireplace and a wood burning stove. Tony said, "Did you notice all the weapons #Steel has scattered around the room?"

Tucker said, "He's ready for unwanted visitors and won't be captured without casualties. I bet he stores ammunition in the bedroom. Send the photos to Jimmy. Let's figure out who we're dealing with."

Forty-five minutes later, Jimmy called Tony on his satellite phone. "His name is Maxx Steele, former Navy Seal Sergeant, and honorably discharged. He's 82-years old and worked for a firing range for twenty years in Frederick, Maryland. He has no police record and no history of non-military violence. He was married to the same woman for 45 years until she passed away three years ago from heart failure. He has no offspring or other family. That's all I've got."

Tucker said, "Something triggered his current lawlessness. Keep digging."

Tony said, "What do you want to do now boss? I don't recommend we knock on his door."

"Does the drone have audio capability."

Tony said, "Yes."

"Let's wait until he calls someone. That could be useful."

May 29, 2024
Fairfax, Virginia

Star was unable to convince the Fairfax Adult Detention center to allow Ram to accompany her to interview Denver Jones of Manakin Sabot, Virginia; the man who tried to attack her on the back porch at her home. She left Ram in her SUV with a window open and water and told him she would not be long.

After Denver's attorney joined Star in the visitor's room of the jailhouse, she asked the attacker, "Mr. Jones, why did you invade my property with a firearm?"

The attorney said, "Don't answer that, it's an admission of guilt."

Star asked, "OK, Mr. Jones, you said, 'You can't stop us. You've only scratched the surface. There will be more tomorrow.' What did you mean by that? What is it you think needed to be stopped?"

Jones looked at his attorney who nodded approval to answer the question. Jones said, "You want to stop the *Deadly Gray* vigilantes from achieving justice."

Star said, "Yes, that is true. You know, don't you, that vigilante violence is illegal, right?"

The attorney said, "Don't answer that."

Star asked, "Where did you learn of my involvement with the FBI's attempt to stop vigilante violence?"

Again, Jones received approval to answer that question. Jones said, "On a web site."

Star asked, "Do you know #Steel?"

Jones answered, "Only as a participant of the website blogs."

"What do you know about #Steel?"

"Only that he is a leader and a *Deadly Gray* justice warrior."

Star asked, "Did he ask you to visit my home?"

"No."

"So, you came to visit me on your own free will. What did he say in his blog that made you want to visit me?"

"Only that you were an enemy of the *Deadly Gray*."

Star asked, "Why are you a supporter of the *Deadly Gray* senior movement?"

The attorney said, "Agent Cherokee, what's in it for my client to answer that question?"

Star said, "I could encourage the prosecutor to drop charges against him or ask for leniency if Mr. Jones helps me find and bring to justice #Steel."

The attorney asked Star to leave the room while he and Jones discussed his options. When Star returned the attorney said, "He refuses to answer your questions and is prepared to accept incarceration rather than help you find #Steel. Do you have any other questions?"

Star said, "No. So be it."

Star left the detention center, got into her vehicle, and said to Ram, "Well that was a waste of time. The *Deadly Gray* vigilantes are committed to their cause. That scares me to death."

May 29, 2024
Houston, Texas

At the Marriott Marquis Houston, attendees of the Carbon Capture 2024 Conference gathered in the Texas Ballroom to discuss technologies and methodologies to reduce carbon dioxide emissions generated by the power and oil industries. Representatives included executives, engineers, and journalist from around the globe.

Joeng Qi who represented the Peoples Republic of China (PRC) attended the evening mixer and banquet along with his two Chinese bodyguards. Mr. Joeng was speaking with one of the representatives from the European Union while a journalist from *Environmental Newswire*, Abe Stansfield, waited ten minutes for his turn to shake the hand of the PRC power broker.

One of Joeng's bodyguards observed Stansfield's agitated state and whispered in his boss's ear that the man in line to meet with him next appeared untrustworthy. When the conversation with the Europeans ended, Joeng turned his back on Stansfield and began a conversation with a U.S congressman from Wyoming.

Before the bodyguards could react, Stansfield pulled a 2.5-inch polycarbonate T-Handle push dagger knife out of its sheath and jammed it into the Chinese environmental leader's back.

Joeng screamed, the bodyguards tackled Stansfield, and the conference mixer was in chaos. The bodyguards overpowered Stansfield, but he managed to stick a ball-point pen into one of the bodyguard's eyes and kick the other bodyguard in the groin. But to no avail.

Joeng was rushed to a Houston hospital emergency room where he was ultimately saved to live another day—avoiding an international crisis.

The climate change apostle, Abe Stansfield, suffered a broken neck as a result of the retaliation from the one-eyed bodyguard.

Later, upon review of his laptop, FBI investigators learned that Stansfield wrote articles to be posted in the next three editions on the *Environmental Newswire* entitled, "China Operates 1,000 Coal-Fired Power Plants", "A Study of China's Dishonesty In Fighting Climate Change", and "China Calls for Stronger Action on Climate Change By Others but Takes No Action Itself."

Star Cherokee investigated the case and discovered that 66-year-old Stansfield frequently wrote blogs on #Steel's web site, *DanielWebsterWorldView.* She called SAC O'Connor and said, "POTUS may hear from Xi. The Houston fiasco turns out to be a case of a *Deadly Gray* vigilante attempted murder. Be prepared to be called to the White House."

O'Connor said, "What Houston fiasco? What are you talking about?"

An exasperated Agent Cherokee said, "You have hereby been forewarned. Duck for cover."

◆ ◆ ◆ ◆ ◆

May 29, 2024
Las Vegas, Nevada

Tank and Jolene's company, White Knight Personal Security, LLC, had offices and agents all over the country and in several nations. Tank called his Phoenix, Arizona office and asked them to send three of his White Knights to his hotel room in Las Vegas where Tank held captive three middle eastern people. He gave one of the security agents instructions as to how to pretend to be someone he wasn't.

Tank gagged and kept the three captives immobile the entire time it took his people to drive from Phoenix to Las Vegas. Tank ate and drank in front of them and did not allow any of the captives to visit the restroom or have water. He wanted them weak and miserable.

The three former Special Forces White Knight officers entered Tank's hotel room with a large suitcase, a toolbox, and refreshments for Tank and themselves. One of the men stood guard in the hallway while one stood guard with his weapons prominent in Tank's hotel room. The last White Knight pretended to be Daniel, the Mossad interrogator.

Tank ate a juicy hamburger in front to the captives and said, "Which one of you wants to go first? Moe, here, knows what's in store for him so I'll use Daniel to help me interrogate Moe first in the other room unless either of you want to volunteer.

"But first, help me put the lady in the suitcase so we can transport her to the warehouse. Did you bring the acid?"

Daniel, the pretend interrogator, said, "Yes, it will be my pleasure to treat the Jew-hater to my trade. Martyrdom won't be pleasant for her."

Mohammed tried unsuccessfully to scream something to Tank through his gag.

Tank said, "Moe, I'll take your gag off if you promise not to scream or make enough noise to alert the hotel guests. If you violate my request, that large man over there will remove most of your teeth in one blow with his hard-as-a-rock fist. Do you understand?"

Mohammed shook his head, 'yes.'

Tank removed his gag and said, "What is it you want to say?"

"I will tell you everything you want to know if you will release Daria."

"So, the woman has a name, and she means something to you. He looked at the other male hostage and said, "Apparently, you are not important or valuable to Moe, here. Good to know."

Tank said, "In your culture, you'd have to kill Daria if I strip her naked in front of other men; is that correct?"

Mohammed said nothing but looked completely defeated.

"Take Moe into the other room; we'll delay taking her to the warehouse until I think we have all we can squeeze out of Moe."

Daniel sat Mohammed on Tank's bed and opened his toolbox while Tank sat on a chair in front of the immobile and petrified terrorist.

Tank said, "Every time you give me a bad answer or lie to me, I'll remove a piece of Daria's clothing. Why does the Iranian Revolutionary Guard Corp want me dead?"

"You are too close to the truth."

"About?"

Mohammed answered, "Our deal with Stephen Paddock that went bad."

Tank's eyes lit up and said, "Tell me the entire story as you know it."

"Allah, forgive me.

"We want to destroy the United States, the Great Satan. We know we can't destroy you militarily in war. We know the Great Satan is much too powerful for us to openly attack America. We had a plan to defeat you from within. It is a long-term strategy, but it starts with small Jihadist cells."

"Let me get this straight," said Tank, "The weapons Paddock brought here to the Mandalay Bay Resort and Casino were supposed to arm a terrorist cell. You've got to be kidding? That's not enough firepower to do shit. Off with her blouse, Daniel."

Mohammed said, "I tell the truth. I never said the plan was to use the weapons to stock an IRGC cell. Please."

Tank yelled, "Stand down. Maybe he is telling the truth. Explain."

Mohamed said, "The weapons were not intended to arm an Iranian cell, they were intended to be used to kill the Saudi Prince."

"The mission failed, what happened?"

Mohammed took a deep breath and said, "A rogue Revolutionary Guard did not trust Paddock; he had a, 'how do you say', premo…"

Tank interrupted and said, "Premonition?"

"Yes, premonition or extra sense thing. He confronted Paddock and accused him of being CIA. He said Paddock looked like a deer in the headlights and was obviously guilty, so he killed Paddock in a rage of anger. He also knew that the CIA was on to us and that the mission had failed.

"He went crazy and decided to kill as many infidels as he could. So, our rogue soldier shot as much ammunition as possible out the Paddock's hotel window at the people enjoying the concert.

"He regained control at some point and stopped, left Paddock's room, and fled."

Tank said, "Where is the killer now?"

"We don't know. No one was angrier about the massacre event than the Ayatollah. He feared that if the United States learned that an Iranian committed the greatest mass murder ever in the United States, that America would launch war against Iran—a war Iran could not win and where millions of Iranians would die."

Tank said, "The quickest way to end a war is to lose it. Tell that to the Ayatollah.

"What is the rogue soldier's name?"

"Abdalhamid Mafi."

"Do you or one of your partners in crime have a photo of him?"

"Yes, I do."

Tank said, "You're doing well and saving yourself from Daniel's handiwork. The next question is why did the IRGC kill two Chicago private investigators at exactly the same time as your alleged rogue soldier was massacring innocent people enjoying a country music concert?"

Mohammed's face displayed complete confusion. He said, "What?"

Tank thought, *Either Moe is a good actor, or he really doesn't know what I'm talking about.*

"Daniel, take Moe into the other room and bring Daria in here."

Moe begged, "Please, I told you the truth. Don't hurt her."

Tank said, "Gag him."

Daniel brought Daria, a twenty-something petite woman with dazzling and intelligent eyes into the suite's bedroom and sat her down where Moe had previously sat."

Tank asked, "Are you part of Iran's goal of world dominance and the death of anyone that is a non-believer?"

She said, "Is this a trick question?" Her English was perfect.

Tank said, "Yes, and your answer is?"

"What I'd really like is for Muslim women to have equality with Muslim men. But I'm realistic and would settle to live in a country where such things are possible. I do what I must do to be here and not back home."

Tank said, "And that something includes killing me if your masters so instruct."

"Yes."

"Are you Mohammed's wife?"

"No."

Tank said, "He is very protective of you."

"I am his younger sister."

Tank said, "How well do you know Abdalhamid Mafi?"

She said, "Only by reputation. I never met him. He is now on the Iranian equivalent to the FBI's 'Most Wanted List'"

Tank acknowledged that Moe told him the truth. Tank said, "You are very articulate in English; where were you educated?"

"Princeton."

"Whoa, how'd that happen."

Daria said, "Just like America, it's about who you know. Our parents knew the right people."

Tank said, "During the massacre of Americans by Mafi, two Americans were assassinated by someone else. That implies that the assassin knew the massacre was going to occur. Your brother implied the massacre was spontaneous, not planned. Which is it?"

She said, "I know nothing about the assassination of which you mention. Are you saying that during the massacre, another assassination was ongoing?"

Tank thought, *She's a little too cool and too cold.*

Tank asked, "Who is your partner in the other room? The one you pretended to be drunk with last night. What is his role here?"

Daria said, "He is less informed than Mohammed and me. Interrogate him as you see fit, but he knows less than I do. Do as you wish, but Draconian measures will not yield fruit for you."

Tank said, "Let me decide that."

She asked, "May I go to the bathroom?"

"No. Daniel, it's time to exchange Daria with the last captive."

Tank's line of questioning was entirely different with the final soldier, "How well do you know Sheriff Lakota?"

He answered, "I know who he is."

Tank leaned in and asked, "Since he knew Abdalhamid Mafi was the real Las Vegas massacre shooter, how did the IRGC contain LaKota, keep him from disclosing the truth?"

The soldier headbutted Tank as hard as he could. It stunned Tank, made his eyes water, but didn't render

Tank unconscious. Daniel planted a round house punch into the nose of the IRGC soldier, clearly breaking it.

Tank said to the headbutter, "That was dumb. How do you say dumb in Farsi? Never mind. Gag him, put him in the suitcase, and we'll deal with him later. Bring Moe back in here."

As they brought Mohammed back into the room with Tank, Moe watched the former Special Forces men put his co-conspirator into a suitcase. Tank applied a handkerchief to his head wound and said, "Your friend is not so bright. He'll pay for his foolishness. You, on the other hand, have a chance to redeem your team's current situation. I'll give you the benefit of the doubt that you don't have control over him. So, I will ask you the question I asked of him. Since he knew that Abdalhamid Mafi was the real Las Vegas massacrer, how did the IRGC contain Sheriff Lakota, and keep him from disclosing the truth to American authorities?"

"Threats and money. We offered him money and threatened his family if he ever told anyone what he knew."

"And Adam Heinz?"

"Mr. Heinz was a different story. He approached us. He said he knew about our deal with Paddock. He knew we intended to kill the Saudi Prince and that he suspected it was a deal gone bad. But I don't think he knew an Iranian RGC soldier committed the massacre. We discussed among ourselves the option of killing him, but we decided to pay him off instead."

Tank said, "We could kill you. We could continue to interrogate you. But, instead, my men will drop you off in the town of Kayenta, Arizona. Here is your phone, Moe. Send me the photo of Abdalhamid Mafi, now." He did and Tank took his phone back from him. "If we see you around here, we will not be so forgiving."

Before the three White Knights left with the middle easterners, the one who pretended to be Daniel reached into his toolbox and handed Tank the audio recorder. He said, "That voice recording is probably worth more than the national debt."

◆ ◆ ◆ ◆ ◆

May 29, 2024
Maysville, West Virginia

Tony said, "The battery is just about spent on the nanodrone, Florence, and I don't see a way to get Red inside the cabin. We have less than ten minutes."

Tucker contemplated the situation and said, "Get online, go to his website, pretend to be a blogger and, assuming he is online, send him an unusual message. Tell him something that will make him go outside."

Tony said, "Like what?"

"Like there is something unusual in the sky, or an eclipse or something."

Four minute later, Maxx Steele exited his cabin, swinging his shotgun from side to side, and looked like he was ready to kill someone. The backup nanodrone, Red, entered the cabin while Tony instructed the original drone, Florence, to leave."

Tucker asked, "What the hell did you say on his blog page?"

Tony said, "Only that Tucker and Tony are outside his cabin to speak with him."

Tucker looked apoplectic.

Tony laughed and said, "What I really said was that a rumor has it that Grant County, West Virginia is infected with rabid squirrels."

Tucker said, "Poor squirrels within sight of Steele."

Tucker and Tony waited another 75 minutes in their Ford F-150 until finally, Maxx made a call on one of his satellite phones. They could hear only one side of the conversation:

"It's me. Maxx."

A few seconds went by until Maxx said, "Because I want you to know that I think I should shut down for a while. As you said, it is self-sustaining. We don't need to build a *Deadly Gray* following; the media and governments are doing it for us. I estimate that 1,730 *Deadly Gray* crimes were committed worldwide in the past six weeks and it's growing exponentially. So, I want to shut down my systems and disappear; I'm too old for this shit anyway. I'm in a rabies invested area. You're younger."

Whoever Maxx spoke with took about two minutes before Maxx said, "God bless America" and hung up.

Tucker said to Tony, "Some younger guy either leads the *Deadly Gray* mission or picked up the baton from Steele."

Tony said, "Can I remove Red the first time Maxx opens the front door. I don't want it to get trapped inside?"

Tucker said, "Yes, of course. Let's call Star."

Star answered her FBI supplied satellite phone and said, "Hello, this is Agent Star Cherokee."

Tucker said, "No caller ID?"

Star said, "Hi, Dad. You never call me on my FBI phone unless it is important so this must be all business."

Tucker said, "True. Can you record the call or take notes?"

"I'm ready."

Tucker said, "Here are the coordinates for the location of #Steel." Tucker gave it to her. "His name is Maxx Steele, former Navy Seal and though old, still dangerous. I fear an attack on Mr. Steele will result in agency loss of life and his suicide by FBI SWAT."

Star said, "This is fantastic but how do I explain to the decision makers how I know that this guy is #Steel?"

Tony said, "The FBI Cyber Division legally retained us. We did what the FBI asked us to do. Why is that a problem?"

Star said, "You're right, Tony."

Tony said, "I now have your testimony on tape that I was right. I'll frame it or something. Anyway, I recommend SWAT uses a helicopter. He'll be hard to catch on his dirt bike otherwise."

Chapter 25

May 30, 2024
Wiscasset, Maine

Tank set up a conference call with Jolene, Maya, Sonja, and Jimmy Ma to discuss the path forward on the investigation of ATF Adam Heinz and his role in the coverup of the truth about the Las Vegas massacre. This time, Jolene allowed Stanley to listen to the conversation without him having to sneak within earshot.

Tank explained what he'd learned and how he'd learned it. He played the audio recording of the confessions by the Iranians for the others on the phone to hear firsthand.

Maya said, "There are holes in their story. We need to plug the holes before we even consider going public with what you learned, Tank. We don't have enough actionable intelligence."

Tank said, "Jimmy, I sent you a name and photo of the alleged real Las Vegas shooter. What have you learned that you can share with us?"

Jimmy said, "For one, I learned not to put myself in a position where you interrogate me, Tank. That story about the sulfuric acid was quite imaginative."

Sonja interrupted Jimmy and said, "The technique Tank threatened the terrorists with has been used before."

Jimmy said, "Oh." Jimmy shivered before saying, "Good to know. What I learned about Abdalhamid Mafi is that he is a hunted man by the Iranian Revolutionary Guard Corp or IRGC. His face has shown up in

Matamoros, Tamaulipas, Mexico. He sold himself as an enforcer with the Nuevo Progreso cartel and changed his name to Jose Trevino."

Sonja said, "Jimmy, if you discovered this, then the IRGC and or the CIA with NSA could discover this. My guess he's a dead man walking. Tank, if you want to interview him, you need to do it soon."

Jolene said, "That's way too dangerous, Tank. Are you kidding, penetrate a drug cartel? Pump the brakes a little bit. You don't even speak Spanish."

Stanley said, "I speak Spanish, I could go with you and be your spiritual advisor. We could get some good bean burritos."

Maya said, "I can't tell you what to do, but questioning a cartel enforcer in cartel country would not be the smartest thing you ever did. You have a proclivity to take risks."

Sonja said, "Unless…"

Tank said, "Unless what?"

"Unless it was a joint CIA and Mossad mission. I'm sure the CIA wants him dead, and Mossad would like to interrogate him for real."

Maya said, "Invade a sovereign country?"

Stanley said, "It wouldn't be the first time and it won't be the last. Just like the Las Vegas massacre."

Maya said, "Back to the holes in the story you heard from the Iranians in Las Vegas, there is too much strategic ambiguity; a spontaneous, unplanned outburst by a crazed jihadist is inconsistent with the two American's assassinated by a sniper rifle shot from a different angle at exactly the same time. That's what you discovered, right Sonja?"

"Right."

Maya said, "It's the chaos theory."

Stanley said, "Which means the massacre was not spontaneous but rather planned. I bet at the end of the day, the people you set free in Arizona were the planners and this mafia guy was set-up for the fall. Damn them, they made a mockery of us. ."

Jolene said to Stanley, "He's not a mafia guy, his last name was Mafi."

"Whatever."

Jimmy said, "Though the truth appears illusive, the failure to kill the Saudi Prince plays into it somehow. The same snipers that killed the American private investigators could have done the same to the Prince. They didn't need all the weapons bartered by Paddock to kill one person. We're missing something."

Maya said, "Heinz, he's the missing piece to this puzzle and why Manion put us on to him. He approached the Iranians after the massacre? Bullshit."

Tank asked, "Path forward, anyone?"

Sonja said, "Joint CIA/Mossad interrogation of Mafi."

Jolene said, "Another visit with the Arizona jihadists."

Maya said, "Jimmy to keep digging."

Stanley said, "Find out what the Saudi Prince knows."

Tank said, "Maybe all of the above."

Jimmy said, "This is a genuine clusterfuck. Uh, sorry ladies."

Deadly Gray

♦ ♦ ♦ ♦ ♦

May 30, 2024
San Francisco, California

San Francisco Chronicle Headline: **A New Trend: Kill at the End of Your Life**.

A new cultural revolution has emerged as an unintended consequence of the internet and social media: terminally ill seniors exact vigilante justice for perceived unfairness' in their lives. An American Psychiatrist Association study suggests that many seniors jumped on the vigilante bandwagon for four reasons. The first reason is because the seniors believe they or someone they love was harmed and they want justice. The second reason is an unfulfilled life bored with the daily grind whereby the senior wants to do something meaningful as the autumn of their life approaches. The third reason is that religion plays less importance in their lives, and they feel no consequence in the afterlife. The fourth reason is due to mental health issues such as dementia, Alzheimer's Disease, and other psychopathic deviate behavior. As of this writing, it is estimated that 82 end-of-life crimes were committed in the past seven weeks in California alone.

May 30, 2024
Maysville, West Virginia

Old man Maxx Steele placed video cameras on the dirt road of Outlaw Trail on the way up to his safehouse cabin. At a point a quarter mile away from his safehouse, a vehicle passed over a cable and triggered an alarm. Maxx had less than a minute to make important survival decisions. The video proved to him that it was the government, probably FBI—they hustled up the road at a good clip in a Humvee followed by a Mine Resistant Ambush Protected vehicle or MRAP.

"Fuck." He flipped a toggle switch, pulled a cord, and used a mouse to activate a fail-safe system. He grabbed his old M4, slung it over his once-powerful frame, went outside, and pulled the tarp off his ATV.

Maxx smiled when he heard the explosion; the Humvee crossed the fail-safe activated landmine. He figured he had 30-seconds to hit the escape trail. His old body did not cooperate, but he managed to hobble onto the ATV, and started it on the first try. He could hear the MRAP get closer

He maneuvered the ATV down a trail he cut for just this purpose. As expected, a gigantic explosion blew material into the air, pieces rained down around him even though he was a good 50 yards down the trail; his cabin and shed blew up from the C4 he pre-positioned. As planned, his electronic hardware, weapons, and ammunition were destroyed by the explosion.

Maxx Steele felt good that his plans worked; the land mines, the cabin and shed explosions, and his escape ATV. No way the MRAP could follow him down this narrow trail between oak trees and fallen pine trees.

Though his hearing wasn't the best, Maxx thought he heard something that, if he was right, would end his chance of escape. He thought he heard a Blackhawk helicopter.

"Fuck."

Maxx knew the Sikorsky UH-60 Black Hawk could carry 10,000 pounds of armament including rockets, missiles, and 50-caliber gun pods. He knew he would not escape so he stopped the ATV, pulled out his favorite cigar, lit it, and took a couple of enjoyable drags. He thought, "*I will die a soldier's death.*" He pulled the 5.56×45mm fed M4 Carbine and began to fire in the direction of the Blackhawk.

The 50-caliber rounds shredded the trees and bushes around him until they reached him and cut him in half. Maxx Steele, #Steele, apparent leader of the *Deadly Gray* vigilantes was dead.

But his legend was likely to live on.

Jimmy Ma called Star; she picked up after the fourth ring, "Sorry Jimmy, I was on the phone with the FBI SWAT team leader who just terminated #Steel."

Jimmy said, "Yes, Maxx Steele, former Navy Seal, and proverbial tough guy. I bet it wasn't easy. I predicted the SWAT team would lose some agents in the process of raiding Steele. Did they?"

Star said, "Don't know yet. Two are in critical condition but alive from a landmine planted by Steele."

Jimmy said, "Well, I hope they make it. Listen, the reason I called is that we have good news. I haven't been able to reach Tucker, so I thought I would call you. We have completed the algorithm. We now know, thanks to Suzzanne, the people who logged onto #Steel's website, *DanielWebsterWorldView.* With a little quantum computing, we can now prepare a list of *Deadly Gray* visitors to the website, the visitor's illness or malady, their specific grievance, and the likelihood they may commit a vigilante crime."

Star said, "Fantastic. You all are unbelievable. Can you prepare a list of the top 10 candidates?"

"Already done."

Chapter 26

June 1, 2024
New York City, New York

The Wall Street Journal Headline: **Backbone of Deadly Gray Vigilantes Broken:**

An FBI SWAT team raided the hideout of a former Navy Seal in the small community of Maysville, West Virginia. The FBI received a tip from an anonymous informer of the coordinates where Maxx Steele, the alleged mastermind behind the Deadly Gray movement, hid out. Steele died in a shootout with the FBI and two FBI SWAT team members were flown to a hospital in Winchester, Virginia where they remain in critical condition. Director Naylor of the FBI said, "It is our hope that with the elimination of its founder, the overall Deadly Gray movement by our senior citizen will subside.

June 1, 2024
Washington, DC

Brad Naylor met with SAC Chris O'Connor before their scheduled meeting with the President in the Situation Room. Naylor said, "Let's go over the plan outline."

O'Connor said, "I spoke with Agent Cherokee and Special Agent Winemiller late last night. Two major developments occurred just yesterday that should be in our favor to change the atmosphere of the meeting. The termination of the *Deadly Gray* leader must be good news and a kudo for the FBI. Also in our favor is the completion of an FBI algorithm that predicts vigilante crimes before they occur. We can walk into the lion's den with progress, not just a plan."

Director Naylor said, "I see; item one of the plan was to find and contain #Steel. Item two is the development of an algorithm that will help us stop some crimes before they happen. What's item three?"

O'Connor said, "Item three requires cooperation from the mainstream media and journalists worldwide. We need to flood the television, radio, news outlets, and social media with propaganda that stigmatizes the *Deadly Gray* vigilante movement. Whereas, today, seniors embrace the idea, we want them to later think that people who are vigilantes are stupid, selfish, hateful, and lawless fools."

POTUS called Naylor and O'Connor into the Situation Room before they finished their discussion about their plan. It made no difference.

President Lamb said, "You guys have a serious problem. As if the *Deadly Gray* uprising wasn't bad enough, we now have a super angry group of *Deadly Gray* followers. You have dropped a pile of crap on me with your elimination of #Steel. We have an image crisis worse than 'Ruby Ridge' and 'Waco Davidian Cult' combined. Did you have to cut him in half? Couldn't you have just arrested him? And apparently, he wasn't the lone puppet master. Someone else is blogging on #Steel's new website energizing the people who follow it. The *Deadly Gray* movement is now a religion, and we just crucified their Christ.

"Shut that site down.

"Now!

"You're excused."

June 1, 2024
Atlanta, Georgia

"Good morning, I am Nancy Jordan, and this is CNN Breaking News. The world grieves today about the brutal assassination of a United States veteran who started the *Deadly Gray* justice movement with websites entitled *DanielWebsterWorldView* and *DeadlyGrayJustice*. He was known as #Steel to his followers, but CNN has confirmed that his real name is Maxx Steele, a former Vietnam era Navy Seal.

"Unfortunately, his assassination is another blemish on the FBI legacy of abusive use of force. Riots have broken out in assisted living and nursing homes around the world. Congressional switchboards are overloaded with threats of an increase in vigilantism. We here at CNN strongly discourage violence by seniors. Now, a word from out sponsors."

June 1, 2024
Vero Beach, Florida

Three seniors from a nearby Melbourne assisted living community slowly entered a twenty-year-old

Lincoln Town Car and drove to a local Home Depot. They collectively went down the home cleaning section and placed in their basket every cleaning fluid they could find that said 'flammable.' They stocked up on briquette grill fire starters and filled an empty grill propane tank.

The senior driver no longer had a driver's license but at least could see and hear well enough to catch each stop light without running a red light. She said, "I need to rest before we get there and J. Edgar Hoover the house. I'll pull over into the next strip mall."

The oldest of the seniors said, "I need to pee. Stop somewhere I can pee."

She said, "OK, There's a Mickey Ds in the next shopping center. We'll wake up John when we get there; I love to play tickle monster on him."

The Town car pulled into the parking lot and the oldest senior hobbled into the rest room before he wet his adult diapers.

The woman swung her thick legs out the passenger seat and opened the back door with her fleshy arms to tickle and wake up John.

John said, "Stop it, lady, you're as mean as a copperhead. Are we there yet? I don't think I can carry the propane tank by myself."

She said, "No and we didn't expect you to with your worthless knees and Asthma symptoms to carry it alone. Do you want anything to eat at McDonalds before we leave?"

John said, "No. Do you know how to get there and have the right address?"

She said, "How hard can it be to find?"

The oldest member of the group returned from the restroom. The woman said, "Don't you know how to zip up your fly by yourself? Get in the damn car will ya, baldie?"

He said, "I never understood what the big deal about hair is anyway. By the way, am I getting older or is McDonald's finally playing great music?"

John said, "You are way past 'getting' old. You were getting old a century ago."

She drove the team to the Vero Beach address she'd written down and said, "OK boys, it's action time." She waddled up the driveway with supplies, placed them strategically under the entranceway porch and started back. The two men struggled to carry the propane tank, so she said, "Stop and rest, I don't want to have to carry you back after you've had heart-attacks."

Both men stopped to rest while she got other supplies. As she passed them on her way back to the house, she said, "Will you two mouth-breathers move. We'll get caught and I don't want to have to bring you cookies in jail."

John said, "I thought this would be more fun. I thought I would finally do something meaningful in my life. What is it we're doing again?'

The oldest man said, "We're here to burn down the FBI Director's vacation home because he killed #Steel, remember?"

John said, "Oh, yes. This is fun."

The old men finally dragged the propane tank to the front of the house and placed it on the porch while the old woman poured flammable liquids around the base of the home.

She said, "OK, John, give me the lighter."

John said, "I don't have a lighter."

She said, "Does anyone have a match?"

Both men shook their heads.

"Well, it's a good thing I have matches. What would you two do without me?

John said, "Live a longer life?"

The oldest senior said, "Every day I look down at the daisies is a bonus day."

She said, "Shut up and turn the valve open on the propane tank. And run for the car."

The oldest senior said, "Run?"

"Just move as fast as you can. Are we ready?"

She lit a match, threw it on an area she doused with flammables. It caught fire immediately and the old overweight woman attempted something resembling a run herself."

She only got 25 feet before the propane tank exploded.

In the hospital, the three seniors were treated by emergency medical personnel for second degree burns but survived to learn later from the fire marshal that the house they burned did not belong to the Director of the FBI. They had the wrong address.

Chapter 27

June 2, 2024
Harpers Ferry, West Virginia

Jimmy called the Deputy Secretary of Treasury and said, "Sir, I want you to know before anyone else what I discovered about the counterfeiting of U.S. one-hundred-dollar bills."

"I'm listening."

Jimmy said, "The Kanggye site in North Korea has counterfeited $17-billion worth of one-hundred-dollar bills over the last three years. Here are the coordinates of the Kanggye press." Jimmy gave it to the Deputy Secretary.

"How good is this information?"

Jimmy said, "One hundred percent. Check the satellite photos from the National Reconnaissance Center."

"Mr. Ma, please, keep this under your hat."

"Of course."

After they hung up, Jimmy opened a bottle of Almost Heaven Bourbon Whiskey and entered a website to play the game of 'Go' when he received a call; it was Tucker. Jimmy took a swig, swallowed, and said, "Yes, boss. I'm glad you called. I just got off the phone with our Treasury customer. He's happy; I showed him where the facility was in North Korea that pumped out counterfeit dollars. But that is not why you called. What do you need?"

Tucker said, "You know the Treasury Department loves you, right?

"Rightly they should."

Tucker said, "I love your modesty; it's endearing. Back in April, I asked you to follow the money on the person who took photographs at both Heinz's and Manion's funerals."

Jimmy said. "Blessing."

"Yes, Blessing. whom I understand is CIA and related to the Speaker of the House."

Jimmy said, "Tony helped me gather data on the guy. It took us a while but what we learned is that Spencer Blessing was Heinz's CIA handler. Heinz lived a double life as a high-level muckety-muck in the ATF and an agent of the CIA. He collected two paychecks from the government and handsome payments from other sources."

Tucker asked, "What other sources?"

"Payments from accounts in Belize and Cayman Islands."

Tucker said, "And?"

A bank account in Islamabad, Pakistan wire transferred to the account from Belize; a bank account in London transferred the money to the account in the Cayman Islands."

Tucker waited.

Jimmy said, "Both accounts originated from Tehran, Iran."

"OK, what about Blessing."

"I think Blessing negotiated the payments to Heinz, but I haven't yet discovered any improprieties in his known financial accounts. Tony and I are still digging but we feel like we're pissing into the wind."

Tucker said, "It continues to baffle me how Manion, even with the help from Maxx Steel could have known to pinpoint Heinz as a bad guy. The lack of evidence is somehow evidence of an insulated crime."

"I'm sorry sweetheart, but you can't have Lucky Charms for every meal. You must eat something healthy, so, eat your pears and drink your orange juice."

"Mom, you're mean. Daddy lets us eat Lucky Charms anytime we ask when he's home."

Sonja didn't believe that for a moment and wondered how a four-year-old learned to be so conniving. Sonja said, "I'll ask Daddy about that when he comes home. What do you think he'll do if he learns you didn't tell the truth?"

Sonja's little girl, Li, looked down, pursed her lips like she was going to cry and asked, "He'll send me to bed?"

"And he won't allow you to have any Lucky Charms for a week."

Sonja's phone rang; she had hoped it was her husband, Troy. She watched him play short-stop against the Red Sox on TV yesterday. But it wasn't her all-star who was calling; it was a call from London.

"Hello."

In a thick English accent her father-in-law, Bernard Nazareth, said, "Good evening, my dear Sonja, how are my grandchildren Powers and Li doing?"

Sonja said, "Can I ship them to you for a couple of days so you can learn first-hand? I've managed to spoil them beyond reason. I must be cognitively deficient."

"Oh, my dear, I think not. There is no one that has perfect mental health, especially when under the pressure of rug rats."

Sonja asked, "Do you want to speak with your grandbabies?"

Bernard said, "Yes, but I called for an entirely different reason. We Brits are lost at sea when it comes to the issue of the *Deadly Gray* vigilante movement. I'm investigating the problem here in the UK on behalf of my friends at Scotland Yard. Can you arrange a call or meeting with you and Star and whomever I need to speak with on the subject? We've made no progress linking the murder of a member of the House of Lords by a commoner to the *Deadly Gray* mastermind. What's worse, there is a frightening increase of crimes by seniors since the original killing. We don't know what we don't know."

Sonja said, "I think I can make a joint call happen. How did you get involved with this investigation, Bernard?"

"Because of you, my dear. They approached me because I am related to you. You are still famous within MI-6 and the Yard."

Sonja said, "I'm surprised my reputation is not past the half-life of people's memory."

June 2, 2024
Location Unknown

The mystery man who mentored #Steel—Maxx Steele—felt the need to fan the flames of the *Deadly Gray* movement by appearing as #Star, #Steele's handle after Maxx closed down *DanielWebsterWorldView* and replaced it with *DeadlyGrayJustice.* He wanted to post something that would stir up the mainstream media, receive maximum exposure, and recruit a new set of vigilantes. He wrote:

"I AM ALIVE—RUMORS OF MY DEATH ARE GREATLY EXAGGERATED.

"At least in spirit. Our goal to build an army of seniors who want justice where justice has been elusive remains achievable. The millions of you out there know who you are. Has justice passed you or a loved one by because you were not part of the elite for whom justice is bought and paid for? If you are at the end of your life, now is the time to make a statement." #STEEL

.

◆　◆　◆　◆　◆

June 2, 2024
Washington, DC

President Lamb asked the Chief of Staff to get the Director of the NSA on the phone. POTUS said, "Your colleagues at the FBI have failed to follow my instructions. Their failure reinforces my lack of confidence in them. I'll deal with them later. I now instruct you to shut down the dark website *DeadlyGrayJustice.* Can or can't you accomplish that? The new person claiming leadership over the *Deadly Gray* seniors is having a field day. With arrogant disdain for the U.S. Government, he or she is openly stuffing it up our nose with confident hubris."

The Director of the NSA answered, "Sir, NSA provides foreign signals intelligence to our nation's policymakers and military forces. It is the purview of the Justice Department to enforce our laws."

President Lamb said, "I didn't ask you what your mission statement was; I asked if the NSA could shut that website down. It is counter-intuitive to me that Twitter can block presidents from access to their platform, but we are unable to block individuals from a corrupt site. "

"Sir, you may not know that Tor, the largest dark web browser, was developed at the U.S. Naval Research Laboratory with the Defense Advanced Research Projects Agency. It is financially supported by the State Department, the National Science Foundation and Princeton University, among others. Blocking the dark web is almost impossible, by design. It was invented as a secure, anonymous, unblockable way to get information into and out of totalitarian countries that try to censor the Internet. By the way, a disproportionate number of Tor users are in Iran. To try to remove all the nodes would be like trying to shut down all the servers of the regular internet. In fact, the dark web is larger than the light web.

"However, if you control a web site's content, it's relatively trivial to cause the user's browser to reveal their true IP address."

"If you so direct me, I can flood the specific website so that it is overwhelmed and can't manage the volume of contacts."

POTUS said, "You are so instructed. Don't let me down."

After POTUS terminated the connection with the Director of the NSA, he asked the Press Secretary to enter the Oval Office. Lamb said, "The mainstream media are obviously vaccinated with stupid. All of them, bar none, whether TV, radio, newspapers, podcasters, and our friends in the social media ran and reran this anarchist's post. He might just have well run an ad on prime-time TV or during the Super Bowl; they just helped him recruit seniors into his *Deadly Gray* program. There will be a plethora of new crimes including assassinations and outright murders. In your next press meeting, tell the corps just that. I must say, without the first amendment, we would not know who had chicken noodle soup for brains."

◆ ◆ ◆ ◆ ◆

June 2, 2024
Sioux Falls, South Dakota

Judge Xavier Peabody was serving his 33rd year presiding over civil and criminal cases brought before the court. He had a reputation for being moody and inconsistent with his verdicts. Sometimes he was lenient, sometimes brutal. If you were the defendant, you prayed that he was in a good mood when you stood before him.

In 1998, Truman Reich, a dependable truck driver, sat in one of the courthouse's benches as an observer of the trial of a 19-year-old young man charged with the manslaughter of his mother. It was the young man's second DUI in 18 months. The jury found him guilty, but Judge Peabody gave him the minimum sentence of one year in prison commuted after six months. Of course, it helped that the criminal was the nephew of the Sioux Falls mayor.

Truman wrote the judge five times pleading his case that his mother was worth more than a sentence of just six months in prison. Especially in view that the guilty man was arrested by police for a third DUI six weeks after his release from prison. But his plea fell on deaf ears.

The judge left the courthouse around 4:30 p.m. and got into his Lexus to drive to his home like he did every working day. He pulled up to a stoplight and thought, "*I catch this damned light red nine out of ten times.*" He waited for the light to finally turn green, accelerated, and ……. that was Judge Xavier Peabody's last moment alive.

A Mack Heavy Dump Truck full of gravel hit Peabody traveling at 35 miles per hour. The 25-ton payload crushed the Lexus as if were made of cardboard. Police at the scene took photos of the accident and brought Truman Reich to the station and charged him with reckless driving.

Truman thought, *Maybe I'll get a lenient judge. After all, I'm just another passenger on the Deadly Gray justice warrior train.*

Chapter 28

June 3, 2024
San Antonio, Texas

Though he'd been to America many times, this was Daniel Edelman's first trip to Texas. He was a history nut and couldn't wait to see the Alamo. He was shocked—it was so small. He had a Walt Disney/Fess Parker image of the Alamo as a much larger fort.

He saw Sonja McLeod Vincente stroll up the street with a man he assumed was his CIA counterpart and another man who was the largest Hispanic guy he'd ever seen. He rightly concluded that the man was the person referred to as 'Tank'—it was no wonder.

Edelman greeted Sonja with a peck on the cheek and said, "My dear, you look wonderful; being a mother looks good on you. We miss you terribly. No one can possibly fill your shoes."

"Thank you, Daniel, you haven't aged a day since I last saw you. Let me introduce you to my colleagues. First, this is Jorge Alvarez, better known as Tank."

Daniel said, "An apropos name for you Mr. Alvarez. I intuitively want you on my side for whatever we're here to do."

Sonja said, "And this is …"

Daniel interrupted, "I don't need to know the name he uses today; I know who he is, what he's done, his expertise, and what he had for lunch."

The CIA man said, "I haven't had lunch yet today. Even the Mossad can't predict what I will have for lunch in the future."

Daniel said, "You had a shrimp creole for lunch yesterday at Fridays in Dulles Airport."

The CIA man said, "And do you want me to tell you what I learned about you?"

Tank who wore tight jeans, a large belt buckle, and a 'T-shirt' with "White Knights" printed on it said, "If you two lovers quit bantering and comparing the size of your body parts, I'd like to discuss our proposed mission—should you decide to accept it."

Both men looked up at Tank and decided that they will enjoy collaborating with him. Sonja read the body language of the men and just smiled. She said, "I've secured an abandoned laundromat for our discussion—power is on, and Tank has swept it for bugs. There's one table and four chairs."

"A laundromat?"

Sonja. "At this unused laundromat, no one will overhear our discussion. And by the way, I can predict what you'll have for lunch. I've ordered Chinese food to be delivered. I don't trust a Mexican food delivery person in view of our mission. You just never know. Here is the address. Let's split up and reconvene in 90 minutes."

Tank and Sonja went one way, the CIA man another, and the Mossad agent a third. Sonja asked of Tank as they walked down the street, "Do you have a plan?"

Tank said, "Are you looking to me for a plan when two of the best intelligence agencies in the world are with us?"

Sonja said, "I know inside that huge skull is a brain somewhere, so, yes. The other two will supply the resources to execute your plan."

Tank said, "I have the framework of a plan. Maybe our friends will turn the dull edge of an idea into a scalpel."

◆　◆　◆　◆　◆

Tank's phone rang; it was Tony Vinci. Tank said, "What's up little man?"

Tony said, "You know I'd take offense at that comment coming from anybody else, but you probably say that to New England Patriot defensive linemen.

"I have good news and bad news for you."

"I'll take the bad news first."

"Abdalhamid Mafi, the man you're chasing is not in Mexico working with a drug cartel."

Tank said, "How do you know that?"

"Because the good news is he's been spotted in Los Angeles. You know I'm tied into almost all municipal video cameras in the country. I have good relationships with the contractors who install the cameras and the municipalities that operate them. I previously spread his photo around and though he has shaved his beard and lost some weight, our facial recognition software positively identified him. I'll send you a copy of the video that captured him."

"You know, Tony, you might have just saved our lives. I didn't want to go into cartel country."

Tony said, "At least you look Hispanic, Sonja on the other hand is very blond. Not too many of those down there; at least natural blonds."

"Tony, where in L.A. should I look for this guy."

"He visits or stays in a homeless encampment in Santa Monica."

Tank said, "Wonderful, a petri dish of human folly. A genuine treasure trove of LSD lovers. Thanks again, Tony we obviously had bad intelligence."

Tony said, "I didn't say he wasn't, at one time, involved with a Mexican drug cartel. Don't forget, he's been on the run for seven years."

Tank said, "This guy is definitely a survivor, a tormented contortionist from looking over his shoulder 24/7."

Tony said, "He's bound to be a little complacent by now after all these years. Maybe he won't see you coming."

Tank said, "I don't blend in well in a crowd."

June 3, 2024
San Antonio, Texas

The abandoned laundromat still had a musty, dirty clothes smell to it coupled with the odor of stagnant water somewhere in the building. Though the electricity was on, the air conditioner did not work. It was late spring in southern Texas. A hot smelly old building was a formula for a short meeting. The CIA man was first to enter the structure, followed by Tank and Sonja with

Daniel arriving a few minutes later. All four found the location most unpleasant but perfect for a clandestine meeting.

Tank said, "Before we get started, watch this video on my laptop screen." They did.

Tank said, "Scratch what we planned to do in Mexico."

Sonja said, "I guess someone will have to go undercover at the homeless encampment to spot Mafi."

Tank said, "I've never been successful at undercover work; I'm too damned big and stick out like a sore thumb. Sonja, you would be good undercover person."

"Not doing it. I'd have to constantly fight off the lechers. After I beat up the first aggressive druggie, they'd all know I was a plant."

Daniel said, "My thick Jewish accent disqualifies me as a local person, but we can find someone within Mossad to fill the role."

The CIA agent said, "I'll do it; I enjoy undercover work. It's a lot like acting, role playing. And I'd love to be the guy that captures this prick."

Daniel said, "I bet somebody's therapist knows all about you."

Tank said, "OK, let's meet at the Santa Monica pier in 48 hours. If everyone agrees, let's get the hell out of this smelly place."

Sonja said, "Wait, what am I supposed to do with the Chinese take-out food?"

Tank said, "Let's give it to the San Antonio homeless."

♦ ♦ ♦ ♦ ♦

June 3, 2024
New York City, New York

The *Fox Business News* anchor said to the viewing audience, "Wall Street does not seem to be concerned with the exponential increase in vigilantism by our seniors. It has not affected the financial ecosystem. In fact, the markets have increased in value over the last three or four weeks and is approaching all-time highs. What are we to conclude from this?

"We think investors don't care because the *Deadly Gray* rid us of criminals who do not contribute to consumer consumption; in fact, they are a negative factor.

"We also believe, based on our limited polling, that investors think, maybe, U.S. policies and funding allocations may benefit from the *Deadly Gray* movement. Seniors are putting us in the green by waking up the wokers."

♦ ♦ ♦ ♦ ♦

June 3, 2024
Manassas, Virginia

Special Agent Rusty Winemiller assessed the data presented to him and contemplated what to do with it. He knows Director Naylor will kick his ass when he learns about it. He suspects O'Connor wouldn't know what to do with it. And he fears Star would share the information with her support team which in turn would put even greater pressure on him. From Winemiller's perspective, the data was scary as hell: *Deadly Gray* vigilantism is now beyond the control of either the Government, law enforcement, or the movement leadership.

Winemiller thought, *The movement has become a monster. It's a fatal contagious plague; a pandemic of mental dysfunction at warp speed, and acts that violate the premise of space time continuum.*

CNN covered the subject at the top of the hour with fear resonating in the voice of the reporter:

The number of violent crimes for the month of May 2024 was the highest in recorded history at 502 violent crimes per 100,000 people.

In 2020, a record 17,815 homicides were committed in the United States alone. In 2024, at the current rate, the U.S. is on course to exceed 20,000 homicides. Most of the increase in the murder rate is attributed to the senior demographic over the age of 65.

Winemiller was startled when someone knocked on his door. "Come in, it's open."

Chris O'Connor opened the door tentatively and said, "Have you got a moment?"

"Yes, Chris, but you should have called, first."

"Sorry, but I wanted to show you something I didn't feel comfortable discussing over the phone. Agent Cherokee pointed this out to me. Look at this.

"A 71-year-old woman with breast cancer killed her ex-husband with a small caliber pistol. They were divorced for 27 years. In another case, a 67-year-old man with a serious heart condition murdered his former boss who he learned had an affair with his wife twenty years ago. A third case involved an 82-year-old man with prostate cancer who killed a fellow poker player with a tile knife for cheating. He had submitted a complaint to the local police department without department movement on the case. A fourth case…."

"Stop, what is you point?"

O'Connor said, "The point is, the algorithm prepared for Star by her band of geniuses predicted each of these crimes. I'm uncertain what to do with this information."

Winemiller said, "How many other crimes are predicted but not yet committed?"

O'Connor said, "721. We could save lives if we mobilized a team and contacted each senior on the list."

Winemiller said, "Hmmm, small keys open big doors. This key could sure open some doors for us and make us look a little better in the eyes of the public; I think, though I'm unsure. Maybe the public doesn't want us to catch the *Deadly Gray* vigilantes. Maybe most people are rooting for the commander of the senior army."

O'Connor said, "I fear that they are mad at us for not finding him or her. I know Naylor and POTUS are pissed that he's still out there. At least the website is non-functional at this time, thanks to the NSA."

Winemiller said, "If I were not already in a wheelchair, I would be in one after President Lamb got through with me. He held me personally responsible for not shutting down the dark *Deadly Gray* website. Nothing I said placated him; no explanation satisfied him. I just took it on the chin or rather in my 'O-ring'."

♦ ♦ ♦ ♦ ♦

June 3, 2024
Mount Vernon, Virginia

The cleaning company Star hired did a fantastic job of spit-shining the floors, detailing the windows, and leaving the house 'spic and span.' A catering company professionally displayed the meal which stayed warm in Bunsen burner heated stainless steel trays.

The doorbell rang a little earlier than she expected; she hadn't finished dressing or applying her makeup. She went to the door with Ram by her side and looked through the viewer before opening the door for her mother and father. She said, "I'm sure glad it is you. I was afraid the Attorney General would arrive first. I would have no idea how to keep him entertained until you showed up."

Maya kissed Star while keeping an overly rambunctious and happy Ram from jumping up onto her outfit. Tucker said, "You've done a good job of making this place homey and not stuffy like the first time we were here. Hi Ram."

Ram slobbered all over Tucker. Then he suddenly stopped waging his tail and growled. Tucker said, "Our guests must be here. Good, Good." Ram's tail started wagging again.

Tucker opened the door and said, "Honorable Gannon, good to see you. I thought you were going to bring your wife, is she OK?"

"I've had so many threats against me and my family that I have them safely tucked away. I brought my government provided personal security team with me. They'll stay outside, front and back, if that is OK with your daughter."

Tucker said, "Please, have a seat. I prefer to sit on the back porch overlooking the Potomac if it's not too warm for you. Maya and Star will be out soon. I've poured a glass of Glenlivet for you."

Gannon smiled and said, "You are a gracious host. The idea to meet here at your daughter's home was a great idea. Local to me, no one will see us together, and we can talk in private."

Tucker said, "Is it OK for my daughter, Star, to join in on our conversation? I know that ultimately she works for you but she's far down the Justice Department food chain, and is discreet; she is not a threat to secrecy."

AG Gannon said, "She used to listen to conversations in the Oval Office and War Room as Assistant Press Secretary, so I suspect she can keep secrets."

Maya and Star walked onto the back deck. Gannon started to stand but Maya said, "Please, we love your chivalry but there is no need to stand. Arthur Gannon, meet Star Cherokee."

Star stuck her hand out to shake his and he leaned over and kissed it and said to Tucker, "It is totally unfair that you could have two beautiful and brilliant ladies in your family. It is my pleasure, Star, to meet you."

Star said, "Thank you. I've ordered food catered for us; I hope you enjoy it."

They all fixed their plates and returned to the back deck. Tucker asked the AG, "Are any of the threats on your life from people you know or are they all anonymous?"

Gannon looked at him curiously and said, "Why do you ask?"

"As you know, I have a couple of geniuses on my staff at Entropy Entrepreneurs. I asked them to build an algorithm to determine who might be the next *Deadly Gray* victim or the next vigilante. Your name popped up on the algorithm as a potential victim. So, I was wondering if any of your threats were from your past, or if the algorithm is flawed."

Gannon's face expressed anger as he said, "Who is the *Deadly Gray* vigilante determined by your algorithm?"

Tucker said, "An old man named Egor Chase; ring a bell?"

Star read Gannon's thoughts: *Him again.*

"I was a young prosecuting attorney in Toledo, Ohio. The parents of a 9-year-old little boy accused Egor of pedophilia. I went after him vigorously, with hate in my heart, and with the tenacity necessary to put him away for a long time. The jury gave him 30 years. He always maintained his innocence, but the jury didn't buy it. He wrote me hate mail while imprisoned and claimed his inmates continuously raped him because he was guilty of pedophilia. He blamed me for all his misery and threatened me often for over 20 years. He finally was released by the courts on good behavior.

"He's been out for 15 years but still sends me threatening hate mail. So, based on your algorithm, I assume he is ill. What's he got?"

Tucker looked at Star and she said, "He has a brain tumor and has maybe three months."

Gannon said, "Guess it's a good thing I have my security with me at all times."

Star said, "SAC O'Connor sent an FBI agent to his last known location to interview him. It did not go well, and they arrested him as a parole violation to threaten the United States AG. He's incarcerated again. I expect he'll die in prison."

Attorney General Gannon said, "Why are you sharing all of this with me instead of addressing the issues intended at this meeting?"

Tucker said, "Because we wanted you to be aware that at least one of the threats against you is real and of the power of this algorithm."

Star read the AG's thoughts: *Why am I hearing about this from you instead of the FBI Director?*

Maya said in a soothing gentle voice, "Mr. Gannon, we are concerned for your well-being, our hearts are in the right place. May I refresh your drink?"

Gannon nodded and said, "I need it after this conversation."

Tucker said, "Let's get down and discuss what you came here for."

Gannon said, "I'm not sure my heart can take what I fear you are going to tell me."

Tucker said, "The current leadership within the FBI is clean but unable to avoid their association with past corruption. Trust in the FBI is at an all-time low. To regain that trust, you need to prosecute past leadership for corruption."

Gannon said, "I fear that will cause a media circus and make things worse."

Tucker said, "You have judges that do not follow the Constitution because they are influenced by their ideological predisposition instead of the law."

Maya brought Gannon his scotch and said, "Predispositions contaminates an open mind."

Tucker went on and said, "You have other judges that preside over suits in which they have a conflict of interest. I prepared a spreadsheet for you with names."

Gannon thought, *I'll have to speak with the president to figure out what to do with this information.*

Ram growled as one of Gannon's security guards moved closer to the back deck. Star said, "Good, good." Ram heeled and laid next to Star.

AG Gannon said, "Back to the algorithm, how do you think we should use this to bring the senior movement under control?"

Tucker looked over to Star and she said, "You or we at the FBI have a chance to save lives and prevent crimes before they happen. We know the victim and the senior who will commit the crime. We just don't know when and how."

Maya added, "We can't play GOD and decide which life is worth saving, but we can save a wronged senior from spending his or her final days in jail."

Gannon said, "Why do I feel like I'm at a railroad crossing, the barrier failed to drop, and I'm about to be hit broadside by a fast-moving freight train?"

PART THREE

Chapter 29

June 4, 2024
Santa Monica, California

The four amigos met at the entrance to the Santa Monica Pier and shuffled onto the beach without speaking to each other. It was another beautiful sunny day in paradise as they strolled south while the wind sprayed salt water from the Pacific Ocean onto the sides of their faces. Tank's 310-pound frame made it difficult for him to keep up with the other three on the walk because he sunk deep into the sand and left large impressions that could reinforce the legend of 'Big Foot'.

The unnamed CIA man said, "I set up a camera at the homeless encampment that streams to my cell phone. I check it constantly, but so far, no dice in finding Mafi."

Tank said, "I've assigned three White Knights to troll the area and keep their eyes open. All three are experienced undercover officers; it's unlikely they'll even be noticed."

Daniel, the Mossad agent said, "I have a small armory in the trunk of my car just in case we need weapons. My concern is that Mafi has assembled a gang and is not operating alone."

The three men looked at Sonja for her input. She shrugged her shoulders and said, "I brought my sniper rifle."

All three men laughed. Tank said, "If Abe Mafi shows, he's in deep shit."

They walked the beach for a few more minutes, returned to the pier, and started toward the amusement rides when Tank's phone rang. "Yes."

One of the White Knights at the encampment said, "Got him. We'll switch off tailing him until your CIA friend gets here."

Tank hung up and said, "We're up at bat. Let's take Daniel's car. Sonja, can you set up a blind in case he runs? Don't kill him, though, we need to interrogate him."

Sonja nodded her head and left to drive separately to an area near the homeless encampment.

The CIA undercover agent said, "Daniel, drop me off two blocks away so I can slide into the cesspool of humanity. Tank, how will I recognize your men?"

Tank said, "Actually, one of them is a woman but they have photographs of you. They'll contact you."

Abdalhamid Mafi, the man accused by his fellow Iranians to be the real Las Vegas shooter, was of average height but underweight and carried with him a large nose. His intelligent eyes shifted constantly, and he walked with a slight limp.

Another of the White Knight undercover officer's called Tank and said, "He is a social animal, friends with many of the encampment occupants. My observation is that he is the unofficial homeless encampment sheriff. I talked to an occupant, and he informed me that if someone in the camp stole from another person in the camp, or got violent with a pathetic homeless resident, Mafi steps in and ends the altercation—usually with greater violence than the conflict warrants. Nobody messes with Mafi. Mafi recruits homeless U.S. military veterans and uses them as backups. To all in the camp, he claims to be a refugee from the country of Uzbekistan."

The CIA man wore cut-off jeans, a holey Grateful Dead tee-shirt, sandals, a Dodgers ball cap, and a pair of cheap dime store sunglasses. His hair was muffed up and unruly, his face dirty, and he walked slightly bent over. He was shocked when he was greeted with a hug from a homeless black woman. She said, "He's 25 feet to your right talking to a man in a wheelchair. He goes by the name of Rustam. How do you want to play this?"

The CIA man hugged her back and said, "Audrey, it's so good to see you. I had hoped you graduated out of here by now." He pretended to kiss her ear when he said, "Corner him, I'll go up to him, introduce myself as new to the encampment, ask him for advice, shake his hand, and slap handcuffs on him. He'll go violent, you and your friends, hit him from behind until he goes down."

She nodded, left, and corralled her two White Knight partners. The CIA guy waited until he was sure they had coordinated before he walked up to Abdalhamid Mafi, or rather his alias, Rustam, and said, "Mr. Rustam, I'm sorry for interrupting your conversation with this gentleman but.......Rustam hit the CIA man with a pair of brass knuckles in his right hand before he could finish his sentence. The hit was sudden and shockingly powerful coming from an underweight man. The CIA man hit the deck and Rustam ran.

The three White Knights were equally surprised by the unexpected explosion of violence. The White Knights chased after him but missed the starting gun. One of the White Knights pulled a gun and yelled, "Stop right there or I'll shoot." Rustam didn't stop and the officer didn't shoot—too many people in the crowd. The other two White Knights chased the Iranian, but he had the advantage—he knew the area and the encampment layout. One of the White Knights notified Tank, "He's running."

Daniel was with Tank and headed to his car truck to pull out whatever weapon he thought he needed. Tank spoke to Sonja on comms and said, "He's running. Can you see him?"

She said, "Not yet."

Despite his limp, Rustam, i.e., Mafi, was fast and clever—he predicted this day would come, but he always thought it would be the Iranian Revolutionary Army that would find him. He parked a motorcycle not more than one-quarter of a mile away. He was sure he could make it to the bike before the clowns who chased him caught up with him. He also had a gun of his own if he needed to use it.

He reached his stolen 250cc Yamaha bike, unlocked the chain, started it up and just as he was gaining speed, he fell hard. His head hit the pavement at 15 miles per hour, the bike collapsed on him, and his elbow dug into the asphalt. He tried to stand up, but for some reason couldn't. He wondered if his leg was broken or even more seriously fucked up.

Four people stood over him before he could stand. Rustam reached for his gun, but a size 13 combat boot caught him in the face before he could reach it.

When Rustam woke up, he stared at a huge man he'd not seen at the homeless camp. Tank said, "Welcome back to hell, Abe."

Mafi looked around and saw three other people staring down at him. He tried to move but couldn't; he was strapped to a chair. Mafi looked at his captives and said, "You are not IRGC. You are not LAPD. Who are you?"

Tank said, "And you are not Rustam, an Uzbekistani refugee. You are Abdalhamid Mafi, an IRGC deserter.

"We both know what will happen to you if we turn you over to the IRGC. What you don't know is what will happen to you if we turn you over to my friend, here, Daniel of the Mossad or maybe to the man you attacked in the encampment. Have you ever heard of CIA interrogation techniques?

"But fortunately for you, you may only have to deal with me. That is, if you answer my questions honestly. If you do not, well, you'll have to deal with the lady standing next to me. She shot your motorcycle out from under you. She could have easily placed a round through your heart instead. Keep that in mind before you decide to lie to me. Don't let us down. Are we clear?"

Mafi nodded his head.

"My friend Daniel here has injected you with something I can't pronounce. You will tell the truth; you, chemically, have no choice."

The CIA guy said, "We will videotape the interrogation. But before I turn it on, I want you to know that I am waiting for Tank to give me the nod and reciprocate that sucker punch you delivered to me."

Tank said, "First question to you Abe is why are you AWOL with the IRGC? Why do they hunt for you?"

Mafi said, "I was betrayed, set up for a fall, so I ran."

"Why you?"

Mafi said, "A matter of convenience, I was in the wrong place at the wrong time."

Sonja asked, "You mean in Paddock's hotel room at the Mandalay Bay Resort and Casino?"

Mafi said, "Who are you again?"

Sonja said, "I'm the one who shot your Yamaha instead of you. I would have preferred to shoot you, but I had instructions from this big guy here to keep you alive."

The CIA man said, "Answer the lady's question, were you in Paddock's room during the massacre?"

Mafi said, "That wasn't her question, but yes, I was there."

Tank asked, "Did you shoot out of the Mandalay Bay Resort and Casino window at civilians attending the country music festival?"

"No."

The CIA man said, "Your partners in crime at the IRGC say you did; that you lost control and killed as many infidels as possible in a fit of rage."

Tank added, "And murdered Paddock."

Mafi said, "I want a lawyer. This is the American way, right?"

Daniel laughed and said, "OK, we'll take you to Tel Aviv and give you an Israel lawyer?"

The CIA man managed to get his laughter under control and said, "Under the Antiterrorism Act, you are not granted an attorney. You are a mass murderer with fundamentally no rights."

Tank said, "Worse than that, you probably won't live that long, anyway. I personally may break your fucking neck if you don't answer questions honestly."

Daniel said, "Iranians invented Torture back in the sixth century. But we at Mossad have studied the methods used by Persians over centuries and improved on them. I suggest you answer Tank's questions honestly."

Tank said, "Abe, you speak exceptionally good English. I assume you mastered the language over the past six plus years. Did you shoot out of the Mandalay Bay Resort and Casino window at civilians attending the country music festival?"

"Yes and No."

Tank said, "OK, tell us what really happened."

"Yes, I shot out the window, but I shot into the air, not at the concert goers."

Tank said, "We're listening."

Mafi said, "I was supposed to be a distraction while a sniper killed two American private investigators working undercover for the ATF. It was Paddock who shot into the crowd, and I killed him."

Tank asked, "And his motive was?"

"Money and lots of it. The Saudi Prince contracted him to kill Americans at the concert. The Prince's plan was for the massacre to be blamed on Iran which would drive the United States to declare war on Iran. My own countrymen believed it was me who killed all those people, but U.S. law enforcement pinned it on the right guy, Paddock. Iran paid off Americans to cover it up because even the Ayatollah believed that we were guilty.

"I didn't do it. And to make things worse, because I killed Paddock, the Prince never had to pay him so there is no evidence or record of payments. In your language I think the expression is, 'I was fucked'."

Tank looked over at Sonja and asked, "would you mind getting Jimmy on the line for me while I ask Abe another question?"

Sonja said, "Sure, but he might stress out when he hears it is me."

Tank said, "Abe, why did Paddock have so many weapons in his room? With all the ammunition he had, he didn't need all those weapons."

"Paddock was going to sell them to us."

Tank asked, "What happened?"

"The private investigators happened. We were compromised; there was no way we were going to get the weapons out the hotel without being noticed. So, we, the IRGC, went into Plan B, eliminate the PIs. We never knew the Saudi Prince was about to put us in checkmate."

Sonja said, "Jimmy's on the line."

While Tank was on the phone, the CIA guy asked, "Mr. Mafi, did you learn that the IRGC betrayed you and then you ran. Or did you run which convinced the IRGC that you betrayed them?"

Mafi said, "I ran first but contacted IRGC leaders to tell them I was innocent, but it was too late. They decided I was a perfect scapegoat."

Tank said, "OK, I'm back. Abe let's say the chemicals in your bloodstream are working and your answers are honest. Maybe, just maybe, the U.S. puts you in witness protection, would you be willing to share with us Iran's overall terrorist plans for America?"

Mafi said, "I suspect, but do not know that they have either killed or imprisoned my immediate family. If you can get them out or tell me their fate, I would be willing to share what I know to be true almost seven years ago."

Daniel asked, "And what is the plan for Israel?"

Mafi said, "I'll share with you what I knew back in 2017."

Jimmy Ma called back. "This is your follow-the-money guru. The two private investigators from Chicago were not on the payroll of the ATF, they were on the payroll of the CIA."

Tank thought about the CIA man, *Some people are such treasures, you just want to bury them.* Tank looked over at the CIA man and said, "We need to talk."

◆ ◆ ◆ ◆ ◆

June 4, 2024
El Paso, Texas

"Another fucking photo op; just what we need from the losers in Washington," said retired Border Patrol agent Mack Dubois as he peered through his binoculars.

His friend and roommate at the local senior living center said, "Those pathetic gender vigilantes in Washington need to spend more time protecting the border and less time applying artificial stupidity to get re-elected. Is this the guy you want to waste a bullet on, or do you want to wait for a bigger fish?"

Mack said, "We won't be able to get close enough to the big fish, I'm not that good a shot. Besides, this pariah is a cabinet member, a reptile of the DC swamp, and part of the problem; he'll do."

Mack's friend said, "He won't be here long, so, if we're going to do it, we need to act soon. "

Mack said, "You don't have to join me on this. It's my family I'm doing this for. My Dad fought in World War II to protect the borders of European countries, I fought in Iraq to protect the border of Kuwait, and my son died right here protecting our border from invading Mexican mules. Now, the dragon-breath, woke elite, Rockefeller worshiping, deep state assholes with altered inbred DNA are running our taxed-to-oblivion country with open borders.

"I can't stand it; we must send them some sort of message instead of timidly allowing ourselves to be led by the rings in our noses."

"We've been through this before, Mack, I'm not cowering down and letting you get all the glory while my rotting bag of bones sits in an old people's home and some bleeding-heart nurse brings me a bedpan. Not going to happen—I want us to go out like Butch Cassidy and the Sundance Kid."

Mack asked, "What's rarer than an honest politician?"

"I dunno."

"Me either – you ready."

June 4, 2024
London, England

Bernard Nazareth said, "Don't you just love technology? I can see you, Sonja, in Missouri and you, Star, in Virginia while I'm way over here in the UK. This is bloody cheeky."

Star said, "Good to see you again, Bernie, I understand you are somehow tied in with Scotland Yard to deal with the United Kingdom's version of the *Deadly Gray*."

Bernard said, "Yes, I hope you can share with me what the U.S. is doing and maybe we can learn from it."

Sonja said, "Star, I've been thinking about this a little bit since Bernie's last call. What do you think about asking the algorithm team to build Scotland Yard a British model of the one built at Tucker's instructions?"

Bernard asked, "An algorithm; what does it do?"

Star said, "It predicts who might be a victim of the *Deadly Gray* movement and who might be the perpetrator."

Bernard said, "My God, you have such a thing?"

Star said, "It is not public knowledge, Bernie, and it wouldn't work for you; it requires an entirely different data base. I'm not sure if the algorithm team has the bandwidth to take anything else on, but I thought we'd explore it.

Star said, "It is a good idea, Sonja, but we would have to get permission from the Justice Department, State Department, and Entropy Entrepreneurs."

Bernard said, "You mean your dad, right?"

"Yes, for Entropy; but the other two entities may take longer to get permission. You might want to get the Yard to contact Attorney General Gannon. My parents can work the State Department to see if they would agree to the plan."

Bernard asked, "How much will this cost us Brits?"

Star said, "That's above my pay grade, but my dad probably will be the last word on the subject."

Bernard said, "Thank you very much. You two may have prevented my demise. The Yard talked about throwing me into a mass grave site or using me as an undersea drone."

Star said, "I'll get my quid pro quo."

◆ ◆ ◆ ◆ ◆

June 4, 2024
Location Unknown

The self-appointed commander of the *Deadly Gray* army used a false ID on Gmail and a confiscated computer from an electronic recycling center to send a blanket email to the mainstream media outlets and on Twitter:

> "The U.S. Government made the *Deadly Gray* Justice website unusable. Their suppression of opposing views violates the First Amendment of the Constitution. There must be a price paid for the government's abuse of 'we the people.' I, hereby, encourage all *Deadly Gray* vigilantes to act, make a stand, be relentless, and make it known that even the government is not above the

law without impunity. Make a statement; let your tone-deaf congress representative and senators know about your displeasure. How many times do we have to suffer injustice while your elite policy and lawmakers live in gated communities? All we ask for is justice. We must be the gatekeepers of real America.

"We are not destined to be distraught. We will not tolerate their 'sleight of hand' approach to justice, the government's manufactured moral code, the mainstream media and social media enabling and the Department of Justice's protocol's for circumventing the legislative process.

"Go Deadly Gray."

♦ ♦ ♦ ♦ ♦

June 5-7, 2024
Multiple Locations

The Associated Press offices on 13th street in Washington, DC caught fire at 4:15 a.m. on June 5th and the Senate Hart Building on Constitution Avenue was sprayed with animal blood around 5:20 a.m. Highly radioactive cesium was discovered in the basement parking lot of the Hoover Building housing the Headquarters of the FBI, and five seniors were arrested trying to reach the Vice President's home at the Naval Observatory.

In New York City, a *The New York Times* security contractor prevented a small group of former Vietnam veterans from a New Jersey branch of the American Legion from entering the building. In the Bronx, the abandoned home of a congressperson was spray-painted with vulgar graffiti. A group of 2,300 seniors peacefully protested in front of the United Nations. Posters included: *We Don't Want to be Europe; No One World Government; Love the Country You Live In; Proud to Be an American; There is Only One Race, the Human Race;* and *Go Home if You Don't Like Us.*

In Dayton, Ohio two allegedly *Deadly Gray* vigilantes stabbed a journalist who wrote anti-second amendment editorial articles. The journalist remains in critical condition.

In Detroit, 31 abandoned structures were torched by local seniors who protested the city's spending policies and priorities. A Royal Canadian Mounted Policeman killed a 76-year-old senior farmer who attacked a man in court on trial for stealing his cattle.

Deadly Gray vigilantes attacked the Peoples Republic of China's Embassy in Washington, DC; the headquarters of Black Lives Matter in Vancouver, British Columbia, Canada; The Center for Disease Control in Atlanta; and a branch of The Environmental Protection Agency in Cincinnati, Ohio.

Around the world, there were attacks in France, India, South Korea, Argentina, South Africa, and the United Kingdom."

The Speaker of the House called the Senate Majority Leader for an emergency session of Congress. The Secretary of State conducted damage control with the Peoples Republic of China, the United Nations, and with affected friendly nations.

President Lamb went on prime-time television to make a statement to the American people: "My fellow Americans and colleagues around the world, we deeply regret the recent cowardice violence perpetrated by seniors who believe vigilantism is the way to express their grievances for whatever justice they feel is unfulfilled. One person's justice is sometimes another's injustice. The concept of rehabilitation is not embraced by all.

"Justice for a climate warrior is an injustice for a person who loses his job installing an oil pipeline. An attempt by poor United Nations countries to secure food from wealthy nations is justice for the third-world nation and an injustice to the hand-to-mouth American taxpayer who needs every penny to provide for his or her own family.

"A lenient judge is considered fair to the criminal and unfair or unjust to the victim. But vigilantism is not the solution to the perceived problems. I appeal to all of you seniors who feel compelled to act now at the end of your lives to reassess what you are doing. You helped build this country to be what it is; you may have fought for our nation to defend other nations in wars; or you may be a former law enforcement officer. Whatever your past contributions to America or in defense of the contributions of your offspring, violence as a solution is unacceptable. Please back down. Don't embarrass yourself or your children.

"I have called up the National Guard to protect high probability targets. Your children may be in the National Guard—don't put them in the position of having to confront you.

"And finally, and maybe most importantly, we hear you.

"Thank you and God Bless America."

◆ ◆ ◆ ◆ ◆

June 7, 2024
Las Vegas, Nevada

The un-named CIA man stood before Tank and said, "I've been granted authority to read you in under the condition that you sign this document."

"I don't sign documents without my lawyers buy in."

"Then I can't share with you the information you want to know about the Las Vegas massacre."

Tank said, "I can beat it out of you."

The CIA man chuckled and said, "No doubt you could, but if you do, you'll never see the CIA coming. One moment you are alive, the next you are roadkill."

"What am I signing?"

"It basically requires you to maintain absolute secrecy with the information I share with you. Any divulgence of the shared data is considered an act of treason."

Tank said, "I will not sign that. No way." I'll do without the information. Now get out of my space and if I ever see you again, it will be too soon. Adios MF."

The CIA man did not leave; he stood there for a few moments and finally said, "I did not intend to push your button, I tried to push mute. What I can tell you without your signature on this non-disclosure document is that Adam Heinz was both ATF and CIA."

Tank said, "I already know that. Tell me something I don't know."

"The CIA tried to trap the Saudi Prince in an illegal act to gain influence over him. He was suspected to have funded other assassinations and was already under an Agency microscope. We wanted to catch him so we could leverage what we know to America's benefit."

Tank said, "In other words, you wanted to extort him at will. Nice. Did innocent people have to die to make that happen?"

The CIA man said, "Tank, you totally misunderstand. There is no way we knew the massacre was going to happen. No one saw that coming."

Tank asked, "Who assassinated the two American private investigators under contract by the CIA?"

The CIA man said, "What are you talking about; they were hired by the Saudi Prince to investigate what the Iranians were planning against him?"

Tank said, "If I catch you lying to me one more time, I will break your face. I know you are trained to lie and deceive but I won't put up with it. This is the second and last time I'll ask you to leave—get out of my fucking space."

The CIA man said, "What makes you so sure I lied to you?"

Tank said, "You'll have to sign a nondisclosure agreement where you'll be guilty of treason if you violate it before I'll answer that question. Don't let the door hit you in the ass."

The CIA man left without saying another word.

Tank picked up his phone and pushed a number. Tony Vinci answered, "Hi Tank, have you solved the mystery of the century yet?"

Tank said, "I've sent you a photo of a CIA operative. Find out what you can about the slime ball. I feel like he doesn't want me to discover the truth here."

Tony said, "Gee, what a surprise, a devious CIA guy in the mix. How soon do you need it?"

Tank answered, "It's not urgent but I'd like to know what I'm dealing with before I travel down this road too much further."

Tony said, "I'm on it."

Tank received an incoming call before Tony even hung up, "Yes."

"Mr. Alvarez, this is Mike Tursky with the LVMPD, do you remember me?"

"Of course, Mike, how are you?"

Tursky said, "Sheriff Lakota is AWOL or missing; I thought you should know."

Tank asked. "Any reason to believe that foul play is involved?"

Officer Tursky said, "That is one of the reasons I called you. It could be related to your investigation into the Las Vegas massacre."

Tank asked, "What's the other reason? You said that it is one of the reasons you called me."

"He learned that you discovered he had part ownership in a hotel in Cabo San Lucas. I believe you are too close to uncovering a corruption scandal in which he is involved. He may be running, or he may be dead. Either way, you should know."

Tank asked, "How long has he been missing and is his wife at home?"

Tursky answered, "He didn't show up today for work, didn't answer his phone, and didn't respond to texts. So, he is missing for only four hours. I asked his dispatcher if she sent anyone to the home or checked the hospitals. She said yes to both and concluded no one was home, including his wife, and that he's not checked in to a hospital."

Tank said, "Thanks, Mike, let's keep the lines of communications open. You are right, it doesn't sound kosher. Something is wrong."

Tank called Jolene and asked, "Is everything OK at home?"

Jolene said, "We need to decide about Stanley; he's driving me nuts. When are you coming home?"

In the background Tank could hear Stanley say, "Too late, you are already nuts. Where are the cashews anyway?"

Tank said, "I'll come home soon. Things are coming to a head here. It is convoluted with too many players keeping too many secrets. Misdirection seems to be the name of the game."

In the background he heard Stanley yell, "Hi Tank. Have you talked to the Saudi Prince, yet? You know, he has all the answers."

Tank said to Jolene, "I wish I knew how to make that happen, even Tucker doesn't have that kind of pull."

Jolene said, "You forget, you have one more card to play before you fold your hand."

Tank said, "Ok, what card is that?"

"Maya. She knows the Prince from her days as Science Advisor to the President. Plus, the Prince has a reputation for wanting to be around beautiful western women."

Tank said, "Do you think Maya will do it; reach out to him?"

Jolene said, "All we can do is ask. Let's see if we can conference her into this call."

"Hi, Jolene."

"Maya, I've got Tank on the line from Las Vegas. I think he has a gambling problem because he never comes home anymore."

In the background, Stanley said, "The only problem with gambling is when you lose. No one has a problem when they're winning."

Tank said, "Can you send him on an errand to say, Antarctica or something?"

Maya said, "Listen, I've made an appointment I'd like to keep that starts in a few minutes. Can you call back later?"

Tank said, "Real quick. I'd like to speak to the Saudi Prince. Can you help facilitate that?"

"Will I have to see him in person?"

"No, why?"

"Because I came close to decking him the last time we met in person. He has roaming hands. But I was the ultimate diplomat and pretended like I enjoyed his touch. He'd love to hear from me, but I will never allow myself to be in his presence."

Tank said, "I just need an introduction."

Maya said, "You'll have to go to him in Riyadh or…"

Tank asked, "Or what?"

"Unless you become the excuse for him to return to Las Vegas where he can gamble."

Tank said, "Listen, I also must go; Tony is calling in with hopefully valuable information. Thanks, Maya and love you, Jolene. I'll call again later tonight."

"Yeah, Tony, what do you have?"

Tony said, "I've seen your CIA man before. He was the guy whose image I captured by nanodrone. He performed surveillance at both Colby Manion's and Adam Heinz's funerals. Your CIA man is persona non grata in Langley. He may be CIA, but he is considered a real fuckup. He works alone because no one wants to be linked with him. His name is Spencer Blessing, and he blew a mission in Guatemala for which he has not been forgiven. He needs a win badly and is riding your coattails in the investigation into the massacre as a way to regain favor in the Company. He wants you to succeed as much as you do. You ought to be able to leverage that need somehow."

Tank said, "Good work. Tell Tucker I think he should give you a raise."

"Tank, you know I'm independently wealthy and don't need this job. I don't do it for money, I do it because I love it."

Tank said, "Great, since you love your job, I have another task for you if you have the bandwidth."

"And that is?"

"Locate Moe, the smooth-talking lying Iranian who I think runs the Phoenix IRGC cell and who I should have tortured when I had a chance. Do you know where I can get sulfuric acid?"

Chapter 30

June 8, 2024
Chevy Chase, Maryland

The Secret Service increased their protection of Supreme Court Justice Randolph Atkinson and his remotely located family. Very few knew the location of the safe house in which Atkinson's wife lived. They gave both the Justice and his wife burner phones and changed them out frequently so no one could identify her location.

Contractors hired to reconstruct the burned-out parts of the Justice's home and pool shed were vetted and given special badges to be able to work in and around the mansion.

The lead Secret Service agent assigned to protect Justice Atkinson said, "Sir, are you ready? We must leave now if you're going to make your meeting on time. You know how bad and unpredictable traffic can be."

"Yes and no. Yes, I'm physically ready to leave. Yes, I know how bad traffic can be. No, I really don't want to endure the wrath I'll be subjected to in the meeting. I'm too old for this."

Forty-five minutes later, Justice Atkinson sat in the Oval Office with President Lamb and his Chief of Staff. POTUS was unusually deferential to the Justice and spoke quietly. "Your letter of resignation was as beautifully written as some of your opinions. You made a compelling argument and I respect your position. But the decision will, if fact, set a precedent for other criminals to affect judicial decisions, force other judges to flee, and reinforce the current misconception that justice is applied unfairly. It's only been ten days since your home was the target of an arsonist. Give us a little more time to find and arrest the guy who threatens you and your family."

Randolph Atkinson responded, "The angry man has not just made a threat, Mr. President, he acted on his threat. He not only set fire to my home but did the equivalent to my financial world. He stripped my bank accounts and retirement accounts. I'm ruined. I need to sell my home in Chevy Chase and retire to live with one of my children until I recover my losses. How can I concentrate on lawsuits and make important decisions when I'm in this kind of mental state? If I resign, you can pick a candidate that better fits your ideology."

POTUS said, "Your voting record is just fine, thank you. Tell you what, we explored options on your behalf before you arrived today. Depending on how much money this creep has stolen from you, we think we may be able to find money in the Treasury to cover your losses. We're investigating the legality of this option. Give us ten more days, please. It's in everyone's best interest."

"No, it is not in my ailing wife's best interest. She needs to be near me. Here is what works for me, I disappear for the next ten days. I'll come back and we'll reconvene. Deal?"

President Lamb said, "Deal. See you in ten."

The Secret Service took Justice Atkinson to the Supreme Court Building while the President asked Director Naylor who waited in the lobby for his turn in the barrel to enter the Oval Office.

POTUS said, "Naylor, have you captured the perp that set fire to Atkinson's house and stole his entire life savings? How many people can there be that were affected by the Connecticut eminent domain Supreme Court decision?"

Director Naylor answered, "We know who the affronted property owner is, and we have her in custody; her name is Minerva Garcia Martinez. Her lawyer trained her well. She has said little except that she has retained a mercenary to execute her plan to ruin Justice Atkinson. We have, thus far, not learned who the mercenary is and how he absconded with the justice's financial accounts. The lawyer wants to plea bargain; he is more reasonable than she is. She is 79 years old, her husband has passed, she is childless, and has only one item on her bucket list and that is to get even with the people who voted for the eminent domain ruling."

The Chief of Staff asked, "Do you have a plan?"

"Special Agent Winemiller thinks it would be beneficial if Agent Star Cherokee interviewed Martinez with her lawyer present. She has a good interrogation technique and an incredible track record especially with other women. It can't hurt."

POTUS asked, "And the mercenary?"

Naylor said, "We're batting zero, so far."

June 9, 2024
Las Vegas, Nevada

Tank heard the knock on his Mandalay Bay Resort and Casino room. Though an enemy doesn't usually knock, he took no chances, pulled his Sig Sauer P320, chambered a round, and yelled through the door. "Who are you?"

The CIA man said, "Tank, we need to talk."

Tank said, "No, Spencer, we don't. You need to get your head out of a dark place."

The CIA man was taken aback that Tank discovered his name and finally said, "Listen, if you know who I am, you know my history. I want to help, not throw speed bumps in front of your investigation."

Tank steamed; he quickly opened the door, grabbed the CIA man by his shirt collar, and threw him against the hotel room wall. As the CIA man slid down the wall, Tank grabbed him with one hand by the throat, lifted him so his feet did not touch the floor, and held his P320 to his head. "If you want to help, I want two things from you. One, I want you to tell me everything you know about the ugly events surrounding the Las Vegas massacre. Don't give me any shit about a non-disclosure agreement.

Spencer Blessing said as he gasped for breath, "What is the second thing you want?"

"I want you to bring me two IRGC agents who operate a cell in Phoenix."

The CIA agent began to lose consciousness with Tank's huge mitt constricting his throat. In desperation, he pulled a Beretta APX A1 out of his waistband only to have it taken by Tank.

Spencer Blessing said, "Tank, you don't have to pulverize me to get me to cooperate. I'm not your adversary. I'm with you and I agree to your terms."

Tank let go of Spencer's throat and let him drop to the floor. Tank said, "Every word you say has a 'sounds-of-lies' ring to it. Let's start with everything you know about the Las Vegas massacre. Start with who you think killed all those innocent people at the country music festival."

Blessing said, "Don't hit me or strangle me, but I honestly don't know for sure who was the trigger puller. What I can tell you is that there were multiple conflicting and simultaneous missions ongoing. The Saudi's had a mission, the Iranian's had a mission, and the United States had a mission. They overlapped and conflicted. It was a classic clusterfuck.

"The United States' mission was to catch Iran buying weapons from Paddock who needed the money to pay his gambling debts.

"Iran's mission was to kill the Saudi Prince with weapons provided by Paddock.

"The Saudi's mission was to cause a war between the United States and Iran by facilitating the massacre and blaming it on Iran.

"But the missions were compromised by double agents. The Saudi's had a mole inside the IRGC. The IRGC had a mole inside the United States Government, either the CIA, FBI, or ATF.

"Iran and the United States wanted the real reason for the massacre to be covered up; the Saudi's wanted the real reason, as they want it known, to be disclosed so that the American people would demand retribution against Iran.

"But I don't know who actually pulled the trigger, Paddock or Mafi or someone else."

Tank said, "If we are going to work as a team, bring me Moe and his sister. Here's the address in Phoenix of their terrorist cell."

Spencer asked, "How did you get this address."

Tank said, "I have my sources." He thought, *Thank GOD for Tony and Jimmy.*

Tank said, "I have an opportunity to meet with the Saudi Prince in two days. He's a gambler. Compile your questions for him while you're traveling to and from Phoenix."

Spencer asked, "Any advice you can give me about the two Iranians you want me to pick up?"

Tank said, "Don't fall for the claim Moe has diplomatic immunity. Don't fall for the innocence of his sister—she's a scorpion. Use all the force you can muster—they're well-armed."

The CIA man said, "I think I'll secure some help."

Tank said, "Good idea. You aren't nearly as dumb as you look."

June 9, 2024
Kelowna to Vancouver, British Columbia

Corey Robertson felt bored and unfulfilled; he was at the end of a phase where all he did way lay around his hideout in Kelowna, British Columbia, Canada and did nothing but think and drink. Though he enjoyed his quiet time fishing on Okanagan Lake, he grew angry every time he reminisced about the loss of his teammates and friends in Vietnam fighting the communists. He thought, *All for nothing, because of the fucking lying, dishonest, and hateful media.*

The hardboiled 76-year-old Marine sniper could stand it no longer. The *Deadly Gray* sniper who ridded the world of *The New York Times* and *The Washington Post* traitors locked his cabin down, threw his sniper rifle into his new Ping golf bag, put it in the back of his Ford Expedition and headed south. He thought, *I know I'm a head case. First stop: Vancouver. Hopefully, I'll make it to LA before the cops catch up with me.*

For hours, he tried to find the headquarters of Black Lives Matter in Vancouver until he saw a flyer pinned to a telephone pole. It read: *BLM meeting scheduled for 4:00 p.m., June 9th at Deer Lake Park.*

Corey backed his Expedition onto Cedarwood Street and waited for the crowd to build. He laid down in the back of his SUV, got into position, and conducted reconnaissance. By 4:15 p.m., roughly 30 people were roaming around a platform setup for the speakers. The first speaker didn't look like the main presenter but rather someone who was going to introduce the keynote propagandist. Corey couldn't hear what the presenter said but the lack of crowd response implied this guy wasn't his primary target.

At 4:32 p.m., the crowd got animated when a very tall, well-dressed imposing guy took to the microphone to cheers and whistles. The sniper lifted the hatchback, focused his scope, rounded a chamber into his bolt action rifle and waited for the right moment.

When the speaker lifted his arm with his fist clenched, the crowd went wild; it was Corey's signal to let it loose. He said to himself, *Fucking communist—a racist screaming racism.*

He calmly shut the hatchback, got into the driver's seat, and drove the Expedition in the direction of Richmond and ultimately to White Rock where he stopped at a local high school, pulled into an empty parking lot, and packaged his rifle back into the Ping golf bag with clubs sticking out prominently visible.

When he got to the U.S./Canadian border crossing, he displayed his passport and was allowed to continue to Seattle where his next target lived. At a motel in Ferndale, Washington he turned on the TV and listened to a newscaster say:

> In Vancouver, British Columbia, a Portland Trailblazer basketball player was shot at a Black Lives Matter rally by a sniper who was blocks away from the event. A manhunt for the killer continues. The victim was a successful American entrepreneur, a philanthropist to BLM, and an outspoken communist leader. BLM blamed a white supremacist group and rioted in downtown Vancouver where windows were broken, stores were looted, and fires were set in parked cars. The Royal Canadian Mounted Police has no comments for the viewing audience at this time.
>
> In other news…..

Corey shut the TV off.

◆ ◆ ◆ ◆ ◆

June 9, 2024
Portland, Oregon

Mayor Chappelle paced in the office of Sheriff Wingard and yelled loudly in his honking voice, "It's been five weeks since the editor of the Portland Observer's home was attacked. Are you telling me you have no leads and made no progress in identifying the bomber? What has your department been doing? Do you have your thumb stuck up your ass?"

The Sheriff of the Portland Police Bureau said, "Wasn't it you who supported the movement to defund the police? There are consequences when you pander to the Portland left."

The mayor said, "A Molotov cocktail was thrown through the picture window of the *Portland Observer* editor's home. Does not that crime climb on your priority list to the level that might capture your interest?"

"No one was hurt. Insurance covered his loss. I have more serious crimes to contend with than political crimes."

The mayor said in an exasperated tone, "If you want to get reelected, you need to pay more attention to this particular crime. Keep your foot on the pedal. You have opened the door to let the Observer roast your ass." Mayor Chappelle stormed out of the sheriff's office.

Sheriff Wingard thought, *That man loves himself to death*. He called the detective assigned to the case into his office and said, "Connie, Chappelle put more pressure on us to close the Molotov cocktail case. Any ideas as to how to proceed given that we actually know who the perp is?"

Connie answered, "It's your uncle, not mine. I've dragged my feet but why charge a guy his age and who will die soon of liver cancer? I think we should let him die of natural causes and then announce that he was the bomber after he passes. I understand he only has weeks anyway."

Wingard said, "We don't have weeks. Arrest him, no judge will incarcerate him. They'll let him out on bail, and he can go home."

Connie said, "He's a *Deadly Gray* vigilante. He'll be popular among a certain crowd. Sir, you are about to wade in troubled water. Do you think you'll be able to pick a judge?"

Wingard said, "No. We just have to be lucky."

Connie drove out to the home of the Sheriff's uncle only to find the house empty. Over the police band Connie heard: *Code 2, Proceed Immediately to Deardorf Road.*

Connie arrived ten minutes later to see a house aflame, firefighters struggling to bring it under control and Sheriff Wingard's uncle leaning against a northern red oak tree across the street from the burning house. Connie walked up to him and asked, "Mr. Wingard, this is the home of a *Portland Observer* editorial journalist. Why did you do this?"

The old man said, "There was a time when I trusted what I read in newspapers. There was a time when publishers, editors, and investigative reporters were honorable. Now, a journalist is a step down from a politician and two steps down from a used car salesman. Journalism needs a wakeup call, or should I say a wokeup call. I don't have long to live; it might as well be me to woke them up. They are Nazi derivatives. I'm a *Deadly Gray* vigilante who wants justice; the last man standing as they say."

He looked at Connie with compassion and said, "It's OK if you arrest me; it's your job."

Connie walked away, left the old man still slumped against the tree, jumped in her cruiser, and drove to the Police station. She reflected, *I hope my act of kindness does not fall under the umbrella of no good deed goes unpunished.*

June 10, 2024
New York City, New York

Headline in *The New York Post*: **Deadly Gray Senior Vigilantes Out of Control:**

Yesterday, another vigilante attack on journalist occurred again in Portland, Oregon. Our investigative reporters found that the motive for the focus on journalists to be mass disappointment in the media by seniors who have observed, in their opinion, its regression over last 50 years. Are we to ignore this trend and pretend that the vigilantes are demented people? Are we journalists deaf to the dog whistle? Who are these seniors?

Are they racists? No, thus far the crimes were committed against white people by white people.

Are they criminal by nature? No. Thus far, 95% of the Deadly Gray vigilantes had no previous criminal record.

Are they organized? Yes and No. There appears to be no relationship between Deadly Gray vigilantes. They do not know each other. However, the common thread is a dark web site that encourages seniors to commit these crimes.

Why us reporters and journalists? That is a question, we need to explore. Sixty-seven percent of Republicans have an unfavorable view of the media, and 58% say attacks on the media are justified; that justice can't be achieved without power. We need to reflect on these numbers. Are we parked in a fire lane? We are in a position to sink or swim. There is a lesson to be learned, here. It would be poetic for us to learn something about ourselves from the Deadly Gray movement.

Chapter 31

June 10, 2024
New London, Connecticut

Minerva Garcia Martinez was a stately woman of 66 years of age who carried herself with grace and dignity. She married an American plumber who grew his practice over time into a very profitable enterprise. He died of lung cancer, but his last request was to get even with the people who unfairly stole their property, paid a less than fair price for it, and did it so that they could tax the property at a higher rate. Her husband said, "We can't allow fascists to prevail." Ms. Martinez is determined to settle for nothing less than honoring her husband's last request.

She sat in a small room in the Montville Correctional Facility with her attorney and looked across the table at Star Cherokee and her protector, Ram.

Minerva asked, "Is it common for a German Shepherd to be present during an interview? He is frightening and intimidating. Please have him removed."

Star said, "Mrs. Martinez, Ram is my security blanket. Just weeks ago, he saved my life from a crazed man who wanted to kill me. Years ago, he saved my life from people who tried to kidnap me."

Minerva reminisced, *I miss my Chloe.*

Star asked, "Do you have dog? If so, who is taking care of it?"

Mrs. Martinez's personality changed to one of joy and excitement at the thought of her pet while her attorney looked at his watch. Minerva said, "Oh yes, my sister is taking care of Chloe. I miss her so much."

Star asked, "What kind of dog is she?"

"She's a Schnauzer."

Star said, "I understand they are a great breed."

The lawyer interrupted the conversation and said, "Can we get on with this interview, Agent Cherokee?"

Minerva said, "Are you part Cherokee Indian?"

"Yes."

Minerva thought, *Star is part minority and a dog lover. We have more in common than I thought.*

The attorney said, "Ladies?"

Star said, "OK. Mrs. Martinez, you hired someone to destroy the life of a Supreme Court Justice. I'm sure your attorney has advised you that you have committed a serious crime."

The attorney said, "Is there a question you want to ask?"

Minerva said, "I am fully aware of the seriousness of the charges against me. I would do it again. The Supreme Court Justices ruined our lives. This is payback."

Star asked, "Who is the mercenary you hired?"

The attorney said, "Don't answer that."

Minerva thought, *Joey Crash.*

The attorney asked, "What is in it for my client if she answers that question?"

Star said, "I am not legally able to negotiate a plea, but I will work hard to help you get a reduced sentence if she shares what she knows about him and how to find him."

Minerva thought, *I won't tell this young lady that he lives in Indianapolis.*

Star asked, "How did you learn about him and how did you pay him?"

The attorney said, "This meeting is over. Unless you get some sort of concrete bargain for Mrs. Martinez, there is no sense in continuing this interview. If you don't mind, please, take your dog and leave while I speak in private with my client."

Star said, "Thank you for your time and I hope to meet with you again, Mrs. Martinez, with the prosecuting attorney."

Star and Ram left the correctional facility, got into their rental SUV, and headed to the airport. On the way, Star used the Bluetooth feature to call Tony Vinci, "Can you get me some information on a Joey Crash from Indianapolis? He's a mercenary. See what you can find."

Tony answered, "Is he the Black Lives Matter and *The Seattle Times* journalist shooter?"

Star said, "No, what are you talking about?"

"It's all over the news and social media. The BLM sniper is the same person who took out *The New York Times* and *The Washington Post* journalists. The striations on the bullet are the same. He must have driven down from Vancouver to take out a *The Seattle Times* reporter. We have ourselves a serial *Deadly Gray* vigilante; just what we needed."

Star said, "Wonderful, just wonderful."

"Everyone, down on the floor. Down on the floor, hands behind your head. I mean now.

"We are *Deadly Gray* vigilantes; we have nothing to lose, so, do what I say."

The leader of three bank robbers wearing ski masks said, "You," as he pointed at a teller, "fill this bag with cash." She started to say something, but the leader shot her in the right shoulder before she uttered a single word. The teller screamed and fell to the floor crying and writhing in pain.

The lead thief said, "All of you now know I mean business. You," he pointed his gun at another teller, "fill these bags with cash out of the registers." She did as he instructed but not before she pushed a panic button which notified police of an on-going robbery and added a purple bomb to the bags to stain the cash.

A bank security guard hid behind an encased column, pulled his firearm, turkey-peaked to see if he had a clear shot at one of the robbers, emerged, aimed, and successfully shot a bank thief. The guard then turned his handgun on another but was too late; the guard was hit in the stomach with a 9mm round.

After shooting the guard, the third thief ran to his shot partner and pulled his ski mask off to speak and console the seriously wounded partner.

With his mask off, all could see that the one robber was not a *Deadly Gray* at all; the man bleeding out couldn't be more than 35-years-old.

The St. Louis police arrived before the teller could fill the bag with cash. The lead robber grabbed the bag and ran to the back of the bank only to discover there was no rear exit.

While he ran, the people on the floor got up and ran out the front door to safety. The security guard who was injured was down but not out and shot the lead thief in the throat.

The lone remaining robber stayed with his dead friend crying when the police entered the bank. As it turned out, none of the robbers were over 40 years of age.

Two of the three thieves died, but all bank employees and customers at the scene survived. The injured teller and guard were released from the emergency room with non-life-threatening gunshot wounds.

A new phenomenon appeared—fake *Deadly Gray* vigilantes.

♦ ♦ ♦ ♦ ♦

June 10, 2024
Silicon Valley, California

Six retired people sat at two tables pulled together in The Juke Box Diner eating breakfast. Mark said, "Did we all do our homework?"

Jim said, "I did. Here is a quote by Noam Chomsky: *"Goebbels was in favor of free speech for views he liked. So was Stalin. If you're really in favor of free speech, then you're in favor of freedom of speech for precisely the views you despise. Otherwise, you're not in favor of free speech."*

All at the table nodded their heads in support of the quote.

Mark said, "Perfect. Who's next?"

Bill said, "Mao said, *'Let a hundred flowers bloom, let a hundred schools of thought contend.'*"

Mark said, "What do you think that means?"

Bill said, "That he actually supported the concept of free speech; that he could learn from criticism by others."

Ken said, "I'll go next. Fidel Castro is quoted as saying, *'The first thing dictators do is finish free press. There is no doubt that a free press is the first enemy of a dictatorship'*."

Bill said, "At least he was honest about it."

Jim said, "We're headed toward a dictatorship because social media is finishing free press."

Robbie said, "I guess it's my turn. I have two quotes by Hitler: First he said, *"It is the press, above all, which wages a positively fanatical and slanderous struggle, tearing down everything which can be regarded as a support of national independence, cultural elevation, and the economic independence of the nation."*

Mark said, "Guess he wasn't in favor of our first amendment. What is the second quote?"

Robbie said, *"To conquer a nation, first disarm its citizens."*

All at the table squirmed at the quote. Robbie added, "That's exactly what the idiots are trying to do today in our country."

Mark said, "OK, Steve, you're up; last, but not least.

Steve smiled and said, The founder of Twitter said, *'...it also comes with a realization that freedom of expression may adversely impact other fundamental human rights, such as privacy and physical security. So, we believe that we can only serve the public conversation, we can only stand for freedom of expression if people feel safe to express themselves in the first place."*

Ken asked, "Please, Steve, translate for me."

Steve said, "He was justifying censorship."

Robbie asked, "What has the CEO of Meta Platforms said about their use of censorship?"

Mark answered, "He said 'tech giants shouldn't determine what is censored' as his company determines what is allowed and what is not—hypocritical bullshit."

Bill added, "As six of the local *Deadly Gray* vigilantes, how should we go about censoring the censors?"

Steve said, "Let's cut power to their operating facilities." Steve smiled and added, "Often."

Mark said, "They probably have standby generators."

Robbie said, "That run on fossil fuels—that's poetic justice."

All laughed. Mark said, "At least it's a framework for a plan."

Steve said, "More than a framework; I've created a detailed plan with locations of transformers, switchgear, power lines, and generator fuel tanks.

"It's a night-shift job, though. Can you guys stay awake past midnight?"

Ken said, "Hell no. Can we do it at 4:00 in the morning when I get up?"

Steve said, "That's better yet. Do we all agree on the plan and the time?"

Five yesses were heard.

Mark said, "We *Deadly Gray* vigilantes may not survive this mission but we're old and nothing goes on forever."

Steve said, "Pi does."

All laughed.

♦ ♦ ♦ ♦ ♦

June 11, 2024
El Segundo, California

Corey Robertson drove south from Seattle on Washington, Oregon, and California backroads to avoid the canvass by law enforcement on Interstate 5 looking for him. The old Vietnam sniper decided to bypass Portland and San Francisco despite his intense dislike for the Jane Fonda loving press that live there. His target was the *LA Times* opinion journalists who were the most pro-communist influencers in the country. *Someone must pay for their treason.*

When he arrived at the *LA Times* headquarters, he discovered that there were no tall buildings adjacent to the new facility, so he struggled to establish a good vantage point to set up a sniper blind and take out editors and reporters as the entered and exited the building on 2300 East Imperial Highway. He bought an *LA Times* newspaper, found a Denny's, and ate lunch while he read the rag. A couple of editorials he read made his blood boil which gave him new targets, the writers of these specific article. Now, he wanted to hunt individual reporters down rather than kill random enemies as they arrived or left the front door to the building.

Robertson pulled out his laptop while still at the restaurant, searched, and found home addresses for each of the two column writers that angered him. He thought, *One of the poor excuses for journalists lives in Torrance—not that far from here.* He used his phone GPS and drove to his first target's location. An hour later, he was set up for the shot. He waited three long and boring hours in front of the modest apartment complex until she finally showed up.

He thought, *I'm not a monster.* The female opinion journalist in Torrance had three small children.

Robertson was not about to be responsible for the creation of three orphans, so he packed up and drove to the home of the second target who lived in Huntington Park. By the time he arrived at the second reporter's condominium, it was late and getting dark. He feared the guy was already home and wouldn't come out for the rest of the night. But he waited for a couple more hours until someone knocked on his driver's side window—it was a California Highway Patrol officer.

Corey rolled down his window and said, "Hello, officer."

The young CHP said, "May I see your driver's license and registration."

"Yes, sir."

Corey reached into his glove compartment to get the registration. As he did so, Corey noticed the officer put his hand on the butt of his gun in the holster. Corey pulled his wallet out of his back pocket, opened it, and handed the officer his driver's license.

The officer went back to his cruiser to check to see if there were any outstanding warrants against the driver, Corey Robertson.

Corey thought about his options, *I could kill the cop and run but I'm not a cop killer. I could hope the cop returns, let's me go and everything will be OK, but he'll see I'm from British Columbia and inquire more about what I'm doing here. There is, no doubt, an APB out for the Vancouver and Seattle sniper. I'm too old to run and become one of those famous California car chases. I'll just stand down and hope for the best. I see no way to escape.*

The highway patrolman started to walk back to Corey's vehicle with purpose when the *Deadly Gray* sniper saw the *LA Times* reporter who he was targeting. *If I move quickly, I'll be able to run him over before he gets to the front door.*

Corey impulsively turned on the ignition and put the car in drive.

The CHP pulled his gun.

Robertson put the Expedition's pedal to the metal to run the reporter over. The reporter heard the Expedition coming, turned around to see the grill of the accelerating SUV aimed at him and dove just in time onto the trunk of nearby car. The Expedition rammed into side of the car on which the reporter jumped. The force of the crash threw the journalist onto the pavement and pushed the parked car over the top of the prostrate writer.

The reporter heard a single gunshot.

The CHP officer ended Corey Robertson's sniper rampage with a head shot. The reporter was able to slide to safety between the wheels of the parked car pushed over him. No one else was hurt.

The CHP found the sniper rifle in the Expedition, forensics matched the gun to four murders, and one *Deadly Gray* case was closed.

June 11, 2024
Harpers Ferry, West Virginia

Jimmy Ma said, "Do you see what I see? Is this possible?"

Tony answered, "The data is the data. We can't make it up. I've checked it four times."

Jimmy said, "And I followed the threads at least that many times. I even asked Suzzanne to double check our figures and she confirmed we are correct in our analysis. So, what do we do with this information?"

Tony said, "What we always do when we discover a conundrum; we call the boss. Tucker will know what to do."

Jimmy said, "He won't believe it at first and question our conclusions. We'll have to walk him through it step by step. It's not something we should do over the phone. Is he in the office today?"

Tony said, "Oh, no you don't. Don't put all this on me. I'm not going to be the source of buzzkill. He'll put me on the rack."

Jimmy said, "You always wanted to be taller anyway?"

Tony said, "You, at least, have to be on the phone when we present this information to him."

Jimmy said, "Give me some time to pour a drink."

Fifteen minutes later, Tucker called Jimmy Ma, "I understand from Tony that you two have some news for me. What is it?"

Jimmy asked, "Has Tony told you anything yet?"

"No."

Jimmy said, "We know who the commander of the *Deadly Gray* vigilante group is, who administers the dark web site, *DeadlyGrayJustice*, and who sockpuppets with the hashtag #Star."

Tucker said, "That's great, have you informed Star yet?"

"Ah, no sir. We want your advice before we do that."

Tucker said, "You two are acting very mysteriously; what gives?"

Tony blurted, "It's Rusty Winemiller."

Tucker was silent for a full 30 seconds before he said, "We damn well better be right about this."

Jimmy Ma said, "We wouldn't have come to you with this if we were not damn sure, sir. We even had Suzzanne double check our discovery."

Tony said, "Evidence matters."

More silence.

Tucker said, "Let's get Star on this call."

Tony added Star in and said, "Hold for just a second, it's a 'DEFCON 1' call."

Star said, "Nuclear War?"

Tucker said, "As far as we're concerned, it might as well be."

"Dad, you're scaring me."

Tucker said, "Your boss, Special Agent Rusty Winemiller, is the commander of the *Deadly Gray* vigilantes. He was #Steel's superior. He's #Star. He's the author of the latest plea to mobilize the *Deadly Gray* worldwide. He's responsible for the death of many vigilante targets."

Star said, "No, that can't be true. There must be a mistake."

Tony said, "We all wish it were not true. We've all known Rusty for years; he's almost family."

Jimmy said, "I would have trusted him with my life."

Tucker said, "My first thought is that you need to inform FBI Director Naylor and let him manage the situation, but he'll want proof that only Jimmy and Tony can present. Any thoughts?"

Star asked, "I trusted Rusty implicitly. Now I don't know who to trust? I can count true friends on one hand and Rusty was one of them. How well do you trust Attorney General Gannon?"

Tucker said, "Not as much as I trusted Winemiller. That idea floats like a rock."

Star asked, "Then who can we trust?"

Tucker said, "The top of the food chain, I guess. But I don't think I can get an audience with President

Lamb. The AG and Brad Naylor could but how to pull that off without sharing this information with them is another question."

Star's emotions grabbed her as she said, "No, this just can't be true. Tell me this is not true. No wonder he didn't want to have in-person meetings with me. He didn't want me to read his thoughts."

Tucker said, "I'm sorry, sweetheart. I wish I could do something to make it not true."

Tony asked, "Does Maya have access to the White House?"

Tucker said, "Not anymore."

Star tried to regain her composure and said, "I still have friends in the Press Secretary's office."

Tucker said, "A dangerous route. But Star, you just drew the short straw; we have trust Naylor.

"Jimmy and Tony, the three of us are going to DC to support Star."

Star said, "My head is exploding."

♦ ♦ ♦ ♦ ♦

June 11, 2024
Las Vegas, Nevada

The Saudi Prince owns the Four Seasons Hotels and Resorts chain which, in turn, owns floors 35-39 of the Mandalay Bay Resort and Casino. He rented the entire top floor for this visit and entered wearing a full-length loose fitting white garment with long sleeves, a mandarin collar, and traditional Saudi men's headgear. As soon as he possibly could, he disguised himself by changing into jeans, a colorful western shirt, a leather sleeveless vest, and cowboy boots and hat before he headed to the casino. It is widely known that the Prince is a gambler. In fact, he was gambling in Las Vegas the day of the massacre and left suddenly the next day.

The Prince sat in a chair made specifically for him at a Roulette Wheel placing large bets, when he noticed that two of his bodyguards were forced to block a large Hispanic man from approaching him.

Tank said loud enough for the Prince to hear, "Maya Cherokee said you would speak with me."

The Prince did not look at Tank but said, "Not now, my friend, I just got here and I'm gambling. We'll set up something later."

Two casino security men showed up and stood behind Tank concerned that he was going to make a scene. Five White Knights stood behind the casino security guards looking even more intimidating than either the casino security staff or the Prince's bodyguards.

The atmosphere grew tense.

Yet the Prince remained focused on the Roulette Wheel and not on Tank. Tank said, "I have something you want; something your billions has failed to buy."

Finally, the Prince turned around to see the 6 feet-7 inch tall, 310-pound confronter with five very tough looking men behind him. He asked, "And what would that be?"

Tank answered, "Abdalhamid Mafi."

Though the Prince said, "Who?", Tank could see in his eyes that the Prince knew exactly who Tank was talking about.

Tank said, "You know, the Iranian who claims you are responsible for the death of 59 Americans almost seven years ago. That Abdalhamid Mafi."

The Prince tried to remain calm and said, "We all know Stephen Paddock killed those people. I've heard this conspiracy theory before; now if you'll leave me be, I'll get back to my fun here."

Tank said, "So you're unaware of the mole in your organization?"

A casino security man asked the Prince, "Your Highness, is this man bothering you? Do you want us to remove him from your presence?"

One of the White Knights behind them laughed and said, "Good luck with that? You couldn't do that even if we were not here with him. You don't know who you are dealing with. But we are here and if you touch him, we'll break you like a three-legged mule."

The testosterone level rose to maximum heights.

Tank said, "What have you done with Sheriff Lakota?"

"Mr. Tank, I'm tired of your disrespectful and primitive accusations, but to remove you from my life so I can enjoy my stay here in Las Vegas I'll give you fifteen minutes in my suite on the 39th floor."

Tank suspected that his suite was occupied with armed guards and shook his head, "No." Tank looked at the lead casino security officer and asked, "Do you have a private room we could use here on this floor?"

The officer looked around and said, "Not for all of us; it can comfortably hold six or seven."

Tank said, "That should do. My guys can stay right outside the door."

The Prince nodded at the Roulette Wheel operator and said, "Be patient, I'll be back."

When the Prince and Tank were seated in the small private room, the Prince said, "Mr. Tank, what is it you want from me? I assume you are accusing me of something so I can buy you off. How much do you want?"

Tank said, "Whereas, I am not a billionaire, I am financially comfortable. I do not want your money. What I want is the truth. What role did you play in the massacre on October 1, 2017? Let me tell you what I think happened. You learned from a mole you have in the Iranian Revolutionary Guard Corp that the Iranians planned to assassinate you on one of your gambling vacations here in Las Vegas. I think you hired two American private investigators to find out where the Iranians stayed and what they were up to. I think the PIs learned that the U.S. Government conspired to entrap the Iranians in their weapons purchase mission. I think you learned that Stephen Paddock was involved in the entrapment plan, and you offered Paddock an enormous amount of money if he would defraud the Iranians and do something to bring the U.S. close to war with Iran.

"How am I doing so far?"

The Prince said, "You've read way too many John le Carré spy novels. What you've outlined is just another conspiracy theory. Are we done here?"

Tank said, "One last thing, here is a thumb drive for you to listen to at your convenience, but you should know I have already forwarded a copy to the U.S. Ambassador to Saudi Arabia, to the U.S. Director of the CIA, the head of the Iranian Revolutionary Guards, and a friend of mine with Mossad.

"You have a good gambling day, Your Highness; enjoy it while you can. I'm on the lowly seventh floor if you need me."

Tank left the room and the casino. He took his White Knight contingent out to lunch to discuss tactics and protection tools and waited for Saudi Special Security Forces, the SSF, to bang on his hotel room door.

Tank asked his lead officer, "Did you install the cameras on my floor and in my room?"

"Yes. The video feeds are available on your phone."

Tank asked, "Did you bring one of Tony's nanodrones?"

"Yes, the operator is in our van in the parking lot. It's video and audio feed are also available on your phone."

Tank asked, "Weapons?"

The White Knight said, "Everything from Tasers to RPGs."

Tank said, "I asked a LVMPD officer to join us in five minutes; we'll need law enforcement to know what's going on. So far, this officer has been trustworthy. So far."

Five minutes later, Mike Tursky walked into the restaurant and pulled up a chair to their table. He looked around the table at the cadre of Special Forces and said, "Uh, oh. Do you expect an attack from China or something or are you guys about to rob a bank?"

Tank answered, "These guys will protect me from an attack by Saudi Special Forces. It's good to counter force with force."

Tursky asked, "Why would the Saudis attack you on U.S. soil? Isn't that an act of war?"

Tank said, "Because, I think they got away with it back in 2017, I'm the new target, and I believe Las Vegas is U.S. soil.

"I asked you to join us to get you up to speed with what's going down. But before I do, what have you discovered about Chief Lakota? Has he reared his ugly head or is he still AWOL?"

"The latter. We haven't found hide nor hair of him. Now, tell me, what is going on?"

Tank said, "I confronted the Saudi Prince with accusations about his involvement in the Las Vegas massacre of 59 Americans. Of course, he denied any involvement and accused me of being a conspiracist. Before we parted, I gave him a thumb drive with this audio on it:

This is Tank Alvarez of White Knight Personal Security with Spenser Blessing. We are interviewing two prominent members in the Quds Force of the Iranian Revolutionary Guard Corps or IRGC. Our first interview is with Mohammad Fattahi.

Spencer: Moe, I understand that Tank told you who I am and what special skills I have. Is that correct?

Mohammad: Please, I will tell you everything you want to know.

Spencer: Speak up, it is difficult to hear your answers. Moe, you lied to Tank before. Why should we believe you now?

Mohammad: I am a dead man anyway. I prefer to die by a bullet than be subject to the torture I expect from IRGC or CIA or Saudi Special Forces. I'll answer your questions and then you can just shoot me, and you won't have to interrogate my sister.

Spencer: You were betrayed by someone in your Phoenix IRGC cell. That someone was paid by the Saudis. Can you elaborate or provide details of that betrayal?

Mohammad: Abdalhamid Mafi double-crossed us, approached the Saudi Prince staying at the Mandalay Bay, warned him, and presented his idea of causing war between the U.S. and Iran.

Spencer: How can you know this?

Mohammad: Because he fell in love with my sister, asked her to run away with him, and told her that he was about to come across a huge sum of money.

Spencer: Is that all the proof you have? Are you telling me that you just assumed he was getting that money from the Saudi Prince? Why didn't you or your sister stop him once you learned he was a traitor?

Mohammad: I learned only hours before the betrayal. My sister was tempted to accept his offer and waited too long to tell me.

Spencer: Money has that effect on people. Did he or Paddock kill the Americans?

Mohammad: Since both were working undercover for the Saudi Prince, I suspect they both pulled triggers, but I have no way of knowing for sure?

The microphone on the thumb drive was turned off temporarily. When it was turned back on, Tank was interrogating Mohammad's sister: Daria, your brother just ratted you out. Did you know that Mafi was a traitor?

Daria: We discussed it before this interrogation. We both know how torture works and decided to, how do you say in America, spill the beans. I never understood that phrase.

Tank: You considered running away with Mafi? Wouldn't you both violate Sharia Law?

Daria: I was tempted to run away with him, but in the end, I decided against it. I didn't want to spend the rest of my life running and hiding from the Quds, the SSF, and the CIA.

Tank: What did Mafi tell you about where the money was coming from?

Daria: He said he made a deal with the Saudis. He learned that the Prince had access to $800 billion U.S. hidden in private accounts.

Tank: As a member of the IRGC, you could lie to me just to implicate the Saudis. What proof can you provide me that you are telling the truth?

Daria: Mohammad told me you also have captured Abdal. I hope you have him in a safe place where the SSF cannot reach him. Bring him to me and you will be able to observe the truth.

Tank: I don't see how that would prove anything.

Daria: I will be able to convince him to give you the Phoenix bank account number where the Prince advanced him a down payment for the mission.

Tank: What mission?

Daria: He told Abdal that the missile fired from Yemen at Saudi Arabia sponsored by Iran needed a response. The U.S. is more powerful than Saudi

Arabia and could easily repay Iran for the attack on Saudi Arabia. The mission was to kill enough Americans to start a war.

♦ ♦ ♦ ♦ ♦

June 12, 2024
Indianapolis, Indiana

Special Agent In-Charge Chris O'Connor used the information provided to him by Star and her off-the-books special team to find the mercenary, Joey Crash, hired by Minerva Martinez to destroy the life of Supreme Court Justice Atkinson. He didn't ask where the info came from but trusted her enough to assemble a SWAT team to capture the mercenary.

The address given to him was at a middle-income home in a typical neighborhood with perfectly manicured lawns, children playing in the yards, family's washing late model cars, people playing with dogs, and barbecuing hamburgers on backyard grills. It was the last place you would expect a hardboiled mercenary to live.

It also made it very difficult to develop a take-down plan. SAC O'Connor decided to wait until dark. Before they did anything, he confirmed that Crash was, in fact, home. O'Connor had construction plans of the home and knew where the master bedroom was in the house.

At 0400, the FBI cut power to Crash's place of residence. They used an FBI crash ram on the front and back doors simultaneously. Each member of the team wore night vision goggles and carried assault rifles.

The front door SWAT team members cautiously ascended the stairs to the master bedroom while the remaining members searched and cleared downstair rooms. Two more SWAT team members stayed outside in the event Crash escaped out a window.

One SWAT team member broke the bedroom door open and threw a flash bang grenade into Joey's bedroom.

It exploded.

When the smoke cleared, O'Connor yelled, Joey Crash, put your weapons down and drop to the floor, hands out.

5.56 mm rounds spread from inside the bedroom into the bedroom door opening and through walls until Crash's first 30 round magazine emptied. Crash jammed a new magazine into his AR-15 and continued to fire where he thought the SWAT team was positioned.

The tactical gear worn by the team didn't protect all of them. Two SWAT team members were killed by Crash, but O'Connor's and two others' injuries were not fatal. Though O'Connor was hit in the leg he was able to throw a second flash bang grenade into the Crash's bedroom. This time it threw Crash against the wall and gave O'Connor time to empty his MP5.

Joey Crash never got a chance to cash his check from Martinez.

June 13, 2024
Las Vegas, Nevada

Tank was not in his hotel room when he observed on his phone the video of three men walking down his hotel hallway wearing long robes intended to hide their weapons.

Tank said to his five White Knights, "Ok guys, it's time to move." They left the van parked in the Mandalay Bay Resort and Casino parking lot and entered the casino, walked to a private room on the second floor guarded by two Saudi Special Forces operatives.

Tank said, "Tell the Prince I want to speak with him."

They hesitated.

Tank said, "You're outnumbered and will be overpowered since you sent three of your buddies up to my room. Now tell your master I'm here."

One of the guards reached for his radio to call the three guards on Tank's floor when Tank grabbed it from him, and two White Knights restrained the Saudi guard.

Tank said, "OK, I'll just open the door myself."

The Saudi Prince was the lone gambler at the Roulette table when Tank entered the room. The Prince said, "I sent men to ask you to come down and speak with me. You didn't have to force your way in."

"Yeah, armed to the teeth. Listen, if you kill me, I can't stop the delivery of the recording I sent to the people I mentioned earlier. It's in your best interest to keep me alive."

The Saudi Prince said, "What do you want from me to stop the delivery of the lies told by Iranians? Why do you trust them and not me?"

Tank said, "I don't trust them anymore than I trust you. What I want is the truth. If you admit that you were behind the massacre of 59 Americans and the injury of many more, I'll stop the delivery on the audio MP3s to each person on my list."

The Prince asked the Roulette operator to leave the room. When the Prince was alone with Tank he said, "Yes, I admit that I tried to drive another wedge between the U.S. and Iran. I hoped that the U.S. would tactically eliminate Iran's leadership and with Israel maybe even destroy their nuclear centrifuges. However, I did not authorize the random killing and injuring of innocent people attending the music festival. That, my friend, is the truth."

Tank said, "First of all, I'm not your friend. Secondly, what was your plan to drive that wedge if it wasn't to kill Americans so you could pin the deaths on Iran?"

The Prince looked down at his feet as he said, "I left that up to Paddock and Mafi. They chose the method; I just gave them instructions as to the goal."

Tank said, "It didn't work. It was pinned on an American. What happened?"

The Prince said, "The CIA happened. Sheriff Lakota happened. ATF Heinz happened. The CIA knew it was an Iranian that killed the Americans and decided to cover it up and blame it entirely on Stephen Paddock. The fact is, I think it was Paddock; I don't know for sure. I wasn't there. Mafi killed Paddock, so he is the only one that knows for sure which of them or if both were involved."

Tank asked, "What will your father, the King, do if he discovers that you were the instigator of the massacre?"

The Prince said, "Either have me killed or reward me. I'm unsure which way he'd go."

Tank knew the Prince was lying about some of the information he just learned, but was unsure which statements were honest and which were lies.

Tank said, "I'll think about it before I agree to recover the thumb drives."

As he and the White Knights were leaving, the Prince said, "Mr. Tank, confirm my story with the CIA."

Tank nodded, started toward the door to leave, but instead turned and hit the Prince square in the nose with his oversized fist. The Prince was out cold and laid on the casino carpet when Tank said, "This is not over. I want justice."

Chapter 32

June 13, 2024
Manassas, Virginia

Over their uniquely encrypted video conference app, FBI Special Agent Rusty Winemiller directed his cybersecurity team to close on their investigation into a Romanian national ransomware group operating clandestinely in Klamath Falls, Oregon when his office door was blown open by an FBI SWAT ram. Five agents in full tactical gear with MP5/10 submachine guns yelled simultaneously, "Drop to the floor, hands stretched out above your head."

Winemiller did not move, did not obey. Instead, he calmly said, "Using SWAT to contain a paraplegic is a bit of an overkill, don't you think guys?"

The lead SWAT agent said, "Get down and don't touch your desk. We know you have a loaded 1911 in the top drawer."

Rusty said, "Let me guess, you're afraid I'll commit suicide and deprive our leaders answers as to why I did what I did."

"Get down on the floor, now!"

Again, Winemiller did not move.

The lead SWAT agent nodded at his team and two of the agents went around his desk, grabbed his arms, and cuffed his wrists to his wheelchair.

Director Naylor then entered Special Agent Winemiller's office. Brad shook his head and said, "In a million years, I never would have guessed you to be behind the *Deadly Gray* vigilante movement. Why? Explain this to me?"

Winemiller said, "Brad, I don't want you to get in trouble; you need to read me my Miranda rights."

Brad read him his rights.

Winemiller asked, "What are you arresting me for? What are the charges against me?"

Brad said, "Second degree murder and domestic terrorism. The AG may move to add treason."

Winemiller said, "I want a lawyer."

Director Naylor said, "You damn well need one. I'm going to leave the room now and take the SWAT team outside your office while your greatest fans and supporters come in to speak with you. You have ten minutes with them."

In walked Star, Tucker, Jimmy Ma, Tony Vinci, and Ram. Rusty lifted his chin; he didn't hang his head, but tears welled in his eyes. He said, "Thank you for being here on the second darkest day of my life. I have a lot to say to you but what I say can't be held against me in a court of law."

Tucker said, "We can't promise that Rusty, you need to say nothing to us that you don't want to come out in court. Each of us will be subpoenaed and we can't perjure ourselves, please, understand."

Rusty said, "Got it. But I'm going to take the risk and say things to you that come from my heart. I've known you all since Star was nine years old. I have worked with each of you and have nothing but respect for you. Even you Jimmy, the crazy fucker you are. Anyway, you are the closest people I have to family. We've been through some real shit not to mention the attacks on each of you over the years. I love you guys, especially you Star. You were a joy to be around and work with.

"I've never told you the real story behind my condition, being a paraplegic. I told you that I dove off a bridge into a river as a teenager on a bet. I hit rocks and the rest is history. That is not true. The real story is that I was thrown off the bridge by a high school bully. His name was Robert Whipple. One of the reasons I wanted to be an FBI agent was to find the bastard and get even. I did and I did.

"I thought about the achievement of justice; it felt wonderful. The more I thought about it the more I wondered how many others like me wanted justice that can't be achieved in court, inside the judicial system which is, in fact, not blind and not always fair.

"Recently, I had a beer in a bar with an old family friend whose name I'll maintain as confidential. He told me he had pancreatic cancer and if it was determined to be untreatable and terminal, he was going to take out a politician he hated on his way out.

"The two separate unconnected events became the genesis of thc *Deadly Gray* movement. It grew and it grew beyond my expectations. I assigned you, Star, to investigate the *Deadly Gray* case so that I could keep an eye on things. I knew when you brought in Jimmy and Tony that I would eventually be caught; I just thought it would take longer and that I would have more time."

Star was crying but managed to compose herself long enough to ask a question. "Rusty, did you have anything to do with the man who attacked me, tried to kill me, in my own home?"

"Absolutely not. I never thought something like that would happen. I would never hurt you; I love you like a daughter."

Tucker asked, "Your attempt to rally the *Deadly Gray* against politicians and judges seemed a bit over the top, Rusty. What was that all about?"

"Crimes are committed by the FBI. Crimes are committed by politicians. Crimes are committed by billionaires. Crimes are committed by judges. And they all get away with it. The little guys that commit minor crimes gets the book thrown at them. Our government needs to fix that. I had hoped that the senior rebellion would be a wakeup call."

Brad Naylor reentered the room with the SWAT team and said, "Come on Rusty, it's time."

♦ ♦ ♦ ♦ ♦

June 15, 2024
Wiscasset, Maine

Jolene greeted Tank passionately and said, "I am so glad you are home."

"Me too, sweetheart. I'm exhausted. I just want to plate out, relax, watch a game on TV, and drink a beer."

Jolene said, "That's too bad, I had something else in mind."

Tank said, "I didn't say I wanted to watch TV all night long."

Stanley walked in the room and said with excitement, "Oh, boy, Tankster, you're home." Then he turned serious and said, "How come?"

Tank said, "Because I live here, Stanley."

Stanley said, "Not recently. Who did it, Tank? I bet it was the Saudi Prince."

Jolene said, "Stanley, leave Tank alone; he just got home and he's tired. Go get Tank a Sam Adams."

Stanley said, "We can watch the Red Sox together; they stink this year."

Tank asked, "How good are you at drawing?"

Stanley answered, "I'm better than Leonardo DaVinci ."

Tank said, "Jolene, do we have any large paper so Stanley can design a mother-in-law cottage for Stanley to live in."

Stanley said, "Tank, wouldn't it be a brother-in-law cottage?"

Tank said, "Design it in the dining room; light is better in there."

Jolene returned after she got Stanley paper and a pencil and said to Tank, "Sorry, babe, I'm at a loss as to what to do with him."

Tank said, "Well, he can't stay here forever."

Suddenly, an intrusion detection alarm activated. Jolene confirmed that it wasn't deer this time.

Tank said, "Time to act. Are weapons read?"

Jolene said, "As always."

Both Jolene and Tank entered the war room to view the Closed-Circuit TV camera monitors. The camera that views the entrance to the driveway showed a Buick parked and three men get out.

Jolene said, "Tank, they are White Knights. Why would they not call first? This is unusual."

The driver of the Buick turned the vehicle around and left the premises. The three men hid behind trees and camouflaged themselves.

Tank said, "I'm headed out there to see what is going on. Hand me my PPQ. Before Tank left the house his cell phone rang.

"Tank here."

"Sir, I know you know we're here. We caught wind that the Saudi Prince has ordered the SSF to 'teach you a lesson.' The operator of the drone we deployed in Las Vegas maintained surveillance on the Prince after you left. He recorded his conversation with his security and ran the conversation through a translation program. So, we followed you home in a flight after yours left Las Vegas. Anyway, we're loaded for bear. Do you have any instructions?"

Tank said, "Yes, retreat closer to the house; make sure they are squarely on our property when we trap them. Jolene and I will join you shortly."

Jolene asked, "What is your plan?"

"They could be interesting people to capture and interrogate. Maybe we can torture them with Stanley."

Jolene shook her head but grabbed her semi-automatic shotgun and followed Tank who carried an AR-15, a hunting knife, and his 9mm Walther PPQ.

On comms Tank heard, "Boss, our driver said he just viewed on an FAA app that a Saudi private jet just landed at the Wiscasset Regional Airport. They'll probably be here within the hour."

Tank said, "Come back to the house for 30 minute or so; let's discuss the details of a plan."

Thirty minutes later, the three White Knights returned to their designated positions, Tank and Jolene took up their positions and waited. Nightfall was closing in, so each wore NVGs, installed earbuds, and were cocked and loaded. The driver in the Buick informed the team that the Saudi SSF had arrived—two minutes out.

The Saudi's slowed down, then drove past the Alvarez house entrance for a quarter mile, then turned around and parked 100 yards away.

Wearing western clothes, the three SSF fighters slowly and cautiously walked down the driveway and pointed at CCTV cameras they noticed mounted on trees that lined the driveway. They constantly looked up or side to side for anything that might be security related. They didn't spend enough time to look down; a bear trap sprung on one of the SSF fighters—he screamed like a gutted animal. The other two SSF men came to his aid and opened the jaw of the trap. When they looked up, five heavily armed people were pointing assault rifles, shotguns, and handguns at the SSF trespassers.

Tank said, "Put your weapons on the ground." They did as they were instructed to do as a White Knight collected the rifles. Tank added, "Now, throw the rest of your weapons on the ground."

No one moved until Jolene pulled the trigger on the shotgun pointed in the air. They jumped and each threw handguns on the ground. Again, the White Knights collected the weapons. Finally, Tank said, "The knives, please. Or I'll use this beauty on the person who doesn't forfeit their knife." Three knives hit the ground.

"Now. We're going to pat you down to make sure we haven't missed anything and place plastic ties around your wrists when your hands are together."

Tank said, "You, bear trap boy, come with us; you'll need medical attention. You White Knights stay here and entertain these two remaining Saudis with stories about how we throw captives into a barn with bears. Tell them about the time we threw them in with a mama grizzly bear and her cub. Don't leave any details out."

Tank and Jolene led the limping, whining SSF soldier to their utility shed, unlocked the door sat him down on the seat of Tank's John Deere. Tank reached the drill, installed a long ¼" bit and ran it for a second or two. Jolene took a can of gasoline and started to pour it on the man's wounds when the man screamed, "Please don't torture me, please."

Jolene said, "This is only mild persuasion; the torture comes later."

"I'll talk, what do you want to know?"

Tank asked, "How long have you been guarding the Prince?"

"About 18 months."

Jolene asked, "How about the other two?"

"One about three years, the other about ten years."

Tank asked, "Is the ten-year veteran the one with a little gray in his beard?"

"Yes."

Tank called on the radio, "Bring graybeard here to the shed."

About two minutes later, one of the White Knights marched Graybeard in front of Tank and Jolene."

Tank said to the White Knight, "Take Chester, here back with you, tend to his wounds, and leave the older one here with me and my drill."

Graybeards eyes widened.

Jolene asked, "How long have you guarded the Prince?"

Graybeard said, "A few years."

Tank slapped him with an open hand. Graybeard fell hard to the floor and Jolene poured gasoline on him while he was down. Tank lit a propane torch. The man tried to run but Tank hit him again, this time with a closed fist.

The man was out for a few minutes.

When he woke up, Tank said, "Let's get down to business. Did the Prince order Paddock or Mafi to kill Americans at the country music festival?"

Graybeard answered, "You will torture me, no, unless I answer the question 'yes.' To avoid torture, I say 'yes'."

Tank looked at Jolene and asked, "Is Star in Wiscasset with her family or still in Virginia?"

Jolene said, "I'll check."

Jolene called Maya. When the call was over, she told Tank, "She's coming to Wiscasset, tomorrow."

Tank said to Graybeard, "You're in luck. FBI agent Star Cherokee is a much better interrogator than I am. We'll wait until tomorrow. You will have to suffer the torment of the constraint of time. You'll have to stay in the shed with your buddies until tomorrow. You'll be well-guarded."

Tank said into his radio, "Bring the Saudis here to the shed. You'll need to guard them for another day.

Sorry guys. I'll reward you and feed you. I'll bring you donuts, they are the original hole food you know. One of you needs to go out and capture the pilot. Bring him here and put him in the shed with his buddies. Keep them tied up; we have some dangerous tools in there."

As Tank and Jolene walked back to the house, he said, "You know, you were one crazy mama back there with the gasoline."

Jolene said, "I learned from the best how to be crazy"

Tank said, "You must mean you learned from Stanley."

Jolene said, "Speaking of which, I wonder how far he's come with the design of the house you're going to build him."

Tank said, "In Antarctica."

June 16, 2024
Washington, DC

President Timothy Lamb sat alone in the Oval Office. The big man contemplated about what actions he should take to improve the trust the American people should have in the Justice Department. He thought, *Hell, I don't have trust in the Justice Department myself.*

POTUS, a former military police officer, needed to talk to someone about his dilemma; what action he should take. He chose his Chief of Staff with whom to confide; a calm man who never abused his power and influence. President Lamb said, "Special Agent Winemiller sat in this very office and pretended that he assigned staff whose job it was to capture the leader of the *Deadly Gray* vigilantes. Can you believe that? I bought it hook, line and sinker."

The Chief of Staff said, "We all bought it, sir. He deceived us all."

"But you and I were not close to Winemiller. Shouldn't have FBI Director Naylor or Attorney General Gannon picked up on the fraud? The American people deserve better than an incompetent Justice Department."

The Chief of Staff said, "It might be a good idea to have a press conference to address this issue. What if you announced that it was the FBI itself that uncovered the fraud? Maybe you should say Director Naylor arrested Winemiller; it could engender more confidence in the highest authority for justice or something to that effect. It is at least a baby step forward to improve the current contempt the general public has for the FBI."

POTUS said, "Or I could fire the AG and the Director of the FBI for incompetence and replace them with more qualified people."

"There's that."

President Lamb said, "I have hundreds of advisors. If I ask each of them what I should do, I bet I'd get hundreds of different opinions and conflicting advice.

"Ask Gannon to come to the White House ASAP."

"Yes, sir"

Attorney General Gannon showed up 90 minutes later and said as he entered the Oval Office, "Mr. President, you beckoned me?"

POTUS said, "I need for you to tender your resignation."

Attorney General Arthur Gannon said, "Is this about Winemiller?"

"Yes."

Gannon said, "I must admit, his actions are pretty embarrassing; we should have seen it coming, but we were totally blindsided. His corruption caught everyone by surprise.

"I work at your pleasure, Sir. If you want me to resign, I fully understand, and I will submit my resignation. But before I leave office, I'd like to share with you a couple of things you may not already know. I contracted with the CEO of a company called Entropy Entrepreneurs to secretly investigate corruption in the Justice Department and other agencies. You will want to receive Tucker Cherokee's final report.

"The second item I'd like to mention to you is that you may have been kept in the dark about the real events surrounding the Las Vegas massacre. You need to press the Director of the CIA for what really happened and what they covered up and why."

POTUS said, "I'm sorry Arthur but I'm not letting you out of here until you explain yourself. You can't just drop a bomb like that and expect to walk out the door. Please, embellish on this alleged CIA coverup. What are you talking about?"

"It affects your relationship with foreign entities. The same person investigating government corruption is also knowledgeable about the aforementioned CIA coverup. His name is Tucker Cherokee; my advice to you is that you speak with him."

President Lamb said, "Thank you for your service, Arthur, I'm sorry it had to end on this sour note. Will you, please, ask Brad Naylor to come to the White House?"

Arthur Gannon, nodded deferentially to the President and said, "Thank you, sir, for the opportunity to serve you." He left the Oval Office with his head up. POTUS sensed that Gannon was relieved to leave his position.

FBI Director Brad Naylor arrived at the White House within 30 minutes of Gannon's departure. Naylor said as he was escorted by his Chief of Staff into the Oval Office, "Mr. President, AG Gannon said you wanted to speak with me."

POTUS's disposition screamed anger and disappointment. He said, "It's about Winemiller. Explain to me how or why you didn't see his traitorous actions coming. For crying out loud, he was head of the cyber group; he was supposed to arrest people that were doing precisely what he was doing. Did anybody in his department suspect he was orchestrating the attacks by the *Deadly Gray* vigilantes? How many people died because of him?"

"Yes, sir, many criminals died. It is a tragedy."

"Don't be a smart ass, Brad, there is a thing called due process. But that is not the point, did anyone come to you with suspicions about Winemiller's misconduct?"

"No, Mr. President, not a single person; he was good at keeping his real character to himself."

The President said, "The FBI and maybe even the entire Justice Department is wandering out at sea without an anchor. We need to bring it dockside. To do that, I need new blood, therefore, I need your resignation."

Naylor said, "Understood; I'll have it on the AG's desk before the end of the day."

POTUS said, "I've already asked for the AG's resignation. Tender yours directly to me. Is there anything you want to say to me before we part ways?"

Naylor said, "Yes, sir. I recommend you interview Winemiller behind closed doors with no other ears around you. The *Deadly Gray* seniors were not sheep following a command from a website. They sent America a message; I wouldn't ignore it. You may save our nation by listening to what our seniors are telling us."

June 16, 2024
Wiscasset, Maine

Star listened to a mystery/thriller audiobook the entire trip from Mt. Vernon, Virginia to Maine and stopped only to recharge her electric vehicle and provide Ram an opportunity to do his business. She turned her cellphone and satellite phone off on this trip to avoid speaking with anyone. Star still grieved from the trauma she experienced over the shock and betrayal of one of her best and most respected friends, Rusty Winemiller. The effect it had on her was that she lost confidence in other friends; she felt like she couldn't trust anyone. She saw dishonesty and betrayal before when she worked in the White House, but she never felt it personally, until now.

Star felt like an umbrella in an overpowering wind. When she was surrounded by people, even by loved ones and alleged friends, she still sensed she was all alone. Star thought, *Where do I go for truth and honesty?*

Star yelled back at Ram and said, "I only trust you and my parents. And without Rusty, my mentor, around, there is no one at the FBI I can trust. I've even lost my passion to stay an FBI agent."

Hours later, Star pulled up to the entrance to the Cherokee compound and was greeted warmly by the gate guard who let her through. Star drove another quarter of a mile to the house entrance and pushed the dashboard button that opened the hatch for Ram to get out. She opened the driver's side door, got out, stretched, and nodded a greeting to the house entrance White Knight guard.

Maya flew out the front door, ignored Ram who wanted her attention, hugged her daughter with an unusually strong embrace and said, "I'm so glad you are alright; I've been worried sick about you."

Star was confused and said, "Why wouldn't I be alright?"

Maya said, "I tried to call you; I left you messages. Tank, Jolene, and your dad have tried to call you, but you haven't answered your phone. You've never refused a call from us before."

Star said, "I turned my phone off and listened to an audiobook. I needed some alone time to think. I'm sorry I made you worry. Why is everyone trying to reach me?"

Maya petted Ram as she said, "Tank and Jolene have four hostages in their shed. They need your help to determine if these guys lie when Tank asks them a question. The hostages are Saudi Special Security Forces."

"Mom, they're going to think in Arabic. How am I supposed to read their thoughts? I don't understand Arabic."

Maya said, "Tony Vinci created an Arabic to English audio app for the Department of Defense years ago. All you must do is type onto a laptop the words they are thinking phonetically, and it will automatically show up in English on the screen."

Star said, "The genius strikes again."

Tucker came out of the house with a laptop and a paper bag. Ram jumped up on him and slobbered on Tucker's face with his tail wagging ferociously. Tucker gave Ram instructions to get back into the SUV, kissed Star, and said, "Let's get in your car and drive over to Tank and Jolene's house."

Star said, "What's in the paper bag?"

"Treats for you and Ram prepared by Chef Rhino."

Tucker drove the Rivian EV while Star ate and rewarded Ram with his Rhinotreats. When they arrived at the Alvarez home, Tucker and Star were surprised to see weapons aimed in their direction. The three White Knights assigned to protect Tank, Jolene and the prisoner's shed recognized Tucker and held fire. Jolene came out the front door of her home and yelled, "Stand down."

After the vehicle stopped and all got out, Jolene gave Star a big hug and said, "I'm so glad to see you and thanks for your willingness to help us out. With you, we're going to get to the bottom of the reason for the Las Vegas massacre."

Tank came out of his house, hugged Star, and allowed Ram to jump all over him before he said, "I'm glad you brought the big boy, Ram; we may need him."

After a few minutes of small talk, the five of them went over to the infamous shed. Ram growled slightly at the White Knights until Tank said, "Good, Good." Ram as well as the White Knight security officers relaxed.

Tank said to his officers, "Open the shed door but assume that the prisoners overcame their restraints and converted shed tools into weapons. Assume the hostages think that their only way and time to escape is when we open the shed doors. Each of you have Tasers, use them unless you must resort to using more serious weapons. Jolene and I have our guns at the ready. Star and Tucker, please stand back until I say all is clear. Ram, stand down."

One of the White Knights unlocked the shed, and slowly opened one of the two outwardly swinging doors. The odor from the shed smelled of urine. To everyone outside the shed it appeared that none of the four hostages had attempted to arm themselves with shed tools; they apparently were unable to break their plastic restraints to reach a tool. Tank said, "Well, I see you made use of the bucket I left you. Graybeard and the pilot, get out. We'll resume our discussions of yesterday outside. We have a nice little picnic table for all of us to enjoy.

"White Knights, relock the other Saudis in the shed and guard them."

Tank escorted the two Saudis with their hands still tied together over to the picnic table, sat them on one side of the table and said, "Let me introduce you to our three new guests. First, this lady is FBI agent Star, who has been trained extensively in the science of lie detection by the FBI. Tucker here will explain how the science works."

Tucker said, "We don't have to hook you up to probes to measure your electrical impulses. Instead, we measure wavelength signatures that emanate from your brain. The laptop Ms. Star uses has a sensor rather than a camera installed. She will type on the device as you speak. We'll know if you lie or tell the truth."

Tank added, "The final guest here is Ram. He is a military trained K9. He will do whatever he is instructed by me to do. If I instruct him to remove a body part from your pilot, he will do so. Do you understand?"

Both Graybeard and the pilot nodded.

"Ram," Tank pointed at Graybeard, "Bad."

Ram immediately ran to Graybeard, stuck his snout a fraction of an inch away from Graybeard's face, bared his enormous teeth, and growled ferociously while he awaited his next instruction.

Graybeard was apoplectic.

Tank said, "Ram, stand down."

Ram stopped, moved over next to Star, and sat."

Tank said, "He once removed the genitals of an uncooperative criminal. It was disgusting to watch and listen to. I almost lost it. If you have a low pain threshold, you probably need to cooperate. Do you understand?"

Both Graybeard and a terrified pilot nodded their heads.

Tank asked, "Jolene, do you have anything to add before we get started?"

Jolene said, "Yes, I have a question for the pilot? How long will it be before the Saudi Prince wants to know where his jet is? Did you file a flight plan back to Las Vegas? When will you all be considered deserters?"

The pilot glanced at Ram before he said, "I filed a flight plan yesterday for us to leave this morning and yes, I believe His Highness must already be wondering why no one has reported back to him with good news and why his Learjet is not on the way back to Las Vegas."

Tank said, "All the more reason for us to get on with the interview. Let's start with where we stopped last night. Graybeard, did the Saudi Prince order Paddock or Mafi to kill Americans at the country music festival to have the massacre blamed on Iran?"

Star typed on the laptop before Graybeard answered. He looked over at Ram, then looked at the pilot. He took a deep breath and asked, "What will you do with this information? Will the Prince know the answers I give to your questions?"

Tank said, "The question I asked you was a 'yes' or 'no' question. Answering a question with a question is a stall tactic."

Star continued typing.

Graybeard said, "I don't know."

Tank asked, "OK, does the CIA already know that Saudi Arabia is responsible for the murders of innocent Americans in Las Vegas?"

Star kept typing.

Graybeard said, "I did not say that the Kingdom of Saudi Arabia was guilty of such crimes."

Tucker raised his hand and asked Tank, "May I?"

Tank said, "Of course."

Tucker asked Graybeard, "Is the King aware of the Saudi Prince's plan to start a war between the U.S. and Iran?"

Again, Star typed on the laptop.

"No, I think not."

All eyes were now on Star.

Star said, "Graybeard is loyal to the Kingdom and therefore lied about his answers to each question to protect the Prince and the King."

Tank said, "OK, one last question, who pulled the triggers, Paddock or Mafi?"

Star typed.

Graybeard said, "Stephen Paddock."

Star smiled.

Jolene said, "I have a question. Were you sent here to kill Tank?"

Graybeard said, "Yes."

Tucker looked up into the clear blue sky and said to Tank, "They should be here any minute now."

On que, everyone around the picnic table heard the ubiquitous sound of helicopter rotors beat against the Maine summer like air. It hovered over an adjacent field on Tank and Jolene's property before it landed with a team of U.S. Marshalls whose team leader was known to both Tank and Tucker.

Tank greeted the Marshalls and said, "We have four violent criminals in our custody who came onto my property with malintent. Over here are their weapons. Last night I wrote up my complaint against them and forwarded the complaint to your headquarters. Whatever you do, don't let them lawyer up. They are terrorists who belong in Gitmo. Mr. Cherokee and I will support you with whatever you need. If you run into a diplomatic wall, contact either of us."

Tucker added, "You might want to impound their jet sitting on the Wiscasset Regional Airport tarmac."

Star approached the Marshalls and said, "I am an FBI agent and will testify against these terrorists. Here is my card. Contact me anytime if you need corroborating support."

After the Saudis were cuffed, shackled, and loaded into the government helicopter and flown to Portland, Tucker said, "Let's go to my place and let Chef Rhino feed all of us while Star freshens up before we ask her what we all want to know. Tank and Jolene, you can even bring Stanley and your White Knight contingent."

An hour later, after all were fed a delicious meal prepared by Rhino and imbibed on liquid refreshments, all gathered around Star for answers.

Star said, "As you all know, nothing I give you is admissible in a court of law. We will be unable to prosecute the terrorists with hard evidence but at least we now know the answer to some hard questions.

"Tank, Graybeard lied to you when he said he did not know if the Saudi Prince ordered Paddock or Mafi to kill Americans. He thought when you asked the question '*What will happen to me if I tell these people that His Highness was guilty? I will be killed one way or the other; either by Americans or by Saudis. These Americans cannot know for sure if I lie*'."

Star said, "I conclude from Graybeard's thoughts that the Prince is guilty of planning the attack on innocent Americans.

"He also lied when he said he knew nothing about what the CIA knows. He lied when he said he knew it was Paddock who pulled the trigger. Actually, he does not know who pulled the trigger.

"The only time he didn't lie is when he said he was sent here to kill Tank."

Jolene threw her arms up and asked, "What do we do with this information?"

Tucker answered, "We share it with the President. I recently received a request from President Lamb to meet with him at the White House. I will share this information we learned from Graybeard with him."

Stanley said, "He already knows."

Everyone stared at Stanley as if he was a freak. Stanley shrugged his shoulders and said, "The CIA agents work for him, don't they?"

♦ ♦ ♦ ♦ ♦

June 17, 2024
Wiscasset, Maine

The Acting Director of the FBI, Chris O'Connor, called Star Cherokee on the phone and said, "You have my sympathy about your friend and mentor, Rusty Winemiller."

Star felt the comment by O'Connor was disingenuous; her distrust of others was in control of her emotions. She said, "Congratulations for being selected as Acting Director."

O'Connor said, "Thanks, but we both know it is temporary. I'm calling about the algorithm that was prepared to help mitigate the *Deadly Gray* vigilante killings. I understand it to be quite a powerful tool. I also understand that it doesn't belong to the FBI; it isn't even government property."

Star said, "Yes, that is correct; it is the property of Entropy Entrepreneurs."

O'Connor asked, "What will it take to make it FBI property?"

Star said, "I don't think eminent domain applies to software, so I guess you'll have to ask my father what he'd take for it. I'm sure he'd be reasonable as it is in the country's best interest for the FBI to use it; he is a patriot first and a businessman a distant second."

"Can you ask, intervene on the FBI's behalf?"

Star said, "I'd rather not. Have the FBI contracting organization contact him. I will, however, warn my dad of the FBI's interest in the algorithm."

O'Connor said, "One other thing, Star. We need to replace Winemiller. Are you interested in the job?"

Star was surprised by O'Connor's question. She never contemplated that she would be considered by the FBI for the position. She said, "Thank you, Chris for asking, but honestly, I think that job is a tad over my head. I'm not qualified, I'm still learning the ropes in cyber security. And I don't think management is my thing anyway but let me think about it."

Acting Director O'Connor said, "OK, but don't think about it too long. We need to fill the position ASAP."

A couple of hours later, Star received a call from her best friend, Sonja. Star said, "I am glad you called; I've been thinking about you."

Sonja said, "I've been left in the dark. Since I was helping Tank in Las Vegas, I haven't heard from anyone. However, I heard about Winemiller by watching the news; I wanted to give you time before I called. Sorry is all I can think to say about it."

Star said, "I was blindsided by it, yet I should have known because he refused to speak with me in person. He wasn't about to let it slip and let me read his thoughts. I should have picked up on that."

Sonja asked, "What's the latest on the Las Vegas massacre? Why hasn't Tank kept me in the loop? He's pissed me off."

Star said, "I'm sure you're the last person Tank would want to piss off. To answer your question, three Saudi assassins came to Wiscasset to kill Tank. I suspect he got a little too close to the truth."

Sonja said, "Oh, no."

Star added, "Of course, Tank prevailed and interrogated the Saudi SSF assassins. Bottom line is that they confessed to knowing that the Saudi Prince ordered the Las Vegas massacre."

"It is fantastic that he's solved the case. What will happen to the mega billionaire Saudi Prince?"

Star said, "Undetermined. Dad has a meeting with the President; maybe something will come from it."

Sonja said, "Well, at least Tank completed his mission. Listen, I have something else to cover with you. I want to remind you that my father-in-law, Bernard Nazareth, who we spoke with recently wants to know if Scotland Yard could buy an algorithm from your dad's company tailored for the United Kingdom."

Star said. "I'm sure he'd be willing to have an algorithm built for our friends across the pond, but Bernard will have to negotiate the sale directly with Dad.

"By the way, Sonja, we're having a win party at Dad's house in Wiscasset on Friday, June 21. I know it will be difficult for your baseball all-star short-stop husband to join us this time of year, but if you and the twins would be able to come, it would please everyone."

Sonja said, "Traveling with two four-year-olds is tantamount to hell, but I'll see what we can do.

"Tell Tank I'm pissed." Sonja added, "Hope to see you soon. Luv ya." Sonja hung up.

Star called Jolene and said, "You need to do a little damage control. Tank has failed to keep Sonja up to speed with the status of the Las Vegas massacre investigation after she made the personal sacrifice to help him at his request. Not cool. Help him along, will you.?'

Jolene said, "Sonja is the wrong person to piss off. I'll deal with it. I think Tank's emotional engine is leaking a little oil."

Chapter 33

Star drove over to the Alvarez household with Ram in the back seat. Intrusion alarms went off in Tank's control room, but Tank and Jolene were expecting Star and didn't react.

Upon arrival, Star let Ram out and he excitedly jumped on Tank. Ram loved Tank almost as much as he loved Star because Tank trained Ram before Tank gave him to Star for her protection.

Star said, "Hi, you all."

Jolene said, "You've been in Virginia for how long and you're saying, 'you all' already?"

Star laughed and gave Jolene a loving hug.

Jolene and Tank had no children and treated Star as their surrogate daughter. After 30 minutes of small talk, Star asked, "Did you hear that my former boss's boss, Brad Naylor, was asked to submit his resignation to the President because of the Winemiller crisis?"

Both Jolene and Tank answered simultaneously, "Yes."

Star said, "You might want to consider him to join your company. He'd be a good addition to White Knight Personal Security, don't you think?

Tank said, "Why do you think so?"

Jolene smiled.

Star said, "I think he could bring in business for you; his contacts are incredible. To have a former FBI Director on your payroll must be a plus."

Jolene laughed uncontrollably.

Star asked, "Why are you making fun of me?"

Jolene said, "We're not making fun of you. We're laughing because we've already offered Brad a job. Everything you say are things I've said to Tank as to why we should hire him."

Star said, "That's great. Has he accepted the offer? If so, when does he start and where will he be located?"

Tank said, "He starts in a month or two; he needs some time off. He'll work out of Clifton, Virginia; that was his choice."

Stanley spotted Star and said, "Would you like to see the design of the new house Tank is going to build for me. It's cool. It's a brother-in-law house complete with a foosball room, a 3D game room, a candy machine, and a wide screen smart TV. Outside the house, I will have a fenced in petting zoo."

Star looked at the house design and said, "Stanley, this is excellent. You are an incredibly talented artist, but I think you forgot a couple of things.

Stanley pulled back and said, "Like what?"

Star said gently, "There's no bathroom, no kitchen, and no plumbing. You need to go back to the drawing board my friend."

Stanley's eyes lit up and said, "Are you my friend?"

"Of course."

Stanley said, "Jolene, I have a friend. Star is my friend." He left and returned to the dining room to revise his drawings.

Star asked Tank, "Are you really going to build a brother-in-law house for Stanley?"

Tank said, "In Antarctica."

Nineteen hundred aspiring students, high school teachers, advisors, and scholastic journalists attended the Journalism Education Association and National Scholastic Press Association Summer National High School Journalism Convention. The event included instructional sessions, and keynote speakers from national newsmakers to media critiques.

The conference organizers were excited to get former FBI Director, Brad Naylor as the plenary session keynote speaker. The main ballroom was packed with excited teenagers when Brad took to the podium, "It is my honor to speak before you. Some of you will be Pulitzer Prize winners, some of you will be famous songwriters, others will be TV newsroom anchors, podcasters with multi-millions of followers, number one best sellers, or maybe even writers of FBI press releases."

Most of the young people laughed.

"Your teachers, mentors, and future influencers will most likely tell you that you, yes you, can help change the world. It's true. It's possible. You can be an important cog in the world's constant quest for fairness, peace, and justice for all.

"That quest starts right here, right in this room—you can change the world."

The audience clapped and cheered.

"What is it that needs to change? What change can you affect? It's a matter of trust. You can change the reader's trust in the media."

"A poll cited in a June survey conducted by the Reuters Institute for the Study of Journalism at Oxford that among 92,000 news consumers in 46 countries, the polled found that the United States fared the worst among G-20 nations for trust in the media. The poll ranked American's trust in the media at a pathetically low 29%."

The students stayed silent.

"It will be up to you, you empowered student journalists, to change that. It won't be easy, but all of us look to you to make that change. A YouGov poll for IMPRESS revealed that public trust in the press is also at an all-time low in the UK. Only 11% of people in the UK trust journalists at mid-market newspapers such as the *Daily Mail* and the *Daily Express* to tell the truth while fewer than one in ten trust journalists at tabloids such as *The Sun* and the *Mirror*. Journalists at broadsheets and local newspapers do not fare much better as just 36% of the public trust them to tell the truth.

"It starts right here with you. The public, your readers, want you to receive awards for reporting the news instead of proselytizing your professor or teacher's ideology.

"Report the news. Don't report what you want the news to be. Personally, I stop reading or listening to a report when the word 'may' appear. We readers don't want to know what 'may' happen or what 'may' the impact of the event will be; we want to know what did happen and what the impact is."

The room was silent. Outside the ball room, chants by protestors were heard by conference attendees.

Brad Naylor continued, "Recently, our nation endured attacks on respected media journalists. No sane person condones such violence. But there is a lesson to be learned by all of us from the attacks. Back during the Vietnam War—ancient history for you—the press lied to the public about an action taken during something called the 'Tet Offensive.' The U.S. military won the battle, but the press announced that we lost in hope that the general public would increase their opposition to the war. That news media's conspiratorial lie had both intended and unintended consequences. One of the unintended consequences was the assassination of editors and journalists at multiple newspaper outlets by Vietnam vets more than 50 years later after the lie. Their hate for journalistic lies gnawed at them their entire post-war life.

"Report the news accurately. Learn from the Vietnam veterans and *Deadly Gray* vigilantes whose emotional wounds festered for a half century. I don't know who the abundant humanity is that is protesting outside these halls but don't be surprised if they are seniors reinforcing the same message that I am presenting to you today.

"Be your own person, cut the umbilical cord with your professors in college, try not to allow too much pressure and influence from your editors when they are clearly wrong. Stand up and be the best journalist you can be. Don't be tethered to your ideology whatever it is. Don't allow the obscene social media jerks to influence you; they represent the oblivious opinionated—stay the course. Don't be dishonest. Don't be insensitive to your readers. Be honest with yourself and you will affect the change most journalist aspire to achieve, and you will end the winter of reader discontent as easily as removing oxygen from a candle flame.

"Thank you and I look forward to reading what you write."

June 21, 2024
Wiscasset, Maine

Chef Rhino was in his element. He was more excited than anyone else who attended the 'win party' at the Cherokee Estate. He hired three assistants for the kitchen, two more as servers, and a bar tender.

Sonja's twins, Powers and Li, received constant love and attention. Powers rode Ram like a horse and Li filled in coloring books with Stanley.

Tank jokingly got on his knees to Sonja—which put him eye to eye with her—and said, "Mea Culpa, your highness."

Sonja said, "That's more like it. Can you do that again and this time do it on video so I can replay it whenever I want?"

Tank said, "Seriously, I know I should have called and kept you up to speed. Tell you what, I volunteer to babysit for you to make it up to you?"

Sonja laughed and said, "Are you kidding, my kids would never be the same. I bet Powers would be practicing Ju Jitsu on me when I got him back."

Jolene approached with a glass of champagne in each hand. Tank reached out to receive one of them but instead Jolene handed one glass to Sonja. Tank looked surprised. Jolene said, "You are not a champagne lover, Love, there is plenty of beer at the bar."

Tank left for the bar.

Sonja said, "I'm enjoying Tank's special attention."

Jolene said, "You have no idea what Tank has been through since you last met with him in Las Vegas. In fact, you probably should apologize to him for not protecting him after what he's been through."

Sonja said, "But Jolene, I'm enjoying this; I'm not really angry at him, I'm just having fun with him."

A server came around with a plate of cheese covered Brussel Sprouts. Sonja said, "No thank you, I don't like Brussel Sprouts."

The server said, "Maybe Brussels sprouts don't like you either."

Both Sonja and Jolene looked back at the server with incredulity.

The server said, "Rhino told me to say that to anyone who refused to try one of his specialties."

Jolene said, "Well, I'll have to try it now."

Sonja said, "Not me. Do you have anything with meat in it?"

The server whistled to another server who brought out a lamb kebab."

Tank returned with his beer and grabbed the kebab before Sonja could get it. Tank said, "I'm trying to help you keep your girlish figure."

Suddenly, Li screamed.

Sonja bolted to the sound and found Li looking angrily at Stanley.

Sonja asked, "What happened in here?

Li said, "Stanley colored in a roof, yellow. Who has a yellow roof? No one."

Sonja breathed a sigh of relief and said, "Some houses may have yellow roofs, now don't scream unless you're hurt."

Tank said, "I take back my offer to baby sit."

Sonja said "The only thing free is love. I love my babies."

Tony Vinci rolled in with his special wheelchair and approached Maya. He said, "I always enjoy the parties here. Thanks, as always. Can you and I talk privately before Tucker grabs me?"

Maya said, "Of course, Tony, what's up?"

Tony asked, "How old is Tucker?"

"Tony, there is nothing you don't know about Tucker, including how old he is."

Tony said, "You should keep him in the office, no field work. You know, I love him like a brother or father, but he took chances in Maysville, West Virginia to catch #Steel he didn't need to take. He's way too valuable to all of us for him to be in the field."

Tucker wandered over to Maya and said, "What are you and our brilliant Chief Scientist talking about?

Tony said, "I told Maya that you are too important to operate in the field."

"Tony, why would you deprive me of my fun? I genuinely enjoyed our efforts in Mayville to capture Steele."

"I get it, sir. It's just that you are too valuable as a strategist and tactician to expose yourself to physical risk."

Jimmy Ma arrived at the Cherokee estate last, as always, and said to Chef Rhino. "You know I love you right?"

Chef Rhino said, "Your Heavens Door bourbon on ice is waiting for you."

Jimmy asked Rhino, "Have you seen Suzzanne?"

"Jimmy, you need to give up on her, you're making a fool of yourself."

Jimmy said, "I get that, but I have another issue to cover with her."

Rhino said. "She's talking with her sister on the back deck."

Jimmy said, " Thanks."

He approached the back deck and Suzzanne said, "Damn, Jimmy is here."

Jimmy approached the two sisters on the deck overlooking the Sheepscot River and said, "Suzzanne. May I speak with you privately. I was impressed with your ability but have a concern about your future for the algorithm."

Star was within earshot of the conversation between Jimmy and Suzzanne. She read Suzzanne's thoughts, and it scared her to death.

Tucker approached Tank and asked, "What is your conclusion about the Las Vegas massacre?"

Tank said, "The Saudi Prince is up to his neck in it. He needs to be held accountable for his decisions."

Tucker asked, "Just how do you intend to accomplish that?"

Tank said, "Lethality with prejudice."

Tucker asked, "What do you have in mind?'

"The Saudi Prince must fly home eventually, right?"

Tucker said, "Right. How do you plan to collar the sob?"

Tank said, "We'll protect you from that knowledge, you know, plausible deniability. I suspect the Saudis have a shadow government. I'll try to coax them to take the low road to make sure that His Highness takes it in the wrong orifice."

Bernard Nazareth surprised everyone by entering late that evening. Sonja gave Bernard a big hug and Powers and Li excitedly said 'Grandpa.'

Star cornered her dad and said, "How would you feel if I resigned from the FBI? Over time, it feels like the FBI has been transformed into the Federal Bureau of Insolence?"

Tucker said, "You know I love you and that I'd support you on whatever decision you make. I respect you and know you think tactically."

Star said, "I don't enjoy the job. I'd rather work for Entropy Entrepreneurs or White Knight Personal Security; people I can trust. After Winemiller, I have trouble trusting anyone that is not family."

Chef Rhino entered the family room and with a loud booming voice said, "Dinner is served, everyone please come together in the dining room." A long mahogany table with one chair at the head of the table for Tucker, one chair at the other end of the table for Maya, and six chairs on either side of the table including two containing booster seats. After Maya said a short grace, everyone dug into a delicious meal.

Conversation started around the table with Jimmy Ma saying. "As a family member of the overall Tucker and Maya Cherokee group, I, hereby, inform you that an anarchist hateful crime is about to be committed; I'm about to ask Rhino for ketchup. Tank, can you protect me."

Tank said, "You're on your own with that one; no way I'd take on Rhino."

Jolene laughed and said, "Jimmy, sometimes I think you operate on only one working cylinder."

Tony said, "Yeah but he has one big cylinder."

Sonja said, "Be careful, I don't like where this conversation is going; there are kids at the table."

Everyone laughed except Stanley who said, "Harley Davidson made one-cylinder motorcycles, do you have one, Jimmy?"

Jimmy said, "No, Stanley, are you a motorcycle mechanic?"

Stanley looked over at Jolene and asked, "Can I have a motorcycle?"

Jolene said, "OK, I'll get you a model to put together."

Star read Suzzanne's thoughts again but decided against confronting her.

Tucker tapped his water glass with a spoon to get everyone's attention. Stanley and the twins tapped their glasses like they were playing a tune. Tucker stared at Stanley until he stopped.

"I want you all to know how proud I am of all of you to help our nation manage the *Deadly Gray* outbreak, it is a natural contagious virus that only attacks seniors. What is natural is not always good and you all worked together to stem the tide."

Maya lifted her glass and said, "A toast to the team who put together a powerful algorithm to identify *Deadly Gray* vigilantes and their intended victims before it happens."

Jimmy Ma stood up and bowed to Suzzanne while Tony said, "I'll drink to that."

Tank whispered to Jolene, "I sort of was rooting for the *Deadly Gray* vigilantes."

Bernard Nazareth said, "And thank you for your willingness to build a UK version of the algorithm. I raise my glass to toast all of you."

Jimmy and Tony looked over at Tucker, Tony asked, "What is Bernie talking about?"

Jimmy said, "Oh no, you didn't?"

Tucker said, "Later guys. A toast goes to Tank and Sonja for solving the mystery posed to Star by Colonel Manion about Adam Heinz."

All raised their glasses.

Tucker continued, "Tank and Sonja were tenacious at applying cultural antibiotics on those Saudi butt wipes."

Maya asked, "Tank, how did Manion know Heinz was covering up the real story about the Las Vegas massacre?"

Tank said, "Jimmy, you went through all his emails and texts, did you learn how Manion knew Heinz was guilty of a coverup?"

Jimmy said, "Yes, I'm writing a book about it. You'll have to wait and read it, right after Tucker agrees to send me to Las Vegas."

All laughed.

Tank said, "Hey, I just remembered, there is a $20,000 reward to anyone who unveils the truth about the murder of Manion's granddaughter."

Jolene said, "Looks like you'll need to split it ten or twelve ways."

All laughed.

Star said, "I'd like to toast Dad, my rock, and Tony for finding #Steel."

Jolene said, "I'm going to get dizzy with alcohol if we continue these toasts. I can't handle anymore."

Stanley asked, "Can I make one more toast?"

Before anyone could object, he said, "A toast to Chef Rhino for making such a great meal."

All raised their glasses.

Stanley went on to ask, "Can we take leftovers home?"

June 24, 2024
Mt. Vernon, Virginia

Star sat at home surfing news channels with continuing coverage of *Deadly Gray* vigilantes. The volume of violent attacks by seniors continued to rise. Graphs were presented by pontificators with PhDs in psychology as to why the trend continued. A *Deadly Gray* vigilante in Chicago used an AR15 at a teacher's union meeting. A woman in Buffalo murdered someone she was convinced was an Antifa leader. A man in Beckley, West Virginia stabbed a state politician for his support of the shutdown of a local coal mine. Star thought, *It's always someone else's fault.*

She stopped surfing when she heard the story about the resignation of supreme court justice Randolph Atkinson. He said his reason was due to his and his wife's failing health.

Star typed her own letter of resignation to acting director Chris O'Connor. She gave no reason. She was not going to explain to anyone what her real reason was. Star still hadn't gotten over reading the thoughts of Suzzanne.

Star's doorbell rang; Ram barked. She pulled her Glock and went to the door. She had a Ring Video installed and saw that Brooks, her male friend who she met at the food store, stood at the door with flowers in his hands. Star said to Ram, "Good, Good."

The tall handsome young blond man with a clean close-cropped haircut wearing a sports jacket, khaki pants, and dock shoes said, "I thought I'd drop by and see if you were OK. Haven't heard much from you lately. Is this a good time? I can come back and just leave the flowers."

Star said, "Please, you are a breath of fresh air, I need some time with someone who is not involved with all my problems."

He said, "Problems are my specialty. How can I help?"

She said, "By just being you."

Brooks looked at the weapon in her hand and over at Ram and said, "Maybe your problems are outside my expertise."

Star said, "Just what is your expertise?"

"Running a restaurant. You?"

Star said, "As of today, I'm unemployed. I just turned in my resignation to the FBI."

He laughed exposing his perfect teeth and beautiful smile and said, "Well, at least we have one thing in common."

She said, "That is?"

"We both like Italian food."

She read his thoughts, *I sure like this lady, I hope she doesn't find me boring.*

Star said, "Come on in, maybe we have more in common than food."

He said, "I love dogs."

Star said, "That's a good start."

June 30, 2024
Across the United States

On the dark website, *DeadlyGrayJustice*, #Star wrote:

"The FBI arrested one of its own; someone who, in fact, searched for ways to achieve real justice. That visionary also set up a methodology for passing the leadership role to successors. We will continue to encourage seniors at the end of their lives to achieve justice and rid the world of evil where law enforcement and the justice system has failed. I am the new #Star and will work with seniors to help them achieve justice before they move on to the promise land. I will help violent non-violent seniors find their nemesis and strategize how to best achieve that allusive justice."

Suzzanne Li, Star's aunt, reread what she typed before she pressed 'post.'

Afterwards, Suzzanne called Tony Vinci and asked, "Are you working on the algorithm for Bernard and the Scotland Yard?"

Tony said, "No, not at the moment, I was assessing our FBI model to see who or what might be coming down in the near future."

Suzzanne asked, "What have you found?"

Tony answered, "Have you spoken with Jimmy since the party?"

Suzzanne said, "Yes, Jimmy and I have buried the hatchet since we have to work together and since he gave up hitting on me."

Tony asked, "Did he tell you our discovery using the algorithm to identify new victims and new vigilantes?"

"Yes."

Tony asked, "And?"

Suzzanne said, "We haven't turned the algorithm over to the FBI yet and it's not our job to do theirs. So, I'm for doing or saying nothing about the discovery."

Tony said, "I was hoping Jimmy and I were not going to have a conflict with you over it. Let's let what happens, happen."

♦ ♦ ♦ ♦ ♦

June 30, 2024
Jefferson City, Missouri

Dr. Angel Brown, the *Deadly Gray* veterinarian vigilante and friend of Colonel Colby Manion, was voted chairman of the Las Vegas Massacre Victim's Grandparents Association by the members. Though 84 years old, Angel managed to master the internet and post items on the dark web. One of the 67-member association's goals was to find the truth about the massacre or try to understand the motive behind Paddock's evilness. The grandparents of the massacre victims came from all walks of life, one was a former Air Force B-52 pilot, another was a distributor of fertilizer, another was a math schoolteacher and on and on. However, the skills Angel wanted to focus on today were possessed by a former FAA specialist, a former Quantico marine weapons instructor, and a former explosive ordnance disposal or EOD officer.

Angel called the FAA specialist and asked, "I've got a tail number that you need to track. I hear it currently sits in a regional airport in Wiscasset, Maine. We need its flight plan."

The old FAA man said, "Hold on, I can get that while you're on the phone with me. Let's see, it's no longer in Wiscasset, it's in St. Louis, refueling on its way to Las Vegas. Let's see, it is scheduled to fly out of Las Vegas to Atlanta, Atlanta to Cairo, and Cairo to Riyadh."

Angel asked, "Is there a preliminary manifest."

"Yes, a Saudi Prince and seven others."

"Thanks, I may get back to you before the end of the day."

The FAA retiree asked, "Do your questions mean that the Saudi Prince was guilty after all, and it isn't just a conspiracy theory?"

Angel said, "Yes, it was confirmed a week or so ago or so a little birdie told me."

"Good to get closure."

Angel said, "We won't get closure until this mission is successfully completed."

Angel called his second skilled association member, the weapons instructor. "Are you in a secure location?"

"No, give me a chance to walk outside and pretend to smoke a cigar on the porch. OK, I'm outside."

Angel said, "It's time. Do you still have it, and can you get it to Vegas by 1500?"

"It's in Henderson in an environmentally controlled storage area."

"Can you get there in time?"

The old weapons instructor said, "It takes only a couple of hours for me to drive up there; I'll make it in time."

Angel said, "Are you healthy enough to drive by yourself?"

He laughed heartily and said, "I'll make it if it's the last thing I ever do."

Angel made another call to the EOD technician. He answered the call and said, "Hi Angel."

"Hi Captain. You ready."

"Always. I want this done before I die. Do we finally have the right person? Are you sure; I don't want to take out the wrong person?"

"I will scan and send two photos to you. One is a retired weapons instructor who is on our team. He'll meet you at 1500 at the Extra Space Storage at 1051 Stephanie Place in Henderson."

The captain asked, "And the other photo?"

"Your target, the trigger puller who killed your grandson."

"Where will I find the piece of dog shit?"

Angel said, "A third person will meet you at the storage place and take your package to the killer."

"Can we trust him?"

Angel said, "I am told 'yes' by a very reliable source."

Finally, Angel called Mike Tursky of the Las Vegas Metropolitan Police Department and said, "Today's the day, officer. Are you still on board?"

"Roger that."

"Can you isolate him so that there is no collateral damage."

"Got it all planned out."

June 30, 2024
Las Vegas, Nevada

The Learjet loaded with fuel taxied onto the Las Vegas airport tarmac, accelerated down the runway, lifted above the airport over an isolated desert when a missile was seen targeting the aircraft by local citizens.

The Saudi Prince was looking out the window and helplessly saw it coming. The explosion was enormous; it was obvious no survivors could have lived through the catastrophic ball of fire event.

Tank and Jolene heard about the death of the Saudi Prince from Tucker and celebrated with a primal scream that probably could be heard for miles.

The old weapons instructor left the launcher in place, walked back to his car, and hoped he would make it back home before law enforcement caught up with him.

The *Deadly Gray* EOD officer had assembled a low yield bomb intended to mortally wound just one person. The captain placed the bomb at a location where the policeman told him to leave it and gave the detonator to the police officer.

Mike Tursky walked Abdalhamid Mafi out into an area of the Las Vegas Correctional Facility where the prisoner could get some fresh air. He said to Mafi, "You have 30 minutes out here. I'll come and get you when your time is up."

Tursky watched him from a distance as Mafi wandered alone in the area. He did not get close to where Tursky placed the bomb for the first 20 minutes.

Mafi started to jog and do jumping jacks. He jogged close enough to the package for it to have its intended effect. Tursky pushed the button on the detonator.

The explosion shredded Mafi as if he were cheese on a cheese grater. Tursky disposed of the detonator down the sewer. Though he knew he would be questioned by internal affairs and considered a person-of-interest, he felt vindicated for killing the Las Vegas massacre shooter.

Star, Tank, Tucker, Maya, Jolene, Jimmy, Tony, and Suzzanne heard about the killing of Mafi on the news and all did a celebratory fist pump.

The *Deadly Gray* vigilantes prevailed again.

Epilogue

What happened to:

Abe Stansfield: The environmental activist who attacked the Chinese representative attending a Carbon Capture conference in Houston survived his broken neck after fifteen months in physical therapy at Texas Orthopedic Hospital. Though he would never walk again without a cane, he is able to live a full life as an author and environmental pundit.

Alexandro Rodriguez: The MS-13 gang leader hastily abandoned the headquarters of the Baltimore operation when it was obvious to him that his new young recruit was going to lead authorities to him. In his urgency to desert his place of business, he did not rid the location of evidence of his complicity in capital crimes. He died in prison.

Alice Cloud: The 75-year-old woman from Paris, Kentucky who emasculated a man found guilty of raping her daughter but out on parole served only six months of her 15-year term. A GoFundMe page raised hundreds of thousands of dollars for her to use for legal representation and medical expenses. She was released by the State of Ohio based on her failing health and died a year later while being taken care of by her daughter and great nephew.

Alice Cloud's great nephew: The great nephew searched and discovered where the rapist lived in Cincinnati for his great aunt. He was never interviewed by Star as planned. If she had interviewed the young man, she would have learned that he discovered the rapist's whereabout from #Steel.

Angel Brown: Colby Manion's friend, the veterinarian who saved abused dogs and later became chairman of the Las Vegas Massacre Victims Grandparents Association was never linked by law enforcement authorities to the Learjet explosion containing the famous Saudi Prince or the death of the Iranian shooter, Abe Mafi.

A twelve-person jury found him not guilty of murder of the animal abuser in Jefferson City, Missouri based on his right to defend himself.

Angel died five years later at the age of 89 of natural causes.

Asa Frank: The *Deadly Gray* college professor confessed to Attempted Murder of the Speaker for the House but not guilty to domestic terrorism. He spent two years in a minimum-security federal prison and was released by authorities on good behavior. While in prison, he received 31 proposals for marriage. Upon release, he learned that he amassed $721,000 from a GoFundMe website and offered another $500,000 for a book deal.

Ava Ester: The Australian *Deadly Gray* vigilante was tried for attempted murder in a Melbourne court and found not guilty by a twelve-person jury. She continues to live at home with her daughter who is quoted by interviewers to have said, "I feel very secure with Mom around."

Denver Jones: The man who attacked Star at her home in Mt. Vernon, Virginia lawyered up and pleaded insanity to avoid prosecution for attempted murder of a federal agent. The plea was denied by a federal judge and Denver is now serving a twelve-year sentence.

Drake Earl's Son: The Orangeburg, South Carolina medical examiner's report said the cause of death of a man named Joshua was due to multiple shot gun blasts from the barrel of Drake Earl's 12-gauge Mossberg and not the blunt force trauma from a car lug wrench. Joshua was verified by law enforcement to be the killer of Drake Earl's granddaughter.

Hollywood bartender: A Hollywood Police Department detective tracked the bartender up to Klamath Falls, Oregon where the killer of the high-profile Hollywood producer called home. The detective searched the bartender's home for evidence as to where he might go and found none except that the state inspection for his recreation vehicle was overdue. He put out a nationwide alert to any shop that maintained an RV with a VIN number that matched the bartender's RV. The VIN was identified by an RV dealer in Morgantown, West Virginia but it turned out to be a dead end because it was sold to the new owner four months earlier.

House of Lords Vigilante: A terminally ill commoner murdered member of the House of Lords in the United Kingdom. He was found guilty and faced life in prison without parole if he had lived long enough to serve. Though suspected of being influenced by #Steel, no evidence was ever produced that the killer was a *Deadly Gray* vigilante.

Huda Mohammed: Representative Mohammed's injuries were superficial, and she was released the same day she dramatically arrived at the emergency room. Upon return to Congress, she sponsored a bill to prevent the production of ZAP canes. Her bill was killed in committee and never saw the light of day.

Deadly Gray

Jacob Cohen: The remains of the high school teacher and suicide bomber of an anti-gun activist center in Oakland, California was never found. No DNA of Jacob Cohen was recovered. Only the remains of a suicide vest and unidentified electronic parts were found at the scene of the bombing. Speculation by conspiracy theorists is that Cohen somehow managed to detonate the vest without actually wearing it.

Lynn Barkham: The popular talk radio host returned to her New Jersey radio station after the proposed state law to silence her was defeated by the state legislator. Ms. Barkham is hailed as a first amendment and talk radio heroine and posts frequently in FirstAmendment.News.

Martha Hoffman: After the Secret Service agent secured the petite 82-year-old, she was turned over to the local Minneapolis Police Department for processing. She was charged with aggravated assault on Representative Huda Mohammed and brought before a judge who found her guilty, charged her $15.00, and ordered a police escort home to a cheering supportive crowd.

Maurice Milner: Maurice was arrested on the steps of the police station seconds after he killed the dirty police officer. The lyrics he wrote and gave to his grandson were adopted by a famous rap performer. Maurice's grandson son assumed his grandfather's passion and became a sought-after song writer.

Spencer Blessing: Tank allowed the CIA man to take credit for the capture of two Iranian terrorists. His career was revived, and he no longer was persona non grata in Langley.

Mike Tursky: The Las Vegas Metropolitan Policeman turned *Deadly Gray* vigilante was extensively scrutinized for his role in the death of the massacre shooter, Abdalhamid Mafi but no hard evidence of his complicity was presented to internal affairs.

Minerva Garcia Martinez: She was found guilty of hiring a mercenary to commit arson and attack Supreme Court Justice Randolph Atkinson. She remains an inmate at the low-security women's federal prison, Danbury Federal Correctional Institute.

Roughneck: The *Deadly Gray* vigilante that ran over and killed the Stanford student and identity thief, Kurt Rainwater, stowed away on a freighter that landed in Venezuela. He provided oil-drilling advice to the government until he was murdered by a street thug for the $300 in his wallet.

Rusty Winemiller: The former Special Agent in charge of the Cyber Security Division of the FBI was found guilty of domestic terrorism, second degree murder and treason and is incarcerated at United States Penitentiary Leavenworth.

Sarah, killer of the volleyball coach: The 78-year-old *Deadly Gray* vigilante was arrested and charged with first-degree murder. Her pro bono attorney kept the case from coming to trial before her death of natural causes.

Sean LaKerry: The *Deadly Gray* vigilante incarcerated for crimes he did not commit confessed to the murder of a corrupt defense attorney. As promised, he declared himself to be innocent by reason of insanity. He remains incarcerated in federal prison.

Sheriff Lakota: The Las Vegas Metropolitan Police Sheriff's home was repossessed by Wells Fargo Mortgage. Neither he nor his wife ever made a claim for payment for their share in a five-star Cabo San Lucas Hotel. No one ever saw the sheriff or his wife after Lakota was declared AWOL on June 7, 2024. Theories abound about his fate. Some think the Saudi Prince ordered he and his wife murdered and deposited in a desert grave. Some think he and his wife saw the handwriting on the wall and escaped to a secret hideout. No one knows for sure. His disappearance remains a mystery.

Speaker of the House: She leveraged her near-death experience for sympathy votes and continued to win elections in her district every two years. She survived three additional assassination attempts on her life by seniors.

Portland Sheriff Wingard's Uncle: Old-man Wingard turned himself in to his nephew as the arsonist who attacked local newspaper editors and journalist's. His case never came to trial.

THE END

Cast of Characters

Tucker Cherokee Extended Family

Tucker Cherokee: CEO of Entropy Entrepreneurs; discovered an energy technology with his wife, Maya; entrepreneur; adventurer; and leader. Star's father.

Maya Cherokee: PhD in particle physics; part inventor of a world changing energy technology; former candidate for United States Vice President; former Science Advisor to the President.

Star Cherokee: Daughter of Maya and Tucker Cherokee; formerly Assistant Press Secretary for the President of the United States; currently FBI agent who reports to Special Agent Rusty Winemiller.

Jorge (Tank) Alvarez: CEO of White Knight Personal Security, LLC. Tucker's best friend since childhood.

Jolene Alvarez: Marine, co-owner of White Knights Personal Security and Tank's spouse.

Jimmy Ma: Entropy Entrepreneur employee who "follows the money" as a contractor to the United States Department of Treasury.

Sonja McLeod Vincente: Former Mossad Sniper; currently White Knight Personal Security contractor working for Tank Alvarez. Her father was Tank's mentor and partner before his death. Star's best friend.

Suzzanne Li: Maya's sister and internet technology wizard.

Tony Vinci: Chief Scientist for Entropy Entrepreneurs, LLC.

Chef Rhino : Cherokee family chef

Ram: The Cherokee family's K-9

The following characters became *Deadly Gray* vigilantes:

The Deadly Gray

Abe Stansfield: Environmentalist

Alice Cloud: Kentucky senior who sought revenge on behalf of her daughter

Angel Brown: Veterinarian

Angela Werner: Spouse of former Seal Team Captain

Asa Frank: Professor at University of Missouri

Ava Ester: Australian vigilante

Colonel Colby Manion: First known member of the *Deadly Gray*

Denver Jones: Defended the *Deadly Gray*

Drake Earl: Looked for the killer of his daughter

#Steel (Steelman): Navy Seal in Laos during Vietnam war

Jacob Cohen: High School history teacher

Gregory Jack: New York University bomber

Corey Robinson: Vietnam veteran

Martha Hoffman: Spouse of former police captain

Penny Clark: Autobiographer

Mack Dubois: Retired Border Patrol Agent

Maurice Milner: Retired auto mechanic

Minerva Garcia Martinez: Victim of eminent domain law

Sarah: Achieved justice for a friend

Sean LaKerry: Falsely accused by a corrupt defense attorney

Wingard: Portland, Oregon Sheriff

Other Characters

Abdalhamid Mafi: Member of Iranian Revolutionary Guard Corps

Adam Heinz: Deputy Director of the Bureau of Alcohol, Tobacco, Firearms and Explosives

Alexandro Rodriguez: MS-13 gang leader

Angela Werner: Spouse of Paul Werner

Anthony Dow III: Member of New Jersey State Legislature

Arthur Gannon: United States Attorney General

Bernard Nazareth: Sonja's father-in-law and consultant to Scotland Yard

Brad Naylor: Director of FBI

Brooks: Star's friend

Captain Paul Werner: Leader of Seal Team in Laos during Vietnam war

Caesar Kuffin: University of Kentucky student women's volleyball coach

Chris O'Connor: Special Agent in Charge for investigating the New York City bombing, the Washington, DC sniper case, and the Portland, Oregon Molotov cocktail incident

Daniel Edelman: Mossad Agent

Daria: Moe's sister and member of the IRGC

Egor Chase: Ex-con

Joey Crash: Mercenary

Kurt Rainwater: Stanford post-graduate student

Lynn Barkham: Talk radio host

Mike Tursky: Las Vegas Metropolitan Police Department officer

Mohammad: Moe, an Iranian

Saudi Prince: Son of Saudi King

Stephen Paddock: Alleged Las Vegas massacre shooter

Randolph Atkinson: Supreme Court Justice

Rusty Winemiller: FBI Special Agent in Charge of Cyber Crimes; paraplegic; mentor of Star Cherokee

Sheriff Lakota: Sheriff of Las Vegas Metropolitan Police Department

Spencer Blessing: CIA operative

Stanley Landrieu: Jolene's special needs brother

Timothy Lamb: President of the United States

Victor Judas: Billionaire leftist

Xavier Peabody: Judge

ACKNOWLEDMENT

Thanks go to:

- **Sam Rotolo**: *LightYearStudios.com* for the artistic cover design
- **Shere Day**: My wife for her patience with me and her softer side contribution to the book
- **Brian Day**: My brother for his natural editing talent
- **Colonel Paul Nice**: My friend for helping me conceptualize the storyline.

Beta Testers:

- Paul Nice, Hendersonville, North Carolina
- Tom Cook, Houston, Texas
- Marsha Lindquist, Cave Creek, Arizona
- Bob Twilley, Eden, Maryland
- Ken Landon, Manassas, Virginia

Thrillers by Ed Day as Jed O'Dea
Deadly Cold

A terrorist cleverly formulates a plan to take advantage of the environmental impact of extreme weather for geopolitical and personal gain.

Unsustainable

A terrorist forces California into bankruptcy. Can a modern-day civil war be avoided?

Ed Day

WHA-CKED

Tank Alvarez is blackmailed into investigating a cold case involving the death of a White House Attorney.

Deadly War of Words

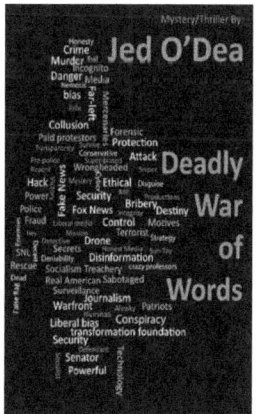

Tucker and Maya form an Illuminati-type organization and solve long standing mysteries.